A Negative

Cassandra Lynn King

CSJ King Publishing
Oregon, Wisconsin

ISBN: 0985622039
ISBN-13: 978-0-9856220-3-9

DEDICATION

To Paul King, my biggest fan.

ACKNOWLEDGEMENTS

First and foremost, as always, I would like to thank my mother and father, Didi and Jeff King, for their never-ending support and encouragement. I would not be where I am today without their help. Second, I would like to thank Deanna Blanchard for her assistance in polishing this novel. I would also like to thank my cover artist, Ashley L. Steinberg, for her hard work and dedication. She never ceases to impress me.

Finally, I would like to thank my family, friends, and professors who have aided in the completion of this novel. Most of all, I would like to thank Brian Morello and the rest of the Beloit College CELEB program for their encouragement as I balance life as a student and a professional writer.

I appreciate the time, support, and commitment provided by those listed above. I look forward to working with them as my career progresses.

Cassie

President Walter Reifert
18 Lemoore Way, Reifert City
Western Continent, Parallel Earth

February 22, 2021
Walter,

The experimentation happening in the United States is getting out of control. The government has managed to keep the existence of the new viral strain a secret, but we're not sure how long that will last. Already there are over a thousand infected individuals with different variations of this new strain, and scientists continue to mutate it, hoping for a result that I can't begin to fathom.

Many of the infected have escaped custody and have sought refuge together in southern Florida, but there are still hundreds in captivity. More are being infected as I'm writing. The lab in Philadelphia (surprise) seems to be the lab in charge, but there are at least three others that we've counted.

The strain is targeting A negative blood this time around, and unlike your strain, this one is not contagious. From our intel, one is infected when the virus enters the respiratory system, and it cannot be transferred from person to person. The doctors force patients to inhale the virus, but once it is inhaled by one person it manifests itself in that person and remains in that body. To our relief, it appears that we will not have another global pandemic on our hands.

But there are still innocent people being experimented on, and it is our duty to liberate them and stop this experimentation before it gets any worse. If other nations discover what the United States has been manufacturing, World War III will be upon us, and I'm not sure if any species could make it through untarnished.

Danny

1

Miriam's Conspiracy

The cafeteria was serving salad again. They served it at least three times a week, and I hated it. There were four meal lines and on random meals they would all serve some kind of salad. It was ridiculous. Salad was disgusting, and I didn't get why the cooks couldn't serve something else in at least *one* line. Most of the time I was so hungry that I would just force it down, but today I was in too bad of a mood to put up with cafeteria crap.

I sat down at my usual table, the one by the huge window overlooking the highway, and located as far from the security tables as possible. To my dismay, even the farthest table could still be seen by them. There were four tables designated for the security officers, and each time I passed by I got head turns and/or insults flung my way. Story of my life.

~~*

Perhaps a little insight into my life will explain why I'm here. I lived a normal, happy childhood with my parents and younger sister until I was sixteen. A few days after my birthday, my high school was evacuated when a massive explosion shook the walls and shattered every glass object. Once outside, we could all see a huge pillar of smoke rising in the distance. It was in the direction of Midtown Manhattan, and we could hear wailing sirens and helicopters and fighter jets for miles around. Whispers started floating through the crowd of students, that they'd overheard some teachers saying that the Empire State Building had just been destroyed by the radical group called ISIL, a long-term enemy of the United States. My heart lurched, and I started running in the direction of the smoke despite my teachers' protests. I was eventually stopped, and a few minutes later my father pulled up in his old truck with Chrissy in tow. He drove the two of us back home and then immediately left to go find our mother, who worked inside the

Empire State Building. He came back in the middle of the night, alone and in tears.

The three of us made it through my mother's death, but two years later, in the infamous year of 2018, my world was shattered again. There was news of a dangerous virus accidentally released from a Philadelphia lab, called the Colician Virus, which infected every single person in the world who had O negative blood. Before we found this detail out, and before we knew what the virus actually was, we were all required to have blood tests. A few days later, our front door was kicked down and men in black riot gear carrying big guns entered our house and dragged my father and sister away. Apparently, as I was told in the hospital later after I'd been knocked out trying to protect my family, they were carriers of the virus. What was left of my family was whisked away by the government to be experimented upon in one of the new laboratories. I was left alone. I never saw them again.

I was granted a full ride to NYU; hundreds of college-age students who had lost family members in the outbreak were granted full scholarships to local universities. I went to school, hoping to start a new life, but after a year I gave the scholarship back. College had always been in my plans, but after losing my family I couldn't continue with my life as if nothing had happened. During 2019 and 2020 I bounced around New York, working odd jobs until I was offered a position that paid a more-than-comfortable income. Of course, the boss was crooked, so things didn't end well. I had always been good with numbers, so I was offered a position keeping track of all the money that came and went. It wasn't the brightest decision of my life, but the boss was surprisingly kind to me and gave me a home.

But after a few months on the job, the FBI apprehended me. I wasn't the only one arrested, but I was pretty much facing my trial alone. My court-appointed lawyer told me I was looking at a life sentence without parole, but before the trial I was approached by the feds and given an ultimatum. Either I could serve out my life sentence in prison, which sounded like an absolute blast, or I could serve ten years in a scientific study, helping scientists find cures and vaccines for new viruses that appeared after the outbreak. It didn't really seem like a fair trade, but the feds seemed pretty serious about it so I agreed to participate in this new study. It wasn't until I was placed in one of the laboratories—big surprise, in Philadelphia, the birthplace of the Colician Virus—that I started to wonder why this was a fair trade for prison. Which leads me to why I sit so freaking far from the security tables.

The study was held on an old college campus, which was permanently shut down during the outbreak. Those who participated in the study were required to live there, so the dorms were a perfect location to house a thousand people. Since the population of participants was so large, the place had a huge security force of over a hundred guards, and each one of them gave me the stink eye and watched me closely. The moment I arrived here I was treated like a criminal. Even with my past record of good and bad things, they only cared about the bad, and were apparently allowed to punish me for it. During my third week, a group of them cornered me in an empty hallway. They were kicking my ass when a young woman intervened and put several of them in the hospital. She was only eighteen, but she had a mean swing and a feisty personality. Her name was Miriam, and we quickly became best friends. She had been here a little over a month when I first arrived in February 2021, and she told me that the guards were all assholes. We started sitting at this table soon after that, both of us now needing to avoid the guards. They didn't bug us as often when we stuck together.

Jeff Robinson, a former comedian from what used to be L.A., joined us in early April. He was thirty-seven, but Miriam and I decided that he wasn't too old to hang at our table. To my and Miriam's surprise, he turned out to be a great friend. Another week passed before Kost Nicholson joined our table. He was forty-five and was a scientist at MIT before his children died during the outbreak, when he lost his marbles and couldn't handle the pressure of teaching any longer. He never had a run-in with a guard, but since he was slightly bonkers he scared everybody else off. He joined our table and the four of us became inseparable.

~~*

I'd been in a bad mood since breakfast, which was probably why I wasn't putting up with the menu today. Miriam wasn't at breakfast or woodworking or even art that morning, her favorite part of the day. If she wasn't around, I wasn't really in the mood for anything.

Miriam made the days at the study bearable for me. The doctors would only call on you once every few weeks, and in between then everybody had to find stuff to fill their days. There were all sorts of activities on campus to do, and you never had to do the same thing every day. We were even allowed to leave campus; we just had to be back by dusk. Of course, I wasn't allowed off campus due to my sentence. If I stepped off campus, I would be in a prison cell within an hour. I didn't want to tell my friends about my criminal past, but I also couldn't leave so I made up a lie that leaving the lab was too hard, that it reminded me too much of my lost family. Surprisingly, they seemed to buy it, and they decided to stay on campus with me. Miriam, Jeff, Kost and I had settled into a routine, and we rarely missed a day. We'd start at breakfast and then build something in woodworking that usually ended up falling apart by the next day. Then we'd go to art and have contests to see who could make the weirdest, prettiest, or most creative piece. After lunch we would go to the chemistry labs to humor Kost, then theater arts for Jeff, and finally we'd head to the gymnasium at the far end of the north building for sports. I found that Miriam was very good at basketball and badminton, so I always made sure we were on the same team. After dinner we would go to the arcade or the bowling alley and then we'd end our day with a movie in the theater arts room. But Miriam wasn't at any of the morning activities today, and even though Jeff and Kost were both there that just wasn't enough. Miriam rarely missed a day, and if she did she'd send a note to our rooms to let us know. Today, we got nothing. No note, and no sign of Miriam.

"Uh-oh," Jeff said as he set his tray down across the table from me and sat down. He had a smirk on his face, and that irritated me even more. "God help us! Austin Rockwell is, yet again, in a foul mood."

"Don't even start with me," I snapped, glaring at the plate of rabbit food in front of me.

"Still no sign of Miriam?" Jeff asked, picking up his plastic fork and attempting to stick some lettuce and spinach with it. That was another thing I couldn't stand about this place: plastic silverware. It was like they were *trying* to make me feel like I was in a prison.

"No," I muttered, slumping back in my chair and glaring at the wooden table.

"She's probably sick or something," Jeff told me, taking a bite and crunching noisily.

"She would have sent us a note," I replied. "Or called one of our rooms."

"Not if she was puking," Jeff said, pointing his fork at me.

"She's not sick," I snapped, now glaring at him.

"She hasn't been called in for a trial in a while. Maybe she got called in late last night and got held up."

"I don't think so," I grumbled.

Jeff stared at me for a few seconds while he chewed, but then he grinned. "You know, they have a diagnosis for what you're experiencing. It's called *separation anxiety*, and I've heard it's actually quite common, particularly when one person is obsessed with another."

"I'm not obsessed with her!" I protested angrily, even though he was probably right. What did it say about me if I couldn't make it through a single morning without her?

Jeff finally became serious, something that didn't happen very often. "Regardless, you need to get over this clingy, overprotective thing you're going through with her. She's a young woman and completely capable of taking care of herself."

"Gee, thanks for the lecture, Dad," I snapped, closing my eyes and dropping my head to the table.

"Oh dear, is Austin not eating his vegetables again?" I heard Kost say, and heard a chair slide out as he sat down next to Jeff.

"Nope," Jeff answered and snickered, back to his comedic self. "He's suffering from Miriam-withdrawal."

"Oh, I see," Kost said, and I felt his eyes on me. "So, Austin, have you two set a date for the wedding?"

My head snapped up and I stared at him incredulously. Kost was known for making us all laugh because he was such a dork. He wasn't known for sarcasm. That was Jeff's department.

Both men started laughing, and Jeff slapped Kost on the back.

"Really, Kost?" I said, shaking my head, and I almost couldn't prevent the smile from coming to my face. "You too? Whose side are you on?"

"I'm sorry," Kost apologized, picking up his fork. "The opportunity was there. I took it."

Even though I was unhappy with Miriam's absence, the carefree energy I was receiving from my other friends was lightening my mood. I decided to poke some fun back at them. "You guys are just jealous that the girl we hang out with is way too young for either of you," I shot back.

Jeff's smile flattened. "I'm sorry to tell you Austin, but my sole interest here is to help people. No interest in girls whatsoever."

"That's bullshit, Jeff! You're a guy! Your sole interest *is* girls!" I didn't realize my mistake until Kost kicked me.

Jeff was staring at his food, his smile gone. I felt awful, because I knew what I'd said had really upset him.

5

Jeff's wife, Amelia, was an O Negative. She'd been taken to the San Francisco labs, one of the big bad ones, along with their two-year-old daughter, Olivia. He hadn't heard from them since.

"I'm sorry, Jeff," I said, poking the watery iceburg lettuce sitting on my plate.

"It doesn't matter," he replied, stabbing veggies with his fork but not putting them in his mouth. "Do you wanna keep going with our schedule if Miriam doesn't show up?"

"Yeah," I said, still feeling guilty. "I'm sure she'll catch up with us in a bit. You're probably right. About her doing a trial."

"Yeah."

An awkward silence passed over the table. Kost looked back and forth between us, oblivious when it came to social situations. Jeff and I both stared at our food, not eating.

Behind us, I could hear the start of a brawl. I heard a female voice, angry and scared, and a couple other voices that weren't as loud or urgent.

"Does the bitching ever end?" I grumbled.

"Probably another lover's quarrel," Jeff replied, glancing over my shoulder. His expression suddenly changed to one of surprise. "Is that Miriam?" he asked.

Kost and I turned. In the center of the cafeteria, Miriam was in a fight with three guards, one female and two male. She was waving her arms frantically at them and speaking in a tone so high I didn't think anyone could actually understand her. The guards were playing it cool, holding their hands up to show they weren't a threat and slowly trying to corner her against a wall or table. They looked more annoyed than anything. Had they been somewhere with fewer spectators, I had a feeling they would be pretty forceful. After all, she had put a few of their own in the hospital before.

"Sounds like a heated argument," Kost mumbled as he looked on with me and everybody else. The cafeteria had gone mostly quiet apart from Miriam and the guards.

"She's really pissed about something," I agreed.

"She actually looks scared, though," Jeff added. "Doesn't she?"

Just then, the guard who was in front and had been speaking to Miriam took hold of her arm and tried to pull her toward him.

"Don't touch me!" I heard her yell, and she attempted to pull away.

"Wrong," I said, jumping up from my chair. I rushed to Miriam's aid, prepared to fight if necessary. I didn't know who started the brawl, and I didn't care.

"Oh, lord," I heard Jeff mutter, but he didn't come after me. He knew anything he said wouldn't make a difference.

"What the hell do you think you're doing?" I snarled, marching right up to the guy holding her and giving him a shove backwards. He stumbled, but he didn't let go of Miriam's arm.

"Stay out of this, Rockwell!" the guy to his left warned, taking a step forward. I recognized him. He was really tall and thin, but he had a good amount of muscle on him. He was one of the guys who had attacked me my first week. I thought his name was Anders.

"You'd better take a hint, pal," the guy holding Miriam growled, still keeping a firm grip on her. "Unless you want a trip to the lab, too."

"You're not taking her anywhere, assholes!" I told him firmly. I wasn't particularly tall or big, but they knew just how much of a fight I could give them. They wouldn't risk getting physical with me, especially since we were in front of a couple hundred people.

"Austin, just leave it," Miriam told me, her voice shaking. "Just go sit down."

I looked at her, surprised. Her expression showed real fear. Why was she so afraid of going down to the lab? It was several floors below ground and was where all the trials took place. Maybe Jeff was right about Miriam having a trial last night; had something gone wrong? Had they given her something that messed her up? Oh, that would really piss me off.

"You should listen to your girl, Rockwell," the female guard chimed in.

"Just walk away before I decide to repay you for Evans," Anders said.

"Don't you all have some mall guarding to do?" I asked. "Or some speeding tickets you need to write?"

"Austin, just go sit down!" Miriam begged. "This isn't something you want to get involved with!"

"Go back to your seat," the first guard snapped, giving me a shove out of the way.

My response probably wasn't as great as it could've been. I kicked the lead guy in the balls as hard as I could. His face froze in surprise, and I quickly took him out with a blow to the face. He fell over backwards onto Anders, finally releasing Miriam. They both fell to the ground, and the woman hesitated. Raising an eyebrow, I gestured for her to walk away. I didn't want to hit a girl, even if she was a guard. She wasn't as big as the guys, and she took several steps back, looking down at her fallen colleagues in confusion.

"What the hell, Rockwell?!" Anders shouted, shoving the other guard off of him and jumping to his feet.

I quickly pulled Miriam behind me. "Maybe now's the better time to repay me for Evans, Andrea," I mocked, daring him with my eyes to attack me in front of everyone.

Anders started to advance, but the lead guard stopped him. "Just let him go," he ordered, rising to his feet gingerly. He was holding his groin and his nose had blood flowing pretty heavily from it.

Anders turned in surprise. "But Diereks—"

"Just leave them," Diereks instructed, eyeing me. "We'll get her later. We'll get them both later."

"Won't we," Anders muttered, scowling at me and retreating with Diereks.

I hoped they would come back for me.

"Come on," I said to Miriam as they left, taking her hand and pulling her back toward our table. She didn't say a word while we went back, but she gripped my hand tightly and didn't let go even when we sat down across from Jeff and Kost. I could feel her fear radiating from her hand to mine, and I knew that something was really wrong. I intended to find out what.

Jeff and Kost were gaping at us. Well, at me. Kost whistled. "Wow," he said. "That was probably the stupidest thing I've ever seen you do."

"Seriously, Austin," Jeff agreed, nodding his head in concern. "They aren't going to let you get away with this one. They're going to come after you."

"Let them," I replied, feeling a bit cocky. My day was suddenly getting better. I also sensed that feeling wouldn't last.

"You should have just left it alone," Miriam mumbled, letting go of my hand and giving me a disapproving look.

"And let them drag you off like they were going to?"

"Yes!" she cried. "Now it's going to be bad for both of us! They're going to come back for me, and you don't want to know what Anders is going to do the next time he sees you."

"Do you really think I give a crap?" I stared at her, trying to get her to understand that I didn't care what they did to me. I had stopped caring a long time ago.

Her expression suddenly became defensive. "Maybe *I* do," she whispered, lowering her eyes to the table.

"What were you guys arguing about, anyway?" Jeff asked.

"Yeah, and where were they going to take you?" Kost chimed in. "You didn't do something wrong, did you?"

"It's not what *I* did," Miriam muttered, keeping her eyes lowered. She groaned and rubbed her temples, her face crunching up in pain.

"Are you all right?" I asked, putting a hand on her shoulder.

She jumped when I touched her but then relaxed. "I will never be all right ever again," she told me.

I blinked in confusion, and felt myself becoming angry again. "What the hell did they do to you? Where were they taking you?"

Miriam sighed. "You wouldn't believe me so I'm not going to bother trying to explain it."

"Try me," I said, folding my arms over my chest.

Biting down on her lower lip, Miriam paused for a moment. A strange look suddenly crossed her face, and her eyes left mine and moved to something over my shoulder.

Turning to see what had distracted her, I saw that the next table over was listening in on our conversation. There were six people, and they were all looking at Miriam with amused expressions.

"What are you looking at, assholes?" I demanded. "I punched a security guard in the face. I'd take on one of you anytime."

All six of them looked away uncomfortably, knowing that I was serious. They started muttering to each other, glancing in our direction occasionally. The four of us were the freaks of the study. Someone was always giving us weird looks or talking about us behind our backs. None of us really cared, but sometimes it could get irritating.

"You were saying?" I turned back to Miriam, but I saw in her eyes that she was going to block me out.

"Not here," she told me, taking my hand under the table again so no one could see. "If the four of us have enough privacy in the chemistry lab I'll think about telling you. But I don't know…"

"Miriam, if you're in trouble we want to help you," Jeff said, just as concerned as I was.

"Yeah," Kost agreed with a reassuring smile. "We're your friends. We want to help."

I looked at each of my friends. Miriam, short, with her black-as-night hair, her chocolate brown eyes and her darker complexion (I had never asked her, but Kost told me that her mother was from Afghanistan and that was why she was darker). Jeff, with his thinning blonde hair, pale blue eyes, and fit upper body. Kost, with his still thick, dark and curly brown hair, dark brown eyes and stocky build. As Kost said, we were friends. And it was the truth. These people were my friends, and were pretty much my family. These were the people I trusted. We all trusted each other, and Miriam could trust us with anything. *Anything.*

"This is a kind of trouble you don't want to get into," Miriam replied gravely, tightening her grip on my hand.

I was stupid to not believe her. I had no idea how serious she was. "Do you want some lunch?" I asked her. "I'll walk you to the line."

"I'm not hungry," she muttered, keeping her eyes on the table.

"Have you eaten anything today?" Kost asked.

"I'm not hungry!" she repeated, her voice rising.

"Just leave her be," I instructed him, not intending for my reply to be as sharp as it was.

Kost nodded and went back to eating his salad without noticing my attitude. Jeff also kept his mouth shut, and none of us said a word for the rest of the hour. At one point, I caught Miriam watching the guard tables, and I looked over as well. Most of them ate at this hour, and four or five of them glanced up in our direction, appearing none too happy. Miriam was still holding my hand, and I felt her shiver and her grip tightened to a point where my fingers crunched together.

"Ow!" I protested, pulling my hand away. I looked at her in surprise, but she didn't look back at me. There was a pained, almost helpless glimmer in her eyes, and I saw a single tear trickle down her face. Sighing, she leaned her head on my shoulder, and rested it there until we got up to leave.

~~*

"So, have you decided whether or not you're going to tell us your big secret?" Jeff asked as Kost messed around with some chemicals and test tubes at a lab table.

"Yeah, what happened with you and those guards?" I chimed in, eager for a reason to start another fight with the guards. I'd been like that since my dad and sister were taken, always looking forward to the next fight. "That wasn't an ordinary argument." Miriam had told us all that we shouldn't know because it wasn't a mess we wanted to get into, but I wanted to help her in any way I could. Especially if guards were going to start dragging her places she didn't want to go.

Miriam looked around the room to see if anyone was listening. It was pointless really. There wasn't anyone close enough to hear. The only other people who ever came to the chemistry lab were five chemistry majors who were doing some research. The chemistry lab had twenty-four tables (I counted the first time Kost dragged us in here, because I was bored and had nothing better to do), and the four of us always picked the table closest to the window. There was just something about windows we all liked. They gave us a sense of freedom. The five college students took two that were on the complete opposite side of the room. There was also a security guard who was stationed inside the room to make sure nobody blew anything up, but he always sat at a desk in the corner by the college students reading his magazine. Probably porn, but who knew.

"Miriam, no one can hear you. It's okay," I assured her. She'd been jumpy and nervous and terrified ever since lunch, and she hadn't calmed down even a little bit. "You can tell us what they did to you."

"Wait, how do you know for sure that they did something to her?" Jeff asked.

"Isn't it obvious?" I said. "If she's this scared and *she* didn't do anything, then what else could have happened?"

"Stop talking like I'm not sitting right next to you!" Miriam cried, shrugging off my hand.

I turned to her, my anger taking off once again. "Please just tell me what they did so I can stop guessing," I begged.

"Why should I?" she demanded, glaring at me. "So you can go pick a fight with them again in front of everyone? There are plenty of other, better ways to impress me than that, Austin."

"Why would you say that?" I asked her quietly, feeling my face flush in embarrassment. I wasn't only hurt by her comment, I was humiliated. Now I knew that Miriam had been thinking exactly what Jeff and Kost always gave me grief about, and it made me feel even worse. I wasn't trying to impress her; I was trying to protect her. She of all people should know that.

"I—I'm sorry," she apologized. That pained look came across her face again, and she put her hand on my shoulder like I had put mine on hers.

"Miriam," Kost started, mixing a dark blue chemical with a bright orange mixture. "If those guards did something to you, then you need to tell us so we can report them and get rid of them so they can't hurt any other people."

"Report them to who?" Miriam asked, almost desperately. "Who is going to listen to us?"

"What about Dr. Hillerman?" Jeff blurted. "He's the head honcho here, right? We'll report it to him and he can deal with them! I'm sure he'd be more than willing to listen to you, Miriam."

"Dr. Hillerman?" I repeated, staring at Jeff in bewilderment.

"Yes, Dr. Hillerman," Jeff said, starting to sound impatient. "You know? The head scientist and doctor here? You can't tell me you haven't heard of the guy."

"Of course I've heard of him!" I snapped. "But have you seen him before? Has anyone here ever seen him? He's four floors underground recreating the Colician Virus for all we know!"

Miriam snickered.

"My point is, none of us have ever seen him around here before," I continued. "If he doesn't associate with any of us, then why would he want to help her? Why would he care? If he wanted to help us, don't you think he would be running the tests with the other doctors? Personally, I wish he would show up, so I could thank him for landing me in this shit hole!"

"Well, I'll give him your message when I meet him tonight," Miriam replied.

"That leads me to wonder, Austin, if you hate it here so much then why did you come here in the first place?" Jeff asked curiously. "And why don't you just leave? It's not like this is a prison."

"Are you kidding me?" Miriam cried, staring at him in disbelief. "Of course this is a prison!"

"Hey! Is there a problem over there?" the security guard called, sounding annoyed.

All four of us looked over in surprise, not realizing we were being so loud. The guard was glaring at us, and the college students were all watching curiously.

"No, sorry sir," Jeff replied, giving a reassuring smile. "Sorry about that. We'll keep it down."

"Believe me, Jeff," I said, lowering my voice. "This was a much better alternative to what I had waiting for me in the outside world." I'd never told any of them about why I was here. I considered telling Miriam some day, but I had no desire to ever tell Jeff or Kost.

Ignoring me, Jeff asked, "Miriam, what did you mean when you said you were going to meet him tonight?"

"Okay, now you really have to tell us what's going on," Kost said, finally setting down his test tubes and leaning in closer. "Spill it, kid. You can't leave us wondering after saying something like that."

Miriam let out a low, frustrated groan and tugged at a stray strand of hair. "I really want to tell you, but I don't want you all to get caught up in this too! It's bad enough as it is! You guys are my friends! I love you. I don't want any of you to get hurt." She looked around at the three of us as tears came to her eyes and started spilling down her cheeks. "Friends are supposed to protect each other."

"Yes, and that's exactly why you should tell us," I told her. "We're your friends. We have to protect you, too."

Sighing, Miriam looked around one last time. "Okay. But you have to swear you will never breathe a word of this to anyone. Because if this gets out, there's going to be a panic, and if they find out you know, they'll come after you, too!"

"Who will?" Kost asked in confusion.

"The guards!" Miriam said. "Don't you see? They're in on it! They're in on everything!"

"In on what?" Jeff, Kost and I all said, exasperated.

"The conspiracy!"

"What conspiracy?"

Miriam looked at me. "You know that joke you said about Dr. Hillerman being underground recreating the Colician Virus? Well, it's not a joke. It's the truth. Haven't you ever wondered what's being tested on us? Hillerman's trying to make a new strain that will affect other people! He's been trying to give us all super powers!"

"That's ridiculous!" Jeff protested. "They're not testing a strain of the Colician Virus on us!"

"See!" Miriam declared folding her arms across her chest. "I told you that you wouldn't believe me."

"They're not testing another virus on us!" Jeff said stubbornly.

"Do *you* know what they're testing on us?" Miriam demanded, raising an eyebrow.

"Yes, of course," Jeff said angrily, but then immediately lowered his eyes and answered truthfully: "No."

"Exactly," Miriam said. "They didn't tell us because they didn't want us to know!"

"Hey, do you guys remember how the Colician Virus worked?" Kost asked, his tone and expression serious. "It had to be inhaled at first, and then it spread by touch."

"Have you all noticed how none of us ever had to take any pills or get any shots?" Miriam asked, seeming relieved that Kost was starting to understand. "It was all 'just relax and breathe in the gas.' That's what this whole study has been about. They want to create more super humans. That's why the government offered you this place instead of prison, Austin. It's a big deal to the government."

"What?" I said, startled "How did you know that?" I was certain I'd never told her about my prison sentence. That's not something I would have forgotten.

"Wait, you were going to prison?" Jeff said, staring at me in shock.

"Don't worry about it," I grumbled, feeling my face going red. Even if I had told Miriam, why would she advertise it to everyone? "It doesn't matter anymore."

"I'm sorry," Miriam said, shaking her head quickly. "Just forget I said anything."

"But why in the name of Christ would the government want to create a new strain of the virus?" Kost asked. I was glad he switched the subject back to Miriam.

"You're the scientist," Miriam reminded. "You tell us."

"They want to study it," Kost said immediately. "They want to understand how it works and figure out a way to kill it."

"Kill it?" I repeated.

"Yes, kill it," Kost insisted. "They want to figure out a way to kill the Colician Strain so they can turn the O Negatives back to humans and bring them back from the Parallel Earth."

I had a sudden, glorious thought. If they succeeded, then my father and sister could come home, and we could be a family again. But that would never happen. What's done is done. I had already learned that the hard way.

"Even if they killed the virus, the Colicians wouldn't want to come back here," Miriam muttered. "It's probably so much better there than it is here."

"There's probably anarchy," I said, a thought I'd had ever since news had broken about the creation of the Parallel Earth. "No sense of government, no leader, no police force…it's probably a hell hole. They're probably worse off than we are."

"I don't know," Kost said doubtfully. "We all saw that speech Walter Reifert gave in front of President Ashton. He sounded pretty confident, pretty level-headed. He took over and is supposedly a really good leader."

"I know that recreating the Colician Virus is bad and all, but I don't understand where *you* come into all of this," I said to Miriam.

"How did you even find out about this?" Jeff asked suspiciously.

Biting her lip again, Miriam said, "Because Hillerman finally found the correct formula to create another strain."

"Wait, he already made it?" I asked, startled. "Are they already infecting people?"

"Not quite yet," Miriam replied hesitantly. "There's only one person who's been affected by it so far."

"Who?" Jeff asked, but he already knew the answer. We all knew who it was.

"Oh, God," I whispered in horror. "It's you."

"Shit!" Jeff hissed, standing up and backing away in fear. "She could contaminate us all!"

"Shut up, Jeff!" I cried, looking to see if anyone had heard.

"I can't believe that you're one of them now!" he said, staring at her like she was an alien. Which, if what she was saying was true, she was. "I *don't* believe you're one of them." Eyeing her, he sat back on his stool. "If you've got super powers, then prove it." He crossed his arms stubbornly.

"Not in the middle of the chemistry lab!" I protested.

"Think of two numbers between one and ten billion," Miriam instructed calmly, ignoring me.

Thinking for a few seconds, Jeff said, "Okay, go."

Miriam gazed at him with this gleam in her eyes that partly scared me, partly fascinated me. It was like she could see into his soul. After about ten seconds, Miriam raised an eyebrow like she was bored. "Of all the numbers you could have chosen, you picked two and thirty-five? And please don't think that I'm crazy, because I'm not."

Jeff stared at her with his mouth half open, his eyes wide in amazement. After a while, he explained, "Those were the ages of my wife and daughter when they were taken by the Colician Virus."

Miriam looked guilty. "Jeez, Jeff, I'm so sorry. I didn't know."

"No, no, it's fine," Jeff assured her, still staring at her.

"Was she right?" I demanded, looking at both of them and desperate for some answers.

"Yeah, she was," Jeff told me, his voice shaking. "Jesus, Miriam. How long have you been able to…you know. *Hear* us."

"It happened last night," Miriam explained. "One of the doctors called on me around ten o'clock and said that I needed to take a quick test. I didn't want to, but I took the gas. It affected me and I've been hearing everyone's thoughts all day. It's so loud and frustrating, and I had such horrible nightmares last night."

"So Hillerman knows about you?" I asked. "He knows you're…changed?"

"I started freaking out this morning when I first started hearing things, and when I heard from a guard what's really going on here I freaked out even more. If I had stayed calm, no one would know about me, but I started screaming at some guards and the doctor who changed me and told them how they were crazy for doing this to more people. They don't know exactly what's going on with me, but they know I'm different. I could hear it in their heads. And Dr. Hillerman wants to *examine* me tonight while everybody's asleep. That's how I know I'm going to see him tonight. The guards are going to come for me again and they're going to take me to him and he's going to dissect me—"

"There will be no dissecting," I promised her firmly. "I'll make sure of that."

"Austin, you can't protect me when they come for me," Miriam told me.

"I can take them down and you can make a break for it—"

"Don't you get it?" Miriam cried. "They're *all* going to come for me. And you can't let them know that you know. They'll keep you quiet using any means necessary. They'll hurt you or maybe even do to you what they did to me. Don't try to protect me when they come again. I mean it, Austin!"

Pursing my lips, I glared down at the lab table. It wasn't fair that Miriam wasn't going to let me protect her. What was I supposed to do when they came for her? Was I just supposed to watch while they dragged her away to be experimented on or tortured? I couldn't do that, and she knew it.

"If you really want to help me, you have to expose this," Miriam told me, like she was reading my mind. I then realized she probably was. "Take this to the press and get it on national news. If the people find out about this, there will be an uprising and they'll have to shut it down.

People won't stand for a repeat of 2018. Once the world finds out, this is over."

"And what happens to you?" I demanded, not meeting her gaze.

She sighed. "I don't want to think about it. I'm the first, and you all know what happened to the first Colicians."

I shuddered. It had been really bad for the first few Colicians who were taken to labs. I didn't want to think about what was going to happen to Miriam when the guards came for her again. Who knew what Hillerman had planned for her?

"I don't know if I can just stand there and watch them take you," I told her through gritted teeth.

"You're going to have to," Miriam replied quietly. "I don't want you getting hurt because of me."

I glanced up and met her eyes for a second, trying to tell her I didn't care. I'd do anything for her. She should know that by now.

"If you knew what they were planning and what they're going to do to you, then why didn't you just leave when you still had a chance?" Jeff asked her, biting his lip curiously.

"I tried, but I had already freaked out at everyone when I tried to leave," Miriam explained. "The guards wouldn't let me out the doors and that was when Diereks and Anders and Parker tried to take me to Hillerman. I told them to stay away from me and they followed me all the way to the cafeteria. I was coming to warn you guys, and I was hoping that if I sat down with you, they wouldn't try to take me. They stopped me before I could get to you and tried to get me to come with them again. I told them I would make a huge scene if they tried to take me, and they didn't believe me. I started screaming at them that they were crazy and people were going to find out about this and then Diereks grabbed me and told me to be quiet and that was when Austin came to help."

"So they're all guarding the doors so you can't get out?" I asked.

"Yeah, that's why I'm saying this *is* a prison," Miriam said.

"If you were coming to warn us in the first place then why wouldn't you talk to us when you got there?" Kost asked.

"I overheard what Diereks was thinking," Miriam told him. "He was thinking that if any of you found out he wouldn't have a second's hesitation to drag you down to the labs as well." She rubbed her eyes. "I was scared that they would do to you what they did to me...but I couldn't go without giving you some kind of warning. That's why I'm telling you that you can't protect me when they come and you can't let them know that you know. You have to figure out a way to get out of here and tell everyone before they turn this into another global catastrophe!"

"How?" I asked desperately. "If they're keeping us all in here like inmates then it's not like we can just stroll out of here."

"I don't know, but you have to find a way," Miriam insisted. "I don't want anyone else to go through what I'm about to go through."

My stomach churned and I bit down on my tongue to keep myself from yelling in frustration.

"Do you think you're contagious like the Colicians were?" Jeff asked cautiously.

"Jesus Christ, man!" I cried in disbelief. "Will you quit worrying about yourself and start worrying about our friend here?"

"Excuse me for fearing for my life!" Jeff shot back.

"Enough," Miriam ordered. "I don't think I'm contagious, but I'm not a hundred percent sure."

"Why do you think that?" Kost asked her curiously.

"I don't think they would let us all mingle together and leave campus if there were possibilities that what they were trying to infect us with was contagious."

"Do you feel really sick?" I asked. "My dad and sister were both throwing up and had really bad headaches before they were dragged off."

"I have a really bad headache," she answered. "But that's about it."

"Do you think this is another blood type virus?" Jeff asked. "I mean, do you know who is affected by this?"

"Well, they've been testing this particular strain on several people, but I'm the first one to have any positive results," Miriam said. "So I don't know if this is another blood type virus. But I'm assuming it will be."

"Yes," Kost agreed. "The original Colician Strain affected those with O negative blood. If they're changing it to affect other people, then the easiest thing to do would be to just change the genetics in it enough to affect a different blood type. It would be easier to still target the blood types than to target something else."

"So what blood type do you have?" Jeff asked Miriam.

"A negative," she answered.

"Shit!" Jeff cried, jumping to his feet again and stumbling over his chair. "That's my blood type! They could do this to me too!"

"Jeff, calm down!" I ordered, sick of him freaking out.

"I can't stay here with this going on!" he continued, his eyes full of panic. He looked like he wanted to start running, but he knew as well as all of us that that would only draw unwanted attention.

"Jeff, sit down and be quiet!" Kost hissed, glancing over at the guard, who was glaring at us again.

"No!" Jeff shouted, but to everyone's relief he lowered his voice. "I can't be turned into a freak! I can't be experimented on like my family was! I'm trying to rebuild my life here! I'm trying to move on!" He glared at Miriam. "This is your fault!" he snarled. "You shouldn't have freaked out at them! Now they know that they have a strain that works and we're all screwed!"

"Jeff, shut up!" I snapped. "We're all in this together, okay!"

"We're not in this together!" Jeff snapped back, still glaring fiercely. "If you think our friendship can help us now, you're out of your mind—"

"I have A negative, too," I told him quietly, raising my eyebrows.

Jeff stopped and stared at me. "You—you do?"

"Yes," I said.

"So do I," Kost put in.

"See?" I said, glad he was finally calming down. "We're all in this together."

"No one else is going to be affected," Miriam said firmly. "You guys are going to get the message out before that can ever happen." She looked around at all of us expectantly.

Kost met my eyes. "I'll do it," he said.

"For you I will," I told Miriam.

Kost looked at Jeff. I did too.

"Jeff?" Miriam asked hopefully.

Sighing, Jeff glared at her. "If I die because of this, I'll kill you," he growled. Turning to Kost and me, he grumbled, "Because we're all friends, I'll help. But I'm leaving all the punching and kicking to Austin. I'll...carry the bags and drive the van."

Miriam smiled. "Thank you."

"You'd better be grateful," Jeff snapped, but then he smiled back and elbowed her playfully. "You're lucky I like you. And I guess I owe you anyway. From helping me when I first got here."

"Well, after this is over I guess we'll be even," Miriam said.

"We'd better be," he muttered, shaking his head.

"We should meet in my room tonight around midnight and we can escape with no one ever knowing," I told Kost and Jeff.

"No," Miriam immediately said. "Don't do it at night. Nobody is out in the halls except for guards and they'll catch you before you can get very far. Plus, security is going to be increased now because of me. Go during a meal, when most of the guards will be in the cafeteria and you can sneak through the crowd and break out through a side door."

"You've really thought this through, haven't you?" Kost asked with a grin.

"I need this to get out," Miriam said. "That's the only way I'm going to survive this."

"Oh, no," Kost muttered, staring toward the door.

The rest of us turned to see that about a dozen guards had come through the door, and one of them was talking to the guard at the desk. He looked over at us and pointed, and they all started walking over to us. Diereks and Anders were among them, and none of them looked very happy.

"Shit!" Miriam whispered, and I felt her body tense beside mine in fear. As they came closer, she slowly rose to her feet and took a step back. I stood up as well along with Kost and Jeff, and Miriam hissed at us, "Don't fight them! Remember what you have to do!"

Tensing in anger, I set my jaw and watched as they marched right up to us and stopped about five feet away. Most of them gave me dirty looks and just waited, eyeing me suspiciously. I was starting to become uncomfortable when I realized that I was blocking Miriam.

"You really don't want to fight us, Rockwell," Diereks told me sharply.

Gritting my teeth, I hesitantly stepped to the side and back, giving a clear path to Miriam.

They all gaped at me in shock, but Diereks and Anders were suspicious. "What, you're not going to stop us?" Anders asked, stepping up to me so our noses were inches apart.

"You're right," I grumbled at him, every word an effort. "I don't want to fight you."

Several guards laughed harshly, and Anders sneered. "What, are you afraid that I'll kick your ass this time?"

"Actually, Andrea, I'm afraid that I'll kick yours again," I muttered, forcing myself to stare back into his eyes. "I need a *real* fight."

"Austin!" Miriam warned in a whisper, shaking her head at me.

Anders glanced at her. "You let your woman do the thinking for you now? Is that it?"

"You better get out of here before I change my mind, Andrea," I threatened, scowling at him.

"Are you going to come with us quietly, or are we going to have to drag you?" a big, tall, blonde guy asked Miriam, watching her carefully.

Out of the corner of my eye, I saw Miriam look at the ground, and my heart broke. As calm as she could be, I knew that she was so scared right now, and I felt awful that there was nothing I could do.

"I'll go," she whispered, her voice barely audible. She didn't raise her eyes from the floor.

"Good," Blondie said, shooting a glance in my direction. He took a step toward her while watching me, seeing if I was planning an attack. He was lucky I wasn't. "Anders, get back in line."

Eyeing me one last time, Anders backed up a few steps and turned away.

"If you hurt her, I'll do to your face what I did to Evans'," I called to him, giving Miriam a reassuring pat on the shoulder.

Anders rounded on me, his expression furious.

"Don't!" Blondie ordered, putting a hand out to stop Anders from advancing. Giving me a disgusted look, he came toward me and stood in front of me as Anders had. "You're a piece of work, you know that?"

I shrugged, the words coming out of my mouth before I could stop them. "At least I'm not working for a complete psycho who tries to recreate global catastrophes."

"Austin!" Miriam cried, her eyes pleading with me again.

Blondie stared at me. "You have no idea what you're talking about," he said.

"Oh, I don't?" I asked. Sometimes I really wished my mouth had a filter.

"Austin, shut up!" Miriam pleaded.

"No, you don't," Blondie growled through bared teeth. "So you'd better stop before I stop you."

"You know what?" I said, sticking my right index finger into his chest. "Why don't you stop me?"

Before I could react, Blondie pulled his right stick out of his belt and slammed it down onto my arm. I heard, rather than felt, my arm break. Crying out in agony, I collapsed to the ground in a heap, clutching my arm. The pain was searing, and I bit down hard on my tongue to keep myself from screaming.

"Austin, no!" I heard Miriam yell, and I think she tried to run to my aid, but I heard her scream as a few of the guards took hold of her.

"You two stay out of this!" Diereks shouted as Jeff and Kost started to come forward.

"You want a real fight, Rockwell?" Blondie asked me, kicking me hard in the gut. I could tell he had been aiming for my balls, but he missed and I brought my knees up to my chest to keep him from hitting them if he decided to kick again. But he didn't, and I was relieved. I was already gasping for breath from the first kick. "I hope that deflated your ego a bit," he said, stepping away from me. "Let's get out of here. We promised Hillerman we'd have her detained over an hour ago."

Gasping in pain, I lifted my head slightly to watch them go. In the end, they did have to drag Miriam out. She wasn't screaming, but she was struggling to break free of them and when she turned to look at me helplessly I knew why. I blew it. I let them know that I knew. Our great escape may not work out after all, and if it didn't, Miriam knew she wouldn't make it to the end. This would all be my fault.

"Damn it," I muttered, and dropped my head back to the floor as I passed out.

2

Hillerman

When Miriam first explained what was happening in this place, I thought I had understood how scared she was. But I didn't. I did now, however. I had done exactly the opposite of what she had told me to do. Instead of just letting the guards take her, I had to intervene with my shitty attitude and let the guards know that I knew what was going on. Now, not only was Miriam screwed, but I was, and Jeff and Kost most likely were too. I blew it for all of us. There was no way anyone would be able to sneak out of here now. Guards would be stationed at all the exits 24/7, and I would probably get taken away the same way she did so they could make sure I'd keep my mouth shut. Which, of course, I wouldn't. Not if it saved Miriam, I wouldn't.

As I had predicted when I first went back to my room, the guards eventually came for me. I went back right after they took Miriam away, because I was too freaked out and in too much pain to go anywhere else. Blondie had really messed up my arm with his metal stick, and that kick in the gut had seriously hurt me. I had assumed the pain would go away in an hour or so, but at 6:00 p.m. it was still just as bad. I was pretty sure that I needed to see a doctor, but I didn't trust any of the ones here so I had nowhere to go. I was certainly in no condition to fight if and when the guards came back for me.

After I went back I paced around my room for a while, until my stomach pain was too much for me to handle and I had to lie down on my bed. That was where I stayed until they came for me.

I had been thinking frantically for a brilliant yet subtle way to escape, but my mind was too scrambled. Kost and Jeff had gone back to their rooms as well, and I prayed they were thinking of some amazing plan to get us all out of here before we were detained too. But I never heard from them, and when a loud rap sounded at my door and made me jump, I could only fear the worst.

"Rockwell!" a gruff voice called from just outside my door. "Open the door and let us in!"

I didn't answer. Maybe if I pretended I wasn't there they would go away.

"Rockwell, we know you're in there!" the voice snapped again. "We can see you on the camera. Now open the door before we open it for you!"

What camera? I looked around, wondering how they'd been spying on me for all this time. "Go away!" I tried to shout, but speaking only made the pain in my stomach worse and I curled up in a ball again, holding my breath in hope it would subside.

"I'm losing my patience!" the guy snapped, trying the doorknob.

"You're going to lose something else if you come in here!" I warned, forcing myself to sit up.

"All right, I've had enough," I just barely heard the guy say to his colleagues. "Open it. Stand back, Rockwell! We don't want any surprises."

"Don't come in this room!" I yelled, easing myself up and taking a few steps toward my door. But I could hear them sticking a master key into the lock, so I stopped and backed away. I was panicking, and I had no idea what I could do once they came through. Trying to recall if there was anything handy to use as a weapon, I looked around desperately. It was hard to defend oneself in a place that banned weapons. But then I remembered; I did have a weapon. Everyone did in their rooms. In the cabinets above the sink were drinking glasses. Going to the cabinet, I opened it, pulled out a glass, and smashed the top against the sink.

When the guards got the door open and started rushing inside, I backed myself into the corner behind my bed, my injured arm held close to me and the other aiming the shattered glass at them. They were all holding some sort of high-tech gun with red target lasers that were dancing all over my chest. Black helmets obscured all their faces and bullet proof vests covered their chests. They were really serious about this.

"Put it down, Rockwell," the guy in front ordered, the one who had spoken to me from outside. He had stopped at the other side of the bed, his gun aimed directly at me. I couldn't see his face, but I could tell by his body language that he was a more experienced guard. There was no way I would win a hand-to-hand fight with him. The others hung back just inside the door, letting the leader do his business. "We don't want to shoot you."

Glancing down at my chest, I saw that the little red dots were still dancing all over my green t-shirt. Would they really shoot me?

"Now, I'm going to come around, *slowly,* to the other side of the bed, and I'm going to take that from you," the leader said, his voice finally calmer. He started to take a few slow steps around the bed, but I stopped him.

"Don't come near me!" I snapped, waving the broken glass in his direction, letting him know that I intended to use it.

"Make this easy on yourself," he told me, gesturing to my broken arm hanging uselessly at my side. "I don't want to break your other arm." He started coming toward me again, and this time the other guards started to move in as well.

"I'm serious!" I warned, waving the glass at him again. "I will kill you if you touch me!"

He snickered. "I'm sure you will."

"You think I won't?" I demanded shrilly, running out of threatening things to say.

"Just relax, kid," he said, and to my surprise he actually set down his gun on my bed and put his hands in the air, just like Diereks had done with Miriam. "I'm not going to hurt you."

"Is that what you people told Miriam before you hauled her off?" I asked weakly, staring helplessly at him. If he wasn't here to hurt me, then what was he here for? He was now around the bed, and all that separated us was three feet of empty space.

"Miriam is fine," he told me, in a tone I suspect was meant to reassure me. It didn't.

"Bullshit," I growled, not lowering the glass.

"Give me that," he instructed, taking another step forward and reaching toward my outstretched hand.

"I'm warning you!" I said, my voice quavering.

"Austin, please." He sounded annoyed more than anything.

I slashed the glass at his hand. He jumped back and jerked his hand away. I saw just before he withdrew that I had cut him pretty deep. He didn't waste a moment of time. Ignoring his wound, he lunged at me, screaming at his colleagues, "Don't shoot him!" He caught me by the wrist and shoved me back into the wall, slamming my hand down onto the bed frame. As pain seared through my wrist, I automatically released the glass and it dropped to the floor, shattering. He then swung me around and threw me onto the bed, pinning my left wrist down with his right hand and grabbing my throat with the other. I tried to kick him.

"Calm down!" he ordered, his grip around my throat tightening as I thrashed harder.

"Get off of me!" I tried to yell, but his grip was so tight that I could no longer breathe. Struggling to break my wrist free of his grasp, I kicked and struggled harder, but I was weak and tired and hurt. This guy wasn't budging. For a while I fought uselessly against him, until I was seeing white spots and my vision was blurring at the edges. Finally, I gave up and slumped down on the bed, sure he was going to kill me. But just before I was about to pass out, he released me and I gasped for air.

"There we go," he said, taking a step away from me while I coughed and caught my breath. "Now," he began, taking his helmet off and setting it down on the bed beside me, "Dr. Hillerman wants to see you."

Breathing hard and clutching my throat, I glared up at him. I considered grabbing his helmet and slamming it back into that smug face of his. He looked to be at least forty, and had short brown hair and serious brown eyes. He had plenty of muscle, but not enough to be body-builder material. I had never seen him before. "Well, I don't want to see him," I muttered back at him, my voice thin and airy.

He smirked down at me. "You don't have a choice in this, son."

"And, what, you're going to drag me down to his lair?" I demanded, rubbing my throat, which was burning inside.

"He heard you were injured while we were retrieving the Lobner girl and he would like to check you out," he explained, narrowing his eyes and watching me closely, like he was searching for something. "He would also like to speak to you about a matter in which I am not at liberty to discuss."

I snorted, and forced myself to smirk back at him through my pain. "I bet he does."

"Let's go," he ordered, grabbing the front of my shirt and pulling me up. "My name is Sergeant Jaeger, and I will be your escort down to the lab."

"Sergeant?" I repeated.

"Yes," Jaeger said, taking me by my good arm and leading me back to the door. "We're a U.S. Special Operations Force."

"Special Forces?" I stopped and stared at him. "Everyone here?"

"No," Jaeger replied, smiling reassuringly at me. "Just us." He gave my arm a tug and led me out the door, his backup men following closely with their guns still at the ready. "We take orders from the very top. We're called CBWDTT: Chemical and Biological Weaponry Defense Task

26

Team," he told me, and then turned to make eye contact. "Not many know of our existence; our existence is classified. We were in Louisiana during the weaponized Ebola threat. We were in Pennsylvania when the Colician Virus first broke out."

My breath caught in my throat for a second, and it felt as if my lungs had frozen. I didn't know why I bothered, but with Jaeger's honesty about what they were working with, I panicked and tried to pull away from him.

Tightening his grip on me as he did with my throat before, Jaeger stopped walking and stared hard at me. "Please don't struggle," he said in a deadly voice, sending a chill through my whole body. "It would be unfortunate if we had to stop you from running."

"Why would you tell me about it if it's classified?" I asked him, staring right back at him. "If not many people know about you, it's because you're top secret."

Jaeger smirked at me again. "You already know something you shouldn't. Something that could be life threatening to you and anyone else who knows about it. I'm sure you'd be willing to keep your mouth shut about it. It would be disappointing if you told all your friends and they disappeared, wouldn't it?" He didn't wait for me to answer. He pulled me along again, leaving me to ponder the threat hanging over my head.

~~*

I wasn't sure how far below ground we were when Jaeger finally opened a white door in a long white hall filled with white doors and shoved me inside. The elevator ride down had felt like forever, but maybe that was just because I was dreading whatever Hillerman had planned for me. After we finally stopped, we walked down several never-ending halls past large windows, beyond which were several large laboratories. There were scientists examining samples of something under microscopes. There were huge white tanks along the walls of the laboratories that looked like portable gas tanks. Jaeger caught me staring at one of the labs, and he told me that this, like his job, was also classified. When we finally reached Hillerman's lair, Jaeger pulled open the door and said, "We'll be right outside, so don't try anything." He shoved me inside and slammed the door.

I pushed my back against the door, wishing I could just fall through it and get out of there. My chest was burning, and I exhaled heavily when I realized I had been holding my breath. The pit of my stomach felt like it was turning to rock. I looked around and relaxed slightly at what I saw. The room I was in seemed to be a normal doctor's exam room, except much, much larger. Instead of the walls being white, they were a dark gray color, making the room appear even darker with its dull lighting. There were dark wooden cabinets lining the interior of the room, with counters underneath them. There were three other white doors leading out of the room. There was a large screen hanging in the corner across from me. In the center of the room was a large exam chair. It was cushioned with what looked like leather and had foot and armrests. Considering what it was probably used for, it looked quite comfortable. The items surrounding the chair, however, did not make me feel at home at all. There was a gas tank sitting beside it with a tube and a mask hooked up to it. My stomach felt even heavier after I took a good look at that. For a moment I was sure I would puke. Beside the chair was a wooden table with trays of surgical equipment. I had just taken a couple steps forward to get a closer look when a door opened to my right.

I had never seen Dr. Hillerman before, and after Miriam's description of what was going on I had pictured him as some mad scientist, mid-forties, with insane hair and crazed eyes hidden by thick framed glasses. I pictured him holding test tubes full of chemicals or holding a giant syringe loaded with who knew what, with scorch marks covering his face and a white lab coat from an experiment gone horribly wrong. So when a man who looked to be at least fifty, slightly overweight with neat graying hair and light blue eyes behind thin, copper-framed glasses stepped through the door, I couldn't help but stare in surprise. Was this seriously Dr. Hillerman? It couldn't be; he didn't look creepy enough. He had the white lab coat, but it was stainless and worn casually over a black shirt and khaki pants. He was holding a clipboard full of papers, and when he glanced up after the door closed behind him, he caught me staring and asked, "Austin Rockwell?"

Still not convinced this was Hillerman, I said uncertainly, "Yeah."

He smiled at me, making his eyes crinkle in the corners. He came a little farther into the room but stopped several feet short of me. "Hello. I'm Dr. Jack Hillerman."

"Seriously?" I asked, still not buying it.

Hillerman blinked at me. "Yes," he replied.

"Oh," I muttered, unable to stop staring at him.

"Why?" he asked.

"You just..." I paused, trying to think of something sensible to say. I wanted to say that he looked normal, but I tried for something a little better. "You're just not what I expected."

Hillerman nodded, but didn't say any more on the matter. Glancing down at his clipboard, he said, "It says in your file that you came here as an alternative to prison. Is that true?"

"Yeah," I replied, narrowing my eyes at him. Maybe if I could scare him he wouldn't do anything to me. He looked harmless enough. "Why? Does it scare you that I should be in prison?"

Hillerman smiled again. "Possibly, but you, too, are not what I expected."

"Really?" I said, trying to sound casual.

"You don't look like the type," he explained, holding my challenging gaze. He wasn't at all intimidated by me. Why should he be? I had one broken arm and there were about twenty soldiers standing just outside the door. "So, Austin, what exactly did you do to end up in this situation? Going to prison, I mean."

"What, your clipboard doesn't tell you that?" I was growing angry. What the hell did he care how I ended up in this situation?

"It does," Hillerman replied. "I was just hoping you would be willing to share that with me. A little patient to doctor trust."

"Well, if I trusted you I would have no problem talking to you about my past," I snapped. Hillerman didn't respond. "What exactly is it that you want from me, anyway?"

"I want to help you," he said.

I snorted. "Why would you want to help me?"

Hillerman turned his head slightly. "I'm a doctor. Why wouldn't I want to help you?"

Setting my jaw, I growled, "It seems to me like you've helped Miriam enough for the both of us."

Something flickered in the man's eyes, something I couldn't identify. "You and Miriam are close friends, from what I've gathered."

"Yes, we are," I said firmly.

"More than just friends?" he asked, raising his eyebrows.

"It's none of your business what she is to me!" I snapped defensively.

"Miriam was exposed to a mistake," Hillerman explained. "One of our scientists created a flawed drug. After she was exposed she became delusional and started having hallucinations."

"She didn't sound delusional when she told me everything that happened here!" I shot back, and stepped back to the door. "Thanks, but I think I'll let somebody else help me. Somebody trustworthy."

"You're not leaving this room, Austin," Hillerman said quietly.

"Oh really?" I said, turning back to him.

He shook his head. "Where would you go? You wouldn't get more than three feet out that door before Sergeant Jaeger stopped you, and I can assure you that you wouldn't be able to win a fight with him, even with *two* good arms."

"You underestimate me." I tried to sound tough, but my shaking voice gave me away.

Hillerman smiled gently at me again. "Why don't you save us all the trouble and take a seat?" He gestured with his head to the chair.

I looked at the chair for a second, and then my eyes flickered to him suspiciously. There was no way I was willingly going to get into that chair. Then my stomach pain began to worsen, and I couldn't help but wince. Hillerman saw it.

"Please?" he asked, holding his smile. "I know you're in pain. I can see it in your eyes. Let me help you."

I regretfully walked around the wooden table. The equipment lying on the trays included several odd looking devices with all sorts of colorful buttons on them, some with little screens at the top. I hesitantly sat down in the chair and carefully pushed myself back so I was lying as far back as I could. As I had suspected, it was comfortable, but I barely noticed as my pain and anxiety spiked. Exhaling slowly to keep myself calm, I stared up at the tiled ceiling and wondered where Miriam was right now.

"Can you move your arm at all?" Hillerman asked me as he came to my side and reached across me to grab one of the devices.

"No, thanks to your goon squad, I can't," I muttered in his general direction, still staring at the ceiling.

"Yes, I spoke to Mr. Tyler about that incident," Hillerman told me, pressing a few buttons on his toy and making it beep.

"What did you do, give him a spanking?" I asked sarcastically, rolling my eyes. I'm sure Blondie enjoyed a little pep talk about how to treat civilians. Very educational.

"No, I gave him a timeout," Hillerman replied.

I turned to look at him and saw that he was watching me with a slight smirk on his face. He seemed to catch on to my personality pretty fast.

"Much more efficient," he added.

Unsure how to respond, I looked back up at the ceiling. It wasn't going to be any fun being a smart ass if he was just going to respond in the same sarcastic way.

Suddenly, three metal bars appeared from inside the chair and snapped over my shins, shoulders, and left wrist.

"Whoa!" I cried, jumping and attempting to worm out of them, but I was held tight. "What the hell are you doing?"

"Hey, hey!" Hillerman said, putting a reassuring hand on my shoulder. "They're just there to keep you steady."

"Keep me steady for what?" I demanded as he picked up another gadget and hit a button, causing all the lights in the room to go out except for a blue one directly above me, which flickered on.

"So the machine can read you," Hillerman explained, pressing more buttons on his first little remote.

"Machine...?" I tugged at the restraints again.

"Please lie still," Hillerman said, and then a long, thin white laser came out of the bottom of his little contraption. He slowly moved the laser over my hurt arm, and when he reached my wrist the device beeped and a 3-D image popped out over it and showed the interior of my arm. The muscles, the veins, the bones. They were all there, and as I stared I saw that there were fractures in both bones of my forearm. Blondie had busted me up real good.

"Well, it is broken," Hillerman informed me.

"Yes, I can see that," I replied, still staring at the picture. I had never seen this type of technology before. It was something out of the science fiction movies of my childhood.

"Let's see if there is any other damage," Hillerman said, and the image disappeared with the push of a button.

I was about to tell him about my stomach pain, but he was already scanning my head and moving the device slowly down over the rest of my body. He scanned every part of me, even my other arm. When he reached just below my belly button, the little machine beeped again and another image popped up. This time, however, I couldn't make out what it was supposed to be. All I saw were multicolored blobs of what I assumed were internal organs, but I couldn't be one hundred percent sure. It could have been a tumor for all I knew.

"You have stomach pain?" Hillerman asked me, although it sounded more like a declaration than a question.

"Was that a question?" I asked, squinting at the picture and hoping it would meld into something I actually recognized. "What's wrong?"

"You have a small rupture in the lower section of your small intestine," he told me, and the image disappeared again. He set the device back down and looked down at me with concern.

"That's bad, right?" I asked uncertainly, praying it wasn't life threatening.

"Yes, it is," he replied, walking around to the other side of my chair. "Especially since you didn't go for help right away. Fortunately I am able to fix this with no problem at all." He reached down beside me and pulled something off the floor. It was the mask connected to the tank full of gas.

"Whoa," I said again, pulling my head away as he tried to put the mask over my face. "Get that thing away from me."

Blinking in that confused way again, Hillerman looked down at the mask and then back up at me. "It's just a gas to help you go to sleep. It's similar to nitrous oxide, just stronger."

"Yeah," I said, nodding to tell him that I understood and still didn't care. "I don't want it."

Hillerman stared at me for a moment before telling me, "Austin, I need to set your arm and perform laser surgery to repair the damage to your internal anatomy. I will tell you right now that it will be very painful and you do not want to be awake for it."

"I'll take my chances," I replied stubbornly.

As if he was reading my mind, Hillerman said, "Whatever Miriam told you about me or what I might do to you is not true." He gave me that reassuring smile again. "I'm only here to help you. I'm not going to hurt you. You can trust me."

"I think I trust Miriam's judgment over yours, Doc."

"Miriam is very sick," Hillerman said, still trying to convince me of his charade. "Now, please." He tried to put the mask on my face again, but again I pulled away.

"I told you I don't want it!" I snapped.

Sighing with a hint of frustration, Hillerman set the mask down on the table and looked down at me again. "Austin, I am a very patient man, but you are running out of time. Either you let me give you the gas willingly, or I can get my 'goon squad' in here to help."

As if entering on cue, I heard the door open behind me, the one Hillerman had entered through, and a gruff voice said, "Do you need some help, sir?"

"I may," Hillerman replied. Peering down through his glasses at me with that searching look, he asked, "So which is it going to be?"

Refusing to give in, I continued to glare at him. I wasn't about to let him poison me with whatever shit he had stored in that tank.

Sighing again, Hillerman shrugged. "All right. Your choice." Looking over my shoulder, he called, "Yes, I am going to need some help."

I heard footsteps approaching me from behind, but I never saw anybody. A pair of hands grabbed my head, one on my forehead and one under my chin, and held me in place.

"Thank you," Hillerman told the man holding me, and he picked up the mask once again.

"Let go of me!" I commanded, attempting to twist my head out of the guy's grip. "I don't want your damn gas!" I fought against the restraints as I had fought Jaeger: pointlessly. I wasn't going to get out of this one.

"This is for your own good," Hillerman told me, putting the mask over my nose and mouth.

"No!" I tried to yell for help—as if there was anyone around to help—but found myself unable to make sensible words anymore. Whatever Hillerman was giving me, it was working fast. I considered holding my breath to limit my intake, but my heart was pounding too fast to allow that. The gas smelled and tasted funny, like a mixture of strawberries and gasoline, and Hillerman's face was starting to drift further and further away. The entire room was pulling away, and I fought as hard as I could to stay awake, but in the end the darkness won. And then I was falling again...

~~*

In the five years since my mother's passing, I have had this recurring nightmare of falling. After my father and sister were taken, the dream visited me more and more frequently. I would fall for what felt like hours, sometimes days, in pitch darkness with no noise other than the wind rushing past my ears. I would shout and scream for help, but I couldn't even hear my own voice. Eventually, after I had completely lost my mind in the dream, I would hit the bottom and jolt awake, sweating and gasping for breath.

I knew what this nightmare meant.

I was falling, spiraling out of control, propelled by the events of my life. Some of my life choices had accelerated this downfall, but much of it was beyond my control. And that was what terrified me the most.

~~*

When I hit the bottom and jolted awake, I thought I was still trapped inside the dream. It was still black, and I searched frantically for any sign of light. I had never been trapped inside the dream after I hit bottom, and now I was scared. I wanted to escape this place, to be free of the darkness. I don't know how long I was trapped there, unable to move, unable to speak, unable to feel. My heart began to race when I heard a voice calling my name. And then the darkness began to lift, and a face was hovering over me. For one, beautiful moment, I could have sworn it was my father, but then the darkness pulled away completely and I saw that it wasn't him. It was Hillerman. I was still trapped. I may have escaped the dream, but I had yet to escape the terror of this place.

"Austin," Hillerman said again, and now that I was mostly conscious I felt that he was holding my face in his hand. "Can you hear me?"

I pulled away from him sharply. I pushed myself upright and glared at him as he took a step back. The lights were back on again, and the bars were no longer holding me down. I found that I could move both arms now, and looking down I saw that there was a dark blue cast covering the length of my forearm. My whole arm felt weak, but I had no more pain and I could move it again.

"How do you feel?" Hillerman asked me, keeping a good distance away.

Reaching down, I ran a hand gently over my stomach. I no longer had any internal pain either. But I felt something strange beneath my fingers. There was a thin line of skin that felt raised, and when I lifted up my shirt I saw that there in fact was a line just below my belly button about four inches long. It was a little darker than the rest of my skin, and it was raised just enough that it looked like a scar from a laser incision. The scar appeared as if I had the surgery months ago.

"Considering the circumstances, I feel pretty good," I admitted, staring down at my scar in awe.

"Good," Hillerman said, smiling down at me. "The scans show that you are perfectly fine. Now, come." He walked over to one of the doors and exited through it.

Sliding my legs off the chair, I carefully rose to my feet. I was a little uncertain on my feet and I swayed for a few seconds, catching my balance on the arm of the chair. I wondered how long it would take Hillerman to realize I wasn't behind him. He was expecting me to behave and follow him, but I was never really one for following the rules. Watching the door carefully in case he decided to pop in again, I began to inch my way to the door from which I had entered. When I was sure he wasn't going to come back through, I rushed the rest of the way and threw the door open. I felt a sudden sense of freedom, but it was soon shot dead when I almost ran directly into Jaeger. I stared at him in surprise. I hadn't been expecting him to still be waiting there. He stared back at me with a stony expression on his face. After about ten seconds, he raised his hand and pointed back at the door Hillerman had left through. Nodding, I closed the door again and went to the other door. I guess Hillerman knew me better than I thought.

When I stepped inside, Hillerman was sitting behind a desk in front of a window overlooking one of the laboratories. He glanced up. "Nice try," he said. He looked back down and continued writing something on several pieces of paper scattered across the desk.

I thought about saying something rude, but I decided against it. Instead, I asked him, "How long was I out?"

"A few hours," he replied, gesturing above my head.

I turned and looked up. Above the door, a clock read 9:45. I was surprised that the surgery hadn't taken longer. Then again, I had heard that Hillerman was a genius at everything, whether it was chemistry, microbiology, or surgery. The man must have gone to school for twenty years. I turned back, and he was watching me again.

He nodded to a chair directly across from him. "You can take a seat."

I didn't move. I cleared my throat nervously and said, "Listen, I really appreciate you helping me, despite how much of an ass I was. I really am grateful."

Hillerman folded his hands neatly upon his papers and waited, knowing there was more coming. This guy could see right through me. It bugged me how some people could do that. Maybe I was just easy to see through.

I hesitated, biting my lip. "But, I really think I should go."

"Go back to your room?" Hillerman asked, his brow furrowing.

I really wished he would stop staring at me. "No," I said slowly. I didn't know why I was so uneasy. What was he going to do to me? Standing up straight to make myself look more confident, I looked him right in the eye. "I want to leave here. This study. I don't want to be here anymore."

Hillerman nodded slowly, studying my face. He shrugged. "You can go if you want to."

Taken aback, I stared at him in confusion. "Really?"

Nodding again, he said, "But where would you go?"

"What do you mean?"

He held up a sheet of paper that had the letters FBI scrawled across it. "This is the ten-year contract you signed," he explained, setting it back down. "You decided to come here in exchange for a fresh start once you finished. So far it's been almost three months. You are not a prisoner here. You are free to leave if you want to, but do you know what's going to happen if you walk out that front door before your time is up? You'll be right back where you started, Austin. If you walk out of this building tonight, I can guarantee that you will be in handcuffs and on your way to a prison cell within a minute of your departure." He leaned back in his chair, watching my reaction carefully. "But it's your choice. Here, or prison."

I thought hard about what he just said. He was completely right. If I left now, the FBI would haul my ass back to prison and I would never get out. I felt completely cornered. Hillerman was offering me a choice, but it wasn't really a fair one. I could stay here and be experimented on and beat up by guards for another nine years and nine months, or I could leave and be thrown in prison for the rest of my life.

"What are you so afraid of?" Hillerman asked me, folding his hands again and peering at me. "Is it me? The guards? Are you just afraid for Miriam's health? I can assure you, we're treating her as best we can. What is it about this place that scares you so much that you would choose prison over it?"

"I'm afraid of your secret," I told him quietly.

Hillerman's expression didn't change. "I'm not sure I know what you mean," he said.

"I'm sure that you do."

"Why don't you take a seat, and we can discuss it," Hillerman offered, again nodding to the chair across from him.

Again, I refused to move. "Why am I still here?" I demanded. "What do you want from me?"

"I want you to sit down," he said, his voice sounding a little more forceful. "I thought maybe we could talk a little, so I can reassure you that you are safe here." He waited expectantly, staring at me with his eyebrows raised.

I knew it was pointless to argue any further, so I walked over to the table, pulled out the chair, and sat down. I glared across the table at him, but he easily held my gaze. Leaning toward him, I said firmly, "I *don't* feel safe here, and nothing you can say will change that!"

"Because Miriam told you it wasn't safe?" Hillerman asked me. "And, oh yes, you trust her judgment over mine."

"You catch on quickly," I said sarcastically. "I like that."

"Let me explain to you what has happened to your friend," Hillerman said, leaning forward as well.

"You already told me your story!" I snapped. "And so did she!"

"I'm sure she did," Hillerman muttered with a chuckle.

"And frankly, she was more convincing!" I finished, ignoring his comment.

For a moment, Hillerman just stared at me with that all-too-happy smile of his. But then he asked me, "Do you know what happens when one becomes delusional?"

I continued to glare at him, not going to let him convince me that Miriam was crazy. I knew that she wasn't.

"The mind begins to draw away from reality," Hillerman began to explain, his eyes never leaving mine. "You begin to see and hear things that aren't real, and soon you become convinced that they are. You even become convinced that there are conspiracies all around you." He nodded to me. He knew exactly what Miriam had told me. "The reason Miriam was so convincing about her theories was because she herself was convinced. Once we treat her she will realize that this place is no different than any other medical study in the country."

I nodded. "So you're telling me that everything she told me was all in her head?"

Hillerman nodded and smiled, thinking that I was beginning to believe him. "Yes, that's right. She created her conspiracy in her mind and she believes it is real. But I can assure you, it is not."

I snickered. "I know how people are when they're delusional. I've seen friends of mine on acid trips. My father, as I'm sure you know, is a Colician. When he was first affected and his ability began to show, he was constantly mumbling to himself about broken gas lines or fried circuits or something he was convinced he had to fix, but there was nothing broken. When Miriam came to me today and told me about what was going on here, she wasn't showing any of the symptoms I had seen before. She was terrified, and this time I can see something that *is* broken. It's this place. There's something going on here that you don't want people to know about, and now you've made Miriam a part of it. She is *not* crazy."

Hillerman continued to smile at me. "Are you a doctor, Austin?"

"No, but I know enough to recognize when someone is lying through their teeth at me!"

"Why don't you tell me exactly what Miriam told you, so we can sort this mess out."

"You know exactly what Miriam told me! Stop pretending to be oblivious!"

"I may be mistaken," Hillerman replied calmly. "And I think it may be best if you told me what *you* think is going on as well. What do *you* think is going on, Austin?"

"Don't you mean what I *know* is going on?" I demanded. "You can stop the act now! I know about your experiments!"

"You mean our medical tests?" Hillerman clarified.

"Yeah, those!" I cried. "I know you've been testing a new strain of the Colician Virus on us, and I know that you finally succeeded with Miriam!"

Nodding again, Hillerman asked, "And you really believe that?"

"I believe Miriam!" I replied.

"You seriously believe that these scientists are all here to recreate the greatest global calamity in human history?" Hillerman pointed a thumb over his shoulder at the window overlooking the lab. "Can you really look me in the eye and tell me you think I would do something like that?"

I looked him square in the eye. "I *know* you're doing this."

"Do you have any idea how delusional *you* are beginning to sound?"

"No!" I cried, pointing an accusing finger at him. "You are *not* going to pin that on me too! You can't convince me I'm crazy!"

"Well, if you go around telling everyone that we're recreating the Colician Virus, what are people going to think about you?"

Hillerman was evil; he was trying to corner me again as he had done when I wanted to leave.

"You know what's funny?" I asked him. "You haven't once denied that you're experimenting on us!"

"That's because we *are* experimenting on you," Hillerman replied. "Just not with what you think." Smiling again, he told me, "Everybody here signed up to be experimented on, Austin. They all knew what they were getting themselves into, and so did you."

"I didn't sign up for what you've been doing!" I said. "I would have chosen prison over this place if I had known what you were doing here!"

Leaning closer to me again, Hillerman asked, "Do you really think we would put our patients at risk like that?"

"If you were trying to find a cure to the Colician Virus, then I definitely think you would put us at risk."

Hillerman actually appeared surprised. Confused. Maybe Kost had been wrong, and they really *weren't* trying to cure the virus. "What makes you think we would be searching for a cure?"

"Isn't it obvious? If you cure the virus, then all the Colicians can come home. All the broken families can be put back together again."

"Well, that is a very thoughtful idea, Austin, but my fellow scientists and I would not test dangerous material on innocent civilians like you are suggesting."

"Let's cut the crap, Jack," I said sharply. "Lieutenant Douche Bag out there practically admitted to me what you guys have been cooking up down here!"

"*Sergeant Jaeger* is a typical soldier," Hillerman replied, not at all offended by my outburst. "At least, a typical modern day soldier. He runs on the fear he creates in others. He works to intimidate everyone. He'll say anything to scare you. And now that you mention it, I will have a word with him for filling your head with even more of this nonsense."

I was now completely frustrated. Hillerman wasn't giving in to anything I tried, and I started to wonder if I should give up. I believed every word Miriam had told me; it all made sense. I would fight for her, whether Dr. Hillerman would admit to his experiments or not. Sighing as I realized how tired I was, I put my elbows up on the desk and dropped my head in my palms.

"What's wrong, Austin?" Hillerman asked.

"Will you stop calling me that?" I said, glaring at him through my fingers. I was sick of him calling me by my first name. The only people who called me Austin were Miriam, Jeff, and Kost. Everybody else called me by my last name. Only my friends called me Austin, and he was definitely not my friend.

Hillerman appeared very confused. "That's your name, isn't it?"

"Everyone here calls me Rockwell!" I snapped. "You should do the same!"

He seemed to understand. "Does it bother you that I call you by your first name? Does it bother you that I treat you differently than everyone else treats you?"

"I'm not here for a therapy session!" I said. I didn't want to discuss my feelings with the likes of him.

"I'm well aware," Hillerman replied. "But part of me thinks that maybe you need one." He looked down at his papers again. "After all, you didn't always used to be this angry, did you? You used to be much happier, with a very promising future."

"Stop!" I warned, starting to feel my emotions take flight as I realized where he was taking this.

"But you stopped being happy after your family was taken by the strain," Hillerman continued in the same calm voice, looking back up at me with a solemn expression. "That was when you threw your life away."

"Shut up!" I cried. I couldn't take it anymore. Slamming my fists down on the desk and making the papers jump, I put my head back in my hands as tears came pouring from my eyes. I became an emotional wildfire whenever my family was brought up. My life ended when they were taken from me.

Giving me a dramatic pause, Hillerman said quietly, "You threw your entire future away after they were taken. You started getting into trouble, even working for a drug dealer."

"I had nothing better to live for," I whispered. "I lost everything after the strain."

"Is that why you're so afraid that we're creating another strain?" he asked me softly. "Because you think you'll lose what you have left? You're afraid to lose Miriam, is that it?"

"It doesn't matter," I said, but then sighed. "Yes."

"And when she told you about what she believes is going on, you panicked, because you couldn't have a repeat of 2018," Hillerman concluded.

Closing my eyes, I nodded. This man really could see right through me.

"Look at me, Austin," Hillerman instructed, and when I did he once again smiled reassuringly at me. "Miriam is going to be fine. You're not going to lose her. I promise you, we are not recreating the Colician Virus."

"If she's fine, then I want to see her," I said.

Hillerman hesitated. "I'm afraid I can't allow that."

"See?" I raised my eyebrows. "That's why I don't trust you. You say she's fine, yet you won't let me talk to her."

"I said she *will be* fine," Hillerman corrected. He shook his head. "She's not fine right now, and that is why I'm not going to allow you to see her. She's in a very frantic, panicked state right now, and has become a danger to both herself and everyone she comes into contact with. Very few people are allowed to see her. But I assure you, tonight my colleagues and I will work as hard as we can to find out what exactly has been done to her, and we'll fix it." He smiled at me yet again. When I didn't reply, he asked me, "Who exactly did Miriam tell about her conspiracy?"

"Excuse me?"

"Well, she told you about what she thought was going on," Hillerman said, but I could tell he was keen on getting this last bit of information from me. "Did she tell anyone else about it?"

"No," I answered, a little too quickly, and immediately knew that Jeff and Kost were in danger.

"Are you sure about that?" Hillerman asked in a soft voice, and gave me this look that made me freeze.

I nodded as a shiver made the hair on the back of my neck stand straight up. "She said I'm the only one she fully trusts."

Nodding slowly, Hillerman gave me one last searching stare before looking back down to his papers. "Okay. You're free to go now."

I wasn't exactly sure what to do, so I just sat there.

He glanced back up. "Sergeant Jaeger will escort you back to your room."

"Okay." I stood up and started walking to the door.

"Oh, and Austin?" Hillerman called after me. When I turned, he said, "If I were you, I wouldn't go spreading details of Miriam's conspiracy around. We wouldn't want a panic on our hands."

"No, I guess we wouldn't," I replied through my teeth.

"And try to get some rest," Hillerman instructed as I walked through the door. "I have a feeling we'll be seeing each other again very soon."

Something woke me one night, a night long after I'd retired to the beach house with my wife. She slept beside me, but as I was startled awake and sat up quickly, she blinked awake as well. My eyes darted across the bedroom, searching for the source of my anxiety. My wife reached up and gently rubbed my shoulder, asking if I was all right. I said I was, even though we both knew I wasn't. I shivered, and she sat up to wrap her arms around me. She asked if it was a nightmare, which was a definite possibility, even after all these years. I shook my head no, and told her I was going to go for a walk. She asked if I wanted her to come along, but I shook my head no again. I just needed some air.

Out on the beach, the wind blew hard, signaling the storm that was about to touch land. I walked barefoot and shirtless on the black sand, ignoring the shivers that kept rippling through my body. Something was wrong, tugging at my mind, taunting me, but I couldn't interpret the message my subconscious was trying to send me.

The crashing of the waves against the rocks couldn't drown out the pounding in my head, the ringing in my ears. I stepped into the surf, the salt water stinging my bare skin, and suddenly it hit me.

It was time.

I ran back inside, despite the protests of my arthritic knee, and went to the little closet in the hallway, outside the powder room. In the back of it, I had buried an artifact from my past. My wife didn't know I had it, and if she found out…that would be a very loud conversation. But I needed it now. I needed it to help someone in dire need of guidance.

The costume was heavy and thick, its artificial fur itchy and hot. Still, I crept into the powder room and slipped into it, pulling the mask over my head. My breath heated up the inside of the mask, making my face hot. Beneath the costume, my skin itched, and I wanted to take it off as soon as I put it on. I ignored my discomfort and stepped in front of the mirror. A black, furry creature stared back at me, an image that haunted my past but was necessary to help the young man who needed me.

Most people wouldn't understand why the costume was necessary. They would ask why I couldn't just tell him what he needed to know. I knew that I couldn't reveal my true self to him, or even use my own voice, because if I did, too many things would become complicated and the young man I was trying to help might not understand what he was seeing. I knew he would be confused because, even though he didn't know me, I knew him very well. He would not understand if he saw my face.

And so, the suit was necessary. It would help guide him to the person he needed to find, and divert him away from a tragedy that would end his life.

Once he found the man who would become his friend, I would direct him from there.

3

Nightmares

When Jaeger took me back to my room, I was unpleasantly surprised to see that my door was gone. Someone had removed it from its hinges. He caught me staring at the doorway and told me, "This way you can't lock us out."

But he was wrong. I *could* lock him out. Once Jaeger and his men left me alone, I took my blanket and my pillow from my bed, walked into my bathroom and locked the door behind me. They hadn't thought to remove this door. It was wooden, so this one would be easy to kick down, but it still gave me a sense of security. The bathtub was tiny and cramped, but at least I felt safer behind a locked door. This way, I would be able to hear if someone came for me again.

It took me forever to get to sleep. Every little sound I heard put me on red alert. I would finally begin to doze off, but then there would be a rustle of air inside the vents or a creak in the ceiling and I was wide awake again. In the time I spent lying awake in the bathtub, I was forced to think about Hillerman, and what else could have been in the gas he had given me. Miriam was infected with the virus this way; it would be so simple for Hillerman to slip the virus into the gas canister along with the sedative.

It must have taken hours before I finally relaxed enough to slowly fall asleep. And even then, the fear didn't leave me. The nightmares started as soon as I lost consciousness, and they didn't stop coming.

~~*

For the first time in almost three months, I didn't have the dream of falling. Instead, I had dreams that were much, much worse. The first dream started with me alone in an empty city. I looked everywhere in every building, but there was nobody. There was complete silence wherever I went. The only sound was my frantic, desperate voice as I screamed and screamed and prayed there would be somebody, *any*body. After what felt like three days of searching, I completely gave up. I collapsed to my knees in the middle of a deserted street and screamed so loud and so long that my throat was raw and I felt as if my lungs were going to come up my throat. I let myself cry and cry, until there was nothing left inside of me. I curled up in a ball in the street and wished something would just come along and kill me, and put me out of my misery. Anything was better than this torture.

Suddenly, out of the silence, out of the empty world, came a voice. It was only a whisper, but I could have heard a butterfly's wings beat. I immediately sat upright. Looking around frantically, my ears strained to hear the slightest sound of movement. When I heard it again, I was sure I wasn't going crazy. Jumping to my feet, I looked to where the whisper had come from. There was a tall building, at least forty stories, looming over me on one side of the street. The front doors were open, and even though there was an empty blackness beyond them I bolted over, not once hesitating at the darkness. Once inside I couldn't see a thing, so I stopped and stood very still, hoping that maybe I would hear the voice once more. I did.

"Austin..." it whispered from above me, a breath in the air.

I couldn't see, but for some reason I didn't need to. I went straight to the stairs, and before I knew what I was doing I was running. I was running up flight after flight until I finally burst through another door and dashed out onto the roof. Considering how long I had been running, I wasn't winded; I was breathing normally.

After being in darkness for that long, the sudden light that met my eyes made me squeeze them shut and shield them with both arms. Blinking furiously and squinting against the harsh light, I peered across the roof and my breath caught in my throat when I saw a person standing at the edge. He was facing me, but he was far enough away that I couldn't make out his face. What I could make out, however, was the blood that was dripping off his entire body. His white shirt and dark blue jeans were completely ripped and tattered, strips dangling off of his gaunt form. There were gashes where the clothes were torn, the origin of all the blood. His entire body was heaving up and down from heavy breathing, and his arms were out away from his sides in a way that made it appear as if he was going to attack me. For several terrifying moments, I stood frozen where I was, staring at the man. His dark brown eyes never left mine. As scared as I was of this injured man, there was something strangely familiar about him. I still couldn't make out his face. Even if I did know him, he was giving off an aura that told me to stay away. Something wasn't right about him. I began to slowly move back into the stairwell. Then the man sucked in a loud, rattling breath and whispered, "Austin…"

I suddenly recognized him. It had been three years since I had last seen him, and his horrifying appearance had kept me from realizing who it was. "Dad?" I asked hesitantly.

His arm slowly extended toward me, shaking the entire time. His ragged breathing was getting louder, as if someone was squeezing his windpipe and he was struggling to breathe.

Realizing what he wanted me to do, I carefully walked across the roof toward him. As I got closer, I saw how his face had changed. He no longer had the constant, joking expression outlining his serious eyes. Now, his eyes were bloodshot and his hair was grown out and hanging in matted clumps around his face. His front lip was pulled back to show his front teeth, which were stained red with his own blood. Several deep cuts lay all across his face, making his skin color appear a dark crimson. He looked completely insane. He scared me.

"Oh my God!" I whispered as I stopped myself several feet away. "What happened to you?"

His terrifying expression didn't change. He stared into my eyes and slowly pivoted his feet so he could point out to the rest of the city. "You sent us here," he hissed, his upper lip pulling back even more.

I looked to where he was pointing, and my eyes widened in shock. The sky was no longer the pale blue it had been the three days I had been here. The sun was no longer shining. There were dark, ominous, orange and gray clouds blocking out the entirety of the sky. They were low and thick and they made me feel like I was getting pushed deeper and deeper into this world, forced to remain a captive inside of this dream. The clouds weren't half of what made the world suddenly appear so terrifying. Every building in the city, every building I had personally searched for signs of life, was burning in a fire that reached toward the sky and turned the clouds those dull, depressing colors. Most of the buildings had already crumpled to the ground and lay in heaps of rubble and ash, but the ones that remained standing were engulfed in the flames licking at the sky.

"What's happening?" I breathed in horror, unable to look away from the destruction. The next time I blinked, the roaring of the fire filled my ears and made me want to scream in agony. I looked to my father, hoping he could provide the answer.

"This is where you sent us," he growled, still not looking away from me.

Looking down, I saw that the building we were standing on was also burning. We were completely surrounded by the flames, but it was like they had created a circle around us. Why was this happening? Why was my father's world burning? Then I remembered something I had thought about ever since my family left for the Parallel Earth. Nobody had heard what became of the Parallel Earth. Once I imagined what it was like, and this was what I had pictured. A world without a government, without a leader, and the people unable to control their powers. I imagined their world burning in a never-ending fire.

"This is where you sent *me*," he said quietly.

"I didn't want you to go," I told him, my eyes pleading with his.

He didn't listen. I don't even think he could hear me. "Now you can burn with me," he replied, grabbing my arm and pulling me off the edge of the roof. Both of us started falling fast toward the ground, but we never struck.

I guess I didn't escape the old dream after all...

~~*

I woke up screaming. At least, I thought I woke up. It turned out I only moved from one dream to the next. One empty world to another. Only this time, I was in a forest.

It was pitch black like the stairwell had been, but I could tell it was a forest by the rustling of leaves. I wondered how many days I would be trapped in this dream.

Unlike I had in the empty city, I didn't start walking in search of somebody. I knew there wouldn't be anyone. Even if there was, things would just end badly like they had with my deranged father. So I stood perfectly still, my quickening breaths and racing heartbeat drowning out the rustling leaves. I didn't know how long I stood there. I couldn't know. I seemed to be trapped in an unchanging pocket of time, a single instant of eternity that I would be imprisoned in forever.

When I first heard the voices, I thought I was going crazy. I was sure I was losing it. The words were indistinguishable, as if the wind was whispering something to me. I must have been there, alone, for so long that I just went completely mad. It was just the wind playing tricks on my mind. There was nothing here, just the trees and the darkness and me. Nothing more, nothing less.

The whispers steadily rose in volume, and it took me a while to realize that whoever it was wasn't whispering, they were screaming. The screams became louder and louder, until suddenly a violent gust of wind hit me full in the face and surrounded me, pushing me every which way. Unable to take it anymore, I collapsed to the ground and curled up in a ball, squeezing my eyes closed. The screams were tearing at my ears, making me wince. They were no longer only in my ears; they were in my head too. When they got so loud that they were echoing in my brain, I started screaming too.

~~*

When the screaming abruptly stopped, I blinked in surprise and lifted my head to take a look around. I had once again jumped to a different dream. Now, I was crouched in a hallway with soft lighting. It looked like a hallway in a hotel, extending for as far as I could see. Wooden doors were widely spaced along the walls with three digit numbers carved into them, and even though the hall was so plain and nondescript, I recognized it. It was a hallway inside a cruise ship. I had never been on a cruise ship, but I recognized it from the commercials I'd seen on television as a kid.

As friendly and inviting as it was, the scene felt off. I expected to hear voices this time, voices of excited kids and exhausted parents, but once again there was nobody. There were soft sounds around me this time though; the rumble of the engine below me, the whirring of the AC. I felt the gentle rocking of the ship as we cruised across an ocean. Where were all the people? This was a strange place to be alone. Was everybody asleep? Was everybody dead? Was there even anyone else on the ship?

"Austin," said a soft voice that sounded almost mechanical.

I stood up quickly and rounded on the person who had spoken my name. When I saw who, or what, was behind me, I nearly burst into laughter. A man dressed in a big, furry gorilla suit stood not four feet from me. He looked so fuzzy that I couldn't take him seriously, even though I knew that I probably should. The gorilla man stood there unmoving, so still that I couldn't believe there was actually a person inside. I stared through the dark, empty holes of the mask, hoping to see a glimpse of the man's eyes. Nothing. Only blackness. "Hello, Austin," he said after several long moments of blaring silence.

I raised an eyebrow at his odd, monotone voice and struggled with my strong urge to snort and laugh. "What do you want?" I asked, beginning to grow uncomfortable with the situation. What kind of weirdo approaches a stranger in a gorilla suit?

"Follow me," the gorilla man replied, but he didn't move.

I was starting to wonder if the gorilla man was whom I was actually speaking to. He had remained frozen the entire time, and I couldn't see his face so how did I know there was even a man in the suit? I leaned to the side to peer behind it, looking for someone standing behind the suit, messing with me. "Where are we going?" I demanded, narrowing my eyes suspiciously.

"Follow me now," he repeated, his tone still not changing.

"No," I said forcefully, glaring at him.

The gorilla man paused for a second, as if struggling to come up with some way to convince me to go with him. Clearly, he was not very good at persuasion, because all he said was, "Follow me, Austin Rockwell."

"What happens if I don't?" I asked, holding my ground. I could barely trust anyone anymore, and I wasn't about to put my trust in a man dressed as a monkey.

Finally moving, the gorilla man raised his furry right hand and pointed at something over my shoulder. Other than that, the rest of his body remained in its frozen position.

Slowly and hesitantly, I turned to see what the gorilla man wanted me to see. I only managed to catch a glimpse of the animal before its teeth were in my face and its snarls cutting through the air around me. I again collapsed to the floor, crying out in terror and covering my head with my arms.

~~*

I hopped again to a fourth dream. I was breathing hard from the animal's sudden attack, but once again I had hopped at the very last, crucial second. The animal that attacked me looked oddly like a German Shepherd, with coarse brown and black fur and a long snout like a dog's. Its breath in my face smelled like dog breath, too. I didn't know what it meant, what any of it meant, but I kept a mental note to talk out my dreams later, when Miriam and I were back together.

There were voices, and these were actual voices instead of just random, ghostly whispers. Lifting my arms away from my face, I squinted up at what was above me. As I stared harder and harder, I realized that I was instead looking down at what was below me. Turning my head from side to side, I saw that I was lying on the ceiling between two florescent lights. The ceiling I was on appeared to be about ten feet off the ground, in what looked to be a large hospital room. There was a flat bed in the center of the room, with arm, chest, head, and leg restraints attached to it. To the right of it, a flat-screened computer sat on a cart and beeped every couple of seconds. Three different canisters of gas attached to masks sat beside the bed, unlabeled, making them all the more suspicious. On a shelf of the cart below the computer, there was a tray filled with the same little gadgets Dr. Hillerman had in the room where he had treated me. To the far left of the bed there was a metal door, and to the far right there was a long counter running along the wall with all sorts of medical equipment spread across it. There was everything from syringes to scalpels to drills, and as I looked around I became more and more uneasy. Three men stood at the far end of the counter, leaning over something and discussing a matter in hushed tones. They were wearing blue surgical scrubs with white masks covering their noses and mouths. One of them had glasses, and I realized it was Dr. Hillerman. That was when I understood that this dream wasn't really a dream. I was observing firsthand what was really going on down in Hillerman's lab. Somehow, I was able to do this.

Hillerman and the other two doctors moved away from the counter and began moving toward the bed. They started talking louder, but it still wasn't loud enough for me to understand them. I strained to hear, but it all came up to me as mumbles and nonsense. I then tried to lift my head off the ceiling and lean down closer in an attempt to hear better, but I found that my body was glued down. I tried pushing myself up with my hands, but accomplished nothing. Growing frustrated, I slumped down and sighed heavily. Since I was actually able to see what was going on under the lab, it would have done some good if I could actually hear the conversation brewing beneath me. Suddenly, with a clarity that caused me to jump in surprise, the volume in the room skyrocketed and I was finally able to understand just how gruesome things were about to become.

"How many more people know besides Rockwell?" one doctor asked.

"Austin wouldn't say," Hillerman replied, his hands sliding into his pockets. "I did my best to convince him of our cover story, but he won't trust any staff here. He wouldn't tell me who else was told."

"Do you think she told anyone else?" the other doctor asked.

Hillerman nodded. "The two of them socialize with two other test subjects: Kost Nicholson and Jeff Robinson. I am fairly certain that the two of them were told as well."

"What do you plan to do about them?" the first doctor asked.

"Austin's already been taken care of," Hillerman assured. "Whatever has affected Miriam will begin to take effect on him shortly. Once we're done here, I plan to make a house call to see the other two."

Shit, I thought in horror. *He did get to me, and now he's going to go after Kost and Jeff too!*

I suddenly could hear loud, terrified screams coming from outside the metal door opposite the doctors, and a moment later the door burst open and two security guards came through, dragging a struggling Miriam behind them. She was kicking and wailing as hard and loud as she could, but the guards each held one of her arms and she was much smaller and weaker than them. She tried to halt herself by pushing her feet into the floor in front of her, but they kept slipping out from under her. She was no longer wearing her outfit from before; she was now in a white shirt and white pants that clearly screamed, "I'M A PATIENT IN A HOSPITAL FOR THE CLINICALLY INSANE." Clinically insane doctors, maybe…

As the other two doctors walked back over to the counter with the medical equipment from the cart, Hillerman pulled two latex gloves out of his pockets. He was watching Miriam struggle with a strange fascination that made me shudder. I had never seen someone look at another human being like that before. It made me extremely uncomfortable.

When the guards finally managed to haul Miriam to the bed, they pushed her down onto her knees so she would stop kicking at them. She went down hard and inhaled sharply, and as she suddenly seemed to feel the intense gaze bearing down on her, she slowly looked up into Hillerman's suppressing eyes. I then understood what the restraints on the bed were for.

"Hi, Miriam," Hillerman said softly as he pulled on his gloves.

Miriam let out a noise that sounded like a cross between a squeak and a moan. I could feel her fear filling up the room, and I tried to call out to her, but found that I could not speak. Her petrified face filled me with terror, but I was still glued to the ceiling and could do nothing to help. I was being forced to watch whatever was about to happen to my best friend, unable to do anything to assist her. It made me want to throw up or scream or something.

Hillerman nodded toward the bed and then the guards pulled Miriam to her feet once more. As one took her by the legs and the other held her arms, they hoisted her up onto the bed. She started thrashing immediately, but two more doctors came through the door to assist the guards as they attempted to strap her down. Once they managed to get her head and wrists secured, Miriam started to give up. She had stopped screaming, and her struggles were no longer effective. Several whimpers escaped her, and her breathing sped up rapidly as a low chatter began amongst the doctors and guards. When she was completely strapped in, the two guards left, leaving Miriam at the mercy of Dr. Hillerman and his assistants.

Her breathing was still heavy and fast, and I could have sworn she was staring up at me. Maybe she could sense my presence there, and knew I was being forced to watch what was about to happen. Hillerman saw how panicked she was, and he pulled one of the masks up from its tank and set it over her mouth and nose. This sent Miriam into another fit, and she began screaming and thrashing all over again.

"Relax, *relax*!" he instructed soothingly, placing his free hand on her forehead to keep her steady. "It's only oxygen. Just breathe…" He glanced over at the computer after another doctor placed a clip over Miriam's right index finger, causing the computer to beep rapidly as jagged lines appeared on the monitor. A large number 194 popped up at the bottom of the screen. "Let's try to get your heart rate down a little," Hillerman said, keeping the oxygen mask over her face.

Miriam squeezed her eyes shut, but I saw that she was struggling to get her breathing under control. She inhaled slowly and exhaled even slower, and she did this for almost a minute before the number on the screen went down to 170.

"Good," Hillerman praised, removing the mask. "It wasn't very wise of you to tell your friends about what's happened to you," he scolded, turning to take an empty syringe from the doctor standing behind him.

"I haven't told anyone," Miriam lied, her voice quavering with her fear. She still hadn't opened her eyes.

Hillerman chuckled and turned back to her. "Now, we both know that's a lie," he said, gently rubbing the skin on the inside of her elbow with a cloth soaked in alcohol and preparing to stick her with the needle. Miriam felt this and her eyes shot open, and she started to squirm away again. "Don't," Hillerman warned as the needle penetrated her skin, and she froze as he started drawing blood. "Who else did you tell besides Austin?" he asked quietly, and I could tell that he was losing his patience. He was running out of time to silence those who knew.

"No one," Miriam whispered, her terrified expression making her seem very feeble and helpless.

"Miriam," Hillerman began, placing his hands on the bed beside her and leaning closer so he could look her in the eyes. "You do understand that if any of this gets out, bad things will happen to the people who talked?" He glanced back to the monitor for a second as Miriam's heart rate rose again. "Are you sure you don't want to tell me who else knows?" When Miriam refused to reply, he nodded slowly. "No? Okay." Stepping away from her, he snapped his fingers at the doctor behind him. The doctor handed him another syringe, but this one was loaded. Hillerman started to inject the clear liquid into Miriam's upper arm.

"What are you doing?" Miriam demanded shrilly, but there wasn't much she could do to prevent the injection.

"This is just a mild sedative to help you relax a little," Hillerman informed as he gave her the shot.

"I don't want to relax..." Miriam mumbled weakly.

"Well, I need you relaxed," Hillerman told her, handing the syringe off again and patting her shoulder gently. He stepped around the bed so he was positioned just behind her head, and he said, "Miriam, I'm going to ask you a few questions, and I need you to answer them honestly."

Miriam's eyes fluttered from the drug and she sighed heavily, but she seemed conscious enough to focus on Hillerman's words.

"Can you confirm for me your blood type?" he asked. "For the record?"

"A negative," she murmured, her eyes drifting closed.

"Stay awake, Miriam," Hillerman said, turning again. "Let's get that IV going now." As two other doctors started hooking up an IV to Miriam's right arm, he looked back down at her. "A negative," he repeated, nodding. "And how are you feeling right now?"

"Scared," she mumbled, blinking up at him as she struggled to focus her eyes.

"Yes, I know," Hillerman replied. "But do you feel sick?"

"I feel tired," Miriam said, her words jumbling together. Her eyes fluttered closed again.

"That's just the sedative," Hillerman told her, glancing up at the doctors preparing the IV. "We need this going now. We're losing her."

"I just started the drip," one of them informed. "See, here she comes."

Hillerman looked back down at her as she started to wake up. She blinked up at everyone gazing down at her, and I could see her chest rising and falling rapidly as her breathing sped up again. Whatever was in the IV, it was having the opposite effect as the sedative. Hillerman saw this new panic in her eyes, and in an effort to keep her calm, he said soothingly, "You're all right."

"What are you doing to me?" she demanded, looking around at all the doctors frantically.

"We're calming your body while keeping your mind alert," Hillerman explained as the fear intensified on Miriam's face. "It's a strange sensation, but it will pass."

"Why?" Miriam squeaked, and I felt horrible that even with all her fear, she was still unable to move.

"We don't want you struggling, but we need you to focus on our questions, all right?" Hillerman did something then that made me very angry and protective. He reached out a hand and smoothed back Miriam's hair, evidently to try and comfort her. I was going to cause him some serious damage for touching her like that. "Now, I know you're scared, but everything's going to be just fine. Can you tell me how your body feels right now?"

"I feel exhausted, and my head has been aching all day," Miriam replied, her eyes still flickering from doctor to doctor.

"That's to be expected," Hillerman said, nodding. "What else?"

"What else *what?*" Miriam demanded weakly. "What else do you want from me?"

"Do you have any other pain?" Hillerman asked, his voice steady to keep her calm.

"My whole body feels like it's vibrating!" Miriam snapped, and her desperate eyes seemed to make contact with mine again. "And I'm starving! What do you care? You did this to me!"

"I'm only trying to help," Hillerman said, and his hands gently brushed back her hair again. He was pushing his luck.

"I don't want your help!" Miriam sobbed as tears spilled out of her eyes. "I want to go home!"

"I'm afraid that's not going to happen for a very long time," Hillerman told her softly, wiping the tears from her eyes. "Don't cry. We're going to help you get through this. Everything's going to be just fine."

The doctor's words were not comforting, and Miriam let out several more sobs after that. She was so scared, and she stared pleadingly into my eyes. I wanted so badly to help her, to reach out and take her hand, but I couldn't move. If only I could wake up, then I could try to find exactly where she was and stop this.

Hillerman shushed her for about a minute before speaking again. "Why don't you tell me about this new ability of yours?"

"I don't want this!" Miriam cried. "I never wanted this!"

"And I can help you through this, but I need you to talk to me," Hillerman told her, peering down at her with prying eyes. "What can you do? Tell me about it."

Trying to swallow down her sobs, Miriam stared up at him through her tears. Her lips quivering, she obeyed him. "I can hear what people think."

"Can you hear what I'm thinking right now?" Hillerman asked her curiously.

Pausing, Miriam gave a slight shake of her head.

"Why not?"

"I don't know," Miriam said in a shaky whisper.

"Is it because you're scared?" Hillerman asked, his gaze practically pressing down on her for his answers.

"*I don't know!*" Miriam repeated, stressing her anxiety and confusion. "I don't know why, and I don't care!"

"Can you try?"

"No! I don't want to! Leave me alone!"

Sighing, Hillerman stopped to think, his eyes never leaving Miriam's terrified face. "Can you do anything else?" he asked her, trying not to upset her any more.

"I don't know," Miriam squeaked, squeezing her eyes closed.

"Are you able to manipulate the thoughts and actions of others?"

"I don't know!" Miriam screamed, but then she cried out in pain and gasped. Her eyes were exhausted, and I knew she needed serious rest.

"What's the matter?" Hillerman asked in immediate concern.

"My head!" Miriam moaned. "It feels like it's going to explode!"

Quickly turning to the doctor on the other side of her, Hillerman waved his hand. The other doctor rushed back to the counter and loaded another syringe, this time with a thick white substance. He handed it to Hillerman when he returned.

"What is that?" Miriam asked cautiously as tears of pain flooded her eyes.

"It will help with the pain," Hillerman assured her, injecting it into her upper arm.

Miriam gladly accepted the shot, and her agonized whimpers died down shortly after. With the pain suppressed, she seemed much more relaxed as well as relieved.

"The headache is caused by the pressure applied to the brain during the transformation," Hillerman explained to her when she calmed down. "It will bother you for the next week or so, but as long as you behave yourself I can relieve the pain. Do you understand that? If you cooperate with us throughout these tests, you won't have to suffer."

Regretfully, Miriam nodded. She didn't want to give in, but the pain must have been so intense that she would rather cooperate with him in return for medication.

"Good," Hillerman said, smiling down at her again. "Now, I can see that you're exhausted, so I'll save any more questions that I have for the morning. I'm going to give you a sedative so you can sleep through the night to rest up for the stress of the next few days."

"Do you want me to set up the MRI right away, sir?" one of the doctors asked as Hillerman accepted yet another loaded syringe.

"No," Hillerman replied, walking around Miriam so he could inject the sedative into the IV. "I want to open her up. I want to see if there are any internal changes that have occurred."

As it dawned on Miriam what was about to happen, her breathing and heart rate sped up again and she began thrashing violently against her restraints.

Seeing this, Hillerman smiled reassuringly. "Don't worry," he said. "You won't feel a thing. When you wake up, you won't even realize that anything happened." He injected the sedative into the IV.

"No!" Miriam screamed, tugging against the straps. "No, no, no! No..."

4

Changed

I woke up after that, but not before I fell from the ceiling, with Miriam's screams filling the darkness that held me. The force I felt when I struck the ground caused me to sit up so fast that I smashed my forehead into the bath faucet. I cried out and put a hand to my head, muttering a couple curse words until the pain died down. At first, my sleep-ridden brain couldn't rationalize why I woke up in my bathtub, but then I remembered. I remembered the horror I'd seen last night. I remembered everything.

"Oh no," I whispered. I jumped up and went to the mirror. I looked at my reflection, expecting to see a monster looking back at me. Maybe the man in the gorilla costume from my dream, or my beaten, bloody father, but all I saw was myself, same as before. The only thing different was the little spot of blood on my forehead.

But I'm not the same. I knew that. I couldn't deny it. I heard what Hillerman said last night. It may have been in my dream, but it had also really happened, and I knew that Hillerman wouldn't lie about something like that, not to his colleagues. I could picture him lying about that to me to intimidate me, but he didn't know I was there last night. This was for real. I was now a…what would Miriam and I be called? Second generation Colicians? Maybe Hillerman had a special name for the strain he used on us and we'd be named after that.

Kost and Jeff! I suddenly remembered what Hillerman said about them last night. He was going to change them too. I had to find them.

I scrambled out of the bathroom and practically ripped my dirty clothes off. My bedroom door was still missing, but nobody was there, and even if there was I doubted I would have cared much. It wasn't like I had a reason to be ashamed.

I smelled awful. My whole body smelled like sweat and grime. Any other day I would have been in the shower immediately, but I had to get to my friends. They were way more important to me than my hygiene. I threw on the first pair of boxers and shorts I found, and then grabbed the nearest t-shirt lying on the floor. It didn't smell too bad. I rushed out the door, almost forgetting to slip into my sneakers on the way. I turned to run toward Kost's room, which was closer to mine than Jeff's.

I ran right into Sergeant Jaeger.

"Whoa!" he said, catching my arm as I jumped back in surprise. "Where you off to, boy?"

"Cafeteria," I answered automatically.

Sergeant Jaeger raised an eyebrow. "I don't think so. Back in your room."

"I'm starving!" I protested, my voice more of a whine than I intended it to be. I *was* starving. I had never felt so hungry in my life. "You're seriously gonna keep me stuck in here and not even let me eat?" My stomach growled along with me.

Studying my face carefully, Jaeger sighed. "All right. But no funny business like last night. I get any of that and you're gonna wish you'd never signed that contract."

I shrugged. "I already feel that way, but okay." Inside, though, I was muttering the f-bomb over and over again. How was I supposed to warn Kost and Jeff if I was being tailed wherever I went? I could try to outrun Jaeger, and I probably could, but he had more of his buddies waiting around to grab me if I tried.

Wait…how did I know that?

A horrible thought pushed that question aside. What if Hillerman already got to Kost and Jeff? What if he was already changing them, like he changed me and Miriam? What if I was too late?

No. I couldn't be. I had to save them. I wasn't about to let anyone else down.

I wolfed down my plate of bacon, eggs, and toast. I wanted to ask Jaeger if I could go get another plate—or maybe another three—but his smirk brought back my stubbornness. He knew what was happening to me as well as I did. That must be what the crazy hunger was: a side effect of the change. I refused to please him by asking for more food. Besides, my stomach was beginning to feel a little queasy.

"You done?" Jaeger asked, still grinning.

"Yeah," I muttered, the nausea sweeping over me like a wave. "I'm just gonna sit for a few minutes."

"Your stomach bothering you?" I could hear the amusement in his voice.

I looked up and saw other guards watching me, whispering to each other and laughing. It made my day to know that seeing a sick man get sicker tickled their funny bones.

Come on, Austin. Look up.

The voice came from inside my head, but I knew it wasn't me. It was Kost's voice. *I'm hearing his thoughts,* I told myself, trying to let the ridiculousness of it settle in. I looked around, trying to pinpoint Kost's location. I found him quickly, even though he and Jeff weren't at our usual table. That was smart; if Hillerman was after them, they'd have to stay under the radar.

I wondered for a moment if they knew Hillerman was after them. Maybe they did. It would make sense. Kost was incredibly intelligent, and if he put all the pieces together, it was clear that Hillerman would come for them, sooner rather than later.

Kost and Jeff were hiding among a big group in the middle of the cafeteria, but I was still able to make eye contact. When I did, Jeff mouthed at me, *Are you okay?*

I nodded slowly, even though I was feeling worse and worse with each passing second.

"Who are you looking at, boy?" Jaeger demanded, stepping in front of me and looking in the direction I was looking. Jeff and Kost quickly ducked.

At that moment, the nausea became too much. I had to distract Jaeger in case he spotted my friends, and I owed him anyway, so I leaned over and barfed on his shiny black shoes.

Jaeger shouted the most profane assortment of curse words I had ever heard in my life—which was saying something considering the mouth I had—as he jumped back out of my putrid pool of puke.

I really wanted to laugh, but I was too busy throwing up. I managed to stop long enough to look up and mouth, *Run!* at Kost and Jeff before I started again. Out of the corner of my eye, I saw them get up and leave, calmly but quickly, and then I realized that just about everyone else in the cafeteria was too focused on me to notice them. They could have sprinted out and I doubt anyone would have known. The guards were laughing, Jaeger's pals were laughing, the other test subjects were laughing, and once I stopped puking my guts out, I was laughing too.

"You think this is funny?" Jaeger snarled, grabbing the collar of my shirt and hoisting me up to face him.

"So funny," I croaked, spitting flecks of vomit onto the front of his uniform.

Jaeger was disgusted, but his anger dominated that. He dragged me out of the cafeteria.

"Where are we going?" I asked as we went down a hallway and got into an elevator, the laughter from the cafeteria still echoing behind us.

"Since you're clearly so sick that you can't control which way your fountain spurts, then I'm going to take you to the doctor."

"The doctor?" I asked, suddenly not finding the situation so funny.

"Yes, the doctor." Jaeger glared at me. "Not so amused anymore, are you?"

I suddenly felt like puking all over again, but I couldn't. Every last bit of food I'd had in my stomach came up the last time. I thought about apologizing, so he'd let me be and not take me to Hillerman, but I could never bring myself to grovel. Especially not to this asshole.

We got off one floor higher than where we were yesterday. What setting would I get to see Hillerman in this time? I thought of the room I saw Miriam in last night and shuddered.

Thankfully, the room we entered simply had a desk with two chairs on either side of it. Jaeger shoved me into one and ordered, "Wait here." He left.

I slumped down into my chair, completely wiped. I stared at the ceiling, wondering where Miriam was. Was she scared? Was she in pain? I didn't want to think about where Miriam could be or what condition she was in, mainly because it hurt too much to think about it, but also because I knew that the same things were about to happen to me.

Dr. Hillerman didn't give me much time to myself. Not long after Jaeger left, he entered with only a clipboard and pen. "Hello again, Austin," he said cheerfully, and I wished that I still had some breakfast left in me so I could barf on him too. He sat down and peered at me. He whistled. "Boy, do you look awful."

"Thanks," I muttered. "It's nice to see you, too."

Hillerman chuckled and set the clipboard in front of him. He folded his hands on the table and leaned forward. "So tell me, Austin. How are you feeling today?"

"Absolutely wonderful," I replied, grinning sarcastically.

"That's not what Sergeant Jaeger's told me," Hillerman said, his eyes dropping to the papers in front of him.

"I'm sorry." If I was going to have a bunch of crap done to me, then I was at least going to enjoy myself a little. "I thought you were able to pick up on my sarcasm. Next time I'll emphasize it a little more."

Hillerman only smiled. "I see your lovely personality traits are still intact. You must not be feeling that bad."

"I told you, I feel wonderful."

"So your stomach's bothering you." Hillerman picked up his pen and started writing.

Oh, so it's symptom time? "I just ate too fast," I lied, even though it was the truth. "I didn't eat dinner last night and I was really hungry this morning. I just ate too fast and Jaeger's shoes paid the price."

"Yes," Hillerman said. "I must say it was quite amusing when he walked into my office with his uniform covered in your vomit. You aimed well."

Whoa. Did Hillerman dislike Jaeger, too?

"Is your head bothering you?" Hillerman asked.

My head actually felt fine. "Not really," I said.

He looked up to my forehead. "What happened there?" He nodded to the bump and the small scab that had formed.

"Uh..." I shrugged. "I was sleeping in my bathtub and I sat up too fast and hit my head on the faucet. But I'm fine."

He nodded again. "And why were you sleeping in your bathtub, Austin?"

"Because I like my privacy and your boys took away my door."

"You know why they did that, don't you?"

"Sure, I guess. Can I go now?"

"No." Hillerman continued to peer at me. "We're not done talking yet."

"I'm not sick," I said, one of the biggest lies I'd ever told. If I looked half as bad as I felt, and I was sure I did, then it was pretty obvious.

"Don't lie to me, please," Hillerman said, a little sternly. "We both know that I'm not an idiot."

"No, of course not," I replied. "You're a genius. The same kind of genius as the guy who created the Colician Strain, right?"

Hillerman smiled. "I suppose there's no point in lying to you anymore, is there?"

Holy crap. Was I really about to get a confession? "I guess not. I'm infected too, so what's the point?"

"Are you hearing things yet?" the doctor asked, watching me closely.

"Nope," I said, a little too quickly. "I'll let you know when I do though."

Hillerman chuckled. "I thought I told you not to lie to me." And then, from inside his mind: *Miriam's dead.*

I blinked in shock, and forced myself not to react. I knew Miriam wasn't dead. I still felt her presence, and Hillerman would in no way allow his prize to die so soon after her creation. So I made myself play along. "I'm not lying to you. What exactly do you mean when you say 'hearing things'?"

Hillerman watched me, and I knew he saw right through me. I wasn't going to confirm the truth just yet. I was going to play human for as long as possible. "You'll know soon enough," he told me.

Neither of us said anything for a little while. I cleared my throat uncomfortably. "So…can I go *now*?"

His eyes narrowing, he shook his head. "No."

My skin was feeling very hot and prickly, and my airways were beginning to compress. I cleared my throat again, louder this time, and coughed as well. "Why? I haven't done anything wrong."

"No, you haven't," Hillerman agreed. "But you're sick."

"I'm not sick. I told you I just ate too fast."

"That's not what I meant."

"Oh yeah," I muttered. "*That.*"

"And also," Hillerman continued, leaning forward, "you have some important information I'm interested in."

"Oh?" I said. "I don't know what could possibly be so interesting that wouldn't already be on your handy-dandy clipboard."

Hillerman smiled again. "Where are your friends? Kost Nicholson and Jeff Robinson?"

"I don't know," I replied, relieved they were still safe. "I've been with you and Jaeger all day. How should I know?"

"We've been looking for them," Hillerman explained. "But we can't seem to find them anywhere."

"Really?" I pretended to act oblivious, praying my friends could find an opening and get out of here before they were changed too. "Well, that's a shame. If you guys with your cameras and tracking devices can't find them, then there's no way I can help. It's too bad, really. We had a lot of stuff planned. They're a lot of fun. And now that Miriam's gone, they're my only form of anti-boredom medication."

Hillerman studied my face carefully. "Where are they, Austin?"

"I already told you I don't know."

"The four of you are close. Where would they go if they were hiding?"

"Hiding?" I peered innocently back at him. "Whatever would they be hiding from?"

We stared at each other for a while. I knew damn well where the two of them would go if they were hiding, but I'd go to hell and back before telling him where.

"Well," Hillerman said, sitting back in his chair, "if you don't know where they are, then there's no point in talking about them anymore. I'll simply have Jaeger come in and escort you to your cell."

I chewed on my lower lip. "So this is how it's going to be? You're just going to lock me up like you did with Miriam? Do experiments on me and cut me open and shit?"

"That's not exactly how I'd phrase it, but yes."

"Wonderful," I muttered, looking down. "Are you going to let me pack my toothbrush?"

"You're much calmer about this than Miriam was," Hillerman commented.

"Thank you?" I said, scowling at him. "I'm not exactly calm, broseph."

"Well, it's for your own good," Hillerman said. "You're responding very differently than Miriam to the new virus so far, and I don't want any unexpected surprises popping up."

"I need to go to the bathroom," I said suddenly, surprising myself.

Hillerman's brow furrowed. "Are you all right?"

"Fine," I muttered, and coughed again. And again. And I couldn't stop.

"Austin," Hillerman said, standing up nervously.

"I'm okay," I choked out, clutching my throat. My airways were tight and I could feel them closing. "I just—swallowed wrong—" Suddenly I couldn't breathe at all, and I fell out of my chair and onto the floor. This horrible sound was coming from my throat; it sounded like the honk of a goose combined with a cat coughing up a hairball. If Hillerman and I had been in each other's position, I would be laughing my ass off right now while he choked on the floor.

"Austin!" Hillerman's hands were on my chest and my throat as he tried to figure out what was happening. He started shouting orders at someone, but I couldn't hear what he was saying. My ears were ringing so loud that for a moment I thought I was going deaf. But my vision soon went out too, and I realized it was because I was blacking out.

~~*

I woke up still on the floor, staring up at Hillerman as he leaned over me. I could breathe again, but my throat was burning and I urgently needed something to drink. My eyes were watering so much that when I blinked several tears rolled down my face. I opened my mouth and tried to say something, but my throat was too dry and it came out as a moan.

"Don't try to talk," Hillerman instructed. He took a glass of water from somebody standing behind me and helped me sit up a little. "Drink this. You'll be all right."

Water had never tasted so good. I drank the whole glass, but still I needed more. "What happened?" I managed to rasp.

"You had some kind of allergic reaction," Hillerman replied, making me lie back down.

"To the virus?"

"No. I'm not sure what it was, but I'll figure it out after we run some tests."

Tests. That sounded like fun.

"Do you feel better?" Hillerman asked.

I tried to nod, but suddenly my head was throbbing. I groaned loudly and clutched my head, the pain unbelievable.

"It was only a matter of time before the headache started," Hillerman said, and then to the others in the room, "Bring in a stretcher. Wheel him to the infirmary. I'll be down to run some tests soon."

"I don't want to go anywhere with them," I said, my throat and head hurting so bad. "I want to leave."

"We've been through this already, Austin," Hillerman reminded. "You're staying here with us."

I found a strength I never knew I had. I don't know where it came from, but it was incredible. My arms shot out and pushed Hillerman away from me so hard that he actually went up off the floor a few inches before sprawling on his back a few feet away. I was on my feet and fighting another doctor and two soldiers a second later, taking everyone by surprise with my strength and speed.

Everything after that was all in flashes. I got away and made it up to the ground floor, and took out six more soldiers when I stepped out of the elevator. I was running down a side hallway when the world went back into normal time and I was able to think clearly. Now that I was me again, my feet tripped up and I fell flat on my face.

"Ow," I mumbled, feeling the strength I'd had just moments ago fade altogether. My aching head and throat came back, as did my nausea. I couldn't muster up the energy to stand, so I simply laid there, wondering how I managed to do that. Was this a result of what Hillerman had given me? Super speed and strength as well as telepathy? Regardless, it was draining. I never realized how difficult it must be for Colicians to use their abilities; how did they fight against so many enemies if they felt this drained every time?

Not too far away, I could hear shouting as more guards mobilized and came after me. It wouldn't take long before I was back in Hillerman's custody. I wasn't going anywhere.

A door opened to my right, out of my line of sight. I heard the sound of shuffling feet and then two pairs of hands took my arms and lifted me up.

"Let go me…" I muttered at them, my tongue in knots.

"Shut up, Austin."

It was Kost and Jeff. I hadn't realized it, but I'd tripped and fallen just inside the theater wing, our favorite hiding place when we wanted to avoid the guards.

"What're you guys doin'?" I sputtered as I was dragged into a room and swallowed by darkness.

"I said shut up!" Kost hissed at me, helping Jeff pull me into a corner of the room and then flicking on a dim lantern. "You need to stop yelling, Austin. They're going to be coming down the hallway any second."

Was I yelling? I didn't feel like I was…

Jeff put a finger to his lips and we listened as several guards stomped past. We waited silently for several minutes, even after their voices were long gone and all I could hear was my ragged breathing. Finally, I dared to speak.

"Where are we?"

"Girls' dressing room," Jeff said. "The old one that no one uses."

I should have figured. There were so many places in the theater wing that weren't used anymore. "Are you guys okay?"

"Yeah, we're fine," Kost said, his expression worried. "We came here as soon as you told us to run."

"Nice job barfing all over that guard's shoes, by the way," Jeff told me, grinning broadly. "You shoulda seen the look on that guy's face!"

"Enough!" Kost snapped. "We can't joke around with a matter as serious as this!"

"He's not a guard," I explained, looking to both of them. "He's Special Forces. Miriam was right. They're cooking up some serious shit down there."

"We know," Jeff said gravely.

"How do you know?" I asked in surprise.

"We heard from your neighbors that guys with big guns came into your room and took you away last night," Jeff explained. "Why else would they do that if there wasn't something dangerous going on? Fighting with a guard wasn't enough to earn you that."

"Yeah." I swallowed. "There's something I have to tell you guys. I'm...I've got whatever Miriam has."

"We know," Jeff said again.

"It makes sense," Kost said. "With the entrance the soldiers made, and with what you know already, you had to be infected too. It's the only way they could silence you, short of killing you."

"They infected you so you wouldn't call the cops on them, basically," Jeff summed up. "Blackmail. It makes perfect sense."

"But there's more," I said, wondering if Kost already knew this too. He did. "They're looking for us, too."

"But the question is; what do we do now?" Jeff asked. "We already checked the exits. They're all guarded. There's no way out. No *straightforward* way out anyway."

"Let me make a distraction," I said. "I'll draw some guards away from one of the side entrances and then you can escape."

"No way," Kost said forcefully. "We're not leaving you behind. You're not going to sacrifice yourself for us."

"And why not?" I snapped back. "I'm sick. I'm *really* sick. I hate to say it, but I think I might need Hillerman's help to make it through this. I almost died a few minutes ago."

"I can help you," Kost insisted. "I'm no licensed doctor, but I did some research on the Colician Strain and —"

"This isn't the Colician Strain!" I cried. "This is something worse. There's no way you can know how to help me, because I keep surprising Hillerman with my reactions to the virus."

"We're not leaving you behind, Austin," Jeff said quietly. "We're bros. We stick together. We'll find a way out together and then get you help."

I sighed. "And what about Miriam? I can't just leave her here."

"She wanted you to get out, remember? She wanted us to leave before we got sick too. You...well, she'd still want you to get out even though you're sick."

I looked at my two friends, knowing that they wouldn't let me stay behind alone. It was all or none. "Okay," I said. "Kost, you're the smart one. What do you think we should do?"

There was the terrible sound of wood splintering as the door was split in two and came crashing to the floor beside us. Light flooded in, its brightness making me shield my eyes. A shadow fell over us, blocking much of the light, but I still didn't look up.

"What you should do," Jaeger's voice growled, fierce and angry, "is lie down on your stomachs with your hands and feet spread. And let's not have any funny business."

I didn't fight back. Kost did for a few minutes, but decided he didn't like getting smacked around and having guns pointed at his face. Jeff, on the other hand...well, Jeff got hurt. I wanted to fight back like Jeff did, but I just didn't have the energy or the willpower to do so. All I wanted was about ten Tylenol, some sleeping pills, and an enormous bed with soft sheets and big, fluffy pillows. That probably wasn't what Hillerman had in mind for me, but a guy can dream, can't he?

5

The Caiten Strain

Hillerman's expression was angry as I was dragged into the same room Miriam was in the night before. I was surprised to see such an expression on his face, given he'd been nothing but calm when I'd been in his company.

Jaeger dragged me over to the examining table in the center of the room, hoisted me onto it, and strapped me down. The restraints were tight and the one around my right wrist was really hurting me. I didn't see the point of them, honestly. I was so beat that I didn't think I'd be able to fight back. I simply laid there, trying to control my breathing as I waited for what was coming next.

"That was a very dangerous thing you did, Austin," Hillerman told me from somewhere behind me, keeping out of my line of sight. "What if you'd had another allergic reaction? You would have died if you hadn't been with me at that exact moment. If you'd had another attack, we wouldn't be talking to each other right now."

"You're the only one talking, Jack," I mumbled back, my eyes drooping. I was so tired, and my throat and head were still killing me.

"Are you hearing me, Austin?" Hillerman said sharply, coming up to where I could see him. His features were upside down as he looked down on me, but I could see he was rather unhappy. "This virus is still very unstable. We're still running tests, but the dose of the strain given to you and Miriam was too high and it's having very negative effects on the two of you. You can't try to run away like that again, do you understand? You could die, and neither of us want that."

"You have no idea what I want," I muttered, glaring at him.

"Regardless," Hillerman said, his expression and voice softening, "I need to ensure your safety. You are in my care now, and I need you to accept that." He turned toward one of the other people in the room and took something from her.

"What is that?" I asked as he came around the side of the table, brandishing a syringe.

"A sedative," Hillerman said, injecting me with it. "It just helps you to relax."

"All right, but it's not like I'm going anywhere," I replied, my eyes fluttering as the sedative started to take effect. A few moments later, I was brought back out of my induced slumber and my mind was suddenly on high alert. I felt the IV needle in my right arm, and I could clearly see Dr. Hillerman looking down on me. This felt all too familiar.

"I'm going to ask you some questions, Austin," Dr. Hillerman said.

"And you want me to answer honestly," I finished, smiling devilishly. My old self was finally coming back. Despite the pains I still had, I felt...better. Different.

Hillerman blinked at my response, but then seemed to accept it and continued. "It's important that you answer honestly so I can help you. Do you understand?"

"Oh, perfectly," I replied, ready to screw with this guy hard core.

"Good," Hillerman said. "Let's get started then. Your blood type is A negative, correct?"

"Yes, sir, it is," I said. "I would have thought you already knew that."

"I do," Hillerman replied. "I just have to confirm it. For the record."

"Can I confirm something with you first?" I asked innocently, although inside I was laughing. Why? I didn't know.

Hillerman hesitated, uncertain of where I was going. "All right."

"You're infecting Kost and Jeff right now, correct?"

The doctor hesitated again. "Yes."

"Why?"

"I don't think that's any of your concern, Austin."

"Oh, it's definitely my concern." I smiled up at him as he slowly walked around the table, trying to figure out what I was thinking. "They're two of my best friends, and I want to know why you're turning them into freaks like me and Miriam."

"Like I told you, Austin," Hillerman said softly. "For now, you don't need to worry about them."

"No, for now I need to worry about all the wonderful things you're going to do to me, right? You're going to cut me open, take brain samples, all that fun shit. Just like you did to Miriam."

"Nobody's going to cut you open, Austin," Hillerman said, forming his words slowly and drawing them out. "I don't know where you got that idea."

"Oh, I think you do," I said. "And you know what? I don't want you to lie to me either. I know everything. What you're doing down here, what you're planning to do..."

"Austin," Hillerman said in a low, warning voice.

"It's the Caiten Strain, right?" I asked, listening to the words flooding my brain. "The sister strain to the Colician Virus. That's what you've created, what you've infected me with. It's intense. Despite all the pain and discomfort I'm in, I think this disease is pretty awesome."

"So you're in pain?" Hillerman asked, clearly wanting to be in control of the conversation.

"Oh, yes. So much pain. But that's okay, because everything else is so crystal clear now. You *are* trying to cure the Colician Strain, just like I guessed earlier. But that's not all, is it?"

"Austin, please."

"No. I'm going to talk now. You want to cure the Colician Strain, yes, but you know it will take time to perfect the Caiten Strain to a point where it's stable and you can infect mass numbers of people. Those of us who get the early, unstable doses, like me and Miriam and Kost and Jeff, are going to be your lab rats. You're just as curious about these viruses as those who made the Colician Strain. You want to know how they work, how it changes us. You're planning to keep the four of us here forever, aren't you?"

Hillerman stared at me, dumbfounded. "That's a lot of speculation, Austin."

I grinned. "No, that's a lot of accusations, Jack."

"We'll talk about your *future* later," Hillerman said, shifting things back to his agenda. "I want to focus on *you* right now."

"Do your colleagues know your wife is a Colician?"

Hillerman's lips pursed. "That's nobody's business but mine."

"This is all personal, isn't it?" I laughed. "You're trying to cure this so you can get your family back! Here's a news flash for you, pal: the four of us have family too. Do you think they won't miss us when you keep us locked in here like zoo animals? Just like the scientists locked up your wife three years ago?"

Hillerman turned away from me and strode to the door. "Take him to a cell," he snapped. "Don't give him any pain medication, no matter how much he begs."

The guards who brought me in carted me out, while I laughed the whole time.

~~*

The sensible part of me returned after Jaeger and his boys threw me into my new room. I was still cackling like a maniac, and I went over to the cot in the corner to lay down because I couldn't breathe. A few minutes passed and I managed to stop myself from laughing, after which I felt like a complete psycho because there was absolutely nothing funny about this situation. I caught my breath and swallowed repeatedly so I wouldn't throw up again, which I felt like doing more than anything in the world. My throat was still drier than sandpaper, and I looked around, desperately hoping for a sink or a cup of water. But there was nothing of the sort. Then, as if I had taken a blow to the skull by a wrecking ball, the headache intensified. I moaned and cried silently for hours, unable to keep the tears from flowing. I threw up violently six times, even though I had nothing left in my stomach. I simply tilted my head over the side of the cot and dry heaved onto the floor.

For days this went on, or at least it felt like days. Water and food were pushed through a little slot under the door, but I was too sick and in too much pain to get up to get it.

The headache was ruthless. It never stopped; it never even got better. I now understood why Miriam would agree to cooperate with Hillerman. I would literally do anything for a couple of painkillers. But I would never ask. I would never resort to begging.

I continued to dry heave. I couldn't sleep. The headache pounded on. If Hell existed, then this was it. I didn't know what in the world could possibly be worse than this.

After what felt like an eternity, I heard my door open and somebody entered, his shoes clicking across the floor as he came to my cot. I couldn't look up to see who it was. The movement would surely make my brain explode.

The person stood by my bed for a while, and finally asked, "Why didn't you eat anything?" It was Hillerman.

"I...can't...move," I mumbled, my stomach lurching with each word.

"Hmm," Hillerman said, clearly smug. "The headache's a killer, isn't it?"

I didn't answer. I couldn't.

"Are you ready to start cooperating?" Hillerman demanded.

I forced out a yes, because I knew it was the only way the pain would stop. And then, mercifully, Hillerman let sleep find me.

~~*

We went through all the basic crap Hillerman went through with Miriam, and now with Kost and Jeff as well. I only cooperated because he kept the pain at bay. But once I was sure the headache was gone for good…Hillerman was going to have a hell of a time dealing with me.

Hillerman eventually took the cast off of my broken arm, but I thought he only did it because he was running out of places to make incisions. I had scars all over my body now from where Hillerman had cut me open. My forehead, my chest, my stomach, and even my back had the thin scars from where the laser cut me so he could take a look at my insides, as if there was anything new there. And then there were the needle marks. My arms, legs, and neck were covered in little red spots from where the injections were given and blood was drawn.

It must have been three weeks since Miriam first became infected, and I was beginning to grow accustomed to this new life, the life of a prisoner. Whether I was in this facility or out of it, I'd be in a cell. I wished I'd picked prison over this. I hated this place. I hated the guards. I hated Hillerman. I hated myself. Most of all, I hated Miriam for getting me into this mess.

I hated life.

"When's this going to end?" I asked Hillerman one day, when we were both in particularly sour moods.

"When do you think, Austin?" was all he had to say. That was the first day I tried to kill myself.

I had become noticeably stronger since being infected with the Caiten Strain, so I broke one of the metal legs off of my cot and tried to cut open my wrists. The edges were dull, and I managed to cut open my left wrist before someone noticed on the monitor and rushed in to stop me. After that, I had to be in a straight jacket day and night.

A few days later—I didn't even know it was possible, but I still did it—I managed to wriggle and chew my way out of it. I used the straps to make a noose, but my attempt was thwarted yet again by the man watching me on the monitor.

I made a couple more attempts, much more feeble than the others, but I was determined. There was no way I could ever escape, and I wasn't going to live out my years as Hillerman's guinea pig. As my good old pal Patrick Henry once said, "Give me liberty, or give me death!"

After seven failed attempts at suicide, Hillerman finally decided to sit down with me and be my therapist. He was pissed at me for a while for what I'd said that day on the examining table, but now he seemed to have forgiven me, or at least moved on.

"What's going on, Austin?" he asked from across the table. We sat opposite each other, me strapped to my chair with multiple restraints. Two guards stood behind me, in case I tried anything. They'd gotten used to my attitude since I'd moved down here.

"Not much. What's going on with you, Jack?" The words came out as a mumble. Barely. My old flare and sarcasm was pretty much gone. All I wanted to do was just die.

"What's been on your mind lately?" Hillerman asked, knowing I'd answer him this time.

"Death," I muttered.

"So it seems. Why are you trying to kill yourself, Austin?"

"Wouldn't you?"

"You don't really want to die, do you?"

"All I know is that I don't want to be stuck down here forever as your experiment."

"So you're going to kill yourself?"

"If it gets me out of here, hell yes."

Hillerman didn't have anything to say to that. He sighed. "I'm really worried about you, Austin."

"Save it," I snapped. "I don't want your sympathy."

"I have to ensure your safety," he told me. "You understand that, don't you? I have to put the well-being of my patients first."

"What?" I couldn't believe this crap. "If you cared at all about my well-being, I wouldn't be here right now! If you cared about anyone other than yourself, you wouldn't have created the Caiten Strain!" I was getting angry, but I was too weak to deal with anger. "Take me back to my room. I don't want to talk to you anymore."

Hillerman didn't seem to want to talk to me anymore either, because he had me escorted out without saying another word.

Since the straight jacket wasn't doing its job, I was now simply strapped down to my cot. It was the most uncomfortable thing in the world. Besides the fact that Jaeger and the other guards liked to tie the straps so tight that they dug into my skin and cut off my circulation, I was forced to lay on my back twentyfour-seven. I was not someone who could sleep on my back. *This must be what pregnant women feel like,* I said to myself one day. *How do they do it? What's their secret? It would be nice to know, because I can't sleep through the night!*

After I was tucked in, Jaeger hung back. He waited for the others to leave, and then he leaned down. "You know you're going to die down here, don't you? You're never going to get out of this place, you little shit."

I turned to look at him, pure hatred burning through me. "You know that one day, someone like me is going to destroy you, don't you? Just like one of the Colicians killed your father."

Jaeger stood up straight and glared at me, his expression the angriest I'd ever seen on anyone. "How dare you get inside my head! What right do you have to do that?"

"I have the right since you people gave me the ability to do so," I countered, returning his hateful gaze. "Now get out before I go deeper and find out all your dirty secrets."

Jaeger lifted up his foot and brought his boot down on my nose. I heard it crack, but I really couldn't feel much anymore. Blood ran down my face in rivers, and that seemed to satisfy Jaeger enough to get him to leave.

I breathed through my mouth since my nose was full of blood, and I stared off into space, trying to come up with a new way to end it all. There wasn't much I could do. These straps were much tighter than the ones on the straight jacket.

Austin?

Yes? I replied, knowing immediately who it was.

Will you stop? I don't want you to kill yourself.

What else am I supposed to do, Miriam? It's not like we're ever getting out of this place.

We will. We're going to get out of here.

My brow furrowed. What did she have in mind? *How exactly are we going to do that?* I asked the voice in my head.

You don't have to do anything, Miriam said. *I can handle it all.*

Why can't I help?

Because you're still on the pain meds. Why else do you think you can't control it?

Can't control what?

The power! The ability! The pain meds prevent you from having any control over it. I've been off for a couple of days. My headache's gone. And I know how to use the ability.

Okay. I wasn't so sure about this. *What exactly do you have in mind?*

Like I said, I'll handle everything. Just be ready to run.

When?

Tonight. I'm sick of this place. We're going to get out of here tonight.

What about Kost and Jeff? They've been changed too. They're somewhere down here too. We can't just leave them here.

I know, and we won't. I'm going to talk to them too. We're all going to get out of here, Austin. And I know just where we'll go.

Where's that?

Home.

6

The Great Escape

The waiting was unbearable. I was sick of laying here all day every day with nothing to do but stare at the ceiling and occasionally piss my pants because the guards wouldn't let me up to go to the bathroom. Plus, I was still on my back, and I couldn't stand it! Every muscle in my body was pleading with me to roll over. It didn't help that Miriam gave me something to wait for. It was like the Chinese water torture, where a drop of water was dropped on a prisoner's forehead at different time intervals, driving the prisoner insane as they wondered when the next drop would fall. That's what this was. I'd hear a noise outside my cell and think, *Oh, there's Miriam now, coming to set me free.* But it was never her.

At one point, I was so wound up, having no idea when Miriam was going to get here and in dire need of stretching, that I opened my mouth and screamed at the top of my lungs for a good ten seconds.

It made me feel a lot better.

My door opened, and Jaeger poked his head in. "You all right, sunshine?"

"Oh, wonderful," I replied, knowing a good fight would make me feel great. "How are you doing, Lieutenant Asswipe?"

"I'd be a lot better if you'd shut up," Jaeger said.

"I'd be a lot better if you'd drop dead," I shot back.

On cue, Jaeger dropped to the floor like a stone. I stared at his limp body, thinking that maybe there was a god after all and he'd finally answered one of my prayers. But then Miriam stepped into the room and I knew Jaeger wasn't dead, just unconscious.

"You just made my day," I told her as she came and undid my restraints. "How'd you do that, anyway?"

"I'll teach you when your headache's gone," she said, helping me to my feet. "What happened to your face?"

I tried wiping the blood off my face, but I knew there was a lot of it and it was all crusted on. "Him," I said, nodding to Jaeger. "We're good friends, he and I."

"I can see that," Miriam muttered flatly. "Let's go. We have to get Kost and Jeff before the alarm goes off."

Again, on cue, lights started flashing and an alarm blared.

"Balls," Miriam said angrily.

I laughed, having never heard her curse before. "Well, there goes that plan," I said through my laughter.

"Shut up," Miriam told me, taking my hand. We started running.

The alarm was much louder in the hallway, making my brain rattle. "Is there any way we can shut that off?"

"I'm not a Colician," Miriam replied. "I can't do whatever I want."

The hallways were all white. What was it with doctors and white? I had no idea where we were going, because each new hallway looked exactly like the last. Several guards attempted to restrain us each time we turned a corner, all of them knocked down by Miriam.

"How do you know where we're going?" I yelled to her over all the noise.

"I just know!" she called back as we rounded a corner, and halted so fast that I ran into her.

At least a dozen guards were positioned at the end of the hallway, guns aimed and ready to fire.

"Holy shit," I muttered, thinking this was the end. Miriam was already taking care of them.

Every single one of the guards dropped in sync. My jaw dropped with them. "Holy crap," I said, turning to her. "You know, the fact that you can do that is *really* sexy —"

Miriam shut me up by stepping forward, grabbing the front of my shirt, and kissing me. It was a good kiss. I was so surprised that when she pulled away from me, all I could do was stare at her stupidly with my mouth hanging open. She laughed at my expression. "Well, at least now I know how to make you stop talking."

"Are you saying there's going to be more of that in the future?" I asked hopefully.

Miriam grinned. "Assuming we get out of here."

"Then let's get the guys and get out of here."

She turned toward the first door on the left, staring at it uncertainly. "I didn't really think this part through," she admitted. "I got you out so easily because your door was already open. We need a key and a thumbprint to get in."

"Just tell the door to open," I suggested.

"What?"

"You made all the guys drop because you told their brains to go to sleep. A computer controls the doors. Maybe you can make the doors open by talking to the computers."

"It doesn't work like that," Miriam told me, frustrated. "Telepathy only works with other people…"

"How do you know that?" I asked. When she glanced at me, I smiled weakly. "Just try."

She turned back to the door, staring at it. She stared at it for a long time, and I was about to tell her to forget it when we heard a *click* and a *whoosh* and the door swung open. We both stared at each other, amazed. "I guess we can do more than we thought," I said. I looked inside. "Kost! Let's go!"

Kost was doing well. He cooperated with Hillerman right from the start, so he had pain meds in his system and could run with us easily. Jeff, to no one's surprise, had not been so cooperative.

"Jeff, get up!" Kost shouted at him, trying to force him to his feet.

Jeff moaned, clutching his head. He refused to budge.

"Jeff, we're going to get out of here but you have to get up!" I tugged on one arm as Kost tugged on the other, but it was no use. Jeff was in too much pain.

"Jeff," Miriam said slowly. "Look at me."

I didn't know if it was Miriam's tone that got him to obey, but Jeff looked up at her, his eyes red and watery. The two of them stared into each other's eyes, and then Jeff blinked and stood up. "Whoa," he said.

"Better?" Miriam asked.

"What did you do?" Kost and I asked her.

"Blocked his pain receptors for the time being," she explained. "The headache will be back soon, but this will give me enough time to find the meds Hillerman gave us. Now let's go."

We ran down more hallways, only stopping once when Miriam made a detour into an observation room to get a bag full of syringes and meds she thought we might need. She injected us all with a dose and then led us to freedom, taking down anyone who stood in our way.

~~*

It had taken forty-three minutes total—starting when Miriam broke out of her cell and ending when we escaped the last of the guards blocking our way—for us to make it out. None of us had been injured, and we were all feeling wonderful by the time we checked into a hotel in Pittsburgh eight hours later. We could have gotten there faster had we stolen a car, and I had suggested we take Jaeger's car just to get back at him, but that would have been too risky. So we boarded a Greyhound bus and sat anxiously for several hours, praying that we wouldn't get caught.

We had no money, obviously, but with Miriam's ability to talk to machines, she managed to get several hundred dollars in cash out of an ATM. We agreed that it would be safer if we all stayed together, so we paid for one suite with three beds and a pullout sofa.

"I'll take the sofa," I offered as we settled in for the night, all four of us exhausted. Jeff was already out cold on one of the beds, and Kost was snuggling up under a bunch of blankets on another. I wasn't about to let Miriam sleep on the sofa.

"You could just share mine," Miriam said, gesturing with her head to the other room with the third and largest bed.

I wasn't about to say no to that offer. I followed her, jumping onto the bed as Miriam closed the door behind us. She looked me up and down from where she stood, a peculiar look in her eyes.

I cleared my throat. "Listen, about before…"

"I'm tired, Austin," she said, coming and climbing in beside me. "This wasn't an invitation for anything else. I just thought we could both use some decent sleep."

"Good," I said, and was completely honest when I said it. "Because I'm really tired, too." We snuggled in together, my arms wrapped around her. "That's not to say I won't be up for anything *later*…"

"Shut up," she said, and we both laughed before dozing off in each other's arms.

~~*

Even with Miriam in my arms, something I'd wanted for a very long time, I still had the dream of falling. I awoke with a jerk, blinking in the sunlight shining on my face. It took me a minute to remember where I was, especially with the blinding sun disorienting me. But then I remembered. I remembered it all.

I rolled over to face Miriam, who was wide awake and staring at me. "Do you have that dream often?" she asked.

I shrugged. "Every now and then."

"You know you can't lie to me anymore," Miriam said.

"If you can just read my mind then why do you even bother asking?" I snapped, sitting up and pushing the blankets off of me. I stood up and stretched, glancing at the clock. 2:33. Great. Now that we were well rested, we could continue on our way to Wisconsin, where Miriam's father and two older brothers would be. Speaking of which, why were we going somewhere Hillerman and Jaeger were surely going to look first?

"It's my great-uncle's cabin," Miriam explained, reading my mind just like I didn't want her to. "He passed away a few weeks ago, and my dad and brothers are going up there to clean it out. We were never close to Uncle Trent, so the people looking for us won't think to look there right away. My family has done its best to stay off the grid since the Colician outbreak; my brother Vincent was in prison for almost a year because they thought he was aiding the rebels. They won't tell anyone where they're going. We can get up there and get the help that we need from my family and then get the hell out of here."

"Where are we supposed to go?" I asked her. "Where *can* we go?"

She paused. "I'm still working on that," she admitted. "But we'll be all right. We're far more powerful than anyone after us. We'll find somewhere where we can be safe and live out our lives as normally as possible."

"Yeah," I muttered. "I guess we'll never get to live a normal life, will we?"

Miriam shrugged. "Normal's boring."

"Well, I'd take it over this any day." My stomach growled ferociously. "I'm starving. Let's order some room service and get the hell out of here."

I didn't know what the young man who delivered our food must have thought. Four ordinary people ordering food enough for ten people would have made me suspicious. But he simply smiled and took our cash before leaving us to wolf down our breakfast. I must have eaten a whole pig's worth of breakfast sausage. Miriam ate at least four of the ten helpings of cheesy scrambled eggs, and Jeff ate over forty strips of bacon. Kost was the only one who didn't seem very hungry. He picked at a waffle in front of him, his chin resting in his hand. His eyes were sullen and tired, and when I looked up at him I noticed that his skin was taking on a grayish tint.

"Hey, man," I said, nudging his foot under the table. "You okay?"

"Protein deficiency," Kost mumbled.

"What?" I asked. Jeff and Miriam looked up as well, curious.

"Protein deficiency," he repeated. "That's why you're eating so much meat and eggs. This new strain must have that as a side effect."

"A protein deficiency would explain *why* we're eating eggs and meat," Jeff said flatly. "It doesn't explain why we're eating so much."

"Many cases of the Colician Strain resulted in patients eating excessively the first two to sixteen days." Kost's eyes drifted shut. "That's one of the similarities the two viruses share. Add that to protein deficiency, and what do you get? Yum, yum, eggs and bacon."

Miriam, Jeff, and I all exchanged dubious looks. "You sure you're all right, Kost?" Jeff asked. "You're a strange dude, but you don't talk like that."

"You haven't eaten much, either," Miriam said, poking his waffle with her fork. "Where's *your* protein deficiency?"

"All cases are different, girly." Kost giggled, and his head dropped to the table so hard that the noise made us jump. "Symptoms are different. Each body reacts differently to the virus. Some bodies respond to it by shutting down altogether."

I suddenly knew where he was going with this. "You're not going to die, Kost," I said, my voice weaker than I wanted it to be. "I won't let that happen."

"How are you going to keep it from happening?" Kost's head snapped up and he stared at me with an intensity that made me shiver. "Who are you? You're insignificant! One out of millions! You can't save me! Baseball! Batman! Babies! Follow me, Austin Rockwell!" His eyes rolled back in his head, exposing the whites of his eyes that were spotted red with broken blood vessels. He fell off his chair to the floor, where he convulsed violently.

"Kost!" Jeff knelt beside his friend, shaking his shoulder. "Snap out of it, bro!"

"Leave him," Miriam said, pulling Jeff's hand away. "There's nothing we can do for him. Just let him get over it." She glanced over at me, still in my chair.

My butt was rooted to the spot. Hearing Kost spill out all those random words was weird enough, but then he had to repeat part of my dream, the dream I had the night it all went to hell. The dream with the gorilla man.

"Austin?" Miriam asked from the floor, watching me nervously. "Are *you* okay?"

"I gotta pee." I bolted from my chair to the bathroom, slamming the door behind me and locking it. I took a good long look at myself. There was still blood crusted on my face from when Jaeger kicked me, and I touched my nose gingerly, trying to feel where the break was. It looked all right, and there was no way I could go to a hospital to get it fixed, so I was going to have to make do with the way it was. I stripped the clothes off my body, dropping them in a pile on the floor and taking a look at my naked body. I looked awful. I had lost a lot of weight, and my skin was bruised around my ribs. My whole body looked as tired as I felt, but my eyes were looking good. They looked more alert and even looked lively and energetic. I must have been getting back to my old self.

There was no way I was getting back into those filthy clothes. I climbed in the shower and turned the temperature up as hot as it would go. The heat was wonderful, and the steam made my skin feel amazing. I stood in the steady stream of hot water until Jeff knocked on the door, annoyed because he had to pee and I was hogging the bathroom. I quickly scrubbed myself, making sure to get all the crusted blood off my face, and stepped out, wrapping myself in a towel and letting Jeff in.

I went into the main bedroom to see how Kost was doing. He was sleeping on his side, his mouth hanging open and a loud, raspy sound was coming from his throat. Miriam stood watching him, her back to me, her arms folded across her chest. I went to her side and put my arm around her. "How's he doing?" I asked her softly.

Miriam shrugged, still gazing at Kost. "Better, I guess. I'm no doctor."

"I know," I said. "Do you have any idea if he's going to be okay? Do you know if…what he said before might be true?"

"That he's dying?" She shrugged again. "I don't know. But I think we need to consider it a possibility."

"I can't let him die," I whispered. I couldn't lose anyone else.

"You probably don't want to hear this," Miriam told me, "but what he said before was right. What are you going to be able to do to stop it? You're no doctor either."

I sighed. "I don't know, but…"

Miriam took my hand. "I don't want him to die either, Austin."

I looked down at her, trying to think of something to say, but Jeff snapped from the bathroom, "Can I come out or will I ruin some romantic moment?"

Smiling and blushing a little, Miriam called, "No, it's fine." She looked up at me. "You might want to put some clothes on, Austin."

Oh yeah. I was still in a towel. Oops. I brushed past Jeff and went back to the bathroom to get my clothes. As disgusting as they were, they were the only clothes I had. Once I was dressed, I went back to join Jeff and Miriam at Kost's side. "So, should we wake him up? We can't exactly carry him onto a bus."

Miriam looked up at me again, solemnly. "We can't move him, Austin."

~~*

But we had to move him.

The only clothes we had were the white scrubs from the lab, which would draw attention. While Kost rested, Jeff and I went across the road to a Walmart and purchased some new clothes for all of us. We gave Kost two hours of rest before we woke him up and helped him get ready to go. He seemed better, but he didn't talk much. He could do what we needed him to do, but he was slow and it took him a good amount of effort. Eventually, with Jeff and I on either side of him, the four of us boarded a bus destined for Madison. We'd be safe for a while and Kost would be able to rest again.

We were on the Greyhound for almost two hours when Miriam finally took a break from fussing over Kost. It was Jeff's turn to sit next to Kost and keep an eye on him. Miriam sat next to me and rested her head on my shoulder, letting out a weary sigh. "I'm so worried about him," she said.

I glanced over at Jeff. "You know, as much as the two of them used to bicker, you can tell that they're good friends. Jeff would be devastated if anything happened to Kost."

"I know. I'm just worried about what we're going to do if something *does* happen to Kost."

"I don't want to think about that."

Miriam drew her legs up and leaned her whole body against me. "Me either."

She dozed off for a while, and eventually, so did Kost and Jeff. I couldn't sleep, though. Somebody had to stay awake, just in case Jaeger and his men found us. I stayed awake through the whole bus ride, until we reached Madison close to noon the next day. I gently shook them all awake and called a cab. We went to a motel, where I made sure everyone was comfortable. Then I passed out on one of the beds and didn't wake for hours.

7

Going North

"Austin!" Miriam hissed in my ear.

I blinked once, groaned, and rolled over.

Miriam giggled. "Wake up, sleepy head."

"*No.*"

"Jeff got breakfast."

That got me moving. I bolted out of bed and into the adjacent room, where Jeff and Kost were sitting at the small circular table in the corner. Jeff was wolfing down bacon, sausage, and eggs, but Kost was the same as yesterday. He picked at some sausage, but he wouldn't eat.

"Feeling any better?" I asked hopefully, sitting on the edge of one of the beds and accepting a full plate.

"Mmm," Kost grunted, poking his sausage around his plate. He looked worse than yesterday. His skin was grayer, his eyes were duller, and he looked as if he was even thinner. His skin was pulled tight over his hands and face.

I looked at Miriam, and I saw in her face what I was thinking; we had to get Kost to a doctor or he was going to die.

"What do you think is happening to you, Kost?" I asked him. "You made an educated guess about the protein deficiency, so you probably have a good guess as to what's going on with you."

The three of us waited for Kost to answer, and when he did, his voice said it all. "My body's rejecting the virus. We were the first four infected; even Hillerman admitted that we all received the first version of it. They still haven't worked out all the kinks yet. That's what they needed us for; they needed to test the dosage and determine the side effects, such as protein deficiencies. So either my body's rejecting the strain, or there's a side effect affecting me but not you."

"Do you know any way that you can make yourself better?" Jeff asked.

"I'm a chemist," Kost said, "not a doctor."

"Exactly," Miriam chirped. "You're a chemist. You could find a way to synthesize something and—"

"I might be able to do that if I understood the virus." Kost looked up at us, his eyes defeated. "I know a little about the Colician Virus, but this Caiten virus is different. It has different properties, different chemicals used in its design. I wouldn't even know where to start." He sighed. "If I had data from the doctors at the facility, I could run some tests, but even then, I don't have a place to work. And judging by the rate of deterioration, I'd be dead before I'd get any results, anyway."

"You're not going to die," I told Kost again, even though my sincerity was growing weaker.

Kost glanced at me. "You're not a doctor either, Austin."

"Then we'll get you to one," I insisted. "We'll find you help. I'm not going to just let you die!"

"None of you are taking me to a hospital!" Kost snapped, the ferocity of his voice startling us all into silence. "Don't you know what'll happen to us if you take me to a hospital? When they find out who we are and what kind of virus we're carrying, they'll quarantine us until Hillerman has us picked up and then we're right back where we started! We're not going to die in that place! Is that understood?"

We stared at him. Even I was at a loss for words. He was right. If we took him to a hospital, we would end up back at the facility, but if we didn't, he was going to die slowly. I wasn't sure what was worse.

"What if..." Jeff suddenly had tears in his eyes. "What if we found a doctor who was willing to keep his mouth shut..."

"Even if we could, there's no way he'd be able to fix me. I'm done. No ordinary doctor can save me."

"No *ordinary* doctor." Jeff's eyes hardened. He rose to his feet and strode toward the dingy little bathroom.

"Jeff, where are you going?" I demanded.

Miriam stood up very quickly. "Jeff," she said shakily. "Don't do it. Please. I'm begging you not to do it."

"Do what?" I asked, suddenly wishing I could use my ability like her.

"No *ordinary* doctor can save him," Jeff growled in the doorway. "So I'm gonna call one who's *not* ordinary."

"Oh, shit," I said. "Are you seriously thinking about calling Hillerman?"

Jeff stared at me. "Yeah, and while I'm at it I'll call Jaeger, too. And maybe Santa Claus and the Easter Bunny." He threw his arms in the air. "No, dumb ass! I'm talking about calling somebody who works first hand with the Colician Virus. Somebody who wouldn't give us away for fear of being caught himself."

I felt like I should know who he was talking about but I still didn't have a clue.

"He's talking about Dr. Shawn Perry," Miriam said quietly.

"The Colician?" I looked at Jeff, bewildered. Dr. Perry, along with Walter Reifert, was one of the most well-known Colicians who gained notoriety after the outbreak. "Why the hell would you call him?"

"He has experience with this sort of thing!" Jeff snapped. "He'll know what's wrong! He'll know how to save Kost!"

"He's a Colician!" I cried. "You know what they're capable of!"

"Really?" Jeff challenged. "You're going to talk that way about your own family?"

I looked away, guilty. Yes, my father and sister were Colicians, and I loved them anyway. But he was talking about putting his trust in a Colician who we didn't know. We didn't know which ability he had. He could hurt us; God only knew what he might do to us. For all we knew, Perry would be just as interested in studying our abilities as Hillerman.

"This isn't about my family," I muttered. "We don't know this man. How do we know he won't lock us up like Hillerman did?"

"He's Kost's only chance!" Jeff said.

"Enough!" Kost said, and then began coughing heavily. "I can hear you, you know! You're not calling anyone! Humans or Colicians. It's my life, and it's my decision."

"Kost," Miriam began gently. "I know going for help seems like the illogical choice right now. If we go to a hospital, Hillerman will find you for sure. If we call Dr. Perry...who knows what will happen. I know either choice seems crazy, but this is your *life* we're talking about, Kost."

"Like I said." He laid down on one of the beds and closed his eyes. "It's *my* life. It's *my* decision."

"No matter where you were taken," Miriam said, "we'd come get you."

"Do you really want me to start yelling again?" Kost demanded.

We dropped the subject, even though we were all afraid of watching Kost die.

We needed more new clothes and food for the drive up north, so Miriam and I went to check out the mall while Jeff stayed with Kost. Since we were on the east side of the city, we thought it would be safer to go to the mall on the west side, just in case anyone recognized us. If they did, they would most likely start looking for us on the west side where we were shopping, giving us time to slip back to the motel and get out of here. We didn't have enough cash left for a cab, so we caught the city bus instead.

"I'll have to talk to an ATM again," Miriam said, giving me a sideways grin.

I smiled. "While you're at it, why don't you talk to Hillerman's computer database and wipe our records. And find a cure for Kost's illness."

"Yeah," Miriam muttered. "I wish."

While we walked from the bus stop to the mall, the giant West Towne Mall sign looming above us, I couldn't think of anything to say. "So…"

Miriam slipped her hand into mine. "I've been wanting to talk to you about something," she said.

"Okay," I said, grateful I didn't have to be the conversation starter.

She didn't say anything for a while, and I was beginning to wonder if she hadn't heard my reply. "Do I seem…I don't know…different to you?"

"We're all different now, Miriam," I said.

"Well, yeah, but I'm talking about personality. Do *I* seem different?"

"Yeah," I replied. "But it's not in a bad way, if that's what you're worried about. You used to be really hesitant and shy. You even seemed scared and sad. You talk more now, you smile more, and you seem…happier."

"Would you think I'm crazy if I said I was?"

I shrugged. "No. I'd ask you why, though."

Miriam was silent again. "I told you my mother died during the Colician outbreak, remember? Well, I didn't tell you everything."

I was confused. I remembered her telling me this, a long time ago when she was upset and finally started to open up to me. I didn't understand why she was bringing it up, though. "What didn't you tell me?"

She looked up at me guiltily. "She was killed because she *was* a Colician."

This surprised me. It never occurred to me that her mother's genes were the reason she was killed. "She was taken to the Madison lab?" I asked.

"No, thank god. She was taken to the Chicago lab, but she was still killed. She died early on, before Walter Reifert's revolution began. She never even had a chance."

"Are you ashamed of it?" I asked. "Is that why you never told me?"

"Ashamed?" Miriam looked at me, her eyes angry. "Why would I ever be ashamed of my own mother? I didn't tell anyone because I hated the world for what they did to her!"

"Okay," I said. "I'm sorry. I wasn't trying to offend you."

"I also didn't tell you," Miriam continued, "because I knew what you'd lost and I didn't want you to hurt any more than you already did."

I looked away. "You don't ever have to worry about hurting me. If you ever need to talk about something, I'll be there for you."

"There's something else, too," she said.

"What?"

"Well, since this virus has affected me. I've felt different. I *am* happier, just like you said. It makes me feel closer to my mother. And this virus has left me thinking about a lot of things." She squeezed my hand tighter. "I've been thinking about *us*, Austin."

Miriam's happiness must have started rubbing off on me, because her words sent a warm feeling through my body and put a smile on my face. "What do you think about us, Miriam?"

"I'm not sure what I think about us," Miriam said. "All I know is that I want to be with you. Considering what's happening right now, I think it might finally be possible."

My brow furrowed and I glanced her way. "How is running for our lives going to give us the opportunity to be together and to be happy?"

Miriam shrugged. "Back at the facility, I was so angry. Scared, too. I hated the world for what it did to my mom, and my anger would have kept us from being together. For some reason, this virus has taken away my anger. It freed me. I'm happy now, and I can be with you."

"I hate to burst your bubble, but we still have to worry about Jaeger and all those other wonderful people."

"I know."

"Can I ask you something? Why are you happier now? What about this virus made your anger go away?"

Miriam looked up at the clouds thoughtfully. "I think it's because when I became infected with this virus, I was pushed away from this world. I don't have to be a part of it anymore. When I did, I think that's what was making me so angry. I had to live with the people who killed my mother and her kind. Now, we're free to go anywhere. We can start over." She smiled at me. "We can be happy."

"But where can we go to escape the world completely?" I asked.

"The Colicians found a place. We can, too."

"The Colicians moved to another planet, Miriam."

"We'll figure something out."

We were at the front entrance of the mall. "Let's shop," I said.

An hour and a half later, we had six bags of clothes for the four of us and six hundred dollars left over from the one thousand Miriam had pulled out of an ATM. We were both wiped, so we were taking a break in the food court. I was enjoying a bean and cheese burrito and a Pepsi from Taco Bell while Miriam picked at her Japanese dish of beef and vegetables. It took me a while to notice, but I suddenly remembered that Miriam hadn't been one to pick at her food these past couple of days.

"You okay?" I asked her, sipping my Pepsi.

She didn't answer. She picked at a large piece of beef, her eyes narrowed.

"Your food all right?" Maybe it was undercooked or something...

Again, she ignored me.

"Miriam!"

She looked up, startled. "What?"

"*Are you okay?*" I spoke slowly and clearly.

"Yeah," she said, confused. "Why?"

"You were glaring at your food," I said. "Did it say something rude?"

"Oh, no, I was just thinking, that's all." She went back to picking at her food.

"You're not eating like we normally do," I pointed out.

"My stomach feels a little funny," she replied.

"Funny how?" I asked, immediately concerned. If she was getting sick like Kost...

"It's fine," she said quickly. "I'm just a little queasy. You know, when you get that feeling in the pit of your stomach that something's wrong—" Her voice stopped abruptly, and her eyes went wide in surprise.

"What?" I asked, panicking.

"Jeff," Miriam said. "He's calling to me. Something's wrong with Kost. He's having one of those fits again, like when he starting screaming random words before..." She paused, listening. "He's saying some of the same stuff from last time. Baseball... Batman...babies..."

I glanced up at one of the enormous televisions overhead, one of the four that overlooked the tables in the food court. The Milwaukee Brewers were playing onscreen. They were up to bat.

"Miriam," I said, nodding to the screen.

She turned and looked, then looked back at me, fear in her eyes. "Something's not right," she said. "We need to go."

I had no reason to argue. Whatever was going on with Kost was freaking me out, and if he was trying to warn us about something, then I wasn't going to stick around here waiting for trouble to find us.

We gathered up our bags, and I asked Miriam, "Should we wait for the next bus or should we catch a cab?"

Miriam was answering me, but I didn't hear what she said. I was too focused on the pair of eyes that had just met mine from across the food court, right in front of the exit.

"Aw, shit," I muttered, and then grabbed Miriam's hand and started running further into the mall. We quickly lost our bags in our flight, but we didn't need to worry about clothes right now.

"What's wrong?" Miriam demanded.

"Jaeger!" I cried, urging her to move faster. I could hear Jaeger shouting commands to his forces, and I knew they were coming after us.

"How the hell did he find us?" Miriam asked shrilly.

"Who cares!" I said. "He did!"

We ran fast, but we both knew we were already cornered. A second group of soldiers was advancing on us from up ahead, and I pulled Miriam to a halt. I glanced around nervously. "What should we do?" I asked as the two groups closed the space between us. There were multiple shops on either side of us, but once inside we were screwed for sure.

Miriam squeeze my hand and took a deep breath. "I'm not sure," she whispered.

"Shopping, eh?" Jaeger walked toward us, leering. "I'll admit, this wasn't the first place I'd expect to find you kids, but I'm not exactly surprised."

"How did you find us?" I asked him.

"Doesn't matter," Jaeger replied. "Where are the other two?"

"Doesn't matter," Miriam said, narrowing her eyes.

Jaeger turned his eyes on her. "You're right. It doesn't matter. *You're* the ones that matter."

Miriam took a step back and looked at me uncertainly.

"It doesn't really matter if we find your friends," Jaeger continued. "You're the ones Hillerman wants. Just the two of you."

"Why?" I asked.

"He found something in your DNA. Something different from the other two." Jaeger started advancing again. "Who knows. Maybe you're the cure."

"Did you ever stop to think," Miriam said angrily, "that maybe the Colician Virus doesn't need to be cured?"

"That's ridiculous," Jaeger said.

"Is it?" Miriam snapped. "Because I'm pretty sure that the Colician Virus, and now the Caiten Virus, are the cures to humanity."

Something drew my attention. I looked up above one of the stores, where another enormous television screen hung, still broadcasting the Brewers game. The game suddenly switched to a commercial break. The first commercial was an ad for the new Batman movie.

I turned around and started backing toward the TV, pulling Miriam with me.

"Where are you going to go, Rockwell?" Jaeger taunted. "There's nowhere left to run. And I should tell you that if you do run, I'm authorized to shoot you. Dead or alive; those were my orders."

"He's not lying, Austin," Miriam whispered.

"I know," I said. "We're not running. Not yet." I glanced back at the TV, where an ad for baby formula was now playing. Multiple images of smiling babies flashed across the screen.

"What are you doing?" Miriam asked me nervously.

"I'm not sure," I said. "But I think we'll be okay."

"Stop walking," Jaeger ordered, raising his weapon. "Both of you are being taken into custody."

"I'm pretty sure that's not what's about to happen," I replied, smirking.

I hadn't realized that the ceiling was made of glass, but I was soon made aware of it. A thunderous crash echoed through the building and a shower of glass rained down on us. The soldiers ducked and shielded their heads, and any shoppers still in the area cried out as well. I shielded Miriam with my body, but there was no need; the TV screen directly overhead protected us.

As soon as the glass shower ended, I tugged Miriam's hand. "Come on!" I cried. Many of the soldiers were hurt, but they wouldn't be kept down for long. We had to get out of here.

Jaeger yelled something after us, but we kept running.

"Where are we going?" Miriam asked.

"There's more than one exit," I said. "We'll leave through one of them."

"Jaeger's men are bound to be at all the exits!"

"Well, we have to *try!*"

Just as we rounded a corner, a pair of hands shot out of the wall and grabbed us. We were pulled into a tiny closet that smelled of cleaning supplies.

"Hey!" I shouted, trying to pull loose.

"Quiet!" I managed to catch a glimpse of a young man in a janitor's uniform before he closed the door and everything went pitch black.

"Who are you?" Miriam demanded.

"Unless you want to end up back in that laboratory," the man said, "I suggest you shut up."

We complied, keeping our ears peeled for signs of Jaeger. There was too much shouting outside to tell.

A dim light flickered on above us, and I blinked at the man in front of me. He was around my age with brown hair, but I knew immediately that he wasn't a janitor. "Listen," he said quietly. "I'm here to help you."

"Did you break the ceiling?" I asked.

He nodded. "I can get you out of here, but you have to do exactly what I say or else they'll catch you back at your motel."

"Who *are* you?" Miriam asked.

"It doesn't matter," the man replied.

"How do you know who we are?" I demanded, confused.

"*Stop.*" The man stared sternly at us. "I don't have time for your questions. I'm trying to help you. That's all that should matter. Now follow me."

We followed him down a narrow hallway, the noise and light all but disappearing behind us. In a minute or two we reached a door, and we saw a sliver of sunlight sneaking in under it. The light was still absent from the hall, but we felt the young man turn to us in the dark.

"Okay," he said. "You have to follow my instructions exactly, or else you're going to end up caught."

"Who are you?" Miriam asked again.

The man silenced her quickly. "No questions. In exactly thirty-six seconds, a bus will pull up twenty-three feet to the left of this door. Wait eight seconds after it stops, then run as fast as you can and get on. At the second stoplight, a pickup will collide with the vehicle in front of the bus, causing the bus to run into both vehicles. The front set of bus doors will be forced open by the collision. Get out as soon as the accident occurs. There will be another pickup—red—going in the opposite direction. Jump in the back as it slows. It will take you back to your motel. Any questions?"

"Several," I replied.

"You have twenty-four seconds," the man said, ignoring me. "Start counting."

We obeyed, even though both of us were unsure of this man. I tried to look into his mind, but I was still learning and was too anxious to do it. From the vibe I received from Miriam, she was having trouble getting in his head, too. I found that curious, because she was already pretty good at getting inside the minds of others.

When our countdown reached five, the man turned the door knob. "Good luck," he said, and opened it.

The two of us rushed out, the sunlight momentarily blinding us. Just for a moment, I turned to glance back at the man, curiosity getting the better of me. I caught only a glimpse of him before he slammed the door closed again, but a glimpse was enough. The brightness of his green eyes remained imprinted in my brain.

~~*

Miriam and I made it all of eight steps before we heard the first shout. "There!" We looked and saw six of Jaeger's men at an exit further down to the left, all sprinting toward us. Miriam hesitated, but I propelled her forward.

It's a trap, it's a trap... was running through Miriam's mind.

No, I told her. *We'll be okay.*

Miriam wanted to argue, but we weren't in any kind of situation to stop and weigh our options. We ran to the bus, jumping aboard moments before the doors swung shut. The soldiers were still shouting outside the bus, getting dangerously close, but the driver was talking on his radio and didn't hear them. He simply put the bus in gear, and took off.

As the bus departed, the soldiers ran alongside it, banging on the side. A couple passengers voiced their concerns and called out to the driver, but the driver waved a dismissive hand at them and said, "The pickup times are clearly stated. If they're not on when the doors close, too bad for them." Passengers continued to protest, but the bus driver just ignored them.

Shocked yet grateful for the bus driver's ignorance, I tossed five dollars into the money deposit box and led Miriam down the aisle to a pair of empty seats. Our fellow passengers were wary of us, knowing that we were in some kind of trouble. A couple of them were even phoning the police. This didn't bother me, but it bothered Miriam.

"He led us into a trap!" she hissed, her eyes afraid. "That Colician bastard set us up!"

"No he didn't," I reassured. "Trust me. It was Walter Reifert."

Miriam's mouth fell open. "Are you sure?"

"Yeah," I said. "It was him."

"Why?"

"I don't know." I gazed out the window, anxious to get out of here. The bus was circling the large parking lot and was about to take a one-eighty to get back on the road heading south. The bus took the first right and we passed through the first stoplight. One more to go.

"Why the hell would Walter Reifert help us?" Miriam demanded. "He's a Colician! He shouldn't want anything to do with us!"

"Of course he should. We're not human anymore, Miriam. We're in the same shit hole he was in three years ago. I don't think he wants anyone to go through what he—"

The end of my sentence was cut off as I heard a tremendous crash ahead of us. Our conversation had distracted us from focusing on the task at hand. The bus driver braked violently as a pickup and SUV in front of us collided, and then the bus struck both vehicles, causing Miriam and I to fall out of our seats. I was momentarily dazed as my head struck the floor, but Miriam was quick to pull me to my feet. We shoved past the frightened passengers who had moved into the aisle, and in a few seconds we were squeezing through the broken doors and running around the accident to get to the other side of the median.

"Oh my God!" Miriam cried, putting a hand over her mouth as she gagged.

"Don't look," I instructed, pulling her along and forcing myself not to look at the bloody mess inside the SUV.

"We have to help!" Miriam squeaked, but she knew that we couldn't. Right now, we had to focus on getting to Kost and Jeff.

My mind was so scrambled from the chaos occurring around me that I completely forgot what we were supposed to do next. What did Reifert say came next? I stopped running in the middle of the road, trying to remember what to do. Four camouflage Hummers with Jaeger's soldiers hanging on the sides got me moving again.

"Come on!" I tugged Miriam forward, racking my brain for the next step in our escape plan. When I drew a blank, I said, "Crap! What are we supposed to do next?"

Miriam started to answer, but a fierce whistle startled us both into silence. A red pickup was pulling through the intersection, going back in the direction of the mall, and it slowed to a steady crawl as it passed the bus. A young woman, probably the same age as Miriam, leaned her head out of the driver's window and gestured for us to get into the back.

"Red pickup," Miriam muttered. "Let's go!" We bolted for the truck, practically diving into the bed. just as we heard the tires of multiple vehicles squealing to a halt. No doubt they belonged to Jaeger's men. As soon as we hit the bed, the girl driving took off again. There was chaos on both sides of the road now. Accidents were happening everywhere; we could hear it happening all around us as the girl weaved the truck in and out of the unfolding chaos. How could this be happening? How did so many accidents happen at once? Was it because the first collision was such a distraction that no one was paying attention to where they were driving? I got my answer when I met Miriam's eyes as we crouched down out of sight, struggling to keep our balance without being seen. Her gaze was frightened, full of terror. "They're causing this!" she whispered, her voice barely a squeak.

"Who?" I asked.

"Reifert!" She pointed toward the cab. "Her! The other Colicians they're with! They're causing the accidents!"

"No way," I said, but even as I said the words I couldn't convince myself of their truth. We both knew the Colicians were causing this disaster. But if they were causing it to help us escape, should we still be concerned? Who were we supposed to fear? The Colicians, who were causing all this chaos, or the humans, who the Colicians were risking their lives to stop.

The girl at the wheel was taking the truck away from the mall, away from the chaos. She was now driving the speed limit, which meant that the soldiers weren't following.

I looked at Miriam again. "I think we're safe. Here, I mean. The soldiers didn't see us get in."

"What do we do now?" Miriam whispered, her eyes still mortified. "We can't stay with them!"

"Okay." Now that I was calmer, I could think more clearly. "Reifert said that the pickup would take us back to the motel, right? Well, that means they know where we're hiding. We'll wait a mile or two, and when she stops at a light we'll get out and run. We can tell Jeff to get Kost out and hide and find someplace to meet."

"Do you really think that Kost will be able to move?" Miriam asked, but even as she spoke, the truck was veering off the road into a parking lot and skidding to a halt in a parking space. A moment later I heard the driver's door open and then slam shut again.

Acting on instinct, I took Miriam's hand and leapt out of the bed, bringing her with me. I pushed her behind me as the driver stopped in front of me, her brow creased in irritation and her arms folded across her chest.

I took the moment we spent staring at each other to study the girl. She had long, straight red hair; a dark red, not a Ron Weasley red. She wasn't very tall; she was shorter than Miriam, but the way she held herself suggested that her size did not speak for her capabilities. She wore sunglasses, so it was difficult to decipher her precise emotion, but I got the vibe that she wasn't very happy. Her blocked eyes also made it difficult to make any telepathic connection, a fact that was clearly annoying Miriam. That was something we had to keep in mind; eye contact made the easiest telepathic connection.

"So," the girl said, her tone flat, angry. "This is the thanks I get for rescuing you? You're just going to run off and hide ungratefully without letting us give you an explanation?"

I was speechless. Miriam seemed to be in the same predicament.

"Didn't it cross your mind," the girl continued, "that if we know where your motel is, we'll be able to find you no matter where you go?"

Oh. That was intimidating.

"Uh…" I stammered for a moment. "It's just…you scared us."

"You don't have to be scared of us," the girl said, her voice suddenly gentle. She reached up and removed her sunglasses, showing us her dark blue eyes that shone like all Colician eyes did. "That's what we've been trying to tell people for three years."

Miriam spoke up. "You made the ceiling come down on top of us.

Your friend Reifert pulled us into a dark corridor without explaining who he was or what he was doing. Then you caused all those car crashes. Why wouldn't we be afraid of you?"

The girl shook her head. "We did all this to help you get away."

"You killed someone!"

Again, a shake of her head. "We didn't kill anyone."

"I saw someone dead," Miriam said sharply. "I saw his face. He was covered in blood. He was dead."

"I assure you, Miriam, that we did not kill anyone."

Miriam shrank away when she spoke her name. It sent chills down my back as well.

I cleared my throat when neither girl spoke. "So…you're a telepath too?" I asked. The question was pointless; she had to be. How else would she have known what we were talking about in the truck? It was too loud for her to hear us back there. To my surprise, the girl shook her head. "How did you know what we were planning to do, then?"

The passenger door opened and then closed, and we heard the shuffling of small footsteps coming around the front of the truck. A little boy appeared behind the red-haired girl, a little boy with blonde hair and big blue eyes. He couldn't have been older than four, but he appeared more mature than a four-year-old. That was the way Colicians were; they had kids early and the kids developed faster mentally and physically than humans.

The boy smiled shyly, showing off his small, white teeth. He clung to the leg of the girl, and the girl put a protective hand on his head. He was her son, and he must have been the telepath in the vehicle.

I suddenly realized something. The girl seemed familiar to me, and when I saw the toddler it all clicked. The short, red-haired girl was Shauna Skyler, Walter Reifert's wife, and that was their son, Flint.

And then another thought struck me: why the hell would they bring their little boy to a place this hostile to their kind?

Shauna smiled as well, seeming to understand that we now knew who she was. "Will the two of you calm down long enough for me to give you an explanation?" she asked patiently.

I looked at Miriam, whose eyes said it all.

I still don't trust her. We should leave. Now.

"Thank you for your help, Miss Skyler," I told her, backing away with Miriam, "but I think it might be better if we just left."

"We can help you, you know," Shauna said, her voice flat again.

"We know," I said. "And you have. Thank you. But right now I think it's best if we just try to figure this out on our own."

Shauna stared at us for a few moments, her expression half bewildered, half amused. Finally, she sighed. "All right, fine. Have it your way. You can have the truck, so you can get to where you're going."

We hesitated. "Are you sure?" Miriam asked. "What about the two of you?" She looked at the little blonde boy, Flint.

"We'll be fine," she promised. "I've got a ride coming as we speak." She tapped the side of her head to indicate that more telepaths were communicating with her. She tossed us the keys. "Seriously. Take it. Right now, you need it a hell of a lot more than I do."

Miriam and I exchanged glances one more time before hastily climbing in, Miriam letting me take the wheel. As we buckled our seatbelts, Shauna came up to the window. "Remember." She tapped her head again. "If you need our help, no matter when or where, you just let us know. Seriously. We want to help you."

I nodded to her and forced a smile. "We'll keep that in mind. Uh…thanks again."

Shauna nodded in return and stepped away, pulling Flint with her as I put the truck in reverse and then drove toward the lot's exit. As I pulled out of the lot, I looked in the rearview mirror at Shauna and her boy. Her expression was one of worry, different from anything I'd seen on her so far. Whether it was worry for herself, her boy, or us, I didn't know.

But I could take a guess.

8

Separation Anxiety

We parked the truck a half mile from the motel, just in case anyone was following. Kost was worse when we got back. Much, much worse. His breathing was shallow, and had a raspy, watery sound to it. It sounded like my sister's breathing when she had pneumonia as a child. His eyes were closed, but when we opened them to look at his pupils, the whites of his eyes were red with blood. His skin and gums were also taking on a yellowish tint, like the color of eggnog.

"Jaundice," Jeff muttered. "His liver's failing."

"You weren't letting him drink too much while we were out, were you?" I asked Jeff, trying to lighten the mood.

Both Jeff and Miriam shot me a dirty look, and Miriam snapped, "Austin!"

"I'm sorry." I lowered my eyes. "I just don't want to think about what's going to happen to him."

"Nothing's going to happen to him," Jeff said sharply, pulling the blankets up over Kost as he slept. "He's going to get better. He's going to be fine."

"Jeff," Miriam said, putting a hand on his shoulder.

"No!" Jeff pulled away, glaring at her and then me. "He's gonna make it! He's gonna be okay!"

Miriam bit her lip to keep from saying any more. Jeff didn't want to admit it, and we would let him tell himself the lie, because it was better than admitting what we already knew.

Kost was going to die tonight.

"Maybe you were right, Jeff," Miriam said after an hour or so of us restlessly milling about the room. She was running a finger across her lip thoughtfully.

"Right about what?" Jeff asked. He looked to me for an answer, but I wasn't sure what she was referring to either.

"When you wanted to call Dr. Perry before." Miriam looked up at us, her eyes eager and hopeful. "Maybe that is the right thing to do."

"That's what I've been telling you two!" Jeff said in exasperation, throwing up his arms. "Why are you siding with me now?"

Miriam and I glanced at each other. We had already told Jeff about our encounter with Jaeger, but not about our encounter with Reifert and his family. We didn't want to give him anything else to be stressed about. Now that Kost's life was slipping through our fingers, and it appeared the Colicians weren't a threat to us but were interested in helping us, I thought it would be okay to fill Jeff in on what happened. The same thought seemed to be going through Miriam's mind.

"We ran into Walter Reifert during our escape from the mall," Miriam explained, clearly uncomfortable talking about it. "He and his family were actually the reason we made it out of there."

Jeff stared at her, his mouth ajar just like Miriam's when I told her the Colician in the mall was Reifert. "Why the hell didn't you tell me this before?"

I told Jeff the story of how Walter and Shauna helped us escape, being careful to give him all the details. He listened silently, only speaking to ask a few questions for clarification. It was unusual for Jeff not to interrupt a story. He wasn't the type to simply sit and listen. When the story was over, he nodded, staring at the floor.

"Why didn't you tell me this before?" he asked again, quieter but angrier than before.

I started to answer, but Miriam took this one. "We didn't want to freak you out by telling you that we have more people looking for us."

"From what Austin just told me, the Colicians already know where we are."

"Yes." Miriam sighed. "With Kost...with the condition Kost was in, we didn't want to put more stress on your plate."

Jeff raised his eyes, glaring. "So the two of you can handle it and I can't?"

"That's...that's not..." I tried to come up with the right words. "We didn't think you couldn't handle it."

"We just didn't want you to have to deal with it," Miriam finished, smiling weakly. "It freaked us out pretty bad when we first found out. Plus, with Kost dy—sick—it's a lot of things to deal with at once. We just didn't want you to have to deal with that too."

It was clear that Jeff was still angry, but he didn't push it further. Setting his jaw, he addressed Miriam: "So you think that we *should* call Dr. Perry? You think we can trust him?"

"I think that if Kost is to survive this," Miriam said, "then Dr. Perry is our best shot."

"Then let's call him," Jeff said, jumping to his feet.

"Hold on a second," I protested, also rising. "Can we talk about this for a second? Before we get too far ahead of ourselves?"

"What's there to talk about, Austin?" Jeff demanded, his voice getting louder with each word. "This is Kost's *life* we're talking about here!"

"*I know that,* Jeff!" I shot back. "But we can't just call a bunch of Colicians here! Think of the attention they'll attract."

"Who gives a *shit* what kind of attention they'll attract!" Jeff shouted.

"Guys," Miriam warned, going to the window and brushing the curtain aside slightly to see if anyone was listening.

"We also have to consider what it is they want with us," I snapped, lowering my voice but keeping the same amount of venom in it as before. "Why are they helping us? They must want something from us. Why else would they risk themselves for us?"

"Maybe because they *care!*" Jeff was on the verge of hysteria. "They were experimented on before they escaped, and those who were left behind are still lab rats! Maybe they just don't want anyone else to go through what they did!"

He had a point. Those thoughts had passed through my mind earlier. But there was still a big chance that Reifert's assistance today was motivated by something other than pure compassion. "I just want to take everything into consideration," I said finally.

"There's nothing left to consider!" Jeff yelled. "Dr. Perry is practically Reifert's right-hand man! Reifert was the one who saved your asses today! Dr. Perry can and will save Kost's life!"

I started to argue more, but Miriam cut in. "You're both right."

"How does that help us?" Jeff snapped.

"We have to call Dr. Perry," she said. "He's the only person who can save Kost that we can moderately trust right now. But we can't trust him completely." She took a deep breath. "I think we should split up."

"What?" Jeff cried.

At the same time, I said, "I think that's a terrible idea."

"Just hear me out," Miriam said, raising her hands for silence. "We can't move Kost. One of us will stay with him until Dr. Perry comes, and the other two will go north to my uncle's cabin. Then in case something happens, at least two of us will be safe."

"Why do I get the feeling that you're planning to be the one who stays behind?" I raised my eyebrows at Miriam.

"Mentally, I'm the strongest right now," Miriam said. "I'm the only one who can control our new abilities, and that's our best shot if something happens."

"Jeff seemed plenty capable of controlling his ability earlier today," I pointed out. "And I'm starting to figure out how it works. It doesn't have to be you."

"Yes, it does," Miriam insisted.

"You're the only one who knows where the cabin is," Jeff piped in.

"I can *show* you how—"

"Stop." I clapped my hands together. "Miriam, I understand that you're the strongest, but you're going north with Jeff. I'm staying with Kost."

"No." Miriam shook her head forcefully. "Not happening."

"I'm not gonna let you stay here."

"You don't need to protect me!"

"I love you, all right!" I took a deep breath as Miriam blinked in surprise. "I love you, and I'm not going to let anything happen to you."

Miriam opened her mouth, ready to continue arguing, but then she gave up. "Okay," she whispered. "I'll take Jeff."

"Take the truck," I told her. "Kost and I will catch a bus or something. You'll have to leave soon. Take whatever stuff we've got and get going as soon as possible." We'd lost our bags of clothes and other necessities back at the mall, so what we had left wasn't much. The two of them got their few belongings together and were heading out within ten minutes of our decision.

"I'll be okay," I promised Miriam as she clung to me. I rested my chin on top of her head. "Just stay safe, okay?"

"Promise me you'll find me," Miriam whispered, squeezing me tighter.

"I'll always find you," I whispered back. "No matter where you go."

Pulling me forward, Miriam kissed me hard. When she pulled away she said, "Don't be long, now. I'll call Dr. Perry when we get going and tell him we need his help. After he helps Kost, you two get your asses up north, you hear?"

"Yes, ma'am," I replied, and then she and Jeff were gone.

~~*

I waited four hours after Miriam and Jeff left to admit to myself that Dr. Perry wasn't coming. I called Miriam just to make sure she called him.

Yeah, I called him right after we got in the truck. She was just as worried as me. *You haven't heard anything from him at all?*

Nothing, I said. *Did you actually talk to him?*

No, she admitted. *I sent him a message. I sent one to Reifert, too.* We were silent for a moment. *What do we do if he doesn't come?*

He'll come, I promised her. *He'll come. I know he will. He's just...busy. He'll be here soon.*

I knew Miriam wasn't buying my lie, but she didn't say anything else. After four hours of constantly checking my watch, the window, and Kost, I was forced to admit he wasn't coming.

I didn't call Miriam to tell her. I couldn't bring myself to. She and Jeff would be heartbroken, as I was right now. Besides, I'd rather tell them in person after Kost... When I joined them up north, I would tell them the news.

Tears suddenly spilled from my eyes. I tried to act tough around everyone, but the wall I'd built around myself didn't go very deep. My past was full of pain and loss, and that had left me wounded. Now my present was full of pain and loss. How could I get through this again? First, my whole family. Now I was losing my friend.

What would happen to me if I lost Miriam?

"I can't do this anymore," I whispered, fighting back sobs. My tears were blinding me, and I stumbled over my own shoes as I went to Kost's bedside. I collapsed on the bed next to Kost, unable to hold back my sobs any longer. "I can't do this anymore!" I searched for Dr. Perry's mind, one among billions, but it was still difficult for me to find the mind of someone I didn't know, especially if he was on the Parallel Earth. I didn't even know if I'd be able to communicate with someone on a different planet. So instead, I shouted at the ceiling. "Why didn't you come?" I yelled as loud as I could. I didn't care who heard me. "You helped us before! Why don't you help us now? You *killed* him!" I laid there beside Kost for hours, sobbing, soaking the sheets with my tears. I laid there until the sun began to set, casting shadows over the room. I laid there until night took over the world, and there was no one left in it but Kost and I.

The last thing I remember before I fell asleep was slipping my hand into Kost's, praying to whatever God existed to filter some of my life into him. It was naïve, but it was the only thing left I could do.

~~*

As I slept, I also fell. But this time, I wasn't alone. Kost was with me. He was falling too.

I called out to him, screamed his name. He wouldn't look at me or even open his eyes. He started falling faster than me. I tried to reach out, to catch his arm and keep him with me. As soon as I got close to him, grazing his arm with my fingertips, he started falling even faster. I struggled to reach him, screaming his name until my throat gave out, but in the end, Kost fell deep into the darkness, out of sight. Out of time.

Out of life.

I struck bottom and forced myself to stay asleep. I had to find Kost. If I found him I could bring him back, save him. I fumbled around the ground, squeezing my eyes closed to stay in the dark. *I'll find you, Kost. I'll save you.* I tried to roll onto my hands and knees to cover more ground, but I couldn't move anything but my limbs.

"Kost," I murmured. "Where are you?" I continued to grope along the ground, searching for Kost, but to no avail. But then, a hand! A hand took mine, squeezed it gently.

"Austin. Wake up."

The voice sounded familiar, but I just couldn't place it. Not while I was so focused on finding Kost. "Kost," I called again, my voice still a murmur.

"He's here with us, Austin. Wake up, now."

I blinked awake, startled to see Walter Reifert standing over me. He was the one holding my hand. He was the one who spoke.

"Hey there, stranger," Reifert said, giving me a small smile. "Glad to see you made it back okay."

The room was dim; the light over Kost's bed was on, and I was on the other bed. Reifert must have moved me while I slept. A few men and women were standing around Kost, their voices soft and drifting over to me. The man in charge, a tall man with a strong build and dark hair, was shining a light in Kost's eyes and giving orders to a woman who was injecting a crimson colored liquid into Kost's arm.

"What are you guys doing?" I demanded, my words slurring. I was still drowsy, and I managed to sit up despite Reifert's protests.

"We're seeing if there's anything we can do for your friend. There's nothing to be worried about." Reifert sat down beside me. "How are you feeling? You were calling out in your sleep."

"Yeah," I mumbled. "I have nightmares."

Reifert nodded. "I know. I do, too."

"How do you make it stop?" I turned to him, desperate to know how he healed himself. "How do you get over something like this?"

"You don't. Not necessarily." Reifert looked down at me, and instead of seeing a man, a leader of an entire race of people, I saw a boy. A boy whose entire family was murdered. A boy who fought his own thoughts of suicide. A boy stronger than me. "I almost did it too, you know."

"Did what?"

"Killed myself. I got a gun and put it to my head. I wanted to do it."

"Why didn't you?"

Walter smiled. "Because I found something that helped me move on. We can't get over what we've been through. Never. But we can move on."

"What was it you found?" I asked, curious.

Walter's green eyes flashed in the dim light. "I think you know what I've found."

I did. Shauna. Flint. His new family. I had a new family now, but I was already losing them. I was losing Kost. I could see it in Walter's eyes.

"You love Miriam?" Walter asked. It didn't really seem like a question. If he was a telepath, then he had to know.

I nodded.

"Then don't ever let her go." Walter patted my shoulder. "No matter what happens, don't let her go."

"I don't think I could," I whispered.

We both looked up as everyone but the man in charge—Dr. Perry—backed away from the bed and slowly left the hotel room. Dr. Perry stood there, gazing down at Kost. Finally, he looked up. I knew what had happened.

"Well?" Walter asked. His voice cracked on the word.

Dr. Perry shook his head before looking down again.

"Shit," I muttered, putting my head in my hands.

Walter put his arm around my shoulders. It felt strange receiving this gesture from someone I didn't know very well, but since we shared similar pasts and he knew how I was feeling, I accepted it without protest.

"It'll be okay," he promised me.

"It doesn't feel that way."

"I know."

No one spoke for a long time. Dr. Perry was the first to break the silence.

"I'd like to take your friend's body, if that's okay with you."

"Why?" I asked. "So you can experiment on him?"

Walter shifted uncomfortably beside me, and Dr. Perry cleared his throat. "Not exactly. We aren't completely sure why his body rejected the virus. We just want to find out why, so we can be sure that it won't happen to you or your friends." He paused, staring at me in a way that told me exactly what he was thinking.

"No," I said firmly. "You can take Kost, but the rest of us aren't going with you."

"You'll be safe with us, Austin," Walter insisted. "You know that. We won't hurt you like they will."

"I don't care. We're not going with you."

Dr. Perry and Walter looked at each other for some time, mentally communicating, no doubt. Eventually, Walter said, "Well, if you're sure. Just remember—"

"I know," I said flatly. "You'll help us. Just like you helped Kost." There was another uncomfortable silence. I glared at Walter. "Shauna told us you'd help us if we asked for it. We did ask for it. Now our friend is dead."

Dr. Perry stammered for a moment. "We can't be everywhere at once."

I snorted. "Right. My mistake." I laid back down and turned my back to them. It was partly out of anger, but mostly because I didn't want either of them to see my tears.

I felt them watching me for a few minutes, but then Walter got up and I heard the door open as the others came back in to help move Kost's body. How they would do that without attracting attention, I didn't know or care. I just wanted to be alone. My friend was dead.

Kost was dead…

They were gone in a few minutes, and the room was wonderfully silent once again. But now it was empty. Kost wasn't with me anymore. He wasn't anywhere.

I'd expected Walter to hang back, to try to comfort me more, but he left with the others. Without a word. I was grateful for it. It meant that he really did understand my pain. He knew that simple words couldn't heal it.

~~*

I awoke to the sound of the motel room door closing. Alarmed, I sat straight up, preparing myself to fight even though I was weak and hungry. But I had nothing to worry about; the room was empty and I didn't see anything suspicious, except for the large blood stain on Kost's bed, which I forced myself to look away from. Still, I'd heard the door close. Rising, I went to the door and opened it, taking a good long look down both directions of the hallway. Nobody, except a housekeeper a few rooms down, was there. Other than the shuffling of the sheets the housekeeper was folding, it was completely silent.

I went back inside, frustrated, angry. As I passed Kost's bed, I ripped the sheets off the mattress, balled them up, and stuffed them in the trash. I willed them to be gone, willed the blood, and Kost's lingering presence, to be gone. Turning back to the stripped bed, I let out a howl of rage, a sound that wasn't human, that terrified me. Kost's blood had leaked through the thin sheets and stained the mattress, something that shouldn't have surprised me but did all the same. I grabbed the end of it and flipped it, sending it to the floor. It knocked the lamp and digital clock off the bedside table, and I heard the sound of shattering glass, but that didn't stop me. I was too furious, too heartbroken, to be stopped by such meaningless things.

Without caring what sounds I made, or how loud those sounds were, I tore that mattress apart. I thought it would be difficult, but it was easy, one of the easiest things I'd done in a while. It made a satisfying ripping sound as I tore it open, exposing the fluffy white stuffing. I flung the stuffing everywhere, and soon it appeared as if the ceiling had opened up and allowed a snowstorm into my room. Still, I didn't stop. I ripped the mattress into little pieces, until it was no longer distinguishable as a mattress. And until my hands were bleeding.

When I saw the blood, I stopped myself, panting. I was hurting myself, and that was going to do no one any good. For a few seconds, my sanity returned to me, and I choked back the lump in my throat that was threatening to become sobs. I'd cut both hands on the springs. They weren't serious wounds; they didn't even hurt; but the blood told me I needed to get myself under control. Then, the blood suddenly reminded me of Kost, of the blood stain that was the only evidence of his existence, and I lost control again. I went to my bed, preparing to do to my mattress what I'd done to Kost's, but I stopped when I saw the piece of paper at the foot of the bed. Fighting back the rage and ferocity I wanted so desperately to let forth, I stooped and picked up the paper, unfolding it to see what it was.

It was a note. I assumed it was from Walter, but there was no name to prove it.

There's a blue Nissan Altima in the parking lot, closest to the exit. The keys are in the glove compartment. Good luck.

And, at the very bottom:

I'm sorry.

A soft, hesitant knock at the door brought my attention to what I'd done to the room. Bits of mattress covered the floor, practically a new carpet, and pieces of it were soaked in blood. I couldn't tell which pieces had my blood, or Kost's, or both, but it would raise an immediate red flag to anyone who entered. Cautiously, I went to the door and looked through the peephole. I sighed, and then opened the door just enough so I could be seen.

The housekeeper, a young African American woman, stood back as I appeared, her back nearly pressed up against the opposite wall. She was terrified of my appearance, I had no doubt. She must have heard me yelling and screaming. I was surprised, yet grateful, that she had not called security or worse, the police.

"Is...everything okay, sir?" she asked, her voice a squeak.

I tried to force a smile, but it just didn't work. "Fine, thank you," I said. "Sorry about the noise. My friend had a nightmare." When she only continued to stare, her face still terrified but also slightly suspicious, I added, "He fought in Philadelphia in one of the first Colician conflicts. He saw some pretty rough shit."

The girl's face immediately relaxed. She even smiled. "I'm sorry to hear that. Is there anything I can get for him?"

"No, thank you," I told her. "I've got it under control. Again, sorry about the scare."

"It's no problem at all," she said. "I completely understand."

I closed the door, heaving a tremendous sigh. Lying was getting easier and easier, and I knew my story would work. People who fought in the Colician conflicts were highly regarded, so people cut them slack if they had outbursts like the one I described. I was certain that people who actually *did* fight in the Colician conflicts *did* see some really nasty shit.

I gathered up whatever things I still had. All I had was the new pair of clothes I put on at the mall, which I was still wearing, a wad of cash, and a plastic bag of crackers, dried fruit, and nuts. I slipped Walter's note into my back pocket and left the room behind, along with the mess. The pain. The grief. All of it. I didn't bother to turn in my key. They'd find the mess and the blood faster if I did, and I needed all the time I could get.

The car was where Walter said it would be. There was a surprise waiting for me inside; every single one of our shopping bags we'd lost was crammed into the backseat. Not a single item purchased was missing. I felt a great swell of relief building inside me. Kost was dead, and the whole world would soon be looking for us, but it was nice to know that there were a few out there who actually cared about us.

I climbed in, fished the keys out of the glove compartment, and started the car. I pulled out of the parking lot and left the motel behind, without looking back.

~~*

The rest of the day was a blur. I didn't know where I was going, at least not consciously. I drove through countless towns, on countless roads, took countless turns, all without a clue as to where I was, or what direction I was traveling. But, deep down, I knew where I was going. I was going toward my new lifeline, the only thing that willed me forward. And that was the way I wanted to go: forward. It was the only way *to* go. The past was too painful to bear. No looking back. I had to keep going forward, and forward would eventually take me to Miriam, the love of my life, the kindest, most beautiful person I'd ever known. The people I loved were dying, and as Walter said, I had to protect what I had left. I would protect Miriam, and Jeff, with everything I had. I wasn't going to lose anyone else. I couldn't.

I only stopped once on my journey north. It was a five-hour drive, but I refused to pull over to pee or eat. I wasn't hungry, and I couldn't will myself to stop to relieve myself. All I wanted was to get to the cabin, where Miriam and Jeff were, so I could feel safe and happy once again. But after about three hours, I tried to force down some of the crackers in my bag, and ended up squealing to a halt so I could throw up out the door. Since I was stopped, I decided to just pee so I wouldn't have to stop again. Then I was up and off again, and I didn't stop until I pulled onto the gravel drive leading up to Miriam's great-uncle's cabin.

I pulled off into the grass and got out, just as Miriam came running down the path toward me. Tears streaked her face, and she might have been angry with me had she not been so relieved.

She stopped a few feet away, doubling over as sobs overtook her. Normally, I would have run to comfort her, but I was still so numb, and now I felt like I could sleep for a week. So I just stood there, staring at her expressionlessly as she fought to speak.

"Where have you been?" she gasped, trying to stand up straight again. Instead, she ended up collapsing to the ground. When I didn't answer, she said, "You were supposed to call me! I couldn't get a hold of you! I thought..." She couldn't finish.

My legs walked me to her, sat me down beside her. My arms pulled her close to me. I felt like a robot, with someone else controlling my body. "I'm sorry," I heard myself say. "I'm sorry. I'm here now."

"Where's Kost?" Miriam hiccupped, hugging me harder than I thought she could. I didn't have to answer. She knew.

I heard shouts coming from the house, and then pounding feet coming toward us. I didn't look. I didn't care who it was.

I felt like I should say something else to Miriam, try to comfort her more, but I couldn't think. My eyelids were suddenly so heavy, and I had trouble keeping them up. I tried to think of something to say, something kind, something reassuring, but all that came out was, "Walter found our stuff from the mall. It's all in the back." That's the last thing I remember from that awful day.

9

The Next Plan

The cabin was both bright and gloomy. All curtains had been stripped from the windows, so during the day the sun filtered in, lighting up the rooms. But the electricity had been turned off before Miriam's family even arrived, so once the sun set the whole place went dark. A few candles and a fire were the only light, making nights gloomy and depressing. Maybe it felt like that because that was how I felt anyway, but the darkness wasn't helping.

I'd been with Miriam, Jeff, and Miriam's family for a day, and I still hadn't told them what happened at the motel. I barely spoke to anyone at all. I mostly stayed in bed upstairs, allowing Miriam to coax food and water into me. At first, she and Jeff tried to get me to explain what happened, but I couldn't answer them. Finally, on the morning of the following day, Jeff had had enough.

He came barging into the room where Miriam and I slept, huffing angrily. "Dude, seriously. Kost was our friend, too. Can you just screw your head on for five minutes so you can tell us what happened to him?"

"Jeff!" Miriam scolded. She was sitting beside me, trying to get me to drink some juice.

"What?" he snapped. "He's been laying there for more than a day! He's not the only one who lost someone!"

Miriam started to snap back, but I stopped her. "He's right," I said, and realized how selfish I was. I sat up, brushing off Miriam's protective hands. Taking a deep breath, I told them what happened.

"Maybe Reifert's right," Jeff said when my story was over. "Maybe we *should* go with them."

"No way," Miriam replied. "Austin was right. The humans want something with us. The Colicians probably want us for similar reasons."

"I don't know," I said. "Even though I'm still upset they didn't get to Kost in time, I'm starting to think that I was wrong about them. That *everyone* is wrong about them."

"Why else would they have taken Kost's body?" Miriam demanded. "He's something new. A new lab experiment."

"Dr. Perry said he wanted to find out what exactly killed Kost so he can keep it from happening to us," I reminded her.

Miriam rolled her eyes. "Like I'm going to believe that. Even if that was the case, it wouldn't do us any good. We've all been reacting differently. There's no saying what side effects could pop up."

"Still," Jeff said, persistent, "they can offer us some protection. They've made it clear that they're better than Hillerman and Jaeger. I think Reifert's being true to his word."

"We're not going with them," Miriam said firmly, as if she were in charge. "We're on our own right now. We can't trust anyone except ourselves."

Neither Jeff nor I responded to her. She seemed to have her mind set, and both of us were still hesitant about trusting anyone.

"Will you come down for breakfast, please?" she begged me. "I'd like you to meet my family."

I agreed. Her brothers carried me up here after I arrived and passed out in the grass, and I hadn't seen them or her father since then. Besides, if Miriam and I were growing closer, it might be good to talk to her father.

A sudden terror clenched my innards. I was not the best at making friends, or being polite, for that matter. What if her dad hated me? What if he threatened to kill me if I didn't leave his daughter alone? Ridiculous, childish thoughts. I was sure our introduction would be fine, and it was doubtful that Miriam said anything about our growing relationship. Even if she did, her dad couldn't simply tell me to stay away from her. We were in this mess together. To split up would be a tragic mistake. Taking a deep breath, I followed Miriam down the narrow wooden staircase to the ground level.

Vincent and Brent Lobner, Miriam's older brothers, were laughing at the small square table in the center of the kitchen. As soon as we entered, however, they both grew silent and stared at me. I felt immediately self-conscious, and could feel my face turning red.

"Hey, guys," Miriam said quietly, uncomfortably. "This is Austin."

Her two brothers looked almost exactly alike. They both had the same high cheekbones and strong chins, and both appeared to be the same height and girth. Like Miriam, they both had black hair, but their skin and eyes were different. That was the only way I could tell them apart. Vincent's skin was darker, and his eyes were dark brown, almost black. Brent's skin was the same copper tone as Miriam, and his eyes were a deep hazel. If I recalled correctly, Vincent was twenty-seven while Brent was twenty-three, but that didn't seem to make a difference with their appearances.

But one way I could tell them apart was the way they looked at me. Brent was clearly a goofball, probably a class clown when he was in school, and smiled at me warmly after Miriam introduced me. He seemed friendly enough, and I could tell that we would get along just fine. Vincent, on the other hand, regarded me suspiciously, looking at me sideways, a troubled frown corrupting his handsome features. He didn't trust me. But there was something else in his gaze that I couldn't quite place. It was almost threatening, and it frightened me. He was bigger than me, and if I remembered Miriam's story about him correctly, he was once a soldier, before the depths of hell swallowed the earth three years ago. If I stepped out of line, even slightly, I was certain that Vincent would be the first to put me in my place.

"Hey there, Sleeping Beauty," Brent greeted, his mouth twisting in a silly grin. "Good to know you're actually alive. There's chow on the stove. Help yourself."

"Thanks," I said sheepishly, letting Miriam lead me by the hand into the kitchen. I could feel Vincent's eyes burning holes through our intertwined fingers.

"Hold up!" a low voice from another room, no doubt Miriam's dad, called. "I want to talk to him first."

"Dad," Miriam sighed. "He's exhausted and starving—"

"I won't take long," her dad replied sharply.

Oh, jeez. This was it. To live or not to live? That was definitely the question.

To my relief, Miriam went into the den with me. Her dad was sitting in a thick, dust covered armchair reading the newspaper, and he glanced over it when he saw two bodies come in. "I'd rather have a private word with your friend if that's okay."

Miriam stood defiantly, hands planted firmly on her hips, eyes glaring. "Anything you have to say to my friends, you can say in front of me."

Mr. Lobner's eyes didn't waver from his daughter's. I could tell immediately that their relationship was rocky, and I didn't want to be the cause of a fight. I placed a hand on her arm. "It's okay," I told her. "I don't mind."

She turned to me, her expression protesting. I gave her a reassuring smile, but it might have had a greater effect if I felt assured myself. With an exasperated sigh, she left the room.

I looked at her father uncertainly. He had put the newspaper down so I could see him. He was younger than I expected, probably only in his late forties. He was thin, too. Lines and creases covered his tired face, particularly around his eyes, probably from too many sleepless nights after losing his wife and then his daughter. His brown hair was graying, and his hazel eyes were dull. Even though he seemed tired, his expression was hardened.

He sized me up carefully while I studied him. I wasn't tall, and even though I came across as tough, I really wasn't all that strong. He made me feel suddenly puny and worthless, and maybe that was what I was. I hadn't exactly done much to help our situation since it started.

Clearing my throat as the silence went on for too long, I said quietly, "I'm Austin Rockwell." I reluctantly extended a hand.

Mr. Lobner met my gaze, his expression still hard. A moment later his guard fell, and his expression sagged into one of gratitude. "Jerry Lobner," he replied, shaking my hand. "Please, sit down."

Startled by this sudden change, I plopped down into the chair beside him. Mr. Lobner now looked as tired as his eyes, and for a moment I thought he might start crying. He took a deep breath and said, "Thank you so much for helping my daughter. Things between us haven't been the same since her mom passed away, but..." He shook his head. "I would die if something happened to her."

"Sure," I said. "The four of us...well, now the three of us...knew we had to stick together if we were going to make it."

Mr. Lobner nodded. "I can't believe the government allowed this to happen. After what happened in 2018, you'd think they'd be more careful. And now this..." He gestured to me and the kitchen, where Miriam and Jeff were no doubt listening to our conversation. "How could they want to recreate what they did? If this spreads like last time..."

"It won't," I promised. "When Miriam was first infected, she didn't give the virus to us. It's something that has to be administered to take effect. None of us were infected until we were forced to breathe in the virus."

"That's disgusting," Mr. Lobner said, wrinkling his nose. "When this is over, I'm going to find whoever did this to my daughter and..." He stopped himself. "Of course, this is a major problem for you and Mr. Robinson as well. Do you have any idea what you're going to do or where you're going to go?"

I wished I could give him the answer he wanted, the answer that would light the hope sparking in his eyes, but in the end all I could do was shake my head. "No. Not a goddamn clue. Er—excuse me."

Mr. Lobner laughed. "Hell, I've heard worse coming out of the cat's mouth! Don't worry about a thing, son. You say what you like."

"You have a cat?" I asked, surprised.

"She's outside," Mr. Lobner explained. "She's a hunter. She'll come in later for some water and the litter box. She's friendly, don't worry," he added upon seeing my hesitant expression.

"I don't mind cats," I said. "It's just..."

He sighed. "You're allergic."

"Yeah."

"Well, I guess I can keep her outside for the time being..."

"No," I said quickly. I didn't want to impose my needs upon them. "That's fine. I'm only slightly allergic. I'll just be sure to avoid her."

"Well, if you're sure..."

"I'm sure." I took a look around the sunlit living room. "Nice place. Going to keep it?"

Mr. Lobner shrugged. "Don't know yet. We'll have to see how things work out." I knew he was referring to our situation. He paused for a moment before saying, "I'm sorry to hear about your friend. You don't think...you don't think that will happen to any of you, do you?"

His eyes were afraid, afraid for his daughter. I took it upon myself to reassure him. "Kost said that everyone responds differently to the virus. We've all had different side effects so far, so I don't think anyone else is going to die." *At least not from the virus,* I thought, but I didn't tell him that.

"That's a relief," he said, and he even smiled a little. "Miriam won't tell me anything."

Before I could stop myself, I blurted out, "What happened between you two, if you don't mind me asking?" Then: "I'm sorry, that was rude."

"No, it's fine," Mr. Lobner said.

"It's just...she seemed so driven to come here. I thought things would have been better between you two."

"It doesn't surprise me that she was driven to come to us. It's a place of safety, familiar and promising. Miriam always had a good relationship with her brothers. It wasn't me she was compelled to reach. But, there is a story behind that. Things between us weren't always this bad." He sighed. "I don't know if she told you that her mother was a Colician."

"She did."

"Well, that situation was very complicated. Vincent was a soldier, and he was supposed to detain Colicians. We all had a huge fight over what we were supposed to do about our predicament. Vincent could have been killed if he didn't turn over his mother, and if we all took off and were caught, we would all have been killed. I didn't know what else to do. So I..." He trailed off, closing his eyes. "*I* turned my wife in."

I gaped at him. "You did *what*?"

"I know, I know," he said, waving a hand at me to stop my accusations from flying at him. "It's horrible, but we both agreed to it, my wife and I. Neither of us were going to do anything that would jeopardize the lives of our children, so I called the labs and turned her in. 'Everything will be okay,' she said. 'They'll find a cure and then everything will be back to the way it was.' But that wasn't how it happened. There was no cure. The doctors started conducting experiments on prisoners. My wife...she died during one of them. And Miriam...well, she never forgave me. *I* never forgave me."

I understood Mr. Lobner's reasoning for what he did, and even sympathized with him a little. But there was something very different about the two of us; I would have never turned in my family, no matter what the consequences. Maybe that makes me selfish, but that's what love does to you. "I understand," I said, but I didn't tell him that what I understood was why Miriam was so angry with him.

Just then, Miriam came barging in, her brown eyes stormy. "Can he please get something to eat now?"

With a heavy sigh, Mr. Lobner gestured for me to join his daughter. I stood up, bowed my head slightly to him, and went to join Miriam at the table.

Jeff had already eaten, and had decided to go for a short walk on a trail through the woods. Brent and Vincent just finished as I arrived with Miriam, but Brent said he wanted to get to know me so he sat with us, chattering away as Miriam and I nibbled on hash browns and oatmeal.

Vincent leaned against the counter, sipping coffee. I swear he was staring at me the entire time. Taking advantage of the gift I was given, I called Miriam.

Hey, is it just me or does your brother look like he wants to rip my throat out?

Miriam inhaled sharply, obviously not expecting my voice in her head, and we made eye contact briefly before she shot a glance at her brother. *Oh,* she said. *He's very protective. Just ignore him, and don't grab my ass in front of him or anything like that.*

I wasn't planning on doing that! I snapped, stabbing my fork into my plate instead of my hash brown and causing a horrendous screechy sound. Everyone winced. "Sorry," I muttered. I directed my thoughts back to Miriam. *Could you just tell him to chill out? I may not be the nicest guy in the world, but I know how to treat a girl.*

I caught Miriam grinning, even though she tried to hide it by wiping her face with a napkin.

"Austin."

I looked at Brent, startled. He was staring at me expectantly, waiting for me to answer the question I hadn't heard. "Uh…" I started, embarrassed yet also amused. Brent didn't have a clue that Miriam and I had been ignoring him and having our own private conversation. I ventured a guess at what Brent asked me and answered, "Yes."

Brent stared at me.

Holding back her laughter, Miriam said, "He was there for three months. He got there about a month after I did."

"That's what I meant to say," I told Brent.

Brent and Miriam laughed, and then Vincent spoke up for the first time. "It's okay. Brent doesn't know when to shut his mouth. It's easy to zone out when his lips start flapping."

There was an uncomfortable moment of silence, where Miriam looked at me in surprise and Brent turned to his brother. "At least I know *how* to talk!" he snapped back.

I assumed this would escalate into a louder argument, but Vincent didn't reply. He just continued to stare at me. Helplessly, I looked at Miriam again. She shook her head, her eyes saying, *Just ignore him.*

Clearing my throat, I said, "I'm going to step out for a walk, if that's okay." Miriam and Brent said that was fine, so I stood up and picked up my plate to clear my leftovers into the sink. Before I had time to react, Vincent was upon me, grabbing me by the throat and shoving me up against the far wall. My plate fell out of my hand and shattered on the floor, but this didn't faze him.

"Vincent!" Miriam cried, jumping to her feet. She didn't come to my aid; she stood there staring in fear. Even *she* was afraid of him. "Vincent, stop!"

"Dude!" Brent was on his feet too.

"Vince, get your hands off of that boy." Mr. Lobner had come from the other room and was standing in the doorway, glaring at his son.

Vincent ignored them all, staring intently into my eyes. *You listen to me, boy, because I know you can. I've seen the way you look at her, and I've seen the way she looks at you. If you break her heart, or do anything at all to hurt her, I'll haul your ass back to Philadelphia myself. Blink three times if you understand me.*

I gave him three rapid blinks; I just wanted him to let go. His fingers were digging into my throat, and in a few moments I wouldn't be able to breathe at all. Vincent released me, straightening out my shirt and then his own. Looking down at the mess of shattered glass and potatoes, he said, "You made a mess. You ought to pick it up." And then he left.

The room was silent until the front door slammed, and then everyone seemed to simultaneously breathe a sigh of relief. "I'm so sorry about that," Mr. Lobner said, going to a small utility closet and pulling out a broom and dustpan. "He…uh…well, he does that sometimes. Don't take it personally."

"I'm just glad I'm not dead," I replied, dazed.

"I'm sorry about that," Mr. Lobner repeated. "No, no, no," he said as I reached for the broom. "Don't you worry about it. I'll take care of it. Go ahead on your walk now."

I reconsidered that idea, now that Vincent was out there, too. "I think I'll just go upstairs for a bit."

Mr. Lobner nodded, sweeping shards into the dustpan. "Whatever you need to do."

I felt bad leaving him to clean up my plate, but I was so discombobulated by what just happened that I had to get away from everyone. I sprinted up the stairs, sat down on the bed, and stared out the window. Miriam came up a few moments later and sat down beside me. "What did he say to you?" she asked softly.

"The typical big brother warning," I replied. "Don't mess with my sister or I'll mess with you."

Miriam groaned. "Of course he did. Well, at least he didn't hurt you."

I looked at her with fake seriousness. "I'm scared for my life, Miriam."

Laughing, Miriam rested her head on my shoulder.

~~*

That night, Jeff, Miriam, and I sat around the kitchen table, all of us silent. Miriam's family was in the den watching a movie on a battery-run portable DVD player, no doubt straining to hear what direction our discussion was going. So far, it was going absolutely nowhere.

"So," I said, hoping to break some of the tension in the air.

"So," Miriam echoed.

"So what do we do?" Jeff cried, and I heard the movie pause in the other room momentarily before it turned back on.

"Jeff," Miriam said in a low voice.

"Getting here was the plan!" Jeff declared, still louder than Miriam wanted. "We're here! But we can't hide here forever! Where do we go now?"

"Hey." I took his clenched hand in mine and gave it a squeeze. I willed him to look at me. "It's going to be okay. I'm not going to let anything happen to either of you."

Normally, Jeff would have argued back, but the sincerity in my voice and eyes caught him off guard. I took Miriam's hand with my other hand, and then she took Jeff's other hand. We sat around the table, holding hands like children around a campfire. I felt loved around these two wonderful people, and I knew they felt the same way.

We basked in the wonder of the moment, and we were brought back to reality all too soon.

"If you'll accept my help," Mr. Lobner said, leaning against the door frame, "I think I can contact someone who can help you."

~~*

So Mr. Lobner knew some people who were in league with the Colicians. It was kind of ironic. Why would he have that type of connection after turning in his infected wife and having a former soldier as a son? Redemption, perhaps, for the death of his wife?

The people he knew were humans and had aided Walter Reifert after the outbreak, but I still had trouble putting my trust in them. Despite the fact that they were complete strangers, they were humans; there was no knowing whose side they leaned toward.

"Do you really think we should trust them?" I asked Miriam and Jeff. We stepped aside for a moment after Mr. Lobner told us about the humans, needing a few minutes to talk it over. "He said they sneak information to the Parallel Earth from the U.S. government. What if they do the same to the other side?"

"I agree," Jeff said. "But I don't see a lot of options right now. If these people are on the Colicians' side, then we're safe."

"And if they're not, we're back in the lab," I pointed out.

That silenced Jeff, but only for a moment "Maybe we should just go. Just run. Go south. Or north. It really doesn't make a difference to me."

Miriam, who had been silent up to this point, spoke up. "I think we should have my dad call these people."

Jeff and I looked at her. "Are you sure?" I asked hesitantly. "If these people are easily corrupted…"

"I don't think they are," she said. "I've heard of these people and others like them. Their actions are purely aimed toward a Colician advantage."

"But what if this particular group isn't like that?" I whispered, uncertain.

Looking up at me, Miriam asked, "Where else are we supposed to go? We tried running on our own, and Jaeger found us. If we keep playing this cat and mouse game, we're going to end up dead."

Jeff and I looked at each other helplessly. Our options were pretty shitty, and we all knew it. Jeff gave in to Miriam's proposal. "I think we're screwed with either option, so we might as well give this one a shot." They both looked to me for my answer.

I sighed, completely agreeing with Jeff's statement. "Whatever," I said. "Tell your dad to call his guys."

Mr. Lobner called his connections, and we passed the next day waiting for them to get here. Finally, at about 9:00 p.m., his cell phone rang and we all jumped out of our seats, gathering around him to try to hear the conversation. It was the man in charge, a man who wouldn't give any of us—and hadn't even ever given Mr. Lobner—his name, in case we were captured and interrogated. He was at a motel in town, so Mr. Lobner, Vincent, and Brent all went out to meet with him. Jeff wanted to go too, but Mr. Lobner insisted it was too dangerous for any of us to be out in public, even if it was late.

"If you're caught on any security camera, you'll be tracked down and detained in a day," he said. "Just stay here. We won't be more than an hour."

That was roughly an hour ago. Jeff had resorted to pacing the living room, huffing and puffing like the big bad wolf because he was left behind. But, after not too long, the loveseat had started looking pretty comfy to him. Now he was asleep, snoring with his mouth hanging open.

Miriam and I sat quietly in the kitchen, playing various card games at the table. It was just a way for us to kill time, though. Neither of us was focusing on the game in front of us, and neither of us cared who won. We could both hear each other's thoughts, anyway, so we knew what was in each other's hand. We eventually started playing a repetitive game of War, because that was a game of luck instead of skill. We couldn't mentally cheat at it.

Finally, around 10:45, Miriam scattered her cards across the table and said, "I'm sick of this."

"Me too," I muttered.

She heaved a sigh and stared down at the table for a few minutes. I didn't interrupt her thoughts. I didn't have anything worth saying to disturb her. Eventually, she looked up at me. Sadly, I thought. "Will you come upstairs with me?"

Startled, I sputtered, "Uh...sure."

"I want to show you something." She led the way up to the room we shared and sat down on the bed. I took a seat beside her.

"Are you okay?" I asked after she just sat staring at the floor like she did at the table in the kitchen. "Are you nervous about—"

Miriam suddenly burst into tears.

I quickly wrapped my arms around her, shushing her sobs that were causing violent tremors throughout her body. "Jesus, Miriam," I said, not having a clue what to do or say. "What's wrong? Did someone do something...?"

"I miss my mom!" she cried, her sobs growing louder.

Afraid that she would wake up Jeff, I tried shushing her again. "It's going to be okay. I know you miss her. I'm sorry this happened to you." I held her close.

Miriam cried until she couldn't anymore. Still shaking, she said, "I found her in my dad's room."

"What?"

She pulled something out from under the pillow and showed it to me. "My dad had this in his room. I shouldn't have been snooping, but... I needed to see her."

It was a photograph of a woman. A *beautiful* woman. I recognized her right away to be Miriam's mother. The woman in the picture looked like an older, darker version of Miriam. She was wearing a type of scarf or shawl over her head (Miriam had told me she was a Muslim), and was smiling a smile full of white teeth. She was standing in front of a car, the same car that Mr. Lobner had now, and she held her hand over her protruding belly.

"She was pregnant with my sister in that picture," Miriam said softly.

I looked up at her. "Your sister?"

"She died before she was born." Miriam looked away. "She would be turning thirteen this year."

I felt a swell of pain for Miriam, and a stab of guilt for myself. I acted as if I was the only person who knew loss, while my best friend was sitting beside me telling me that she had suffered just as much.

I thought of Kost then, and wondered if this was how the rest of our lives would be. Losing everyone we loved. Our lives had certainly led us down that path already. Would we keep losing everyone, everything, until it was just the two of us, or maybe just *one* of us? How were we supposed to keep fighting when our lives were being pulled out from under our feet?

"I'm sorry," I said, not knowing what else to say. "Your mother was very beautiful." I turned to her, glad to see her smiling a little. "Just like you."

Our eyes met briefly before our lips met.

I had taken the mask off about ten minutes ago to catch my breath. He had responded better to my first appearance in the costume than I hoped. I didn't hold too much optimism for the next few times he would see me, because they wouldn't be in his dreams. This next time would definitely startle him, but I had to remind him of this image so he wouldn't miss his upcoming opportunity.

My wife was still in our bedroom, but I knew that if I didn't return soon she would come looking for me. I had to get this done quickly. One more time, and I would return to bed. I would complete my next visits at another time. Slipping the mask back over my head, I stepped in front of the mirror again.

10

In League

When I awoke the next morning to Brent pounding on the bedroom door and shouting for us to wake up, I barely had enough time to register that I slept dreamlessly.

"Get up!" Brent cried, rattling the knob. "They're here! The soldiers are *here*!"

Upon hearing the word *soldiers*, I was on my feet and quickly throwing my clothes on. I was momentarily grateful that Miriam had remembered to lock the door last night. I was sure that anyone stumbling upon us naked in the same bed would cause a big stink.

"Miriam!" I said as I pulled on my shorts and shirt. "Wake up! We gotta go!"

Miriam mumbled something in her sleep but didn't move.

I shook her as I fumbled to get my head through my shirt. "Wake up, baby! Jaeger's here!"

A low moan escaped her throat, and she winced and turned her head away from me. She whimpered something that sounded Arabic.

"*Miriam!*" Now fully clothed, I shook her hard. "*Miriam!*"

"No!" She gasped and opened her eyes, staring up at me.

"We gotta go," I repeated, tossing her some clothes. She hesitated for a moment before dressing, and then we were running downstairs.

Jeff was waiting for us, practically jumping up and down in distress. "Jesus!" he said as we reached the bottom. "Take long enough?"

"Sorry." I glanced at Miriam, whose gaze was distant and troubled. "Miriam had a hard time waking up."

"Yeah." Jeff rolled his eyes. "Sure."

Brent, Vincent, and Mr. Lobner all held an automatic weapon in their hands—a perk of Vincent once being in the military, no doubt. They all stood pressed up against the wall on either side of the front door, being sure to keep out of sight. Outside, as we could see from peeking out the front window, were dozens of military vehicles and soldiers. Every soldier was aiming a weapon at the house, all except for Jaeger, who stood in front of the group with a megaphone in hand.

"There are soldiers behind the house, too," Mr. Lobner told us, just as I was about to suggest we duck out the back door.

"Great," I muttered. "So we're all screwed, right?"

Jaeger's amplified voice answered me. "Lobner, Nicholson, Robinson, and Rockwell. Step out one at a time with your hands behind your head and nobody has to get hurt."

Jaeger didn't yet know about Kost's death. No one knew except for us and the Colicians.

"What a little bitch!" Brent scoffed.

"I know, right?" I agreed.

"Shut up," Vincent snapped, keeping his eyes on Jaeger.

Jaeger and his men waited for a minute before he spoke again. "This is your last chance. Come out now or we'll come in after you."

"Move," Mr. Lobner ordered, pushing past his sons and opening the door.

"Dad!" Miriam whispered. "What the hell are you doing?"

Mr. Lobner ignored her. He closed the door behind him and stood on the porch, automatic rifle in hand.

All weapons were immediately trained on him. Shouts were passed between soldiers, but it was Jaeger who addressed him. Putting the megaphone down, Jaeger called up to Miriam's father. We had to strain to hear him.

"Sir, please put your weapon down," he said, raising his hands in front of him.

"This is my family's property," Mr. Lobner replied sharply. "I want you off of it."

Did he really think saying that would make a difference?

"I'm going to ask you one more time, sir," Jaeger said. He was losing his patience. "Put down the weapon."

"You stay away from my daughter!" Mr. Lobner's grip tightened on his weapon, and for a moment I feared he would raise it. Apparently the soldiers thought the same thing.

"No!" Miriam cried.

I expected it to all end right there. Jaeger's soldiers would open fire on Miriam's father and he would fall dead. But that wasn't what happened. Instead, Mr. Lobner jerked on his feet and let out a grunt of surprise before slumping down on the porch, a dart sticking out of his neck. I breathed a sigh of relief, but Miriam started screaming.

"*Shh*, Miriam, *shh*," I soothed, pulling her to me. "It's okay. He's just drugged, that's all."

Miriam sobbed into my shoulder. "No, Daddy, no!"

"It's going to be okay," I whispered. I looked to Jeff. "We gotta get out of here."

"How?" Vincent demanded. "There's no way we can get around them. They'll tranq us the second we step out the door."

"Those aren't tranqs," Miriam whimpered.

We all looked at her. "What are you talking about?" Brent asked, but suddenly we all knew. We leaned forward, straining to see Mr. Lobner without exposing ourselves to the soldiers outside. He was laying spread eagle on his back, his open eyes glossy and staring up at the overhang above the porch. He was dead.

"We can't go outside!" Miriam's sobs were so hard that her whole body jerked with each one and she was gasping for air. "They've been given orders, Austin!"

I felt the fear pumping through us all. I swallowed back the lump in my throat, remembering what Jaeger had said to us in Madison.

"What orders?" Vincent asked.

"They don't need us anymore!" Miriam whispered. "They've been given orders to bring us in, dead or alive. They're cleaning up their mess!"

"So what do we do?" Brent demanded.

"One," Miriam said.

"I'm not going to wait around to get killed!" Brent shouted.

"What do you think we should do, genius?" Vincent snapped.

"Two," Miriam said.

"Guys, stop!" I cried. I grabbed Miriam, who was staring into space, her eyes glazed over. "Miriam?"

"Three."

The explosion in the front yard rocked us all, nearly sending me sprawling face down on the floor. I heard every window in the house shatter, and I was sprayed with glass from the window in the front door. My ears were ringing and I was momentarily disoriented. I looked out at Jaeger to see what was going on. One of his big Hummers was on fire; well, what was left of it, anyway. The remains smoldered on the front lawn while Jaeger and other soldiers danced around it, shouting to each other.

Miriam took my hand before I had time to react. She pulled me toward the back door. I was surprised at first, but then I realized she knew what she was doing, just as she knew about the explosion. I didn't know how she knew, and I didn't really care. I just wanted to get the hell out of here. *Alive.* "Hey, guys!" I called as Miriam and I rushed to the back of the cabin. "Come on!"

"There are soldiers out back!" Vincent yelled, but I heard him following all the same.

We reached the back door and Miriam ripped it open, not even hesitating before bolting outside. I realized why the moment my eyes adjusted to the bright sunshine. Funny, how a day as scary as this could be just as cheerful as any other.

"They all went up front to see what the ruckus is!" I called back to them as they paused in the doorway. "Quick, before they get back!"

Jeff caught up to us as we darted into the trees. He gripped my shoulder, his fear flowing from him to me. We were only a few yards in when we heard the exchange of gunfire behind us.

"Shit!" Vincent said as we stopped and turned. "Brent!"

"Stop!" I cried as he ran back toward the house, but Vincent yelled back at me, "Go! Get her out of here!"

I felt so guilty when we turned and ran, but he was right. I had to get Miriam out of here. Jeff, too. We had to stay alive long enough to…what? What were we supposed to do? Was there anything we *could* do? I pushed aside my thoughts of the future and tried to focus on the now. There was no way we could outrun Jaeger on foot. We were in the woods right now, but we would have to come out eventually. When we did, we couldn't outrun Jaeger's Hummers. Not for very long.

Just keep moving, I instructed myself. *Just don't stop. You'll find a place to hide.*

More gunshots behind us. I was beginning to think that Miriam would lose her entire family today. Remembering how she was last night, talking about losing her mom, I knew she wouldn't handle it very well.

"Where are we going?" Jeff asked uncertainly.

"I don't know," I replied, my breathing coming out in great huffs. "But she knows. Let's just follow her."

I wasn't sure how far we ran. Finally, when the sounds of gunfire could be heard no more, I slowed to a halt. Miriam tried to keep going, but I made her stop too. "We have to stop," I told her. "We need to take a break."

Her eyes still had that glazed look to them. She didn't speak or look at me, and I was really worried.

"What's up with her?" Jeff asked.

"I don't know," I muttered, taking Miriam's face in my hands and trying to get her to look at me. "Miriam? Are you okay? Why are you acting like this?" When she didn't answer, I said loudly, "Miriam!"

She jumped and blinked, the glazed look in her eyes disappearing. She met my eyes. "Austin?" Looking around, she suddenly became frightened. "What happened? How did we get here?"

"You're okay. I promise." I heard rustling leaves and snapping twigs behind us, so I took her hand and grabbed Jeff's arm. "I can't explain right now. We have to go."

"No, wait!" Miriam said, tugging back. She gazed expectantly toward where the noise was coming from.

"We have to go!" Jeff insisted.

For the first time in a while, I tried using this new ability Hillerman gave me. I realized that there were a lot of situations where I could have used it, but I was so unfamiliar with the concept and the ability that I just forgot or couldn't figure out how it worked. But it was getting easier each time I tried. I couldn't exactly hear the thoughts of the person running toward us, but I could sense the terror in his thoughts. I suddenly realized who it was.

"Vincent!" I called, not too loud but loud enough for him to hear. "Vincent! We're over here!"

A few moments later, Vincent stumbled into view and collapsed to his knees in front of us. Miriam dropped down beside him and hugged him tightly. "What happened?" she asked him, almost hysterically, but Vincent was too out of breath to answer.

I gave him a few moments to gather himself, but I had to ask him something, even if I already knew the answer. "Where's Brent?"

Vincent looked up at me. He didn't reply or shake his head, and he didn't need to. I saw it all in his eyes.

Miriam didn't say anything. She just hugged Vincent tighter and cried silently. I may not have particularly liked Vincent, but I was really glad he made it. Miriam needed him.

I wanted to give them more time, but it was time we didn't have. "I'm sorry, but we have to go." I helped them both to their feet. I addressed Vincent: "Do you know how far behind they are?"

Shaking his head, Vincent said, "They didn't follow me in. They went back to their trucks. But they'll find us. I know their type. With the technology they have, there's no way we can evade them forever."

"We can't give up," I replied. "We can't. We have to keep going."

"What's the point, Austin?" Miriam asked, her voice cracking on every word. "Vincent's right. They keep finding us. No matter where we go, Jaeger will find us."

I wanted to argue with her, but she was right. No one could deny it. Jaeger would always find us. I sighed and leaned against the nearest tree, not knowing what else to do.

Jeff's head suddenly snapped up. "Do you guys hear that?"

"Don't start," I snapped.

"No, seriously." He started jogging forward.

"Jeff," I called, but he didn't stop. "Jeff! Come back!" I ran after him, and I heard Miriam and Vincent following. I'd lost sight of Jeff, but he couldn't be too far ahead of me; I could still hear him.

"Come on!" he said from up ahead.

I picked up the pace, and a few moments later I stumbled out of the trees and almost went rolling down a steep ditch into a road.

"Whoa!" Jeff caught my arm as I started to lose my balance.

"What the hell are you doing?" I demanded. Jeff was grinning. He nodded down toward the road.

An old pickup was parked on the side of the road down below us. Two teenage boys were leaning against it. One was African American and the other Caucasian. The African American boy called up to us.

"How's it goin'?"

I didn't reply, and I almost punched Jeff when he called down, "Not so great."

"Well, get on down here so we can get out of here," the other boy said. "Your soldier friends will be around here any minute."

Jeff started to pick his way down the ditch, and I grabbed him. "Are you that stupid?"

"They're our ride, genius!" he shot back. "They're who Miriam's dad called to come get us."

"How do you—?" I didn't bother finishing the question. "*Them*? They're just kids!"

"That's why no one will suspect them," Jeff replied. Miriam and Vincent stepped out of the trees, looking at us skeptically. "Come on," Jeff told them. "Our ride's here."

~~*

The African American boy's name was Danny Bennett, and he was only a couple years younger than Miriam. The other boy was his friend Reis Quincy; he was a year younger than me. They were both from Philadelphia, and they both secretly aided the rebels living in the abandoned military installation outside of Hatfield during the Colician Revolution. Or at least that's what they said. The rebels of the installation included Walter Reifert, Shauna Skyler, Dr. Perry, former President Ashton's son, and the famous—or infamous, depending on your point of view—Patrick Lemoore, who helped Reifert begin the Revolution. I'd have bet that lots of people claimed they helped Walter Reifert and company.

"So why are you guys involved in stuff like this?" I asked them. We'd been driving all day, and it was now dark outside. Miriam, Vincent, and Jeff were sleeping in the bed of the truck under piles of blankets and tarps, but I was too wound up to sleep. Two more people were dead. Two more friends. Plus, I wasn't entirely sure I trusted these two punks.

"Our parents started a fundraiser to buy food and clothes and stuff for the Colicians at the installation," Danny explained. "We just got involved, too. It felt like the right thing to do."

"But you guys are just a couple of kids," I said. "Why aren't you in school or scoring babes or doing drugs or something?"

Reis, who was behind the wheel, laughed loudly. He laughed a lot, and his laugh was annoying. "High expectations you have for us, Austin."

"I just don't get why you'd risk your lives like this when you're so young," I replied. "I can't believe your parents let you do this…"

"Our parents do it too," Danny said. "They said that if we want to save people's lives, they wouldn't try to stop us." He shrugged. "Besides, cops and soldiers are expecting older people to be smuggling Colicians and…what did you say you're called?"

"Victims," I muttered. "The strain they used is called the Caiten Strain. So I guess we're Caitens now."

"Colicians and Caitens." Danny looked back at me. "Well, at least they both start with the same letter. It will be easy for people to remember."

"That's good to know."

The boys took no notice of my attitude. "So are you guys gonna like, go live with the Colicians or what?" Reis asked.

I opened my mouth to snap, "No!" but I stopped myself. It had been a thought on my mind a lot lately, and I was sure it was also on Miriam's and Jeff's minds as well. What was stopping us? It would be safer and be a fresh start. Human society sucked, to say the least. Why were we trying to hide within it, where we weren't wanted and where we didn't want to be? I thought back to the nightmare of my father and the burning world, and wondered if it really would be safe to go there. No one knew what it was really like. "I don't know," I muttered, not knowing what else to say.

"You should," Reis said. "I wish I could go over there."

"Why?" I asked.

He shrugged. "It just seems like there would be a lot of opportunities over there, you know? A whole new world that is practically untouched. Can you imagine it?"

"Yeah." I bit my lip. "I had a dream about their world. I dreamed it was on fire. Burning. It was chaos and everyone was dying."

The boys looked back at me skeptically. "Dude," Danny said, "it's nothing like that."

"How the hell would you know?" I demanded. "You just said you wish you could go there, so you obviously haven't *seen* it…"

"We have Colician contacts," Danny explained. "They're doing just fine. They have order and a legal system and good health care and everything."

Hearsay. I wanted to say it, but I kept that comment to myself. The boys chattered on and on, but I was too busy thinking over what Danny said. They're doing just fine. Was that true? I really hoped it was. If my family was safe, it would make my current shit hole of a life just a little bit better. "Do you know anyone by the name of Nathan or Chrissy Rockwell?"

Reis scrunched up his face, his one million freckles making him look ridiculous. "Can't say that I do. Are they Colicians or humans?"

"Colicians. They're my dad and sister."

"Oh." Reis's expression sagged. "Sorry, but I don't know any Rockwells. At least not off the top of my head."

The truck was silent for a few minutes, but then Danny suddenly turned to Reis and said, "You remember when Walter and Dr. Perry and the others were making the rift? That one time we brought supplies and we heard about what was going on?"

"Yeah," Reis said. "What about it?"

"Walter told us that there were a couple of mechanics and engineers working to make the rift. One of the mechanics came and asked him something, and I think Walter called him Nathan."

I leaned forward. "What did he look like?"

"Oh, jeez, I can't remember—"

"What did he look like, Danny?"

Danny's eyes widened at my ferocious expression and tone of voice. "Uh…he was a little older. He had gray hair, longer and messy. He wasn't shaven. I think he had glasses…"

"Did he look at the ground when he talked?" It sounded like my dad, but there were lots of people that could fit that description.

"Yeah, actually, he did," Danny replied. "He didn't make eye contact once."

"That's him," I said. "It has to be. He rarely ever makes eye contact with anyone. It was a weird phobia of his. That has to be him."

"Look," Danny said. "I don't want you to get your hopes up."

"It has to be him," I repeated.

"It was almost three years ago," Reis said "Even if it was him, there's no saying that he's still…you know, there."

"You mean *alive*." I glared at him.

"Sure." He didn't look at me.

It has to be him. He made it out of the labs. He's okay.

Danny was right; I shouldn't get my hopes up, but my hopes were all I had. Even if it was Dad, what about Chrissy? I leaned back in my seat and sighed. For the thousandth time, I checked behind us to make sure I didn't see any flashing blue and red lights or Hummers. All clear. "Where are we going, anyway?"

"Don't know," Reis said. "The coordinates were plotted into the GPS ahead of time, in case someone got caught. Then no one could give it away because no one would know. We're just told when to turn."

"But if they got their hands on the GPS, couldn't they just look up the coordinates?" This sounded like a really dumb idea.

"Nope. They're transmitted through a computer from another rogue. He's really good. They'd have to get his computer if they wanted to know the coordinates. I don't know much about computers or how this thing works. I just know that it's damn near impossible to hack into."

"Good enough for me." I closed my eyes, only intending to rest for a few minutes, but the chatter of the boys and the movement of the truck lulled me right to sleep.

I awoke later to one of the doors slamming shut. It was still dark out, but I could see some color on the eastern horizon. The clock in the truck read 6:24.

Danny and Reis were helping Miriam and Jeff out of the bed of the truck, glancing around every couple seconds to make sure no one was watching them. I opened the door and hopped out. "What's going on?" I asked, stretching my back and my legs. I cracked my neck, a good kink knotting it up.

"Potty break," Reis replied. "If you want a snack or a soda, ask Danny. He's got change for you."

I looked over and saw we were at a rest area along the side of the highway. My stomach growled and I had a nasty taste in my mouth. I turned to Danny, and he was already holding out a handful of quarters and singles. "Thanks," I said. "How long are we stopping for?"

"Ten minutes. Whatever business you need to do, get it done quick."

I walked inside with Miriam. She was very quiet. "How are you?" I asked her, even though I knew the answer wouldn't be *fine*.

She shrugged, and pulled her hand away when I tried to take it. She walked into the ladies' restroom without looking at me or saying a word. It frustrated me, but I had to give her time. Losing family wasn't easy.

I used one of the dirty urinals, being careful not to touch it. There was only one other person in the restroom; he was in one of the stalls. The other guys hadn't come in yet. When I finished my business, I went to the sink and soaked my hands in hot water. It felt wonderful, considering the cool, early-April temperature outside. I bent down and splashed some of it on my face. It made me feel slightly more relaxed, but that feeling left me the moment I looked up into the mirror. The man who had been in the stall was now standing behind me. It was the man in the gorilla suit from my dream in the lab.

I whipped around, my heart pounding, but when I turned I only saw an ordinary man. I didn't even recognize him.

He raised his eyebrows at my frightened expression. "Excuse me," he said flatly.

I looked back into the mirror, but all I saw was the man's reflection. I looked back at him one more time, to make sure he wasn't Gorilla Man messing with me, and then I stepped aside. I felt him staring at me as I left the restroom.

"Dude, are you okay?" Reis asked when we bumped into each other in the lobby.

I was breathing hard and I was probably as white as a ghost. Why had I seen Gorilla Man in the mirror?

"Is everything all right?" He looked toward the restroom door warily.

"Fine," I said hurriedly. "I'm just tired." I ran out to the truck, forgetting my hunger, and practically leapt inside. Vincent was in the seat next to me. He must have been done sleeping. "You didn't have to go?" I asked him.

"I pissed out back," he replied, without a hint of emotion on his face. "Old habits die hard, I guess."

When everyone got back, I finally remembered how hungry I was. I pushed my thoughts of Gorilla Man aside for a minute. "I'll be right back," I told them, jogging around the side of the building to the vending machines. I got a Mountain Dew, a bag of chips, and tried to get a Butterfinger, but the damn candy bar got stuck. "Are you kidding me?" I muttered, trying to shake the machine. It was little things like this that royally pissed me off.

"Need a hand?" a woman's voice from behind me asked. She stepped up beside me and waved her hand at the glass, and the candy bar fell into the bottom of the machine.

Startled, I jumped back and looked at her. "What the hell are you doing here?"

"Well, it's nice to see you too," Shauna Skyler said, brushing back her red hair. "You're welcome."

"Are you following us?" I demanded suspiciously.

She shrugged. "We're keeping track of you. We don't need to follow you to know where you are, you know."

"Gee, that's comforting," I muttered.

"What's got you in such a rotten mood?" Shauna asked, even though her expression suggested she was expecting it.

"Oh wow, where to begin?"

Shauna looked different than the last time I'd seen her. She looked...happier. Also, she kept a protective hand over her stomach, which was just starting to noticeably stick out.

"Whoa," I said, making the connection. "Congrats, I guess. Does Walter know?"

"Thanks." Shauna smiled down at her little baby bump. "And yes. We've known for a while. We usually know right away."

"Do you know what it is yet?"

"A girl."

"What are you going to call her?"

"Katherine Tracy Reifert. She's due in about two months."

I blinked in surprise and had to remind myself that Colicians gave birth in three months instead of nine. "Good name," I replied.

"What about you?" Shauna asked me. "What are you going to name your baby?"

My eyebrows went up. "What?"

She was smiling slightly in a sly, taunting way. "You and Miriam. What are you going to name your baby?"

Now, I'd never hit a girl, especially one with the ability to throw me off a building, but I was seriously considering it right now. "We were just changed into mutant weirdos by some psycho doctor, we're being chased by soldiers who want to kill us, and a bunch of our friends are dead. *We're not thinking about babies right now!*"

Shauna laughed.

"Besides," I continued angrily, "our relationship is none of your business."

"So what are you guys going to do?" she asked, as if she didn't hear me.

My hands were twitching. "What did I just—"

"No, I mean what are the three of you going to do? Where are you going to go?"

"You seem to know everything," I shot back. "Why are you asking me?" Out front, the truck horn beeped twice. "I gotta go."

"Austin." Shauna caught my arm as I turned to leave. Her expression was very serious. "I'm not playing around anymore. We're really concerned about you. Danny and Reis don't know where they're going. What are you going to do if something happens?"

She didn't have to clarify; I knew what she meant. "I don't know. We're just kind of improvising right now, I guess."

Rubbing her belly, she said, "Our offer still stands, you know."

I thought about what Reis and Danny said about the Parallel Earth. It really seemed like the best option right now. And if my dad was alive...I could have him back, and potentially Chrissy too. But then I thought about my dream, and then I thought about what Miriam said back at the cabin. We couldn't leave yet. We had to find a way to stop Hillerman before he made any more of us. Odds were he already had. "We can't," I said. "Thanks, but no thanks."

"Austin, what the hell—" Jeff came around the side of the building and froze when he saw Shauna, his eyes wide.

"Hey, Jeff," Shauna said. "Sorry I've been keeping him. I was just checking in."

Jeff nodded, his eyes still bulging. "Cool," he replied.

She turned back to me. "I brought a bag of stuff for you guys," she said. "I know you were forced to leave in a hurry, so I brought some of your clothes. The soldiers burned the house to the ground, but we managed to get in and get a few things before it was completely destroyed." She turned and grabbed a garbage bag sitting against the wall. She handed it to me. "It's not much, but at least you'll be a little more comfortable."

"Thanks a lot," I said, and handed the bag to Jeff. "I'll be back in a minute," I told him. He hurried away without another word. I turned back to Shauna. "What are you guys gonna do about Hillerman?"

She shrugged. "We don't know. We have a few moles, but not high enough up to get where we need to be. We still haven't got anyone inside."

"Why don't you just blow the whole place up?"

She raised an eyebrow. "We don't like killing people, Austin, no matter what your media says."

I looked away. "Right."

"Once we figure out how to get our people inside, we'll shut it down. Since your escape, security has been tightened. You have to take a blood test just to get onto the property."

"Shit," I muttered. I grabbed the Butterfinger out of the machine. "Well, thanks again, but I really gotta get going."

Nodding, Shauna called after me, "Remember, if you need us, just give us a call." She tapped the side of her head.

"No problem," I replied, and then ran back to the truck.

"What the hell happened?" Reis demanded when I got in. He was holding a very large gun. I hadn't a clue where he got it from, but I didn't trust that he knew how to use it properly.

I looked back toward the vending machines, but they were out of sight and Shauna was nowhere to be seen. "Put that thing away before you shoot yourself," I snapped. "I was talking to Shauna Skyler."

"Shauna?" Danny turned around, skeptical. "Why would she be here?"

"She's checking up on us," I said. "I don't think Walter trusts you to keep us safe."

"He should," Reis said angrily. "We've helped him a lot and have never let him down once!"

"Let's just get out of here," I replied. "She's gone, and getting pissy isn't going to make anything better."

Reis was still muttering to himself when Danny put the truck into gear and drove back onto the Interstate. The two of them had switched places so Reis wouldn't fall asleep and drive off the road. For some reason I felt safer with Danny behind the wheel. I felt safer with Danny in general. Something about him made me trust him.

We drove for several more hours, and I watched the sun rise while I ate my snacks. Miriam and Jeff were still sleeping in the back. Apparently, neither of them were feeling well. Who could blame them? Miriam just lost a brother and father, and the stress of our entire situation was enough to make anyone vomit. Vincent, too, didn't look so great. He said he felt fine, just a little tired, but his face was gray and he shivered constantly. He stared out the window for the entire ride, only speaking when spoken to.

When we reached Ohio around noon, we stopped at a Subway for lunch. We opened the back to find Miriam covered in her own vomit, and Jeff unconscious.

"Jesus Christ!" I shouted, loudly enough for other people in the parking lot to shoot me dirty looks. "What are we supposed to do now?"

"*Shh!*" Reis hissed at me, looking around nervously.

"Don't you shush me!" I snarled, but I lowered my voice. "My friends are dying! Don't—"

Vincent grabbed me, spun me around, and slammed me into the side of the truck. His hand tightened around my throat, tight enough to make me shut up but not tight enough to cut off my air. "Do you think shouting so everyone knows we're here will do them any good? Think about Miriam for once instead of just yourself!"

I had nothing to say to that.

Clearing his throat quietly, Danny stepped up to us and put his hand on Vincent's. "Can you please let go of him? People are watching."

Vincent let go, but he continued to glare at me. "If you do anything like this again, I'll kill you. Sound fair?"

"Whatever," I muttered, shoving past him so I could talk to Danny and Reis. "So what are we going to do?" I repeated, my voice calmer.

"We'll get food, use the restroom, and get the hell out of here," Reis said.

"What about Jeff and Miriam?" I demanded, my voice starting to rise again.

"We have to get where we're going," Danny insisted.

"What if they don't make it to where we're going?" I snapped. "You two fools don't even know where we're going!"

Reis suddenly looked angry. "Look buddy, we're risking our lives to help you, and all you've been is an asshole. Why don't you start showing a little gratitude or you can find your own way to wherever!" He turned and stalked angrily inside.

I know I should have felt guilty, but I didn't. I was too upset and worried to feel guilty.

"There are doctors where we're going," Danny said, still insistent that we continue on our way. "Doctors we can trust. We just have to get there."

"Yes, but how far?" I sighed. "We don't even know where we're going. It could be in Florida for all we know, or the tip of Maine. They might not even make it a few more hours."

"It's the only hope they have," Danny said quietly, and then went inside to join Reis and Vincent.

~~*

I decided against getting any food. I had difficulty eating when I was upset like this.

We cleaned the vomit off of Miriam and I got into the truck bed to look after her and Jeff. I laid next to her as the hours passed. The strong smell of bile still lingered in the air trapped around us, and their faces were tinted blue from the tarp over us.

Sometime later, maybe four or five hours after our pit stop, Jeff moaned and opened his eyes.

"Dude," I said, propping myself up on my elbow.

"What...the hell...happened?" Jeff asked, rubbing his forehead and wincing.

"You've been out cold for like, the whole day." I patted him on the arm. "How are you feeling?"

"Like crap," he groaned. "My head is killing me!" He looked down at Miriam's unconscious form. "Is she...?"

"She's been out too. Hasn't woken up yet. She even barfed all over herself earlier."

Wrinkling his nose, Jeff looked down at himself. "Please tell me it didn't get on *me*."

"You're fine. We checked."

Jeff's expression changed then. It was halfway between fear and resignation. "What happened to Kost… It's happening to us too, isn't it?"

"No," I said immediately, but I couldn't be sure. "I won't let that happen. I won't let you guys die too."

He lowered his eyes and laid back down. Not too long after, he was asleep again, but he was snoring this time. He seemed to be okay now.

We drove the rest of the day and well into the night. It was almost midnight when we finally stopped.

I was trying not to fall asleep for fear that something would happen to Jeff or Miriam while I was out, but I ended up dozing off for a while. Jeff shook me awake when we stopped. "We're here," he said quietly.

"Huh?" I muttered. The darkness was disorienting; we were still under the tarp and I couldn't see anything. A moment later the tarp was thrown off of us and a blinding light was shined in our faces. "Dude!" I cried, shielding my eyes.

"These are the first?" a woman said from behind the light, ignoring my protests.

"Yep," Danny chirped. "Jeff Robinson, Austin Rockwell, and Miriam Lobner."

"Any complications?"

"Miriam is a little sick. Jeff looks to be okay now…"

Suddenly there were hands on me pulling me out of the truck.

"Hey!" I snapped, trying to pull away. "Get your goddamn, moth-er—"

"Take it easy, Austin," the woman said as I was dragged out of the light. "We're friends. We just need to get you inside before anyone notices."

"Where are we?" I demanded, trying to blink the spots out of my eyes.

"Welcome to the nation's capital," the woman replied, and as my eyesight returned I saw her smiling. She looked to be around Jeff's age and had orange hair and brown eyes. She was tall and slim with hundreds of freckles dotting her face. She was also a Colician.

"D.C., huh?" I stuttered, not sure of what else to say.

"Welcome," she repeated. "Glad you made it here safely."

"Oh my God." Jeff was pulled out of the truck after me, and now stood beside me, blinking rapidly at the woman, as if she would disappear if he blinked enough times. "No way..."

"What?" I asked, looking from his bewildered expression to the woman's now guilty one.

Jeff tried to say something several times, but all that escaped his lips were puffs of air. Finally, he spit out, "Amelia?"

I snapped my head back toward the woman. Jeff had only mentioned her once back at the study, but we knew the story of his wife and daughter. Amelia and Olivia Robinson were infected with the Colician Virus back in 2018. They were taken to a lab and Jeff never heard from them again. He'd just assumed they were dead. But, by the looks on their faces, it would seem that Amelia Robinson was standing right in front of us. "Holy crap," I said.

"Oh my God," Jeff said again. "You're alive. You're okay."

Amelia didn't look like she wanted to talk to him. "Take Miriam downstairs to the infirmary." Her voice was strong, commanding. She was clearly the one in charge. "Make sure she's all right and report any problems to me immediately." She started to walk past us, but Jeff caught her arm.

"Amelia," he said, and didn't say anything else. His eyes were pleading. He wanted her to stay with him.

Amelia's tone immediately changed. "I can't talk right now, Jeff," she said softly, her eyes pained. "Right now we just need to focus on getting you situated."

Jeff nodded slowly, but I think it was only because he was too stunned to do or say anything else. I could say the same for myself.

Vincent joined us and went with Jeff and me into the house in front of which we were parked. It was nestled in a quaint, unsuspecting neighborhood, a few miles from downtown. There were lots of tall trees and shrubs along the street, providing plenty of privacy without drawing suspicion. The house wasn't small but it wasn't big either; a three bedroom with two bathrooms, and a cramped living room and kitchen. The "infirmary," we were told, was the basement, which had been converted into a makeshift medical exam room. Danny told us that we should share rooms because he and Reis were staying the night, and others would be spending nights as well to watch over us during our stay. Vincent volunteered to share with Miriam once she was feeling better, so he had a room to himself tonight. Jeff and I went into our room and crawled into bed immediately. There were two twin-sized beds in the room; I took the bed by the wall because I hated waking up with the sun in my eyes. Jeff laid down on his bed and gazed out the window without a word.

"Hey," I said, kicking my shoes off onto the floor. "Are you okay?"

Jeff didn't respond. I was worried about him. "Dude. Shouldn't you be happy?"

"She never wrote to me," Jeff said through his teeth, still looking out the window. "She didn't call or anything, telling me she and Olivia were okay. She left me thinking they were dead or worse…I still don't know if my daughter is alive!"

"Amelia's here," I said. "That's one good thing. We'll find out about Olivia tomorrow." I waited for him to respond, but it was clear he didn't want to talk to me. I sighed, hoping he'd be better by morning, and rolled over to go to sleep.

~~*

The next morning, Jeff was still in bed when I woke up, but he was wide awake. He stared up at the ceiling with a blank expression on his face. I wondered if he'd slept at all.

Cautiously, I asked, "You…uh, wanna get some breakfast with me?"

No answer.

I tried again. "You…uh, wanna go check on Miriam with me?"

Still no answer.

"You…uh, wanna do *anything* with me?" When I still received no answer, I muttered, "Fine," and left.

There was some sort of meeting going on downstairs in the living room. Amelia stood over a computer and pointed out different things to those looking on. I crept past the doorway and went into the kitchen. Vincent and Reis were sitting at the table eating bowls of Lucky Charms, so I went to join them. I'd only eaten that bag of chips and a Butterfinger yesterday and I was starving, so I poured myself a heaping bowl. Danny was at the stove making something that smelled funny.

The room was pretty quiet, so I asked, "Do you guys know how Miriam's doing?"

Everyone paused. Danny started to glance over his shoulder, but thought better of it and went back to his frying pan. Vincent started tapping his spoon on the edge of his bowl, spraying little droplets of milk on the table. I had to look at him twice to realize that he looked like he wanted to kill someone. I sure hoped it wasn't me. Reis was the only one who looked at me, but the expression on his face wasn't reassuring. He looked like a little kid trying not to poop himself.

"Is she okay?" I demanded louder. Reis just looked back at his food, and Vincent started tapping louder. I shoved away from the table and bolted for the basement.

It was an old house and the basement had a musty smell to it. It was dark and I could hear water dripping somewhere. I followed the soft voice of a woman until I saw Miriam sitting on a table in the center of a big room surrounded by medical equipment. I breathed a sigh of relief; she looked fine to me. Unlike yesterday, when she looked like Kost had before he died, her skin and eyes looked great and she looked alert. Except for the worried expression on her face, she seemed to be back to normal.

There was a woman talking to Miriam; she had long brown hair and was a little larger around the middle. I approached slowly, not wanting to interrupt but really needing to talk to Miriam.

The nurse and Miriam both looked up at me. Miriam quickly looked away, and the nurse asked me, "Are you Austin?"

"Yeah," I said, going over to the table. "Is everything okay?" I looked at Miriam, who was studying her nails intently. "Are you okay?" I looked back at the nurse. "Nothing bad happened, right?"

Pausing, the nurse stuck the back of her pen in her mouth. "Well, I suppose it would depend on your definition of *bad*."

I stared at her. "What the hell is that supposed to mean?"

Tucking the pen behind her ear, the nurse gave me a quick smile. "Why don't I leave you two alone for a while?"

When she was gone, I sat down next to Miriam and put my arm around her. "Oh my God, are you okay?" She wasn't saying anything, so I just continued with my panicked questions. "You don't have what Kost has, do you? You're not dying, right? Oh God, did Hillerman do something to you that's having an affect on you now? What's wrong? Please answer me!"

Miriam didn't look at me for a while, but when she did I saw resentment in her eyes. It was so surprising that I pulled away from her. What had I done to deserve such a look from her?

"You remember a few nights ago, when we..." She gave me a look. "Shared a bed?"

"Yeah," I said slowly. There were a couple nights where we'd shared a bed, but only one in particular that I looked back on quite fondly. Did she really think I'd forget?

"We didn't use any form of protection," Miriam said flatly.

My first thought was that I'd given her an STD or something, but I was clean so that couldn't be it. Miriam heard my thought and groaned in disgust. "It's not an STD, Austin! It's a *baby*!"

"A what?"

"You got me pregnant, Austin," Miriam growled. "We're on the run, fighting for our lives, and on top of that we're going to have to look after a kid too. One night of romance for us, and now we're going to bring a child into this mess." She glanced up at me when I didn't answer. "Well? Say something!"

I suddenly understood why everyone upstairs acted the way they did; especially why Vincent looked like he wanted to kill someone. And, much to my dismay, that someone *was* me.

My response was probably the worst possible thing I could have said in that moment: "Aw, shit."

11

Three Months Later

The following three months were some of the worst in my life. Even the study was better, because there I had friends.

Miriam and I hadn't so much as exchanged a glance for more than two months. Our last conversation went a little something like this:

"Are you even slightly interested in this baby, Austin?" she demanded. We were in the kitchen; I was at the table eating a chicken sandwich and Miriam was at the stove burning something.

"Of course I am," I replied, confused. The question had come out of nowhere; I had been more than supportive since we found out about our baby. I researched prenatal care and made sure she took all the necessary vitamins and supplements a pregnant human would need, and then made sure she took extra just in case; researched how to take care of a child and what needed to be purchased before the baby arrived; and even researched baby names. I didn't understand how she could think I didn't care about our baby.

Miriam rolled her eyes and turned back to the stove, continuing to burn whatever was already burnt.

"Are you okay?" I asked her. She'd been tense and sensitive ever since we found out about the baby, but today seemed worse.

"I'm great, Austin!" Miriam snapped, rounding on me with the spatula raised. "I'm so great! How could this situation get any better?"

"Why are you mad at me?" I asked. "What did I do? I'm trying to help you."

"You have no idea what I'm going through right now!" she shouted, flinging the spatula at me. I ducked just in time. "You don't have to carry this baby!"

"That doesn't mean I don't care about it!" I shot back, growing angry. "Or worry about it! I worry about both of you all the time!"

"Well, you're not very good at showing it!" Miriam turned, grabbed the frying pan, and threw it at me. This time, it hit me and burned my shoulder. I cried out in pain, but Miriam either didn't notice or didn't care. "You don't give a shit about me or this baby! You *never* have! You only care about yourself!"

I was on my feet in a flash. "How can you say that? I've been trying to protect you!"

I didn't know how Miriam moved so fast, but suddenly she was in front of me. She struck me across the face so hard my vision went white for a moment. "Stay away from me!" she screamed. "Don't talk to me anymore!"

That was the last time we saw each other. I didn't know what she was up to these days; I hadn't come out of my room other than for bathroom breaks since that fight.

Vincent hadn't killed me yet, but he hadn't spoken to me either. I didn't think any of us were speaking to each other anymore. Jeff certainly wasn't.

Jeff was even worse off than me. He stopped leaving the room just a few days after we arrived. I couldn't blame him. His whole world had come back to him, only for it to be taken away from him once again.

His Colician wife, Amelia, was gone for a couple days after we arrived, but the moment she got back Jeff tried to get every little snippet of information out of her, especially any information about Olivia. I was in the room when this encounter happened, and I really wished I hadn't been.

Amelia was clearly uncomfortable being around Jeff, and we soon found out why. She was trying to complete her duties while Jeff bombarded her with questions, when a man came in and said, "Miss Westfield, your family sent you this." He handed her a letter.

Jeff, stunned into brief silence, stammered, "You...you changed your name back to Westfield?"

Apparently, Amelia had met her soul mate about a year and a half ago and they had a beautiful little girl named Izzi. Olivia was alive and well and loved being a big sister, and also loved her new daddy. Amelia tried to explain that she hadn't purposely moved on after she and Jeff were separated, that it was fate that brought her and her soul mate together, but Jeff wouldn't listen. He saw this as a betrayal and retreated to our room. Amelia tried to go talk to him, but came back down a few minutes later, tear streaks staining her cheeks. We didn't see much of her after that.

That encounter got me wondering: what if my dad had found his soul mate and had another child? What would that child look like? Would he or she be okay? Would I be angry with my father even though I knew it wasn't his fault? What would Mom have thought were she still alive?

Now, three months after our arrival, Jeff and I spent our days in our room, silent. Neither of us spoke to the other, and neither of us wanted to. We weren't allowed to leave the house, so it wasn't like we were missing anything.

Those three months felt like three years, but I didn't care. For all I knew, we would never leave this house. Ever. While in my room, I laid on my bed and stared up at the ceiling lost in my own thoughts. I ate when food was brought to me, but other than that I just thought. I thought about my mom, wondering what she would think about our family's situation. I thought about my dad and my sister, and wondered if they were happy and had a new family. But mostly, I thought about Miriam and our baby.

I couldn't stop thinking about them, despite the last encounter Miriam and I had. I loved her, and I loved our baby. Even if Miriam hated me, I still loved her.

I was in awe of our baby. I would protect him with my life, just like I would with Miriam. No one had said whether it was a boy or a girl, but I was fixated on a son. I just knew he would be a boy. What would he look like? Would he have dark skin like Miriam and blue eyes like me? Would he have red hair as a baby that would change color later like mine did? Would he develop differently because of the change his parents went through? Would he have the same powers as us? Would he have powers at all? All these questions and more ran through my mind, and I predicted the answers to all of them. But there were two specific questions that kept coming up, and the fact that I couldn't—or didn't want to—answer them scared me. They scared me more than Jaeger or Hillerman.

Would he make it to term?

If so, would Miriam and I be able to keep him safe with the situation we were in?

I was stuck on the name James. James Alexander. It was simple enough, but I loved it, and now whenever I thought of the baby I thought of him as James. My James. My little boy. Of course, I was willing to negotiate names with Miriam; I was just enamored with James Alexander.

Every day I wished that Miriam would come to see me, that she would apologize and tell me she wanted me to be a part of her life again.

Every day I was disappointed. I thought about going to her and telling her *I* was sorry, sorry for getting her pregnant, but I knew that would be a lie. I loved James as much as I loved her. I regretted nothing.

After going so long without speaking to anyone or seeing anything new, I finally got an itch to get up. I went downstairs, unsure of where I was going, but determined nevertheless.

"Dude," Reis said when I went into the kitchen, dropping the bag of chips he was eating.

"Hi," I replied, my voice scratchy from going so long without talking. I cleared my throat and tried again. "Hi."

"What are you doing down here?" Reis said, looking confused as well as suspicious.

"What are you doing *here*?" I shot back. "Shouldn't you be in school or college or something?"

He shrugged. "I quit after high school."

"Why?"

"Why not? Schools have gone to shit since the outbreak, just like the economy. I couldn't afford it even if I wanted to."

I nodded, understanding his reasoning. I wouldn't have gone to college at all if the government hadn't given me the full ride.

"You still haven't answered my question," Reis said, stooping down to pick up his chips.

"Got bored," I replied, and then decided what it was I really wanted to do. "I'm gonna go for a run."

"But you can't go outside!" Reis protested.

"Watch me."

Nobody else was on the ground floor. I could hear noises coming from the basement that indicated some meeting was taking place. No one tried to stop me from leaving.

The burst of fresh air that hit me in the face as I stepped outside was wonderful. Jeff and I usually had our window open because of the warm temperatures, but that wasn't the same. It was mid to late July by now, and it was a perfect day. Eighty to eighty-five degrees, partly cloudy, and a slight breeze. I started jogging immediately, not sure of my destination, but confident I could make my way back. All I had to do was listen to the familiar thoughts of people in the house and I would make it back just fine.

I wasn't really in running clothes; I had a t-shirt on but I was also wearing jeans, and the denim soon began to rub the skin on my ankles and hips raw. By the time I stopped — miles from the safe house — I was in considerable pain. It hurt to even take a step. Thankfully, I had stopped running in a park and limped over to a vacant bench. As I sat there, my raw skin throbbing, I wished I'd brought some money along so I could buy a pair of running shorts. There was no way I was making it back in my jeans. Because of my recent lethargic lifestyle, I'd put on some weight, which was why my pants were bothering me so much. Also, I didn't have a phone or even a number I was supposed to call, so I couldn't have anyone come get me. I was pretty screwed by my lack of planning ahead, again.

Then I recalled how we managed to survive on the road before meeting Danny and Reis; Miriam could talk to an ATM to get money from it. If she could do it, I could do it.

I looked around. I didn't see any ATMs anywhere, but I was close to the heart of the city; I could see the Washington Monument from where I was. There had to be one close by. Gritting my teeth, I got up and walked in the direction of the obelisk, taking in its magnificence. I'd only ever seen it on television, and never had a chance to visit it in person. After I got some money and some shorts, I was going to go see it up close.

I couldn't have walked more than a quarter of a mile before I stumbled upon a gift shop containing an ATM. It was strange being around people again; while I was running I didn't really notice, and there weren't many people around anyway. Now that I was in a crowd, I hesitated in the doorway, but I was guilt-tripped inside when a woman held the door for me on her way out. I froze after stepping inside, startled to find so many people inside the small shop, but I forced myself to snap out of it. Appearing nervous only made people suspicious. I had to act like I was anyone else in this shop.

Going to the ATM in the back corner, I glanced around quickly to make sure no one was watching. People were too busy bustling around to pay attention, and no one would see what I was doing if I stood real close to the machine. Placing my hand on the screen, I told it I wanted fifty bucks. I felt bad stealing, so I didn't go overboard on the cash. I waited, but nothing happened. I sent my thoughts to it again, but still to no avail. What had Miriam done? I thought this was exactly what she did! Maybe my ability wasn't as powerful as hers. She seemed to have gotten the hang of it quite quickly, but Jeff and I still couldn't do much but listen to other people's thoughts. Frustrated, I was about to give up, but decided to give it one last try. I stared hard at the screen, focusing my mind on the machine. I felt my mind reaching out, crawling inside the ATM. I saw each little gear and switch in my head. *Fifty dollars, fifty dollars, fifty dollars.* It was a truly remarkable experience, and I thought I'd finally figured out how to control my ability, because a moment later two twenties and a ten popped out of the machine.

"Cool," I said, grinning. Three years ago, I would have abused this ability and taken unreasonable amounts of money, and I probably would have right after we busted out of the study. But I was different now. My baby, Miriam, and Jeff had become my family, and I cared about them more than anything on earth. No amount of money could be worth their value, or could replace them. They were mine.

I took the money and looked around the store. The first thing I picked up was a baseball cap to pull down over my eyes. Next I went to the small section with souvenir shorts with different images from the city. I was about to pick one with the White House stamp on the upper thigh, but then I thought better of it. If I was caught, I didn't want anyone knowing I'd been spending time here. It was best not to wear anything that identified a specific place. I could rip off the tags once I purchased them. I found a pair of plain white ones, and then grabbed a pair of plain black ones just in case. I wanted to also pick out a clean t-shirt, but there weren't any without a symbol, phrase, or logo on them. Disappointed, I started to head to the register, but stopped as I was passing a dessert section. My eyes landed on a pack of a half dozen red velvet cupcakes. I didn't particularly like red velvet, but I didn't want them for me. Something was telling me to get them for Miriam. Did she like red velvet? I hadn't a clue, but I was learning to listen to my gut. Usually it was my ability talking, and it had yet to be wrong.

I took my shorts, the hat, the cupcakes, and a bottle of water to the register and laid it all out for the guy behind the counter. He gave me a quick glance before scanning the items. "On the run?" he asked without looking up.

I was so startled that I just stared at him until he looked up at me with an expectant expression. "What?" I stammered.

"You look like you're on a run," the guy said. "Are you?"

"Oh," I said, and laughed. I must have misheard him the first time. "Yeah, I am."

The guy looked me up and down and shook his head, smiling. "Jeans and running don't go together, bro."

"Tell me about it," I replied. "That's why I need the shorts."

"Well, you chose well," the guy told me. "These are very comfortable running shorts."

"Good to hear," I said, paying and taking all my stuff that he put into a bag. "Thanks, man."

"Take it easy, Austin," the guy called after me.

I stopped in the doorway and turned around, surprised at the sound of my name. The guy was already speaking to the next customer and didn't notice my surprise. When the customer looked down and reached into his pocket, the guy at the register looked over at me, smiled, and winked. He was a Colician.

They're still following us, I realized, and suddenly felt really stupid. Amelia had been at the safe house with us for a few days, and there were probably other Colicians in the house or watching out for us nearby. Maybe this guy knew I was going out alone, something I shouldn't have been doing, and stationed himself in the area to watch out for me. It made me feel safe. Just because we hadn't seen them in a while didn't mean they weren't still around. When I was outside, I sat down on the curb for a minute, needing to let my shock wear off before I could think straight. I had a sudden urge to look in my bag, so I did. Wrapped up in one of my pairs of shorts were two vials of clear liquid with a dropper attached to the cap. A tag was tied to one vial; it read: **FOR MIRIAM. TWO DROPS OF EACH THREE TIMES DAILY.**

The vials made me suspicious. What was in them? Was this guy trying to poison Miriam? I quickly calmed down, telling myself that his intention was to help us. The Colicians had been nothing but kind since we first came across them. Whatever was in those vials, they would benefit Miriam in some way. Maybe they were supplements Miriam needed for her pregnancy, but how would the Colicians know what she needed? And why was he giving them to me? Couldn't he drop them off at the safe house?

I got up, my questions bugging the hell out of me. They would have to go unanswered, because I was not going back in there. I walked on until I came across a public restroom a few blocks away. Inside, I took a leak and changed into one of my new pairs of shorts. The guy from the shop was right; they were very comfortable and my legs felt much better. I rolled up my jeans and put them in the bag, and continued on my way to the Washington Monument.

It took me about a half hour to get there. It wouldn't have normally taken me so long, but I was getting tired so I slowed my pace.

I ran all the way up to the base of the monument. Panting, I reached out and put a hand on it to steady myself as I caught my breath. *This is what three months of zero exercise does to you*, I told myself, and vowed to never go inactive for so long ever again. I took a swig from the water bottle and then craned my neck back, looking toward the top of the monument. It was impossible to see it this close to the base. Looking at it the way I was, the tower looked like it was tipping, tipping, tipping over.

I gave the old stones a pat before I stepped away and jogged over to a bench. The security around the monument was tight, and they got suspicious if anyone stood around too long. I didn't need anything that would get me noticed. Besides, I could get a better view of it from the bench.

For a while, I sat admiring the monument. I didn't know what it was about it that had me so intrigued, but I couldn't stop staring at it. I wanted to go up to the top, but I knew that was impossible. One had to pay a small fortune just to get to the first security checkpoint, and after that they checked ID, blood, and even brainwaves. All three of the checkpoints would pick up on what I was. It wasn't going to happen. At least not now.

I grabbed my bag and started to stand up to leave, but I froze when I looked across the grassy field at a group of kids who had started going ballistic over something. Someone was handing out balloons and little bottles of bubbles, and they were all screaming and laughing and tugging on the outfit of the person passing out the goodies.

It was Gorilla Man.

At first I thought I was hallucinating again, but this was real. *Gorilla Man was real*. He was right there in front of me, interacting with a bunch of kids. The kids were called away by their parents, and the Gorilla Man gathered up the spare containers of bubbles and started walking over to me. He was walking *directly toward me*. I stared with my mouth hanging open, expecting him to say something, but he wasn't even paying attention to me. He plopped down on the other end of the bench, heaving a sigh and pulling off the hat of the gorilla suit. He set the hat in his lap and reached into a hidden pocket of the suit, pulling out a wad of singles. The guy had curly blonde hair, blue eyes, and lots of freckles. He looked to be in his forties, and didn't seem to notice me staring at him. For a while he sat counting his bills, but eventually he caught my gaze. He stared back at me for a moment before laughing. "I know," he said, in a much higher voice than I expected. "The suit's ridiculous. But you'd be surprised how much kids love it. It's an act to promote the zoo. Hell, it helps pay the bills."

I didn't answer right away, and he stared at me expectantly. Finally, I stammered, "Right. Cool."

The dude in the gorilla suit continued with his counting, but he glanced at me again, curiously, and I forced myself to look away from him. I wanted to get up, to run away from this nightmare creature that was now my reality, but my butt was glued to the bench. Once again, my shock had paralyzed me.

There was one thing in particular that kept me from fleeing: my strange series of dreams I had during my first night of infection, the first time I encountered Gorilla Man. In the dream, the guy in the suit told me to follow him. When I asked him why, he pointed over my shoulder and I was attacked by a big dog. At least I thought it was a dog. Regardless, that dream had sent me a message: follow the man in the gorilla suit or I would be killed.

Should I say something to him? I wondered. I started to say something, but he was back on his feet and replacing his mask.

Shit. I rose as well and followed him as he trotted down the path. I shot one last longing glance at the Washington Monument, silently bidding it farewell.

Gorilla Man walked very fast. I had to keep breaking into a jog to keep him in my sight. He waved at kids as he passed; he seemed to be very good with them. I wondered why he hadn't become a grade school teacher, but then I remembered what Reis said. It was so hard to get into college these days, and even harder to actually get a degree. He might have the skills, but that didn't mean squat in today's world.

I followed him for several miles, and he didn't seem to notice me. He kept on trotting to wherever he was headed. Whoever this guy was, he was quite cheerful. I didn't see many people with that kind of skip in their step.

For a few minutes I considered forgetting about him and going back to the safe house, but I was too scared of what might happen if I didn't stop following him. Would I be mauled by a dog on the way back? Would this man in the gorilla suit end up saving my life one day? My determination to stay alive kept me moving.

We reached a questionable looking area of town, with lots of rundown shops and apartment complexes, and people in raggedy clothes who gave me creepy sideways looks. I didn't know why I was surprised that this was where we ended up; if he was working as a dude in a gorilla suit selling balloons and bubbles to kids, he couldn't be making much money. He rounded a corner several yards ahead of me, and I jogged to catch up so I wouldn't miss him round another. But when I turned, he was waiting for me. He grabbed me and slammed me against the wall of an apartment building, putting a knife to my throat before I could cry out in surprise.

"Dude!" I said when I found my voice.

"Why are you following me?" Gorilla Man demanded, pressing the knife harder into my throat.

"Look man—"

"Who are you with?" he shouted.

"*With* ? I'm not *with* anyone!"

"What lab are you from?"

"Dude, you're crazy—"

Gorilla Man's knife was close to drawing blood. "I swear to Christ, I will cut your throat right here!"

I suddenly realized what he meant when he asked what lab I was from. Closing my mouth, I used my newfound talent. *I'm not from a lab, bro.*

He let me go so fast that I fell to the ground. "Whoa!" he said, astonished.

"Thanks for not killing me," I muttered, climbing to my feet and brushing the dust from my shorts. I massaged my throat where his knife had been moments before.

"Sorry..." Gorilla Man mumbled, but he seemed too distracted to know what he was saying. He stared intently at me, a mixture of disbelief and excitement on his face. "I can't believe it..."

"Neither can I," I said, losing my patience. "Who are you? Why the hell have I been seeing you everywhere?"

He ignored me, never taking his eyes of my face. For a while he studied me, and then he whispered, "Are you one of the new ones?"

"One of the new *what*?"

His lips didn't move, but I heard him all the same. *One of the new Colicians.*

My mouth fell open. "Holy shit," I said. "You're a *Caiten*?"

12

Hillerman's Secret

Gorilla Man's name was Lee Stewart. He was living under an alias, because the same people who were looking for me were also looking for him.

"I used to be an engineer," he explained when we were in the safety of his apartment and he had changed out of the suit. It was a rundown, dingy little place, but as Lee put it, it was better than living on the street. Or in a lab. The place was dim because all his windows faced other nearby buildings, so the sunlight he received was minimal. He liked it because no one could keep an eye on his apartment from the street. Still, he kept thick curtains over every window. He didn't have much furniture; only a sagging sofa on which I sat, an armchair with a broken leg where Lee sat, and a small coffee table between us. He'd brought me a dusty can of Dr. Pepper, but my stomach was too unsettled to drink it. Knowing there were more Caitens was upsetting my entire body; my leg was twitching, my head was throbbing, and I couldn't seem to get comfortable. I didn't know whether to blame that last bit on my anxiety or the couch.

Lee himself seemed a little off his rocker. I hadn't noticed them before, but now that he'd brushed his hair, I could see scars on both his temples. Surgical scars. On his arms, there were dozens of fading spots where needles had been inserted. Lee was jittery and kept jumping out of his chair without warning, would walk a few laps around the room, and then sit down again. Another odd thing he kept doing was rubbing his wrists together before rubbing them on the sides of his face. If I hadn't put the pieces together and realized that Lee had been in a lab for a long time, I would have thought he was weird. I just felt sorry for him now. I knew that I would be the same way had I not escaped.

"What kind of engineer?" I asked, taking some deep breaths to ease the tension in my body.

"I built cruise ships." Lee reached under his chair and pulled out a book. He handed it to me. "Are you familiar with the New Age cruise line?"

"Yeah," I said. "I remember wanting to go on one when I was little." I took a look at the cover of the book. I guessed that Lee thought he was handing me a book about engineering ships, but what he actually gave me was an old copy of *The Very Hungry Caterpillar.* I nodded and opened the book upon his awaiting gaze. I hoped that maybe there would be diagrams of ships inside, disguised by the cover, but all I saw were pictures of the little green caterpillar eating watermelon, pie, strawberries, and other things. Something sank inside me when I opened the book. My mom used to read it to Chrissy and I when we were little and it reminded me of them both, but it also made me feel pain for Lee. What was done to him to make him like this? Who could do such a horrible thing to him? Hillerman's name was the first to pop into my head, but there were plenty of others out in the world who'd taken pleasure in the torture of the Colicians, and would have loved to have new victims to experiment on.

Lee took the book back and slipped it under the chair again. "I loved it," he said. "I lived for it." He paused, a strange look crossing his face. He looked confused, and for a moment I thought he would start crying. But he rubbed his wrists together, rubbed his wrists on his face, and continued. "I spent my life building ships. I was living in Miami when the Colician Virus hit. For the first few weeks, business continued as usual. But when the virus began to spread, and cases were reported in northern Florida, all construction stopped. I lost my house. Once the Colicians left through their portal, the economy crashed, and so many people lost their jobs. Thankfully I got mine back. I wish now that I'd left Florida like I planned to when I first lost my job. Just days before Georgia declared war on Florida, a large group of soldiers came by my construction site. We'd just begun construction on the newest, biggest cruise liner ever built. I wish I could have seen its completion… You've probably heard of it. The *Majesty*?"

"Oh, yeah," I said. "I know that ship. I've never seen it in person, but I've seen it on TV. Wow. It's cool that you got to work on it."

Lee was beaming with pride.

"So what did the soldiers want?" I asked.

"The soldiers rounded us all up, and their leader ordered an immediate halt in construction." Lee's expression became very serious. "He introduced himself as Sergeant Jaeger."

I suddenly knew how this story was going to end. "Oh jeez," I said.

"He informed us that there was a very serious gas leak coming from the ship and he needed to evacuate us. We were skeptical, because there wasn't anything we were using that could cause said gas leak, but he was insistent. But once we were loaded into the trucks, we weren't allowed to leave. They kept on driving and wouldn't let us out of the truck for more than a day. When they finally opened the back, they cuffed us and dragged us into a large building. I caught a glimpse of the sign in front of it: Philadelphia University."

"Oh my God," I muttered, not wanting to hear any more but at the same time needing to know.

"Several levels below the school, there was a laboratory. We were separated and put into white rooms. A few days later, after my throat was raw from yelling to be let out, a man finally came to talk to me. He was a doctor. Dr. Hillerman. I take it you know him?"

"Yes," I said through my teeth. "All too well."

"He told me that I couldn't leave. None of us could leave. We were going to help our nation, our *species*. And... well, you know the rest." He pointed to the scars on his temples, and then showed me large scars on both his wrists.

"What are those from?" I asked.

"Pulling on my restraints." Lee did the weird wrist thing. "My procedures were most likely far more painful than yours. Hillerman didn't like giving us pain medication."

"Jesus Christ," I said, feeling nauseous.

"That's not the end, though," Lee said. "Hillerman managed to cover up our disappearances. Everyone he abducted, he claimed to be dead from the gas leak. No one would go looking for us."

"How the hell did you get out?" I asked.

"That's the best part." Lee's eyes gleamed with excitement. "You probably think you're the first newbie, don't you? Well, you're wrong. *I'm* the first. Well, myself and the rest of our crew are the first."

This couldn't be right. Lee's statement didn't make any sense. "If you're the first, then why is he still running tests to figure out how to make a new virus?"

"Because the virus he created was just like the Colician Virus. It would have spread around the world so fast that there would be no way to contain it. He didn't want another pandemic; he just wanted enough of us to try to find a cure."

"So how did he prevent it from becoming a pandemic?"

"He found a way to contain the virus within our own bodies. Now, there's no way I can infect another. He had to do it to everyone who had contact with us too. Just like the Colician Strain, this new virus had the ability to spread through people who weren't affected. They would carry it and spread it to everyone they came in contact with. That's how the Colician Virus spread so far so fast. He figured out how to keep us from spreading it, and ever since he's been trying to create a strain that wasn't contagious. He finally succeeded with you."

"So all the tests he was running...he already found a way to infect people...he was just finding a more efficient way of doing it."

Lee held up a finger to stop me. "There were two hundred and sixteen of us construction workers, engineers, designers, and crew members who were taken to the lab. Out of all of them, only sixty-three of us survived being infected."

My nausea returned. "He killed the rest of them?"

Shrugging, Lee said, "In a way. His virus did. The virus that infected me and the other sixty-two workers was fatal to everyone without A negative blood. That was how Hillerman picked the blood type to target. Myself and the other survivors all had A negative blood. When he started running the current, larger lab, he only allowed people with A negative blood into the facility. That included patients, doctors, and soldiers."

I opened my mouth to ask another question, but stopped. This new snippet of information was far more extreme than anything I'd heard so far. "So...you're saying that Hillerman is...*one of us?*"

Lee nodded. "And Jaeger. And everyone else inside. But they're not exactly like us. Not yet, anyway."

I had so many thoughts and questions running through my mind at that moment that I had a hard time spitting anything out. "Hillerman's an A Negative?"

"Yeah," Lee said.

"But if he was infecting you with a contagious virus...then he's infected too."

Lee nodded. "He and a few of the other doctors there are. None of the soldiers are. I don't even know if they know they're at risk."

I couldn't believe it. The very doctor who had infected me with the Caiten Virus was a Caiten himself. "What's going to happen to him if people find out?"

"Oh, they already know." Lee looked as equally pissed by this statement as I felt. "The government knows about him. They fund his study. They only continue to fund him because he's made progress. He's had positive results."

"I wouldn't exactly call them *positive*," I muttered.

"Regardless, he's successfully infected people with a new virus. That's what the study was all about; infect people with a sister virus and find a cure for the original. So far, Hillerman's completed half of his goals."

I shook my head. This was all so much to take in at one time. "I'm sorry, I just need to go over all of this again. You're a Caiten."

Lee nodded.

"You and sixty-two others were infected with this virus that I and three others were recently infected with. We are all a new species."

"Yes."

"The doctor who infected us is one of us."

"Yes."

"Answer me something else, Lee. Where are all the others?"

Lee only stared at me at first, and then he glanced around quickly, as if a piece of furniture might eavesdrop. He leaned in and whispered, "They went back to Miami."

That was surprising. "To the middle of a war zone?"

Lee bit his lip and looked around carefully again. "They're building something."

My curiosity was back. "What are they building?"

Grinning slyly, Lee shrugged. "What were we building before?"

It suddenly hit me, and then I was confused again. "They're rebuilding the *Majesty*?"

"Not the *Majesty*, per se," Lee replied. "But something very similar."

"Why aren't you with them?"

Again, Lee shrugged. "I wasn't in agreement with them."

"Agreement about what…?" I shook my head quickly. "Never mind." I wanted to know more, but there was a question that had been nagging at me for months. "What I really want to know is why I've been seeing you everywhere."

Lee blinked. "Seeing me? I haven't seen you before in my life!"

"I've been seeing you everywhere in your gorilla suit! It's been scaring the shit out of me! Can you imagine going into a public restroom, looking in the mirror and seeing a dude in a gorilla suit staring back at you?"

Lee seemed to be pondering this new information carefully. He did the wrist thing a couple of times before speaking. "I don't know why you've been seeing me, but I swear it wasn't of my doing. I didn't know you existed until today. I wasn't calling you."

"Then why the hell have I been seeing you?" I whispered hopelessly. I just wanted answers, but everything had to be so damn complicated.

"Hmm." Lee sat back in his chair and was lost in thought for a moment, and then he quickly sat forward. "Maybe you were supposed to find me. Did my gorilla suit say anything to you?"

"Uh…yeah. When I first saw you, it was in a dream I had the first night I was infected. You told me to follow you. 'Follow me, Austin Rockwell,' you said."

"Your name's Austin?" Lee asked. "That's a nice name."

I realized I never told him my name or anything about me at all, and winced with guilt. "Sorry, man. Yes, my name's Austin. I'm twenty-one years old and am originally from New York. My father and younger sister are both Colicians, and their infection led me to Hillerman's study."

"Hmm," Lee said again, and then launched back into our conversation as if I hadn't said a thing aside from it. "Well, you did follow me like my suit said in the dream, and you ended up here with me. The other times you saw it must have just been reminders to follow me when we crossed paths."

"But why was I supposed to follow you in the first place?"

"You ask these questions as if I have the answers, my friend, but I'm just as skeptical as you."

I sighed in frustration, slouching down in my seat. This was really pissing me off. I finally found Gorilla Man and he didn't know his ass from his elbow.

"You said there were four of you, right?" Lee asked.

"There are only three now," I mumbled. "Our friend died a few months ago."

"Oh no," Lee said. "That's too bad. What about the other two? Where are they?"

"They're at a safe house."

"When was the last time you spoke to them?"

I shrugged. "A while. We don't really talk anymore."

"No." Lee leaned even closer. "I mean, do you know if they're all right?"

Again, I shrugged. "Why wouldn't they be?"

Lee's eyes became hazy, and I knew he was using his ability to do something. When his eyes focused on me again, he looked worried. "Something's happening."

"What?" I really wished this guy could figure out how to have a conversation.

"At one of the houses a few miles away. Something's happening. There are...trucks...soldiers..."

I heard the word soldiers and knew something was wrong. "Where are they?" I asked, terrified.

"A few miles away...in a house...I can't tell exactly. I can see a girl...a girl with dark hair..."

Miriam. I bolted to my feet and ran for the door.

"Is she your friend?" Lee asked, alarmed.

"It's Miriam!" I cried.

"Wait!" Lee shouted as I started to leave his apartment. He quickly followed, slipping into his shoes. "I have a car. We'll go together."

"You don't need to get involved in this," I told him, turning to go.

Lee caught my arm. When I looked at him, there was something in his eyes for a moment that made him seem...all there. "We're in this together now, Austin."

We rode to the safe house together in his car—a tiny, rundown blue Smart Car. The engine rumbled and made sounds that made it seem almost alive, but there was no way I could worry about its reliability. All I cared about was getting back to the safe house, to my friends. To Miriam.

And James.

We couldn't even get close.

Several blocks away, roadblocks were in place. One of the officers there approached the car when we refused to turn around. "You can't go through here," she told us sternly. "Please turn around."

"His girlfriend is down there," Lee replied

"There are very dangerous criminals inside the perimeter, gentlemen," the officer said, loudly, as if we couldn't understand her when she spoke normally. "No one's getting in. I'm afraid your girlfriend will have to wait, sir. Please turn around, or I'm authorized to use force." Her hand dropped down to her hip.

Lee looked to me helplessly.

"Just go," I muttered. I'd been trying the entire drive to speak mentally with Miriam or Jeff, but no matter what I did, I couldn't hear a damn thing. I couldn't even tell if they were still alive.

"I'm sorry, Austin," Lee said as we drove away.

"It's my fault," I replied. "I shouldn't have left."

"But maybe you were supposed to."

I glanced at him. "What is that supposed to mean?"

Lee smiled, and it royally pissed me off. "You saw images of my suit in your dreams and even in your reality. Then you suddenly decide to go out and come across me in my suit. That can't be a coincidence."

"What are you saying? I wasn't supposed to be there?"

"Maybe you were supposed to leave, so you could run into me and follow me, so you wouldn't be at the house when the soldiers came. Maybe you would have been hurt, or killed, had you not left. Therefore your subconscious convinced you to leave."

"How can my subconscious convince me to leave, Lee? I didn't know anything was going to happen!"

"Maybe your subconscious did."

"You're not making any sense!"

"Listen." Lee drew in a breath. "Maybe you heard someone's thoughts, someone who knew what was going to happen. But maybe you didn't exactly register those thoughts. You still had the memory of it in your subconscious, which is why you had an itch to leave when you did."

He was beginning to make a little more sense, but I was freaking out too much to care what he was talking about. "Whatever, man. It doesn't matter why I left. What matters is that our safe house was attacked, according to you, anyway. I can't hear a thing right now no matter how hard I try, so I can't even be sure it *was* attacked."

"It was, I promise," Lee said.

"Shut up, dude. I wasn't there when my friends were in danger, and now I don't even know if they're still alive. How do you think I feel right now?"

"Oh, they're still alive," Lee told me.

I threw my arms in the air. "Why the hell didn't you just tell me? Where are they?"

"I don't know. They're blocking their thoughts out of fear. All I know is that they're okay."

I sighed wearily. At least they were okay. I could find them later, when they were being more open and I could actually communicate with them.

Lee steered the car to a halt at the curb and put it into park. "Where do you want to go now? Is there any place you can think of where they'd be?"

I shook my head. "We didn't know of any special hiding place to go to if our safe house was compromised."

We sat in silence for a while. "Do you want to crash at my place until we can find your friends?"

"If it's not too much to ask," I whispered, feeling guilty for taking up his space. "I can crash on the couch, if that's cool."

"That's fine," Lee said, putting the car back into drive and heading in the direction of his apartment. "I have spare pillows and blankets in my closet you can use."

"Thanks."

We drove for a while. When Lee pulled into the same parking spot that he had backed out of, he cut the engine and gave me a reassuring smile. "We'll be okay, Austin," he said. "Everything will be okay. We'll find your friends."

I wish I felt as confident about everything as you do, I almost grumbled, but kept it to myself. I followed him up to his apartment and collapsed on his couch, the emotions I'd experienced in the past hour leaving me exhausted. I stared at the floor, unmoving. There wasn't anything else I wanted to do but sit there by myself.

Lee stood watching me for a bit and then said, "Do you want pizza?"

I shrugged. I didn't know if I'd be able to eat anything anyway.

Shifting on his feet uncomfortably, Lee said, "Well, I'm going to order one. Is pepperoni and pineapple okay?"

Again, I didn't reply with anything other than a shrug.

Taking the hint, Lee left. I could hear him in the other room, placing his order. I suddenly noticed my bag of stuff I'd bought from the gift shop, resting on the floor beside the sofa. In my panic to get to Miriam, I'd completely forgotten it here.

I laid down, using my arm as a pillow. Would Jeff, Miriam, and I ever be able to stay in one spot? Would we have to keep running forever? I closed my eyes, images of them flickering under my lids. I loved them, and I had to find them. *Where are you?* I thought, hoping I would be heard. *Tell me where you are. I'm so scared. Where are you?*

~~*

I awoke with a start sometime later. I wasn't sure what had awakened me, but whatever it was, I was on high alert. Something was stuck to my face, and in a wild panic I clawed at it until it fluttered to the floor. It was a piece of paper. A post-it note, to be exact. Feeling stupid, I reached down and picked it up. My arm was prickling with pins and needles from sleeping on it, so I sat up and shook it out to the get my blood flowing again. A blanket slid off of me, one that Lee must have draped over me while I slept. I felt grateful to him. I looked at the note. *Piz'Zas iN tHe fRIDge.* Seeing this note made me once again feel sorry for Lee. He couldn't even write four words normally.

I was surprised I'd slept through the pizza being delivered. I figured I'd wake up as soon as I heard the lock unclick. I stood up, picking up the extra blanket and pillow Lee had set on the floor beside me and setting them on the sofa. I went to the old, dusty fridge and opened it. When I did, the smell that came from it almost knocked me off my feet.

"Aaarrgh!" I cried, covering my mouth and nose with my hand. Mold was growing on the sides of the fridge and on a lot of the food inside. I quickly grabbed the pizza box and closed the door, but not before I could have sworn I saw the mold actually *growing.* "Jesus," I muttered, dropping the box on the counter and cautiously opening it. I was expecting to see the mold growing on it, but it was clean. I took a whiff and it smelled fine too. There were only a few cupboards in the kitchen, and I was afraid of what I might find if I opened them. But I needed a plate, so I opened the one closest to me. Letting out a yelp, I slammed it shut, and I could hear the little gray mouse scurrying away. Taking a deep breath, I opened the next one. Thankfully, the only thing wrong inside was a small spider web in one corner. I couldn't even see the spider. There were a few plates there, so I took one out and then scrubbed it with soap and water. Once it was clean, I put the remaining four slices on it and stuck it in the microwave. I was relieved not to find anything disturbing inside.

Lee had some serious issues he needed to fix.

While I nuked the pizza, I checked out the rest of the apartment. There was a small bathroom past the kitchen that was surprisingly tidy given what I'd just seen, and past that was Lee's bedroom. The door was ajar and the interior was dark. I could hear Lee snoring softly inside. I glanced at the clock on the stove: 9:13. I had slept longer than I thought.

I ate my pizza in silence and then rewashed the plate, setting it gently on the counter to avoid bothering Lee. I was about to return to the living room when there was a sudden pounding on the front door. Then, "Austin? Austin, let me in! *Please!*"

It was Danny.

I ran to the door and opened it, pulling Danny inside. "What the hell happened?" I demanded, locking the door again. "Where's—"

"I don't have time to explain," Danny said breathlessly. "We have to go—"

"How the hell did you find me?" It didn't make sense. He couldn't have known where I was and didn't have the ability to find me.

"Walter," Danny said. "Now *listen*. I think he followed me. We have to get out of here."

"Who followed you?"

"The guy who ratted us out!" Anger blazed on the boy's face. "The guy who played us and sold us out to the soldiers!"

Before I could ask who that was, Lee hurried into the room, looking frightened. "What's going on?" he asked.

Danny backed up, but I reassured them both. "It's okay, guys. Danny Bennett, meet Lee Stuart. He's like me. Lee, this is one of the humans who was harboring us at the safe house."

Lee still looked a little uncertain, but he nodded toward Danny. "Nice to meet you," he murmured.

"If you're like him," Danny started, gesturing to me, "then you have to come too. We need to leave *now*."

He opened the door and started to pull me out, but I said, "Wait!" and ran to the couch for my bag. "Come on, Lee!" I called, but Lee was hesitant.

"What about my stuff?" he asked.

"Don't worry about your stuff. We have to go!" I grabbed his arm and tugged him out with us, and we hurried down and out to the parking lot.

"My car only seats two," Lee told Danny.

"I brought mine," Danny said, and ran to the pickup truck that had brought us to D.C. We followed, but halted when we heard a familiar voice.

"Danny!"

Danny froze and turned to his right. Reis was running toward us, his arms raised.

"Danny, it's cool, man. Leave them."

Danny pulled a gun out of his belt and pointed it at Reis. "Don't you move, man! I swear to God I'll kill you!"

"Dude!" I said in surprise. "Put the gun down, bro!"

Reis and Danny ignored us. "I didn't tell them about you, man. You're safe. Come on! If they see you with them, I can't help you."

I suddenly realized what was going on. "*You* sold us out?" I said, gaping at Reis. "Seriously? What the hell for?"

Reis regarded me warily, as well as Lee. "You're dangerous, Austin. What was I supposed to do? I have a duty to my country and my species!"

"You little prick—" I started forward, but Lee held me back.

"I can't believe you'd do that to me," Danny said, betrayal in his eyes, on his face. "We were friends. How could you do that? You killed innocent people!"

Shaking his head, Reis replied, "They were harboring dangerous fugitives."

"What the hell were *you* doing then?" Danny shot back.

"My job," was all Reis had to say.

"You didn't give them my name?" Danny asked carefully. "You didn't tell them I was involved, or my family?"

"No, man."

"You're sure?"

Reis nodded. "Like I said, we're—"

The end of his sentence was cut off as Danny pulled the trigger of his gun three times, shooting Reis in the chest. He crumpled to the ground, dead.

"Come on!" Danny cried. "Both of you, in the back now!"

I was so shocked to see Danny kill someone that I stood frozen for a moment. Snapping out of it, I helped Lee up into the bed of the truck and climbed in myself. We pulled the tarps over us to stay hidden.

For the first several miles, Lee and I were being thrown around in the back as Danny whipped around corners and sped through intersections. I knew he was blowing stop signs and red lights; there were lots of car horns and squealing tires. After fifteen minutes or so, we made it to a freeway and Danny sped down it for a long time.

When the truck finally slowed to a stop, I waited for Danny to get out and come talk to us, but nothing happened. Eventually I sat up and looked around. We were in the middle of nowhere, or so it seemed. A steady trickle of cars passed us where we sat on the shoulder, each pair of headlights blinding me as they passed, but other than that all I could see were trees. We were far out of the country's capital now.

I turned and opened the sliding window that separated us from Danny. "Yo. You gonna tell us what the hell happened?"

"Not right now," Danny muttered in the dark, barely visible in the minimal light provided by the moon and passing headlights of cars.

"What are we doing here?" I asked.

"We got no place to go," he replied. "I need to sit and think for a while. Get some sleep. I won't leave until morning."

"When are you going to tell us what happened?" I said softly.

There was a long pause. "I don't know," Danny said finally.

I sighed and closed the window, settling down next to Lee. "We're going to stay here tonight."

"Are we safe?" Lee asked, and I realized just how scared he was.

"Yes." I tried to give him one of the reassuring smiles he gave me earlier, but I didn't think he could see it in the dark, so instead I patted his arm. "We'll be all right. In the morning we'll find somewhere to go, okay?"

I felt Lee nod, and then settle in next to me.

~~*

I awoke again with a start several hours later. Dawn was creeping toward us from the east, and something didn't feel right. Lee was still dozing beside me, and when I sat up slightly. I could see Danny nodding off in the cab. What was wrong? Everything appeared to be all right, but I knew it wasn't. I peeked over the left side of the truck. Nothing. I shifted until I could peek over the back. Again, nothing. Carefully, I leaned over Lee and peeked over the right side. My heart skipped a beat when I saw the form of a man slouched on the ground, resting against the back tire. I was scared at first, then confused, and then I was just amused. I knew who it was.

I found myself laughing. Lee stirred under me, and the man on the ground tilted his head back to glare at me.

"Hey there, Lieutenant Asswipe," I greeted, still laughing.

167

13

Befriending the Enemy

I'd never seen Jaeger look so shitty. I hopped out of the truck to get a better look at him, struggling to get my laughing under control. Jaeger didn't move anything but his head; he was still slumped against the tire and the rest of his body appeared to be immobile. *Jesus,* I thought as I looked him up and down. *What the hell did Hillerman do to him?*

The thing was, I knew *exactly* what Hillerman had done to him. I could see it in his body, in the betrayal in his eyes. Lee said that Hillerman only allowed people with A negative blood inside the study. Hillerman had betrayed the man who was trying to kill us, and now that man was here.

Jaeger had discarded his uniform top and now only wore his cargo pants and black t-shirt. He had no weapons on him; in fact, he didn't look like he had anything other than the mud-stained clothes on his back. His eyes were red, exhausted, and pained. His hair had dirt and grass in it and was matted to his forehead. He had cuts and needle marks in both his arms, and had a mark on his forehead under his hairline that looked just like the mark on my stomach where Hillerman had performed laser surgery. That made me shudder.

He made a noise through his nose, and it took him a few tries before he could speak. "What the hell's so damn funny?"

I wasn't laughing anymore. The mark on his forehead took all humor of the situation away. "Dude," I said. "What the hell happened to you? What did he *do* to you?"

"What does it look like?" Jaeger muttered, his chin dropping to his chest.

"What's going on?" Lee was awake and looking over the edge of the truck. "Who's that?"

"An old pal of mine," I replied. "He's one of us now."

We informed Danny of the situation and I told him that Jaeger would be coming with us. He was less than pleased by my decision, but I wasn't about to leave the former sergeant behind. We couldn't leave one of our own behind, even if he was a prick, because we knew what would be done to him. I was not about to trust him; when we got to wherever we decided to go, I would figure out what to do with him. But for now he was our companion.

As we were getting ready to be on our way, we were all startled by a loud bark behind us. A small German Shepherd trotted out of the bushes, tail wagging and tongue hanging out. It paused before going to Jaeger, licking his hand.

"Is that your dog?" Lee asked him.

"No," Jaeger replied. "But she's been following me for hours."

So we had another companion joining us on our journey to...somewhere. Lee sat up front with Danny and I sat in back with Jaeger as he rested. He named the dog Kyla, and they seemed pretty attached. She kept her head resting on his belly the entire ride and eyed me warily.

I had a lot of questions for Jaeger, but I knew he must be exhausted. I let him sleep for an hour and a half before I poked him awake. This earned a quiet growl from Kyla.

"Whadya want, boy?" Jaeger snarled sleepily as he tried to wake himself up.

"What do you think I want?" I replied. "What the hell happened? How the hell did you find us?" I stared at his face, receiving the same hateful gaze I'd always received. "Why didn't you kill me while I slept?"

"I can't kill you," he mumbled, rolling onto his side so his back was to me.

"What?"

"I said I can't kill you."

"Why the hell not?"

The soldier sighed. "Because we're the same."

I stared at his back for a while. "What does that even mean? You can't kill me because we're both infected? What about when we were both human? You didn't seem to have a damn problem doing shit to me then!"

He paused. "It's different now."

"How?" I demanded. "How is it different?"

Jaeger rolled over so fast that I shrank back into the corner instinctively. For the first time since I'd met him, his expression was soft. He seemed...*sad*. "The virus... changed me. And not just in the way it changes everyone. It gave me a sense of clarity." He sighed again and sat up stiffly. "I didn't volunteer for this. Hillerman was never really one to ask for permission. If I'd had a say in it, I would have said no. Hell no. He wanted to make super soldiers, to track you and the others down. We lost track of you after Wisconsin and there was absolutely no trace of you anywhere, so Hillerman did the last thing he could think of to clean up his mess.

"There were two others he infected along with me. Your old pal Diereks and another who you never met. Kingston is his name. Hillerman only wanted to start with a few with leadership experience, and then if it went as planned he would start infecting more. Eventually he did, and there are well over forty of us now. He had us practice using our abilities on a variety of people inside the study, and it was clear that I had the most talent out of all of us. But with that talent...this *gift*...my mindset started changing. I could hear everyone's thoughts, and the worst were the doctors'. They're going to do horrible things to the others still inside the study, and to other people as well."

"Have they started infecting the other people in the study yet?" I asked.

"No. Hillerman didn't want to start infecting more citizens until you and the other three were killed."

I figured it would be okay to break the news to Jaeger, given our mutual predicament. "Kost is dead, Jaeger. He died while we were in Madison."

Jaeger stared at me, his expression skeptical. "Why? How?"

I shrugged. "We're the result of Hillerman's test strain, I guess. His rough copy. It was unclear to anyone how humans would react to the virus, and Kost's body ended up rejecting it. He died."

The sadness in Jaeger's eyes surprised me. He looked as if he'd known Kost for a long time, like they'd been friends. He looked away. "I didn't know. Nobody knew. We all assumed the four of you were still together."

I shook my head. "It's just been Jeff, Miriam, Vincent, and I for a while."

Jaeger's brow furrowed. "Vincent? Vincent Lobner?"

"Yeah, Miriam's brother." I didn't want to tell him about the baby yet. I wasn't about to trust him with that precious information. "He escaped with us when you killed Miriam's dad and other brother, Brent." I added some bitterness into that last sentence.

Jaeger once again surprised me when I saw the guilt cross his face, creating an ugly expression. He didn't talk for a bit. "I've done a lot of bad things," he whispered. "And I'll never be able to escape that fact."

I nodded, agreeing with him. "So how did you find us?"

"How did I find you at the house or in the ditch?"

"Both."

"Well, Hillerman was using the three of us super soldiers to try to find you and the others. I found you right away, but by then I was beginning to have doubts about what I was doing. I lied and said I couldn't find you, but I could tell that Hillerman knew I was lying. Before either of the others found you, a kid in D.C. reported your whereabouts, so that's where we went. Hillerman ordered me to be in charge of the attack on your safe house. I refused. I was demoted and Diereks was put in charge. He set our dogs loose inside, and anyone who ran out was shot. I saw two people shot before I turned and ran. A few shots were fired in my direction, but they were more focused on the house than on me. I ran and ran and ran. When I made it out of the city and onto the open road, I noticed Kyla following me. Night came and I couldn't run anymore, but I knew I had to keep going, so I walked on for hours. Sometime last night, when I couldn't go on anymore, I saw your truck sitting in the ditch. Something in my gut told me to go to it. I went and collapsed beside it, and who should be in the truck but you."

Just like when I ran into Lee, I thought. It just seems to be complete coincidence, but that's not it. Something's drawing us all together...

"So what's your plan now?" I asked him.

Jaeger shrugged. "Don't have one. I figured I'd stick with you until you find your friends. I can help you get there."

"And then what?"

"I'll have to go my own way I guess."

"Why? You don't wanna stick with us? I'm insulted."

Jaeger snorted. "I'm sure your girl Miriam would love that. After what I did to her family, there's no way I can face her. I can barely look at myself in a mirror anymore."

I didn't reply. I knew Miriam would be outraged to see Jaeger with me, but we couldn't just leave him. It was hard to survive on our own. We had to at least get a good distance away from D.C. before we separated.

"I'll figure something out," Jaeger said, lying back down and closing his eyes. "We'll all figure something out."

I let Jaeger go back to sleep, running over his story in my mind. I was shocked at how much this man had changed in such a short time, but at the same time I was suspicious. Something inside me was warning me not to trust him, and for good reason. Even if this man had changed and his intentions were suddenly pure, he had still murdered innocent people, Miriam's family in particular. We couldn't just let that slide.

After a while, the only part of Jaeger's story I could focus on was Diereks letting the dogs loose on the house. In my original dream of the Gorilla Man, the first time I ever saw him, I asked him why I should follow him and he pointed over my shoulder. I turned and an animal with big teeth attacked me. I thought it was a dog, and now I knew for sure. Had I been in the safe house when the attack happened, I would have been mauled by one of those dogs. My subconscious *had* saved me after all.

~~*

I didn't remember falling asleep, but the next thing I knew Danny was shaking me awake. "What's goin' on?" I muttered, trying to push off the heavy haze of sleep. The sun was beginning to set, the first streaks of orange and pink coloring the sky. "What time is it? Where are we?"

"It's 8:50," Danny said. "And I don't know where we are. Lee just told me to stop."

8:50. I'd slept all day. I glanced over at Jaeger and Kyla, who were both asleep and snoring softly. I decided to let them sleep. "Leave him," I said when Danny went to shake the former soldier awake as well. "He's been through a lot the past few days. Just let him sleep."

After climbing out of the truck, I stretched my stiff back and legs. We were on the side of the road at a tiny wayside, so small that the bathrooms appeared to be outhouses. It was very hot and muggy, even though the sun was going down. I could feel sweat already forming on my forehead and back. I looked around. The landscape was very flat with lots of trees, and one of the trees in particular caught my attention. I looked closer, and realized that it was a palm tree.

"Are we in Florida?" I asked in disbelief.

"Yep," Danny replied, shaking out his wrists. "I don't know where exactly, but we're in Florida."

I suddenly realized that Lee was leading us to his old home, to Miami. He was taking us to the other Caitens. I felt like I'd known it all along. It was the only logical place *to* go. "How did you get across the Georgia/Florida border?"

"Back roads," Danny said. "They aren't as heavily guarded. Lee instructed me where to drive and when to stop while crossing."

"Great," I said, looking around at the seemingly untouched area. "We're in the middle of a war zone. That's just awesome."

"Lee seemed pretty intent on coming here." Danny turned and looked at Lee, who was standing on the double yellow line in the middle of the road and looking north. His arms were crossed and he seemed to be waiting for something.

"Yeah," I muttered. "He's got friends in Miami."

"Are those the others who were infected with him?"

"Yep. I guess he wants us all to be together, which makes sense. We're stronger when we're together."

Danny watched me for a minute without speaking. "Walter never told me about the others. Lee and the engineers. I always assumed you were the start of this virus."

"So did I," I muttered. "Maybe Walter didn't know either."

"How could he not know?" Danny's brow furrowed. "He's very skilled at his ability. He hears about everything."

"No one can know everything," I replied. "Not even Walter Reifert." I looked over at Lee again. "What's he waiting for?"

"No idea," Danny muttered. "He's been standing there since we pulled over." He glanced at me. "I gotta pee. I'll be right back. Keep an eye on everyone for me, will you?"

"Yep," I said. Danny jogged over to the outhouses and I walked over to Lee. "Hey, man. What are you waiting for?"

Lee quickly put a finger to his lips and shushed me. "They're almost here!" he hissed, staring intently north.

"Who's almost here?" I asked impatiently.

Lee looked at me skeptically. "Your friends, of course."

My eyes widened and my stomach jumped. "You found them? They're coming?"

"I've been talking to them for a while," Lee said, as if I should know all this. "We have to go to Miami and be with the others. It's the only way we can be safe. I called your friends to tell them how to find us."

"Why didn't you tell me earlier?" I demanded angrily.

Again, Lee gave me a skeptical look. "I thought you knew all this."

I didn't reply. I looked north along with Lee, wondering why I couldn't hear anything in my head. I hadn't heard anything for a while, and it was bothering me that Lee was able to communicate with Miriam and Jeff and I couldn't.

We waited for what felt like an hour. The sun had finally set in the west, leaving the sky painted with patches of orange and red. It looked like the sky was on fire. It was at that time that we heard the rumbling of an engine from up the road.

My whole body was tense in anticipation of being reunited with my friends, and it felt like an eternity passed before I finally saw the pair of headlights appear from around a corner up ahead. I exhaled and suddenly felt lightheaded, not realizing I'd been holding my breath. "They're here," I whispered. "That's them, right?"

"It is indeed," Lee answered.

It took every ounce of self-restraint to not go running down the road to greet them. A sudden thought crossed my mind, that Miriam would still be mad at me and Jeff would still be practically catatonic. I realized that I didn't care. As long as they were safe, I didn't care about any of that. I would even be glad to see Vincent. But as the dark blue Trail Blazer SUV pulled up beside us, I knew there was something wrong. Jeff was driving, a troubled look on his face, and Vincent was in the passenger seat. I didn't see Miriam.

I pulled Vincent's door open for him. "Where's Miriam?"

"Back seat," was all he said.

I almost wrenched the door off to get to her. She was laying on her side, her skin paler than I ever thought possible. She shivered so hard that she looked like she was having convulsions. Her eyes were squeezed shut and her lips were purple. Her arms were wrapped around her, and I saw that her stomach was round, much rounder than expected at three months. I remembered that the incubation period for a Colician pregnancy is only three months. Maybe Caiten pregnancies would be faster than humans' as well.

"Miriam," I sighed, gently pulling her out of the car and setting her on the ground. "How long has she been like this?"

"About a week," Vincent said, for once not directing hate at me. "Nobody knows what it is. All the Colicians had to leave two weeks ago, and we haven't had contact with them since. We've only had access to human doctors, and they don't know what to do with her. They tried giving her different drugs, but nothing's worked. She gets worse every day."

She rested against me and shivered. Her teeth began to chatter, and a soft moan escaped her lips. I stroked her hair and whispered her name in an attempt to rouse her, but she didn't respond in any way. She wasn't unconscious, but she wasn't conscious either.

"I don't suppose you have any idea what to do," Jeff said, crossing his arms and looking down on us.

I suddenly remembered the vials that the Colician in the souvenir shop had put in my shopping bag. He must have been sent to meet me and give me the vials. At the time, I hadn't a clue what they could do for Miriam, but I did now. "I have something that I think will help her," I replied, waiting for Vincent to take my place with Miriam so I could run back to the pickup and get my bag.

Vincent and Jeff were silent at first, but then Jeff burst out, "Out of all of us, how is it that *you* know what to do?"

Any other time I would have defended myself with vulgar language and facts about my grades, but I couldn't care less about insults right now. "A Colician gave two vials of liquid to me yesterday, with a note saying they were for Miriam. I didn't know what they were for at first, but they must be to help her." I grabbed the bag out of the truck, Jaeger and Kyla still snoozing away, and ran back. I took out the pair of shorts the vials were wrapped in, and paused when I realized the shorts were wet. "No," I whispered, and carefully unrolled them. One vial was completely smashed, the medicine all soaked into my shorts. The other was cracked, but not enough to allow the medicine to leak out. "Shit." This must have happened when Danny was speeding through D.C.

"They're both broken?" Vincent asked, the fear in his voice exponential.

"Just one." I picked up the note, which was wet and withered, and read it a few times. I thought about giving four drops of the one remaining vial of medicine to her, but I didn't know what it was and didn't want to poison her. I could only hope the one vial would make her at least half better. I wished Kost was here; he would know what to do. "Can you open her mouth, Vincent?"

He did, and I squeezed two drops of the medicine into Miriam's mouth. "Now what?" he asked nervously.

I shrugged. "We wait, I guess."

"That's it?" Vincent demanded. "What did the Colician tell you?"

"He didn't tell me anything. He gave me the vials and a note. That's it."

"Why didn't he just come by the house and give it to the doctors there?"

"I don't know, Vincent. I've told you everything that I do know."

Vincent muttered several obscenities and stood up, pacing around anxiously.

"So what do we do now?" Jeff asked. He looked over at Lee, who was watching the scene silently. "Is that him?"

"That's Lee Stewart," I said. "He's the one who led you here. He's also the guy I've been seeing everywhere."

"What guy? You've been seeing him?"

I realized I hadn't told anyone about Gorilla Man. "I never told you because I thought you'd think I was crazy, but I found him in D.C. and he saved my life. He's a Caiten, too."

"He's one of us?" Jeff looked at him in astonishment.

"Yeah." I waved Lee over. He did his wrist thing and turned away, walking back toward the truck. I looked back to Jeff helplessly and shrugged. "He's a little…I don't even know a word that describes him."

"I just assumed he was a Colician while I was communicating with him," Jeff said, the look of wonder still on his face. "I didn't realize he was one of us." He sighed. "So Hillerman's made more Caitens? How many has he made since us?"

"Actually," I said, "Lee was made before us."

Jeff only stared at me, his mouth half open.

"Do you remember the New Age ship, *Majesty*?" I asked. "In 2019 the whole construction crew at the scene was declared dead one day due to a serious gas leak. Did you hear about that?"

"It sounds familiar," Jeff replied. "Weren't there, like, over two hundred people killed?"

"Yeah," I said. "Only they didn't die from a gas leak. Jaeger and his men abducted all of them and took them to Hillerman's lab. He infected them all with the Caiten Virus, but the original strain killed anyone who didn't have A negative blood. Sixty-three of them lived, and Lee was one of them."

Jeff sputtered for a minute. "How did he get out?"

"Same way we did."

Shaking his head, Jeff said, "This is way too confusing. Can you just…?" He held out his hand to mine. I knew what he was implying, so I took it.

"My ability hasn't been working for a bit," I told him. "You're going to have to do all the work."

Once Jeff was finished looking at my thoughts to understand Lee's story and its connection to ours, he whistled. "Holy crap. Hillerman's a Caiten. How about that?"

"It's insane," I agreed. "This conspiracy is just as big as the one that led to the Colician outbreak."

"What the hell are we gonna do?"

I shrugged. "Lee's taking us to Miami, where the other sixty-two Caitens are."

"What are they doing in Miami?"

"Lee said they were building something there, but he didn't say what. It seems they're building another cruise ship, but...that just doesn't make any sense."

Jeff nodded and scratched his chin. "So after we connect with the other sixty-two Caitens...then what?"

I opened my mouth to answer, but then realized that I had no idea what we were supposed to do after that. "I don't know," I said. "I guess I hadn't thought that far ahead."

"What about him?" Jeff asked, nodding to Lee. "Does he know what we're gonna do?"

"If he does," I replied, "he hasn't said so." We stood in silence for a little while before I dared ask him, "So, the attack at the safe house...is Amelia...?"

"She wasn't there," Jeff said dismissively. "So unless something else happened, she should be fine."

"I'm sorry," I said.

"For what?"

"For what happened to your wife."

Jeff shook his head and snorted. "She's not my wife," he said. "She's with someone else now. She's someone else's family. My own daughter calls someone else Daddy."

I wanted to say more, but thought better of it. "How many people died?" I asked.

"I don't know," Jeff muttered. "I didn't stick around to count bodies. Didn't you ask Danny?"

"Yeah, but he wasn't in the mood to talk about it." I winced. "Reis was the rat. He sold us out and then Danny killed him."

"Yikes," Jeff said.

"Guys!" Vincent called. "She's waking up!"

Jeff and I rushed over; I knelt beside Miriam and took her from Vincent. "Miriam?" I said as her eyes opened a little. Her lips were no longer purple, and her discomfort seemed to be mostly gone. She still shivered, but nowhere near as violently as before. "Hey, baby." I kissed her on the forehead. "I'm so glad you and the baby are okay. I was so worried about you."

"You're okay," she breathed, so soft I almost didn't catch it. "I thought you were dead."

"I'm okay," I whispered, kissing her lips this time. "We're all okay."

"Austin." Vincent tapped me on the shoulder and nodded toward Danny's pickup.

I looked over. Danny and Lee were leaning against it, and Jaeger was poking his head out of the bed to observe the scene.

Jaeger…shit.

"Yeah," I said slowly. "About him…"

~~*

Well, after the conversation that followed, Vincent finally reestablished his hatefulness toward me. He wanted to kill Jaeger, and I didn't blame him, given what had happened to his family. Miriam didn't have much to say about it, but she was still groggy and weak. Jeff was silent for most of the argument, pondering over what to do. In the end, Vincent and I decided to let Jeff make the final decision about what to do with Jaeger. After careful consideration, he decided to let Jaeger come with us. I was glad for it. Even after what Jaeger had done to us, I couldn't stand the thought of leaving one of our own behind. Plus, if it turned out he really was on our side, we had him as an advantage. As long as we kept a careful watch over him, we should be safe.

We were all exhausted, but Lee insisted on going all the way to Miami before we stopped to rest. Most of us were tentative, but we eventually agreed it was the safest choice. Who knew what we could run into here? This was Florida, the state that declared war on another. It was a place of anarchy and death.

At least, that was what the media had led us all to believe.

Lee, Danny, and Jaeger stayed in the pickup while I joined the others in the car. Vincent was so angry with me that he didn't even want to be in the same vehicle with me, but he absolutely refused to ride with

Jaeger, so he had to just deal with me. There was no way I was about to separate myself from Miriam again. I held her in my arms as we followed the pickup, kissing her forehead and placing my hand on her belly. I didn't care if Miriam was still angry with me; I was never leaving her or our baby ever again. I loved them both too much.

"I was so worried about you," I told her again, giving her a light squeeze. "I don't know what I would do if I lost you."

"I didn't know you'd left the house," Miriam whispered, and a moment later a few wet drops landed on my hand. She was crying. "When we left and you weren't with us, I thought..."

"It's okay," I said. "I'm here. I'm okay. I'm not going anywhere."

"I thought you were gone," Miriam squeaked, and choked back a sob.

I became mildly self-conscious that Jeff and Vincent could hear our conversation, but there were things we both needed to say that couldn't wait for a private moment. "I'm not gone. I'm right here."

"I'm so sorry."

"For what?"

"For pushing you away." She buried her face in my chest. "I didn't mean all those things I said. I was just so scared for us and this baby, I didn't know what to do! I just got so scared that I lashed out at you. I pushed you away. But I don't want you to stay away anymore. I want you with me. With us."

"I'm not going anywhere," I promised her again. I suddenly remembered what else I had purchased along with the shorts at the gift shop. I picked up the bag and pulled out the container of cupcakes. "I got these for you. Something told me you might want them."

Miriam's eyes widened at the sight of them. "Red velvet? Those are my favorite! I've been craving them like crazy since I got pregnant." She smiled at me. "I guess we have more of a connection than we thought."

"I guess so."

We were quiet for a while, and Vincent started fiddling with the radio to find a decent station. He eventually found a station with some contemporary music. He kept the volume low, but it was comforting all the same. It gave me a sense of normalcy. We'd driven for a little over an hour when Vincent started nodding off, and eventually began to snore softly.

"He doesn't hate you, you know," Miriam finally said.

"Who?" I asked. "Your brother? Of course he does."

"He doesn't. He's just protective. He knows how much you care about me, and he respects that."

"If he doesn't hate me, then why does he act like he does?"

Miriam shrugged. "It's the way he is, I guess. He was never one to create close bonds with other people. Give him some time, and you'll see. He may even open up to you a little."

I wasn't about to hold my breath waiting for that. "Okay," I said, unsure of what else to say.

Miriam was silent again, but the silence didn't last for long. "I like the name you picked out."

"The name?"

"For the baby. James Alexander. It's a good name."

I smiled. "I didn't know you knew I was thinking of names."

"I do. And I like that name. I think it should be his name." She rubbed her hand over the bump on her belly.

"But we don't even know if it's a boy yet."

"It's a boy," Miriam replied, sounding quite sure of herself. "Trust me; I know."

I put my hand over hers and smiled. "Well, I'm glad you like that name." I looked down at her baby-bump. "Do you know how long the pregnancy will be?"

She shook her head. "It's faster than a human pregnancy, but longer than a Colician's. I'm thinking it will take somewhere between five and seven months, but I can't know for sure. None of the doctors who saw me could make an accurate prediction with the equipment they had."

The spike of fear that had hit me so many times was shooting through me yet again. Miriam was sick because of the pregnancy, and we didn't even know how long it was supposed to last. I didn't know if James would kill Miriam, or if they would both die. The lack of knowledge about our new species was freaking me out.

"It'll be okay," she whispered. "We just have to stick this out, and everything—"

The end of her sentence was cut off as a horn blared in front of us and Jeff swerved back into the right lane. I hadn't noticed until now, but he had been drifting onto the other side of the road.

"Hey, man. You okay?" I asked, putting my hand on his shoulder. "Jesus, Jeff. You're soaking wet! You need a break, dude. Pull over."

"Yeah," Jeff muttered, slowly pulling off onto the shoulder. "I'm not feeling too good."

When the car jerked to a stop, I climbed out and went to Jeff's door. When I opened it, I saw blood gushing out of his nose and down his face, and his eyes were rolled back. He twitched every few seconds, and I recognized this scene. I'd seen it once before.

"Jeff!" I cried, shaking him. "Vincent! Wake up! Help me!"

Vincent jerked awake, looking around in confusion. When his eyes landed on Jeff, they widened and he bolted out of the car to assist. "What happened?" he asked.

"I don't know," I replied, unbuckling Jeff's belt and gently pulling him out of the car. "He wasn't feeling good so he pulled over! This is what happened to Kost! This can't happen again..."

"Keep it together, man," Vincent said as he helped me lower Jeff to the ground.

I looked south, the direction we were traveling. I expected Lee, Danny, and Jaeger to be long gone, having left us behind, but up ahead, about one hundred yards, the pickup had come to a stop on the shoulder and was now reversing toward us.

"What do we do?" I asked Vincent, mortified at the thought of losing another friend.

"Just stay calm," Vincent said, but he seemed scared too. "Tell Danny what's happening."

"I already did," Miriam called from inside.

"Okay." He looked back to me. "Help me get him in the back. I'll drive."

"Are we just gonna keep going?" I asked in disbelief.

"What else are we supposed to do? We have to get him to Miami. Maybe the others know what to do about this. They may be the only ones on this planet who have seen this before."

While Vincent followed Danny at an average speed of eighty miles per hour (a speed I didn't know Danny's heap was capable of reaching), Miriam stayed in back with Jeff. I looked back nervously every few seconds, waiting for another seizure or more blood to come gushing out of his nose. I now had two close friends who were very ill. At the moment I really felt like the world was seeing how quickly I would break. A person couldn't be pushed this much and stay sane. If I lost Miriam and Jeff, I would lose everything.

"Do you know how much farther we need to go?" I asked after about two hours.

"I don't know," Vincent replied grimly.

"At the rate we're going, we should get to Miami in a little over an hour," Miriam said, and then she coughed.

It was only a cough, but it still made me turn around. Once again, I saw something I didn't want to see. "Jesus, Miriam." Her skin was turning a grotesque yellow color, as were the whites of her eyes. This was also something I'd seen before. "Drive faster!" I shouted at Vincent. "Go!"

"Stop yelling at—!" Vincent's shout was cut off by a huge explosion that rocked the vehicle and sent it careening off the road. "Shit!" Vincent cried, a moment before we side-swiped Danny's truck, which had also veered off the road. The force of the impact caused our vehicle to flip, finally coming to rest against a line of trees.

I hit my head at some point during the accident, so my thoughts were pretty foggy. I could tell I was hanging upside down, and I could feel something wet running into my eyes. More explosions were occurring back on the highway; the blasts weren't hitting us, but I could still feel the heat. The car was silent. I couldn't hear anyone move or speak or even groan. I feared the worst, but there wasn't anything I could do. I could feel myself dying as it registered that Miriam, Jeff, and Vincent were probably all dead.

I heard my door open, and the brightness of day shone down on me. How does the sun keep shining when things like this happen? Somebody pulled me out of the car, speaking soothing words to me. Some of the words eventually became distinct enough for me to understand.

"It's okay, Austin. You're all going to be okay. Everything's fine."

"Walter?" I tried to say, but there was blood in my mouth and it came out all garbled.

"Don't try to talk," Walter told me, taking my hand. "You're hurt really bad, but you'll be okay."

"Did you do this?" I asked, but I didn't hear his answer. I blacked out and didn't wake up for a long time.

14

Parallel Earth

Everything after that happened in a blur. I drifted in and out of consciousness for a long time, only receiving snippets of images and sounds to give any clues as to what was going on. The first several times I came around I was on a gurney in an ambulance. I could tell we were moving very fast. Vincent was on a gurney beside me, covered in blood. A section of his femur was jutting out of his thigh, and his face looked like he'd been mauled by a rabid dog. A man in a white jacket was sticking an IV into his arm, and it took me a moment to realize that man was Dr. Shawn Perry. A woman took my chin in her hand and repositioned my head so I was looking toward the ceiling. She had long black hair, sunglasses over her eyes and earplugs in her ears. She appeared to be peering into my eyes. She said something to me, but I couldn't hear her.

The next few times I woke up, we were outside. I was still on the gurney and was being carried across a small stretch of blacktop. I couldn't see anyone around me because the sun was so bright, brighter than it should be. And suddenly the brightness was gone. We were inside. Where, I couldn't say, but I did see a crucifix hanging on one wall. As we moved further inside, I could see a blue light illuminating the walls, the source somewhere ahead. It emitted a low pulse that I could feel in my eardrums and my bones. The light became brighter and brighter, until I couldn't bear to keep my eyes open any longer. That was the last thing I remembered from that day.

~~*

I didn't know what time it was, or even what day it was. In fact, all I did know was that my head hurt like someone had taken a tire iron to it, and the bright lights over me weren't helping whatsoever. With a groan that made me realize just how thirsty I was, I forced my eyes open a crack and gazed around. It took a moment for things to come into focus, and even when they did there wasn't much to see. The room was pretty plain; a boring peach paint covering all the walls and a ceiling with long florescent bulbs. The only thing in the room besides my bed and the medical equipment was a television.

My bed was halfway reclined so I was sort of sitting up, but I wanted to sit on the side of the bed so I could try to stand. Unfortunately, the straps around my wrists prevented me from doing so. "Seriously?" I said, flopping back down. I had a moment of fear, when I thought I was back at the study with Hillerman, but I didn't truly believe that. Despite the restraints, I felt that I was safe. I pulled at the straps for a bit, but I gave up quickly, too tired to exert much effort.

Something off to my left made a buzzing sound. I looked up and saw a camera installed in the wall turning to focus on me. I stared back at it and called, "Room Service!"

The television suddenly turned on. Startled, I watched the final moments of Jeopardy. Some dude won several thousand bucks, and for the first time I didn't feel envious of someone with more money than me. There was more to my life now than just making a living.

A door opened to my right, a door that I hadn't even noticed. The woman from the ambulance, the one with the sunglasses and earplugs, came in with a glass of water and a bowl of something mushy. It looked like applesauce, a luxury I hadn't had in years.

"Hi," she said, stopping just inside the door.

"Hi," I replied.

"My name's Erica. I'm a nurse practitioner here."

"And where is here?" I asked.

Erica set the glass and bowl on the table beside me. "You're on the Parallel Earth."

I raised my eyebrows. "Yeah, no shit."

"We're in Reifert City General Hospital. Dr. Perry's been taking care of you since the accident."

"Reifert City?" I repeated.

"That's what we named our capital city," Erica explained.

"Who named it?" I asked, starting to think that maybe Walter was a bit of a narcissist.

"The people," Erica said. "Not Walter. It was put to vote on what the capital city should be named, and Reifert City was an almost unanimous vote."

"Huh," I said. "So how long have I been here?"

"Six days. You sustained serious trauma to your head and chest, and—"

"What about the others?" I asked. "Miriam, Jeff, Vincent? And what about the guys in the other vehicle? What happened to them?"

"Everyone's fine," Erica promised me, but I sensed the lie in her voice. "Some are still recovering, but everyone will be okay."

"What's up with the restraints?" I pulled at them. "I thought we were friends?"

Erica shifted uncomfortably. "I know it looks bad, but it's just so you wouldn't hurt yourself if you woke up and panicked."

I could tell she was still lying. "Well, I'm perfectly calm. So you can take them off now, right?"

Erica didn't answer.

"Yeah," I said. "Didn't think so."

"Listen, Austin—"

"No, you listen. I want to talk to Walter. Hear me? You bring him here and you bring him here now. I'm not talking to anyone else until I talk to him."

Erica stared at me for a moment, maybe thinking I would change my mind and apologize, but then she turned and left without a word.

I felt a little bad, thinking that I was a bit too harsh, but I was tied to a bed and was being lied to. If Erica wasn't going to tell me what was going on, then I didn't have to be polite.

It didn't take long for Walter to arrive. I thought that maybe they'd just leave me for a while, like Hillerman did at the lab after I pissed him off, but then I reminded myself that these guys weren't human; they were better than that.

"Hello, Austin," Walter greeted, bringing a chair in with him.

"Reifert City, eh?" I said as he came to sit by my side. "You must be so proud of yourself, to have your capital city named after you... You're right in the history books with Washington and Lincoln."

"What's with the hostility, Austin?" Walter asked me, peering down at me with his fine green eyes.

"What's with the straps?" I shot back.

"They're for your protection," he replied.

"Bullshit," I snapped.

"Why are you so angry, Austin?" Walter asked me. "You know we only have your best interest at heart."

"Then why do you keep lying to me?" I demanded, but then my stomach plummeted in realization. "Oh my God. Is Miriam...?"

"She's fine," Walter said, but he turned away and shook his head.

I wanted to strangle him. Before speaking, I managed to get myself under control. "Walter, I know you're trying to help me, but I can't lay here wondering what happened to her and my baby. *Please*. Tell me what's going on."

Walter looked back at me, the stress and fear in his eyes mirroring my own. "It's not just about her, Austin. It's about you, too."

"Me?" I repeated.

Nodding, Walter added, "And Jeff. You're dying. All of you."

It took more than a moment for it all to sink in. "*Dying*? What do you mean, *dying*?"

"I mean exactly what I said. The three of you are dying."

I was flabbergasted. "But why?"

Sighing, Walter said, "It's different for each of you, but it all springs from the same source: the virus. This particular variation isn't working too well."

"And Jaeger...?"

"He's fine. He was given a newer variation that works just fine."

I nodded slowly, trying to comprehend it all. "So with us..."

"Jeff is suffering from the same thing as your friend Kost. It's causing liver failure and internal hemorrhaging, which is why there was so much blood with Kost. Jeff's going to be the first to go. Miriam...well, it's the pregnancy that's killing her. She needs so many supplementary nutrients to sustain the child. The baby is literally sucking all the juice out of her. And you..." Walter shook his head.

"What?" I asked. "Don't flake out on me now! You already told me that I'm dying, so you'd better tell me why!"

"The virus is using up the calcium supply in your body. It's tearing apart your bones to get enough."

"But I feel fine," I protested.

"Try moving your legs," Walter said.

I did, and found that I couldn't. I couldn't even feel them, and I hadn't even noticed until now.

"Your legs have suffered most of the damage. If you put any weight on them, they'll break. That's why we put the restraints on, so you wouldn't try to get up."

"Is there any way we'll survive this?" I asked, but I wasn't getting my hopes up.

Walter hesitated. "You don't want me to lie to you, so I won't. There is a chance, but right now it's not looking good. In your case, the odds are in your favor. Dr. Perry thinks he'll be able to come up with something to save you. As for the others, he's still working on it."

Wow. Yet again, I was about to lose my family to a manmade virus. If I got out of here, I would find Hillerman and kill him. Slowly. I snickered.

"What?" Walter asked.

"It's just ironic," I said. "This is the second time one of these viruses is going to take everyone from me." I shook my head. "Whatever force runs this world hates me."

"It'll be okay," Walter promised me.

"What do you know?" I snapped. "You've got your girl and your kid and everything's just fine and dandy for you!"

"You're not the only one who's lost his family," Walter snapped.

"What are you talking about?"

He let out a bitter laugh. "I suppose you wouldn't know, would you? The press only made me into the bad guy. You never knew that I was a victim."

"What happened to you?"

"I lived in Hatfield, Austin. I lived there when the Colician Virus hit. My family and I were taken to the lab a week after. You remember that day, don't you?"

I nodded. "It was all over the news."

"I was there," Walter said. "And my father and three brothers were all murdered that night, trying to protect me. Do you know what's worse than that? I don't know if you have the same connections to the people you care about, but when each of them died I could feel it. It was like a light went off in my soul. You can't begin to imagine what that feels like. So don't you dare tell me that I don't know what it's like to lose someone."

The guilt in my chest was making it hard to breathe. I wanted to apologize, but instead I blurted out, "What about your mom?"

"She died in a car crash when I was six," Walter muttered, looking toward the wall. It was then that I realized he was holding back tears. His words were sticking in his throat and the rims of his eyes were red and wet.

Personally, I could do plenty of it, but I hated seeing other people cry. "Hey," I said, trying to be playful. "You're the president, or whatever. I thought you're supposed to be all tough and whatnot?"

"I was brought into this position at eighteen," Walter said. "I was still a kid. Sometimes I still feel that way." He got up and turned to leave.

"Where are you going?" I asked.

"I have a species to rule over," he reminded me, forcing a small smile. "Dr. Perry will be in soon to let you know how your chances are looking."

~~*

The next few hours were difficult. I was anxious for my friends and for myself, and I desperately wanted to get up and walk around to let off some of the tension. Being unable to burn off my pent-up energy and frustration was one of the worst things for me right now.

At one point, about thirty minutes before Dr. Perry came to see me, I became so wound up that I almost vomited. I leaned my head over the side of the bed as I tasted bile, but after a few deep breaths the feeling subsided.

After that, I tried some meditation to calm myself down. I didn't really know the proper way to meditate, but deep breathing and happy thoughts seemed to be the key. Thoughts about Miriam and our baby, happy, healthy, and smiling beside me. Just the thought of that made me smile and lowered my heart rate. I'd finally gotten myself into a calmed state when the door opened and my heart started racing all over again. Great timing, Dr. Perry. Great timing.

"Hey, Austin." He was backing in, pulling in a large, strange looking machine on wheels. "Erica told me you weren't in the greatest mood when she came in earlier."

"Yeah," I said, clearing my throat awkwardly. "Can you tell her I'm sorry about that?"

"You can tell her yourself," he replied. Erica was on the other end of the machine, helping Dr. Perry bring it in. The sunglasses and earplugs were still there.

"Oh." Talk about awkward. "Listen, Erica. I'm sorry if I...well, *that* I was rude earlier. You didn't deserve it."

Erica smiled in return. "It's okay. I understand."

"I hope this isn't rude," I started, "but how can you hear me with those in?" I pointed to the earplugs.

"These?" She laughed lightly. "I have extremely heightened senses. If I don't wear these, I could go deaf. I need these glasses all the time, too."

I looked at the machine. "So, uh…what's this for?"

"It's got a long, boring name," Dr. Perry said. "But what it does is model an image of your bones and allows us to predict the results of several possible solutions we've got without actually testing them on you."

"So you can fix my legs?" I asked hopefully.

There was a large hole in the machine, where my legs would be going. I watched as Dr. Perry gently lifted my legs and positioned the machine around me. "Don't get your hopes up. We think we've found a calcium supplement that, if you take it for the rest of your life, will heal the damage done to your bones and keep you healthy. But we don't know for sure if it will work; that's why we brought the machine in."

"I hope you're as smart as they all say," I muttered.

He chuckled in return, but said nothing.

"Hold on a second," I said, staring at Dr. Perry suspiciously. "I thought you had regenerative blood? Why can't you just inject me with some of that? Or was that just another untrue story?"

"We already tried that," Dr. Perry explained. "It healed the wounds you sustained during the accident, but the virus continues to eat away at your bones. We need to come up with a solution to counteract the effects of the virus, and my blood doesn't do so."

For about twenty minutes he and Erica took a look at my bones, testing five possible solutions on the holographic display that popped up in front of my face. With each test, my heart slowly sank deeper. By the time the fifth test came around, I knew what the results would be.

"Negative," Erica muttered, for the fifth and final time.

There was a moment's silence so intense that I could hear everyone's breathing.

"So that's it," I said, resigning myself to the fact that I would be in this bed until every last bone in my body turned to mush.

A pause, and then Dr. Perry confirmed it for me. "Yeah. That's it." He stood staring at the hologram for a minute, and then a strange look suddenly crossed his face. He went back to the keypad where he and Erica had been punching in data, and began adding more.

"What are you doing?" Erica asked, leaning over his shoulder to watch.

"I just had an idea," he replied, his face scrunched up in concentration.

"Dr. Perry," I said. "Just forget it. It's over. I'm done."

He ignored me. They both did. Dr. Perry was punching in data while muttering information to Erica. Erica nodded periodically and after a minute her eyes widened and she started pointing to something on the screen, saying, "Yes! Yes! Try that! Right there!"

I looked up at the holographic diagram to try to see what they were doing. As I watched, my bones, which looked like splintering wood, suddenly reformed. I wasn't a doctor, but they looked strong and healthy.

"That's it," Dr. Perry said, beaming ear to ear. He looked down at me. "This solution will work. You're going to be okay."

I couldn't help but laugh. I was so relieved. "What did you do?" I asked. "What did you add in?"

"Your baby," Dr. Perry said. "Your son is going to save your life."

~~*

So my unborn baby was going to save my life. Dr. Perry had examined the development of James, and the way he grew was different from both humans and Colicians. His stem cells were causing his bones to become stronger than normal. He was literally unbreakable. And because of the way his bones were forming, Dr. Perry factored James's cells into his third equation and the results came back positive. The only reason it would work was because James had my genes. If he was someone else's child, it wouldn't have worked.

Dr. Perry started my treatments immediately. The injections were extremely painful, but I stuck it out and after a few days I could finally move my legs again.

The two weeks following Dr. Perry's discovery were rather dull. Dr. Perry insisted that I sleep a lot because of the healing process I was going through, but truth be told I wasn't all that tired. I asked him if I could see any of my friends, but he said for the time being he'd rather I didn't. Besides, Miriam and Jeff were the ones I really wanted to see, and he specifically said I couldn't see them while they were ill.

Finally, after two weeks of seeing no one but Dr. Perry, Erica, and Walter, I got a surprise visit.

"Well, well," I said, grinning as Vincent walked in. "Look who no longer has a bone poking out of his leg."

"I'm so glad I wasn't awake for any of that," Vincent muttered, plopping down in the chair by my bed.

"How is it that you look as if nothing ever happened?"

"Dr. Perry's regenerative blood works wonders." Vincent ran a hand down his cleanly shaven face. "I was told I was quite a mess."

"Yeah," I said. "You have no idea. Have you seen Miriam and Jeff? Do you know how they're doing?"

Vincent shook his head and his expression turned somber. He averted his eyes from mine.

"What's up, man?" I asked him.

He shrugged. "I'm just worried about my sister, I guess. She *is* the last person I have in the world."

I nodded. "I'm worried about her, too. But Dr. Perry found a cure for my condition when my odds were slim; I think he'll find a way to save her. And Jeff. We shouldn't be too worried."

"Listen, Austin." Vincent shifted uncomfortably in his chair. "I'm sorry for treating you like the enemy all this time. I'm just really protective of—"

"You don't have to explain yourself, Vincent," I said. "I was just as protective of my little sister."

Vincent's brow furrowed. "You have a sister?"

"*Had*," I emphasized. "Haven't seen her in three years. Don't even know if she's alive."

"Oh," Vincent muttered. "Regardless, I just want to apologize for being such a prick. You and Miriam are having a child together, so I have to start acting like we're family. She loves you, and I want us to be friends." He held out his hand.

I shook it and smiled. "Of course."

"How are your legs feeling?" Vincent asked.

"They're all right," I said. "Dr. Perry says I can't walk for at least another week, and even then I have to be very careful. He says in two to three weeks I should be just fine. My bones will be even stronger than before."

"Yeah." Wariness was the best word to describe his expression. "So your mutant baby saved your life, huh?"

"Hey now," I said, prepared to defend my son.

"I'm just kidding," Vincent replied, grinning. "He's my nephew. I'll love him no matter how weird he is."

I laughed.

"Do you know what the deal is with him?" Vincent asked. "I know right now he's killing Miriam, but if Dr. Perry comes up with something to save her, will the baby be okay?"

"I don't know. I was hoping you had news for me."

"I guess we're both in the dark."

Vincent stayed for a while longer. Before he left, I asked, "Where are you staying? I know Colicians don't particularly like humans, so where does Walter have you living for now?"

"I'm staying with Lee and Danny in a suite on the top floor. They're normally for nurses and doctors who work around the clock during emergencies, but Dr. Perry's letting us stay there for now. He says that's the safest place for us."

"And what about Jaeger?" I asked. "Where's he?"

Vincent's jaw tensed, and the anger on his face scared me.

"Dude," I said. "I know you hate him, but he's one of us now—"

"You're seriously defending him after—" Vincent stopped, his anger suddenly turning to confusion. "Oh my God. You don't know what he did, do you?"

"What are you talking about?"

"Jaeger manipulated us. He's the reason we were attacked on the highway. He fooled us into believing he was a changed man, and then he told his people where to strike. It was the plan all along. After the attack on the house in D.C. failed, Hillerman knew you would take pity on one of your own, even if it was someone we didn't particularly like. Jaeger was sent to find us on the highway, trick us, and then get us killed. Oh, and his dog? She was his attack dog. He was keeping her under control, and when Lee ran to help us after the car flipped, Jaeger set her loose and she almost killed him."

I was utterly astounded. How could I have been so stupid, offering him another chance? I'd wanted so badly to believe him! "I can't believe I was so stupid," I said, hating myself.

"Don't worry about it," Vincent said. "He fooled Miriam, too."

"God damn it!" I shouted. "I feel like the stupidest imbecile on the face of the planet!"

"Chill," Vincent said firmly. "It's not your fault. If he could fool Miriam, there's no way any of you could have known. You know how strong Miriam's ability is."

"Yeah," I muttered. "But I still feel like an idiot. I was the one trying to convince you all to give him a chance. He must be back at the study, laughing his ass off with Diereks..." I wanted to punch something.

"Well, he didn't kill any of us, so I guess we're lucky."

I suddenly realized something that could jeopardize the Miami Caitens. "Oh crap," I said.

"What?"

"We told Jaeger where we were going. We told him about Lee." I looked at him in horror. "If he knew about Lee, then he knows about the others. He knows about Miami."

~~*

I told Dr. Perry and Walter that I needed to go to Miami. Of course, they refused, but I still put up a pretty good fight. I didn't know how I forgot to mention Miami, but thankfully Lee told them right away the first day. A group of Colicians was already in Miami looking for the first Caitens.

"What then?" I asked. "What happens when you find them?"

"I don't know," Walter said. "We're taking this one step at a time."

The following week was as dull as the last. I received daily visits from Vincent, Lee, and Danny, but other than that nothing really happened. Dr. Perry was still refusing my requests to visit Miriam and Jeff. The day I was allowed to walk for the first time, matters took a frightening turn.

"Now, just ease up," Dr. Perry told me for the fourth time. "If you feel any pain, any at all, just sit back down."

I was sitting on the edge of my bed with my legs slung over the side, surrounded by Dr. Perry, Walter, Vincent, and Lee. I was overwhelmed with excitement and nervousness. Slowly, I set my feet on the floor and started to stand, bracing myself on the bed in case my legs gave out. My knees were shaky after being unused for so long, but they seemed like they would hold. I managed to stand fully upright without experiencing any pain. I grinned boldly.

"There he is," Vincent said, grinning as well.

"How does it feel?" Dr. Perry asked, reaching a hand toward me as I teetered a little.

"Fine. I'm fine." I swatted his hand away and took a careful step forward.

"Wait a minute now." Dr. Perry brought me the walker he wanted me to use the first few days. My pride wouldn't allow that, and when I thought about it I really felt that I didn't need it.

"Just give me a minute," I said, taking a few more steps on my own.

"I really think you should—" Dr. Perry started, but Walter cut him off.

"I think he's okay," he said.

Dr. Perry allowed me to walk around on my own for a few minutes, and then he insisted that I lay back down.

"Please," I begged. "I've been stuck in that bed for three weeks. Just a few more minutes."

Sighing impatiently, Dr. Perry gestured for me to step out into the hall. It was the first time out of my room.

The hall looked like any other hall in a hospital. It was white, clean, bright, and had several nurses and doctors bustling about. The wall opposite of my room was composed of floor-to-ceiling windows, allowing an amazing view of the city. Because of my species and condition, I was near the top floor, where other serious or puzzling illnesses were dealt with.

I walked over to the window to look out over the Parallel Earth for the first time. The view was incredible. I could see for miles. Many buildings were still under construction, but the ones that were finished were remarkable. The structures were so unique, so different from anything on Earth that it took my breath away. And the city was clean! No trash or litter of any sort on the streets, no smoke or other pollutants poisoning the air. When I looked down I noticed that there were close to no cars in the street. Crowds surged below, an occasional emergency vehicle picking its way through them.

"We only use vehicles for emergencies or for traveling long distances," Walter said, stepping up beside me. He must have heard my surprised thoughts. "We walk, bike, use horses, or, if necessary, teleport."

"Wow," I said. "It's impressive, Walter. Good work."

"Thanks."

As I watched the busy city, marveling at it's excellence, it's peacefulness, I suddenly laughed at myself.

"What?" Walter asked.

"It's just funny," I said. "I was always so worried about my family, imagining all the horrible things that were happening here. I had this dream back at the study that your whole world was on fire, and everyone was dead. It's just funny looking back at it now, after seeing that it's exactly the opposite of what I imagined."

Walter shrugged. "No one really knew how we were doing on the other side. You probably weren't the only person thinking our world was in ruins."

I looked past the city, at the mountains in the distance. Their snow-capped summits were partially obscured by low clouds, but it was still a beautiful sight to behold.

A commotion to my left attracted my attention. Nurses and doctors were running past us, worried looks on their faces.

"What's going on?" I asked.

"I don't know," Walter replied. "Doesn't seem—"

I didn't hear the rest of what he said. My whole body went rigid and everything went white for an instant. An image of a baby crying came to me, and a moment later I could hear its screams in my mind. I stared at the baby, knowing that it wasn't just any baby. It was James.

Something was terribly wrong.

My vision suddenly returned. Walter was holding my arm, staring at me. Dr. Perry, Vincent, and Lee were all gone.

"Are you okay?" Walter asked me.

"My baby's here," I said, and started running in the same direction as the doctors and nurses.

"Austin, wait!" Walter cried, following me. "You shouldn't be running!"

I ignored him. I ran until I found the room I could see in my mind, where I knew I would find Miriam and James.

I could hear my baby crying long before I reached the room. I shoved my way in once I got there, and I could have sworn my heart stopped. The first thing I saw was not James; it was Miriam, and that was probably the most horrifying sight I'd seen in my entire life. Blood was gushing from between her legs and pooling on the floor below. Blood was coming out of her nose, eyes, and ears. Her eyes were rolled back and she was convulsing violently on the bed. Her skin was this sickly gray color, the color I associated with zombies in cheap horror flicks. Her arms were bent at the elbow, and her fingers were curled up into bloody claws. The heart monitor beside her was going crazy, beating at fast, irregular rhythms and flashing a red light on the screen.

"Austin!"

Erica took my arm and dragged me out; I was too stunned to protest. "You can't be in here right now."

"What's happening to her?" I whispered. "She's dying. What's wrong with her?" I was mumbling to myself, but Erica answered me anyway.

"The baby came early. He came so fast there was no way to stop it. Miriam's body couldn't handle it, Austin."

"No." She couldn't die. She had to stay here with James and I. She couldn't leave me now. We were finally a family. This wasn't fair.

"Out of the way!" Dr. Perry cried, barging through the crowd of doctors and nurses, cradling a swaddled bundle in his arms. I couldn't see James, but I could hear him crying from inside it.

"Let me see him," I demanded, reaching for him.

"Someone get him out of here," he ordered, trying to shove past me.

"I said let me see him!" I was so scared and so angry that I did something I hadn't done in a long time; I grabbed hold of the doctor's mind and made him stop.

Dr. Perry's eyes widened, and he halted abruptly. He looked at me, and I, realizing that what I was doing was wrong, released him.

"I have to get him to an incubator, Austin," Dr. Perry told me slowly, and I saw in his eyes that he was afraid of me. "He's too little."

"Why is this happening?" I whispered, looking at the tiny, squirming bundle in his arms.

"I'll let you know as soon as it's okay to see him," Dr. Perry said, and then hurried away.

"What's wrong with him?" I yelled after him, the tears streaming down my face. I couldn't lose my son, too.

Miriam's heart monitor started shrieking a single, constant tone.

~~*

Six hours later, I was surprised that *my* heart hadn't stopped beating. My stress levels were high, and I paced back and forth outside of Miriam's room, fighting the urge to puke, and praying for a miracle. Dr. Perry had gone straight back inside after taking James to an incubator and hadn't come out as of yet, so Miriam must still be alive. Plus, if he left James then he must be all right, too. That was what gave me hope. Finally, Dr. Perry came out.

He looked exhausted. His expression was troubled, but he didn't look as if he was about to tell me that Miriam was dead.

"Well?" I asked, the suspense unbearable.

"Sit down," he said quietly, rubbing his eyes and gently pushing me toward a row of chairs. When we were both seated, he said, "She's stabilized. It took us a long time to stop the bleeding. She lost so much that she needed a transfusion. Normally, I would have given her O negative, considering it's the universal donor type, but since our DNA is so different I'm not sure how her body would have reacted to too much O negative blood. Thankfully, I had a pint each of Jeff's, Lee's, and your blood to give her."

My eyebrows went up. "You took a pint of my blood and didn't even *tell me?*"

Dr. Perry shrugged helplessly. "I was trying to figure out a way to save you! Of course I had a pint of your blood. Besides, with this new virus, the only way to predict anything is to run blood tests. I'm trying to help you and your people, Austin. You're not my lab rat."

"Look," I said, "I don't want to argue about that right now. I just want to know how Miriam and James are doing."

"That's your baby's name?" Dr. Perry asked. "James?"

"James Alexander," I replied hurriedly. "But seriously, how are they?"

"Well, the bleeding in Miriam's abdomen and brain has stopped, but as of now she's comatose. We're uncertain what caused the premature labor, but my guess is that Miriam's body knew she was dying, so it pushed James out as soon as it could without killing him, so that they would both survive."

"So James is okay?" I asked hopefully.

Dr. Perry hesitated. "Okay isn't the right word. He's alive, but he's not okay."

"What's wrong with him?" I asked, expecting the worst.

Sighing, Dr. Perry stood up. "Come with me. And don't strain yourself. You've been on your feet way too much already."

"I'm fine," I insisted, following him to an elevator. "My muscles are a little weak, but my bones feel fine."

We got in the elevator and descended a floor, and once we stopped, the elevator began moving *sideways*.

"Your elevators move *sideways*?" I asked.

"The hospital's big," Dr. Perry said. "The NICU is a long way from where we just were."

"How far?" I asked as we halted and then descended two more floors.

"*Far.*" Dr. Perry added extra emphasis to the word.

When we finally stopped, we walked down several hallways, the cries of infants ever-present. At the end of a very long hall, we entered a single room with the label NICU over it. "Why's it so small?" I asked skeptically.

"Because we never needed it until now," Dr. Perry replied.

There were three nurses and one other doctor in the large room, busying themselves with many tasks. Two nurses were futzing with tubes hooked up to a large glass incubator. I knew immediately that that was where I would find my son, where I would gaze upon him for the first time. I started to go forward, eager to see him, but Dr. Perry caught my arm.

The look on his face was...apologetic. "Just...prepare yourself," he told me.

Oh God. What could be wrong with him? I went to the tank and peered down at my firstborn for the very first time.

He was small. I saw that immediately. The nurse beside me said he was two pounds, six ounces and fourteen inches long. A tiny baby, but they said he was big enough to make it. The troubling matter took me a minute to recognize. James's skin was translucent, almost transparent. I could see the blue veins running under it, could see his heart pumping in his little chest. I could see the outlines of all his organs. The only places where his skin wasn't like this were the top of his head, his hands, and his feet. It was shocking to see this, but for some reason I wasn't worried. I wasn't even focusing on that.

James had my blue eyes. There they were, gazing up at me. He looked at me for a moment and then his face broke out into the biggest smile. He reached his little arms up toward me.

"Hey," I whispered, putting my hand to the glass beside him. He put his hand up against mine and made a funny sound in his throat. "I love you," I told him.

"Are you okay?" Dr. Perry asked me softly.

"I'm fine," I said, and found that I was crying. "He's beautiful. Do you know when his skin will get better?"

"We're running some tests on him. I'm hopeful we can figure something out to help him. He wasn't developed enough inside the womb when he was born, which is why he's like this. Thankfully his organs and bones were fully developed, so other than this, he's healthy."

"Great." I grasped Dr. Perry's hand in mine. "Thank you so much. And I'm sorry about what I did earlier. I wasn't thinking clearly."

Dr. Perry forced a smile. "It's fine," he said. "And if my theory about your boy is correct, his skin may develop fully on his own if we give him time."

"Can I hold him?"

He shook his head. "Not for a while. Not until he gets bigger and looks better. I don't want to risk an infection or another illness."

I nodded. "What about Miriam? Since James is out, she should be fine, right?"

Dr. Perry shrugged. "Right now, it's hard to say."

My stomach clenched. "She'll be fine," I told him. "She has to be."

"I'm going to run more tests and get her body pumped full of the nutrients she's lacking. After that, we'll just have to wait and see what happens." He glanced in my direction as he took a pen from a nurse. "You said his name was James, correct?"

"Yes," I said. "James Alexander."

"What last name are you giving him? Lobner or Rockwell?"

"Uh…" I shrugged. "Miriam and I hadn't talked about that."

Dr. Perry nodded. "I'll put your last name down for now, and you can change it later if you like." He wrote *James Alexander Rockwell* on a card along with his birth date, weight, length, parents, and species before sticking it to the glass dome. He then tapped the glass with a finger. "Welcome to the world, little man."

~~*

The next morning, I received remarkable news. Miriam was awake and doing well. It turned out that after Dr. Perry started an IV with the nutrients she was lacking, she quickly got better. Upon hearing the news, I asked when I could see her.

"I'd give her a day to recuperate," Dr. Perry told me. He saw my expression and said, "She's been to hell and back, Austin. Give her some time."

The wait was almost as bad as the other night. I paced around my room, even though I'd been given strict instructions to stay off my feet. How could I lay down when the girl I loved had almost died and now I wasn't even allowed to see her?

I wished my dad was here. I realized I hadn't thought of him in a while, and hadn't even thought to ask Walter if he was alive. But now, I really wished he was here. He had been my rock, even before Mom died. I would give anything to have him by my side through all this.

Walter popped his head in the door early that afternoon. "Hey," he greeted as he came inside.

"Hey," I muttered, not really in the mood to talk.

"I thought you were supposed to stay off your feet," Walter commented, going to the chair in the room and taking a seat.

"It's kinda hard to sit still right now," I replied impatiently, continuing my pacing.

"Are you okay?" he asked after a moment's pause. When he saw my expression, he rephrased. "Sorry. I guess that was the wrong question. How are you doing? This isn't easy to handle."

"I suppose you would know?" I grumbled.

"I do, actually," he replied. "When Flint, my son, was born, he and Shauna both almost died. It was the most difficult thing I've ever been through."

"What happened?" I asked, finally managing to take a seat.

Walter hesitated. I could tell this was a very intimate part of his personal history. "Have you heard of Dr. Donald Rudolph?"

"Yeah, sure," I said. "He was one of the original scientists who worked with the Colician Virus, right?"

"He was also one of the doctors who experimented on us in the Hatfield lab." He took a deep breath. "He was also my uncle."

My eyebrows went up. "Your uncle?"

He nodded. "He experimented on Shauna when she was in captivity, and he shot her during the Hatfield breakout. She was nearly full term with Flint at the time. If Dr. Perry hadn't been there…" He shook his head and looked away. "But anyway, this isn't about me. This is about you."

"Can I ask you something?" I asked. "Do us Caitens have soul mates like you? Do we make that same type of bond?"

"It's hard to say. Dr. Perry examined your brains and didn't find the same connections that we have. Plus, you and Miriam reproduced through sex, so if you do make that kind of connection, it's not the same as ours." He peered at me. "Why do you ask?"

I shrugged. "Miriam's the closest thing I have to a soul mate. I just don't want anything to happen to her."

Walter gave me a weak smile. "I think the universe has it's own way of protecting those who are important to it. If you and Miriam are important to it, and I believe you are, you shouldn't have anything to worry about."

"Thanks," I said, climbing onto my bed. My legs were beginning to hurt, so I figured I should give them a rest.

"Dr. Perry told me about what happened yesterday," Walter told me, his voice taking on a more serious tone.

"Which part?" I asked.

"The part where you took hold of his mind."

"Oh," I muttered. "That part."

"You're new to this, so I'll let it slide this time, but here there's a law in place that says we are not allowed to use our abilities to control or harm anybody else, unless you're being threatened. Do you understand?"

"Perfectly," I replied, humiliated. "It won't happen again."

"I know," Walter said. He stood up. "I have to go. Take it easy, okay?"

"Do you know when I can see Miriam?" I asked him.

Walter shook his head. "It's not up to me," he said.

~~*

Lying back on my bed made me realize how tired I was. I wanted to stay awake, to wait for my chance to talk to Miriam, but my eyes kept drifting closed and after a while I could no longer force them back open.

My dreams were ominous. I kept seeing flashes of people, some I knew, some I didn't. I saw myself and Miriam on a huge ship, sailing across a vast ocean. We were much older, probably in our forties. Beside us was a young man, with Miriam's hair and skin and my eyes. When he smiled, I knew he was James. He was very handsome and had that same look of mischief about him that I had. I saw kindness and ferocity in his eyes. The next few flashes were of Walter, Shauna, and a blonde man I knew could only be Flint grown up. Walter looked to be the same age as I was in my vision of myself, so whatever I was seeing must happen in the same time period.

For the first few moments my visions of them were happy, but they quickly changed. I watched them all die, quickly yet slowly at the same time. Shauna died in a burst of fire and heat; Flint went slowly after taking a piece of shrapnel through the chest, while others ran around him, terrified; Walter was murdered with a quick slice to the throat, but at whose hand I couldn't see. My next visions were of a beautiful girl about Miriam's age, with long brown hair and Walter's eyes. I wasn't told, but I knew this was Walter's daughter. Was this Katherine, the child Shauna was carrying? That seemed logical, but something in my gut told me this wasn't Katherine; this was a future child, someone who wasn't yet thought of. Even though she was smiling, I knew she was in trouble, that she was going to suffer more than her family had. Beside her appeared a young man who looked just like my vision of James, the only differences being that he was younger than James and had brown eyes, like Miriam. This was my son, too, my future son. Just like the girl. He and the girl were together, like, *together* together. I saw flashes of small children at their feet, but their faces were hazy and I couldn't make them out, save for one: a toddler with curly brown hair and Walter's eyes. This child was important; no one needed to tell me that.

Everything I saw that followed happened very fast. The girl was screaming in agony, the toddler was crying, my second son was dead, the ship I was on started firing missiles out of the sides, a massive city was burning, and a pair of icy gray eyes appeared before me as everything went black.

As the lights started returning, I gasped for breath, scared out of my mind. I was standing on top of a building, looking out over the city on fire. Tears prevented me from seeing clearly for a moment, but I blinked them away and took a closer look at the city. It was the same city from my dream all that time ago in Philadelphia, the one where my father told me everything was my fault. But my father wasn't here this time. I looked around the rooftop, but I was alone. I recognized the city this time; it was Reifert City. It was all but burned to the ground. My visions from earlier helped me understand this dream better than I had the first time. My father hadn't been blaming me for something that had already happened; he was blaming me for something that was *going* to happen. Sometime in the future, Reifert City was going to burn, along with the rest of the Parallel Earth. And it was going to be my fault.

I sensed the presence of someone behind me, so I turned. A man somewhere in his forties or fifties stood a few feet away, glaring at me with his icy stare. He was the person with the gray eyes I'd seen in my last vision. I didn't know who he was, didn't recognize him at all, but I knew that he was the one who was going to destroy this place. Somewhere, in the midst of it all, it would be my fault that he did.

"Who are you?" I whispered.

The man smirked at me. "You don't know?"

"I don't know you," I said.

"Think a little harder," Gray Eyes instructed. "You'll remember."

"*Austin ...*"

The raspy whisper was familiar. I glanced behind Gray Eyes and saw my dad standing there, at the other side of the roof. His face was bloody, his hair tossed about his face, just like the last time I had this dream.

"*It's your fault...*" he told me.

"No," I breathed.

My father fell backwards off the roof.

"Dad!" I cried, starting to run forward. Gray Eyes pulled out a gun from his belt and shot me square in the chest. The blast threw me backwards, and I tumbled off the roof as well. I closed my eyes, knowing where this dream was going.

Falling, falling, falling...

~~*

When I struck bottom I blinked awake and gasped so hard I had a coughing fit. I pounded my chest until I could breathe again, and then I tried to calm myself down. My mind was full of the images I had seen: Reifert City ablaze, my son and Walter's daughter happy together before being torn apart, my grandson's importance to the future, the man with the gray eyes destroying the Parallel Earth.

How could it be my fault? I no longer had any bad feelings toward Walter and his people. I had no desire to destroy this place. And if my son was going to be a part of this place, I would never do anything to hurt him or his family. I would never do anything to hurt the Colicians regardless. How was this going to be my fault?

"Jesus," I muttered, rubbing my eyes. They were tearing up from this horrid knowledge, and my emotions were getting the best of me. I took a few deep breaths and rubbed my chest, where my anxiety had left a painful knot. I sat up, deciding that I needed to walk off my dream. My eyes widened. Standing at the foot of my bed, furry mask and all, was Gorilla Man.

He put a fuzzy finger up to his gorilla lips, signaling for me to be quiet.

"Lee?" I whispered. What the hell was he doing?

My door suddenly opened, and I looked over, startled. As my visitor popped his head inside, I looked back to Lee, but he was gone. This was not only creepy; it was annoying. With an irritated sigh, I glanced back to the door.

A little boy was peeking in, a big grin on his face. It took me a moment to recognize him. "Hey, Flint," I said, smiling back.

"Hi," he said quietly, trotting inside. Another little boy followed him, this one with black hair, blue eyes, and a large pair of wings growing from his back.

"Who's your friend?" I asked, studying the pair of wings curiously.

The other boy stood up straight and looked me in the eye. "My name is William Richard Ashton!" The kid couldn't quite say all his letters yet, so his name came out sounding like "Wiwwam Wichode Ashton." It was kind of adorable.

I laughed. "Hi, William. Do you go by Billy or Willy or Will?"

William shook his head hard. "Just Wiwwam."

"So can you fly?"

"A little." He looked back at his pair of snow white wings. "They're a little too big for me right now."

"Hmm." I looked at Flint, who was climbing onto my bed. "What's up, buddy?"

"I wanted to see you," the boy replied as William climbed up beside him.

"Why?"

"'Cause I like you!" Flint crawled up next to me and hugged me.

"But you hardly know me," I protested, patting the kid on the back.

Flint shrugged and sat beside me, and soon William was sitting on the other side of me. Neither boy said anything, and the silence soon became unbearable. "So…what have you boys been up to? What are you doing in the hospital?"

"My sister's sick," Flint replied. "So she's seeing Dr. Perry."

It hadn't even crossed my mind that Shauna must have given birth by now. "Oh," I said, trying to mask my surprise. My surprise quickly turned into concern for Walter and his baby. "What's wrong with her?"

"I don't know. Her face keeps bleeding."

How wonderful. The baby's face bleeds. Before I could ask the kid to elaborate on that, the door opened again and Erica came in, followed by Shauna with a swaddled bundle in her arms.

"There you boys are," Erica said, her voice full of relief but with a touch of anxiety. "You need to stay with us! You can't just wander off without telling us."

"We came to visit Austin!" Flint explained, patting my shoulder.

"Yes, I see that," Shauna said as Erica picked William off the bed. "How are you?"

"Fine," I said. "How's the baby?"

"She's all right. Just some nosebleeds I wanted checked out." She leaned the bundle toward me so I could see the baby.

She was sleeping, but even then I could tell that she looked way older than she ought to. "How old is she?"

"About six weeks." Shauna saw my confusion and explained, "Our babies develop quicker inside the womb and out. The process will slow down in a few months."

"She's cute." The baby had chubby cheeks and bright red lips, and a bit of dark hair growing on her head. "Katherine, right?"

"Yep." Shauna beamed down at her. "My baby girl."

I looked at Erica. "Is William your son?"

She nodded. "Mine and Cole Ashton's. He works in Walter's Cabinet."

Cole Ashton. The son of former President Richard Ashton. Why hadn't I realized that before? The boy said his name was William *Richard Ashton*. He was the grandson of the most disgraced man in the world.

"And yes, he is the grandson of former President Richard Ashton," Erica confirmed, clearly seeing the shock on my face.

"Cool," I replied, having no clue what else to say. "Uh...so the wings actually work?"

"They're not working so well for him right now," she said, gently stroking the feathers on William's wings. "They're not growing at the same rate he is, so he can't stay in the air for more than a few seconds. I'm not sure when he'll be able to use them like his father can."

"His dad has wings too?"

"Yeah. Cole can't wait until he can take William flying with him."

Just then, Walter popped his head in.

"Daddy!" Flint cried, jumping off the bed and running to him.

"Hey, buddy," Walter said, smiling and picking up his boy. The sight gave me a longing to hold my own son.

"Excuse us, Austin," Erica said, and left with William, saying hello to Walter as they passed.

"How's my baby girl?" Walter asked as Shauna passed Katherine to him.

"Dr. Perry's still trying to figure out what's going on," Shauna said. "But he said she seems perfectly fine other than the nosebleeds."

Walter's face was creased with worry, even though he was trying his best to smile down at his baby.

"I guess we're both worrying about out infants, huh?" I said to him. My vision was still on my mind, but I couldn't bring myself to tell him about it now. It would have to wait.

"I'm probably not as stressed out as you are," he replied.

I shrugged.

"Oh." Walter handed his baby back to Shauna and came over to my bed. "I spoke with Dr. Perry. He said you can see Miriam in about an hour."

"Really?" I said, sitting bolt upright.

"Don't get too excited," Walter said, putting a hand on my shoulder. "She's doing much better, but she's still completely exhausted. Dr. Perry thinks she's going to pull through fine in a couple of days."

"That's great!" I almost shouted.

"And there's more." I could tell that Walter was trying to hide his excitement for me. "James's skin is darkening, and Dr. Perry thinks he'll also be fine in a few days."

I could've cried right there. "Thank you," I said, rubbing my tired eyes. "Thank you so much. You don't know what they mean to me."

"Trust me. I do."

When I opened my eyes, I saw Walter smiling at his perfect little family.

~~*

The next hour was probably the longest hour of my life. I'd look at the clock beside my bed about every ten seconds, feeling as if it had been ten minutes. By the time forty-five minutes had rolled around, I was pacing around my room, feeling as if I were about to jump out of my skin. Finally, Dr. Perry came in to get me.

"I think we need to work on your anxiety," he said as I bolted past him.

When we got to Miriam's room, she was still pretty groggy, but she was awake enough to smile for me as I went in.

"Hey," I said, sitting in the chair beside her bed and taking her hand. She had tubes in her hands, arms, and nose, but she looked a lot better. Her skin was a healthy light brown color again, and her eyes were clear and bright. It was truly a miracle. I never really believed in God before, but I was beginning to.

"How's our baby?" she asked, her voice barely a whisper.

"He's great," I said, kissing her forehead. "He has a weird skin thing going on right now but he should be fine in a few days." I smiled more broadly. "Just like you."

"What about everyone else? How's Jeff and Lee and Vincent?"

"Lee and Vincent are fine," I said. "And Jeff..." I looked to Dr. Perry, realizing I didn't know how he was. I'd been so concerned with Miriam and James, so caught up in what was wrong with them, that I hadn't even taken the time to find out how my friend was doing. I really hated myself sometimes.

"He hasn't improved, but he hasn't worsened either," Dr. Perry told us. "It's hard to say whether he'll get better or not."

We both knew without him telling us that *or not* meant death for our friend. I smiled weakly at Dr. Perry. "Do you mind if we have a few moments to ourselves?"

"Sure," he said, turning and closing the door behind him.

"How've you been?" Miriam asked me, reaching up and stroking my cheek.

"All right. I had a weird condition that was tearing apart my bones, but Dr. Perry used James's cells and cured it. Other than that, nothing real interesting has happened."

"What about Jaeger and Danny? Did they make it out okay?"

I realized that Miriam didn't know about Jaeger yet. "Miriam...Jaeger used us. He was the one who got us attacked in Florida. I shouldn't have trusted him. I should've just left him by the road."

A flash of anger crossed through Miriam's eyes, but it left just as quickly. "It's not your fault," she said. "I couldn't get a proper reading on him. I didn't know either."

"But he's gone now," I said. "Back with Hillerman, working on some new scheme, no doubt."

"Do they know about the Miami Caitens?" Miriam asked, worry in her voice.

"I think so. We told Jaeger about them. There's no way he wouldn't have told Hillerman."

She bit her lip. "What are we going to do? I mean…we can't hide on the Parallel Earth forever. We can't abandon the others."

"Walter told me that he had a team out looking for them, but I haven't heard anything about it for a while. Apparently, they're good at hiding. They'll be okay. If they can hide from the Colicians, they can hide from Hillerman."

Miriam paused before asking her next question. "When can I see James?"

There were a lot of tears in her eyes, and I didn't want to see her cry. "Soon," I promised. "As soon as you're both better."

Miriam fell asleep soon after that, and I couldn't bring myself to leave her. I continued to hold her hand, sitting beside her bed and dozing off now and again in my chair. I was startled awake at dusk when someone tapped my shoulder.

"What?" I wiped the drool off my chin and blinked in the fading light. I had a kink in my neck, but I ignored it. "What?"

Lee was standing next to me, rubbing his wrists together. He didn't say anything, so I spoke first.

"Why were you in my room earlier?" I asked him.

"What are you talking about?" Lee asked, confused.

"You were at the foot of my bed in your gorilla suit," I snapped, quickly losing my patience. "I didn't think you brought it with you."

"I didn't," Lee insisted. "I didn't have time, remember?"

I did, but who else would have been at the foot of my bed in a gorilla suit?

"I swear I wasn't in your room earlier, and I don't have my suit. It wasn't me."

"Then who was it?" I demanded.

Lee shrugged. "I don't know. Maybe it was another warning."

"But why…?" I didn't understand it. My original visions of the Gorilla Man were telling me to find Lee in order to save my life. I did, and now he was with us. So why was I still having visions of him if he was here with me?

"I just came to tell you we have to go soon," Lee said, still rubbing his wrists together. I wondered how he could continue doing that without rubbing his skin completely raw.

"Go where?" I asked.

"To Miami. We have to leave soon. We can't wait much longer."

"Why not?"

"Because it's starting soon."

This last time I had contacted him in the middle of the day. My wife was out with a friend, and the house was otherwise empty. Still, I locked the door to the powder room, as if what I was doing was an illicit activity. I knew if I was caught by my wife she'd be upset, but I wasn't doing anything wrong. I was trying to help.

It seemed like I was getting through to him. He'd spoken to me this past time, thinking I was his friend, but I could tell he was beginning to realize that my appearances were now holding a new meaning. I sure hoped that was the case, because I couldn't say any more than I already had.

Why couldn't I? I found myself asking this question again. I hadn't really answered it myself, but something in my gut told me not to push him too hard in any one direction. Maybe if I did, I would cause a massive alteration in his destiny, something that could drastically change the course of history, and not for the better.

15

The Miami Caitens

Two days later, Miriam was up and walking around, a little weak, but definitely much improved. Our son was also much better; we couldn't see through his skin anymore. It was still paler than it should have been, but Dr. Perry said he should have Miriam's skin tone in another few days. It was that day that Miriam got to see James for the first time.

"I've got a surprise for you two," Dr. Perry said as he brought a squirming bundle into the room.

Miriam gasped, stretching out her arms toward him. Dr. Perry handed James to her and then left, knowing we would need this moment to ourselves. Miriam cradled our baby in her arms, crying silently over him.

"My baby boy," she kept saying. "My little baby boy."

James grinned up at her and made lots of baby sounds. He reached up a hand toward her and she held it in hers.

"Isn't he beautiful?" I said, sitting beside her and putting my arm around her.

"He's perfect." Miriam was beaming ear to ear. She looked up at me, the tears streaming down her face. "I couldn't ask for anything better than this, right here." She kissed me, and I didn't think I'd ever felt happier than right there, in that moment.

"Dr. Perry put his name down as James Alexander Rockwell, since we hadn't discussed last names yet," I told her. "I didn't know if you wanted it changed or..."

"That's okay," Miriam said, still cooing over our son. "He can have his daddy's name."

We were interrupted by someone clearing their throat at the door. It was Vincent, frowning, his eyes annoyed yet playful. "Sorry to interrupt," he said, "but I heard I could finally hold my nephew for the first time."

Miriam held James out to him, still grinning. "Here you go, Uncle Vincent."

"That'll take some getting used to," he said, smiling down at his little nephew.

Lee came in a few minutes later to see James as well, and soon we were all laughing and joking as if the past few months had never happened. Since everyone in our group that could be here was here, I had Lee tell us what he'd told me a few days earlier.

"We have to go to Miami," he said when we were all seated around Miriam's bed. "We've waited far too long as it is. We have to go as soon as possible."

"What about Jeff?" I demanded. "We can't just leave him here!"

"Jeff can join us once he's better."

"There's no saying if he *will* get better!"

"We can't wait around any longer!" Lee exclaimed. "We have to join the others! It's the only way!"

"The only way to what?" Miriam asked.

"Survive." Lee looked around at all of us. "Listen. Jeff will get better. When he does, he can come join us. But we have to collaborate with the others *now*. Something's about to happen, and we have to be there for it."

"What's about to happen?" Vincent asked warily.

"I don't know," Lee said with a sigh. "All I know is that we have to be there for it."

"Does any of this have to do with what they're building?"

Lee nodded.

"What are you talking about?" Vincent looked at me curiously.

"Lee told me back in D.C. that the Miami Caitens were building something," I explained. I glared at Lee. "I just wish he'd tell me more about it. Especially since he's insisting we go where it's being built."

Lee rubbed his wrists together nervously. "I can't talk about it. I swore I wouldn't."

"I thought you didn't agree with what they were doing," I said, my patience all but gone. "Now you're saying we all need to go there? I can't agree to this! Especially since Miriam and James aren't ready yet!"

"Look at them," Lee said, pointing to Miriam and the baby. "They're fine. They'll be fine. They'll be safe where we're going."

"How can you promise me that?" I snapped.

"We're the same," Lee said. "We need to be together."

"I think he's right, Austin," Miriam said, seeming distant. "I have a feeling that we're supposed to be there. We'll be okay, Austin."

I closed my eyes and pictured the vision I'd had of James as an adult, and Miriam and I together as a middle-aged couple. I prayed that no decision I made would ever endanger that vision from becoming reality.

~~*

"So you're leaving?"

I was having trouble trying to explain our situation to Walter, and those three words basically summed up my three minutes of stammering. "Yeah," I muttered. "That's what it seems like."

For some reason, I was expecting Walter to become angry and declare that we were not allowed to leave, but he simply looked at me calmly and said, "If that's what you need to do, then that's fine."

I nodded, surprised by his reaction.

"Did you really think I would keep you here?" Walter asked when I didn't say anything. "That's not the kind of people we are. You haven't done anything wrong, and Dr. Perry says you all seem to be in good shape, so there's no reason to keep you here."

"I don't know," I said. "I guess I just make too many presumptions about you guys."

"It's easy to do when the media feeds you lies," he replied. "I do have one question though: why are you leaving your friend behind? Why not wait until he gets better or…" He shrugged, not wanting to go in that direction.

"We love Jeff," I insisted. "We really do. But Lee is confident that he'll get better, and he's been right about these things before. He says we have to go to Miami right away, because something is about to happen that we need to be a part of. At least, that's what he says."

Walter nodded, a look of uncertainty about him. "I can have a convoy escort you through the rift and to Miami tomorrow morning." He paused. "Can I give you some advice?"

"Sure."

"Watch your back. I have a feeling about these Miami Caitens, and it isn't good."

"You think something's wrong with them?"

"Not wrong, necessarily." Walter's face scrunched up as he thought. "I just feel that they might have an agenda they don't want us to know about. We had no idea of their existence until recently, and even now we can't get a reading on them, and they won't let us across the border into their settlement, not even just to talk."

"Maybe they're just afraid of you," I suggested. "I mean, we were scared of you at first. Maybe it's the same with them."

"It's not the same as it was with you," Walter said. "I could tell you were afraid. But these guys…they're hiding something."

I trusted Walter, and I wanted to believe him, but they were my people. I couldn't be against them. "Well, humans are still unsure of Colicians, and you guys are okay. Maybe this is the same thing."

Walter nodded slowly, considering this. Even as we parted ways, I saw the uncertainty in his eyes.

~~*

"Is there something you want to tell me, Austin?"

It was the next morning, and the rest of my crew was getting settled in a small bus. The Colicians even provided a car seat for James! I hung back, wanting to tell Walter about my vision.

"Yeah." I cleared my throat, but every time I opened my mouth to tell him, I found myself speechless. I kept picturing the figure in the gorilla costume, holding a finger to his mouth. He wasn't just telling me to be quiet; he was telling me to keep my visions a secret.

"What's troubling you?" Walter asked me.

I tried one last time to tell him, but I just couldn't. "Maybe now's not the best time," I said. "I'll see you 'round, Walter."

Walter offered me his sincerest of smiles. "Good luck, Austin."

As I climbed into the seat across from Miriam and James, I saw Dr. Perry sticking a dropper under Lee's tongue and squeezing out a few drops. "What are you doing?" I asked as Lee's eyes fluttered closed.

"It's a mild sedative," Dr. Perry explained. "Humans have difficulty crossing the rift while conscious. I don't know how Caitens are affected, but I don't want to take any risks, especially after what you've all gone through the past few weeks." He emptied a dropper into Vincent's mouth and then came to me with a full one. "Trust me. You're going to want this."

I shot a hesitant glance toward Miriam, who gave me an encouraging smile. Sighing, I opened my mouth and Dr. Perry emptied the dropper under my tongue. It tasted bitter and strong, but a few seconds later my vision faded completely and I was unconscious.

~~*

"Austin!"

The hissing in my ear woke me up. I opened my eyes, feeling as if a wall of concrete was sitting on my eyelids. I was so tired, yet I felt as if I'd slept for days.

"Hey." Danny's face slowly came into focus. "We're almost there, Austin. You probably want to start waking up."

"Where are we?" The words came out slurred and my own thoughts were incoherent. For a moment I forgot where I was going and who I was with.

Danny snickered. "We're in Miami, dude. Rise and shine."

Miami. We were finally uniting with the other Caitens. My stomach did a flip in anticipation, but my grogginess still kept me lethargic. I glanced over at Miriam, who seemed a bit more awake than I was. James was still sleeping in his car seat, a thick stream of drool trailing from his mouth. "You ready?" I asked Miriam.

She smiled sleepily at me. "I'm pretty excited."

A Colician woman came back to us and handed us each a heavy backpack full of supplies. "Hello," she said brightly. "My name's Carrie. Drew, Danny, and I are your transport team. We just wanted to give you these packs before you departed. They're full of medicines you may need and instructions on what to do if you or your baby gets sick."

"Thanks," I said. "How long until we get there?"

"About seven minutes," Carrie said, and went back up front before I could say anything else.

I figured the Colician driving the small bus was Drew. He looked to be in his forties with a scruffy beard and light brown hair.

Vincent turned around slowly in his seat to look at us, a pained expression on his exhausted face. "Got any aspirin in those packs?"

"You look like shit, dude," I said.

"Don't you have this headache too?" He groaned when I shook my head. "I don't know what was in that sedative, but it was not meant for humans."

Miriam giggled, but covered her mouth when Vincent glared her way. "I'll see what I have," she said, opening her pack and digging around. After exploring her pockets, she pulled a few pill bottles out and examined them. She murmured the names to herself, and paused as she read the name on a particularly large bottle. "I think this is for our headaches, Austin." She glanced up at me. "That's what's being described on the label."

"Give it here, then!" Vincent snapped, holding out his hand.

"I'm just not sure if it's too strong for you," Miriam said hesitantly.

"I don't care!" Vincent snatched the bottle from her, dumped four into his palm, and swallowed them dry before either of us could do anything.

"Vincent!" I snapped.

"Do you want to kill yourself?" Miriam cried.

"Whoa," Vincent said as he handed the bottle back to Miriam. His eyelids started drooping. "I feel better. A *lot* better."

"That's because they weren't meant for you!" Miriam was glaring at him, but I knew she was scared for him. "I'd be surprised if you didn't just OD!"

"I'm fine," Vincent muttered, rolling back into place. His words were beginning to slur. "Really…"

"Don't let him fall asleep, Austin!" Miriam said urgently.

I leaned forward. "Dude." I slapped his cheek a few times. "Stay awake, man."

Vincent suddenly sat up and turned toward us. His eyes were open and he looked fine. "Wow. I feel awesome."

Miriam groaned loudly. "I hate you sometimes," she snapped.

"You can't scare us like that, man," I told him, but I was too relieved to actually scold him.

"Sorry," he said, stretching his arms and legs. "But I feel great now. That stuff works wonders."

"Don't think you're going to get it for just anything," Miriam said sharply.

The rest of the drive was passed mostly in silence, one of us occasionally making a short comment. I checked on Vincent about every twenty seconds to make sure he hadn't died, but he seemed to be okay. When we reached the far side of the city, buildings started thinning out. I could see foundations where buildings used to be, but all that remained in the area was rubble. As we continued, we saw a large chain-link fence with huge signs displaying warnings such as **KEEP OUT** and **TRESPASSERS WILL BE SHOT**. I glanced at Miriam warily, and she had a similar nervous expression on her face. "Is this it?" I asked.

She bit her lip. "I wish it wasn't."

The bus approached an entrance, and as we came to a stop in front of it, the gate slid open to allow us passage into the security checkpoint.

"I guess it is," I muttered.

At the front of the bus, Carrie stood up and called back to us. "We've arrived at the entrance to the Caiten settlement. There's no saying how they may respond to us, so please exit the bus slowly." With that said, she and Drew stepped off once we pulled to a full stop.

Lee and Vincent followed them. Miriam and I took longer, both of us fighting over who should carry James. In the end I won, despite Miriam's protests. Danny was waiting for us at the front of the bus. "Both can't get enough of him, eh?" he said, smiling as we passed.

"Have you seen him yet?" I asked, turning the car seat so he could see.

Danny peered down and smiled at James.

Miriam clung to my arm, and I felt the uncertainty in her. I kissed the top of her head to reassure her as we followed the others to the other side of the bus.

Carrie and Drew positioned themselves in front of us to shield us from any impending danger as a large, navy blue cargo van approached. I saw that we were enclosed in a chain-linked box, several dozen yards square. There wasn't much inside; it was mostly flat cement, with some shipping containers and two forklifts in the far corner. Beyond the fence, there was a stretch of road, and then the buildings started again. They were small, mostly crappy-looking one-story houses, but there were two that were larger and about seven stories tall. All in all, this place didn't look so great.

The van pulled up and several armed men in ski masks jumped out and aimed their weapons in our direction. This position was held for several moments, until a woman who looked to be about thirty-five stepped out of the side door. She had long brown hair tied back in a loose ponytail, and light brown eyes that studied us all closely. She was of average height, with an athletic build, and a thin face with an expression that suggested she was easily annoyed. She eyed Carrie and Drew. "Is this them?" she asked.

Carrie nodded, her and Drew's bodies both rigid and poised for a fight.

The Caiten woman looked past them and smiled warmly at us. "Welcome," she said. "It's nice to finally meet you."

"Lois!" Lee's face broke into a huge grin and he ran to her. They embraced and exchanged a few words. Lois then gestured to the armed men and they lowered their weapons. Lee looked back at us. "It's okay!" he called.

Carrie and Drew relaxed and allowed us to go through to meet Lois and the others. As we came forward, Lois extended her hand to me. "Hello. I'm Lois Royalty. I'm the head physician here."

"Physician?" I repeated, confused. "I thought you were one of the first to be infected?"

Lois smiled again, and this time I could see the tight lines on her face. Her kindness and excitement were all an act. "The shipyard wasn't the only place Hillerman took his subjects from." Before I could question her further, she asked, "You are Austin Rockwell, correct?"

"Yes," I said.

She looked down and actually provided a real smile for James. "And this must be Baby James, the new arrival."

"Yep, that's our little man," I replied proudly.

"How sweet," she said. She turned to Miriam. "And you're Miriam Lobner?"

Miriam nodded and they shook hands.

Lois turned toward Vincent and her expression changed drastically. "Who are you? What are you doing here?"

I had a moment of confusion, but then immediately jumped to Vincent's aid. "He's Miriam's brother, Vincent. He's been helping us survive these past several months."

"We don't allow humans here," Lois said, and she had a tone that suggested there would be no persuading her otherwise.

I heard a thud off to my right, and I looked down to see Vincent sprawled on the ground, unconscious.

"Vincent!" Miriam rushed to her brother's side, trying to wake him.

"Shit," I muttered. I turned back to Lois. "Listen," I said quickly. "I don't have time to argue with you. Vincent is very important to us and he's overdosed on some pain pills. Will you please help him?"

I expected Lois to immediately refuse and watch Vincent die at her feet, but instead, her gaze softened and she hesitated. The sound of an approaching vehicle caused us to both look back. Three white pickups were roaring toward us. Lois looked at me, fear suddenly in her eyes. "Help me get him in the van," she said, taking Vincent's legs. "Don't say a word about him to Perkins."

"Who the hell's Perkins?" I asked as I set down James and took Vincent's shoulders to lift him into the van.

"Call him *Captain* Perkins," she hissed as the trucks drew closer. "He's in charge. He'll kill you with no hesitation if you piss him off."

My stomach clenched. Was this really what our species was like as a collective? Violent, short-tempered, and unwilling to listen? I guessed I was going to have to get my mouth under control if we were going to be staying here.

We got Vincent into the van and Lois quickly climbed behind the wheel. "If he asks," she said, "tell him I had an emergency at the hospital." The armed men stayed behind and the van sped away.

I went back to Miriam, whose eyes were wide with panic and confusion. She was holding onto James's car seat, clutching it so hard her knuckles were white. I stood in front of her, shielding her from the new arrivals. Lee also shrank closer to us, clearly frightened of this Captain Perkins. "Do you know this guy?" I whispered to him as the trucks drew to a halt in front of us.

"Stay out of his way," Lee replied.

"Who is he?" I hissed.

"He was going to be the captain of the *Majesty*. He was at the site when we were captured by Hillerman. The virus went to his head, but none of us dare say it."

"You just did," I said.

Lee put a finger to his lips and then rubbed his wrists together.

A man hopped out of the back of the middle truck and strutted toward us, his eyes searching each of us individually. His gaze lingered on Miriam longer than anyone else, souring my mood even more. This man, who I assumed to be Perkins, was about fifty-five, with long blonde hair pulled back in a ponytail. He had a scruffy beard and mustache, giving him an unpleasant look. His clothes were camo and dirty, the color quite faded. The only thing that suggested he was a ship's captain was the captain's hat he wore, very clean and bright, unlike the rest of his outfit. His eyes were constantly squinting, and when he smiled he revealed crooked rows of yellowing teeth.

"Well, well," he said, striding up to us. "Lee Stewart, as I live and breathe." He grabbed Lee roughly and gave him a great big man-hug. "Glad to see you finally made the right choice. Are you here for good, this time?"

Lee glanced at us, fear clouding his eyes. I don't know how Perkins didn't see it. Maybe he just chose not to. "Hopefully," Lee answered. "We'd like to stay for a while, if that's all right."

"Of course. You're all welcome!" Perkins turned his gaze on me, his crooked smile still blazing. "Austin Rockwell! Pleasure to meet you." He grasped my hand, his palms dry and cracking. "Captain Nathaniel Perkins. Welcome to Rebellion."

"Rebellion?" I repeated.

"That's what we call our town," Perkins explained. "We've rebelled against the humans by escaping and gathering here. I thought the name fit." He turned to Miriam, and his smile widened. "Miriam Lobner. Welcome." He gazed into the car seat, where little James gazed back. "James Rockwell. Our newest arrival. You look like you'll grow into a strong young man." Perkins's gaze was redirected to me. "You're missing one, yes?"

"Yes," I said. "Jeff Robinson can't be with us just yet. When he's better, he'll join us here."

"Where is he currently taking refuge?" Perkins asked, confused.

"On the Parallel Earth," I said. "With the Colicians."

Perkins immediately changed. His jaw tightened, his eyes became even more squinty, and his whole body tensed. "You're in league with the O Negatives?" he growled, and I thought he would lurch forward and strangle me right on the spot.

"Not exactly," Lee said, stepping in as he sensed an outburst. I stopped him before he could make up a believable lie.

"Yes," I said, finding my bravery. "President Reifert has saved our lives on multiple occasions, and he's —"

The knife was to my throat before I could react. Perkins got real close and whispered, "Say one more word, and I'll end you."

I almost said, "Okay," but realized that wouldn't have benefited me much.

He looked at Lee. "Explain yourself."

Lee was frantically rubbing his wrists together. "We were in an accident on the way here a few weeks ago and the O Negatives rescued us," he said. "We were staying there until we were well enough to travel again. We left Jeff Robinson behind because we were eager to join you here. The O Negatives agreed to escort him here once he recovers. We were simply seeking temporary asylum with them, nothing more."

Perkins eyed Miriam. "Girl! Is this true?"

I sensed Miriam's hesitance, and then she nodded. "Yes, sir," she said. "It's true. Austin likes to joke, that's all. He meant no offense."

Perkins released me and I took several steps back, rubbing my neck where the blade had left a shallow cut.

"Let that be a lesson to you, boy," Perkins snapped, pointing at the wound he'd left. "I don't like jokes. Don't mess around with me again, understood?"

I nodded, unable to force out the words "Yes, sir." I looked at Miriam, surprised at her quick lie. She glanced back at me and quickly looked away. *I'll explain later,* she told me.

I feared for Carrie and Drew, who were several yards behind us but still within sight of Perkins. If Perkins had reacted in such a way because he thought we were in league with the Colicians, what would he do if Colicians were actually present? And why did he call them O Negatives? That term wasn't even used anymore.

"Are these the O Negatives who brought you here?" Perkins demanded, scowling at Carrie and Drew.

I thought about lying, but Lee answered before I could do so. "Yes," he said. "That's them."

Perkins drew a pistol from his belt, raised it, and fired two rounds. Miriam screamed and I shouted, "What are you *doing*?"

Carrie took her bullet to the chest and went down immediately. Drew was hit in the arm and dropped to one knee, but he was up just as fast and running around to the other side of the bus. As he did so, Danny emerged from the other side and started to run to Carrie's aid, but Drew grabbed him and pulled him back onto the bus. Moments later, they were speeding away through the gate that had reopened for them.

"Who opened the gate?" Perkins screamed, his eyes wild and crazy.

"Why would you do that?" I shouted at him, and in response he punched me in the mouth. It wasn't that hard of a blow, but it still made my lip bleed. I grabbed Miriam and pulled her away from Perkins, sheltering her and the baby. Lee followed us. I looked around, panicked, searching for any place to run, to get away from this psycho. The gate was closed again. There was nowhere to go. I looked at Carrie where she laid, twitching, barely clinging to life. I wanted to run to her, but I was rooted to the spot. I couldn't leave Miriam and James.

Perkins jabbed a dry, cracked finger at us. "Get them out of here," he growled.

"Yes, sir." A man who looked about Lois's age came forward and gestured for us to follow him to one of the pickups. We all hesitated, fearing what was about to happen to Carrie, but the look the man gave us suggested that we not go against Perkins' wishes.

I led the others to the truck, having to drag Miriam part way. She stared at me, shocked at my actions. *We can't go with them!* she snapped. *They're going to kill her! What's going to happen to us if we go with them?*

They'll kill us if we don't, was all I could say. I didn't want to go with these people any more than she did, but I had to think about her and our son. Miriam gave in, but I sensed her fury and fear.

James was beginning to fuss. I thought that maybe even he could sense what was about to happen.

We all squished into the backseat, none of us wishing to sit up front with the man who ushered us inside. Miriam rocked the car seat on her lap, a little too quickly, trying to quiet James. The man climbed behind the wheel and quickly drove away, looking into the rearview mirror every few seconds. Soon, we heard the inevitable crack of gunfire, and we all winced. I had been holding onto Carrie with my mind, praying she would somehow be okay, but now I felt her fade away, a peculiar, disturbing feeling.

The man driving us had a pained expression on his face. He felt guilty about what just happened. I felt that we could trust this man, so I decided to open up to him. "What's your name?" I asked.

I soon saw that he didn't just look to be about Lois's age; he actually looked like Lois. Similar features, same eye and hair color. "Quinn Royalty," he said, offering us a weak smile in the mirror. "Lois's twin brother."

"You don't seem to support Perkins' actions," I pointed out.

"It doesn't matter what I support or don't support." Quinn had driven us out of the fenced-in area and we were now headed toward the cluster of buildings we'd seen earlier. "All that matters is surviving. Disagreeing with Perkins won't make that happen."

"What's his deal?" I asked. "How the hell did that nut end up in charge?"

Quinn looked back up to the mirror, his eyes full of fear. "His power drove him mad. He's the most powerful of any of us. Others have tried to take him down, and they've all ended up dead or crazy. Don't get any ideas, Miriam." His eyes shifted to hers, giving off a flash of warning.

I glanced at Miriam, whose brow was furrowed. She seemed determined, and had stopped rocking James as she lost herself in thought. James stopped fussing and turned to gaze at her, curious as to what was going on with his mother. I saw in her eyes what she wanted to do. "Don't," I said. "I'm begging you. If not for me, for James."

She looked at me, the creases on her brow softening. "I won't do anything. Yet. I have to figure this guy out first. That's why I went along with Lee's lie; I can't do anything until I understand him better."

I closed my eyes. "Please. I don't want you to get killed trying to stop this man."

"How many more people is he going to kill?" Miriam demanded. "Maybe you can do nothing and live with yourself, but I can't. I can't stand by and watch someone kill innocent people. It's not right."

"What about us?" I whispered fiercely.

She glared at me. "This is bigger than the three of us, Austin. It always has been."

We sat in silence for the remainder of the ride. Quinn took us down what appeared to be the main street of the...what was the proper word for this place? Town? Settlement? All the buildings on the right, the tall ones with multiple stories, were unlabeled, plain and dull gray. They didn't appear to be living quarters, but I had no clue what else they could be used for.

The buildings on the left were labeled, even colorful. One was labeled "Chuck's Tavern" in neon orange letters over navy blue siding. Another was "Ulysses's Hardware, Home Maintenance, & Other." The sixth building was "Anne and Gary's Food Market," and it was the biggest on the block. The last was a faded pink, run-down shed with "Ingrid's School & Nursery" painted on the front.

When I saw the school it was clear that Perkins didn't give much of a crap about education. As I thought about it, I started wondering why the hell there were Caiten children. James was an exception, being born a Caiten. But why were there other children? Any children born here would not be old enough for school.

Quinn saw me staring. "Everything will be explained tonight, after you're all settled," he assured me.

As we parked next to one of the unlabeled buildings on the right, I thought back to Walter's words. He was right. Why had I ever doubted him? *If you can hear me,* I said, projecting my thoughts as far as I could, *you were right, and I'm sorry. I'm so sorry.*

I wondered how he would react to Carrie's death.

We all got out and followed Quinn inside. Turned out I was wrong;

these buildings *were* living quarters. From what I could see, they appeared to be a series of cinder-block apartment complexes. Three numbers following the letter L were on every door. We ascended two floors. I had to take James from Miriam, despite her protests, because she began panting and lagging. On the third floor we walked down the hall and took a right before coming to a door labeled L327. Quinn produced a key and unlocked the door. He gestured for us to enter.

The moment I stepped inside, I was greeted by a stench so foul, I gagged. It smelled like something had died. A mouse or a rat maybe, that had been left to rot for months. Miriam covered her mouth and nose as she followed, and James made an uncomfortable sound from his seat. There was a single bed, definitely not big enough for Miriam and I, and a cradle made of wood next to it. Along the closest wall there was a small kitchen with a stench of its own. A single door was in the corner, leading to what I assumed to be the bathroom. I didn't check it out, knowing that whatever was behind it would be just as revolting. Miriam and I stared in disgust, knowing all too well what this place was.

"Here you go," Quinn said, holding his nose and handing us the key.

"Do you really think this place is suitable for an infant?" Miriam demanded, whirling on him.

"Personally," Quinn replied, "absolutely not. But my opinion doesn't matter. All that matters is surviving." He nodded to us apologetically before turning to leave.

As soon as he was gone, I pushed Miriam outside and set the baby down. I glared at Lee, who was standing in the hall, rubbing his wrists together. "What the hell is this?" I hissed. "I thought we were supposed to be living together as a community, not in a dictatorship!"

"I'm not letting my child sleep in there," Miriam said firmly.

Lee shrugged helplessly. "Do what you want. But there are always consequences for that. No matter what you say to Perkins, he won't give you a better place. The better living places are for him and his soldiers and informants only."

I got right in his face. "What the hell is going on, Lee?" I demanded, speaking slowly and clearly. "Explain it to me, because I don't understand."

"I can't," Lee said. "I can't explain anything to you. That's for Lois and Perkins to do."

"Why did you bring us here?" I snapped, ignoring him. "You said we had to be here, that we would be safe here. I do not feel safe here at all."

Lee opened his mouth to reply but his gaze moved past me and his eyes widened. I turned. Behind us a few yards was a woman with bright blue eyes and black hair in a pixie cut. She was staring back at Lee, just as shocked as he was. She looked to be in her thirties, at least a decade younger than Lee, but I saw something in her eyes that trumped their age difference.

"Annabelle," Lee said.

Annabelle strode forward. The love I saw in her eyes made me think that she was going to start kissing him, especially when Lee held out his arms to her, but instead she slapped him hard across the face. Stunned, Lee stared back at her. A moment later they were both hugging each other and crying.

16

The Ugly Reality

Annabelle Lawrence was Lee's fiancé. Lee told us the story as we all crammed into Annabelle's apartment on the first floor. Her apartment was one of the nicer ones Lee had described, much larger and cleaner than ours. I wasn't sure what that meant regarding Annabelle's status.

"We were both on the design team of the *Majesty*," Lee explained, squeezing Annabelle's hand. He sat on an old arm chair with her on his lap, facing Miriam, James, and I where we sat on Annabelle's bed. "That's where we met. We argued a lot over structures and layouts, and because of that, we would have to stay late many nights to work out an agreement. They went on as arguments for weeks, but then things started changing. We would purposely stay late to work on designs, going out for dinner and drinks. We thought we hated each other at first, but we realized that wasn't the case anymore. Soon..." He looked at Annabelle. "Our relationship became much more.

"We were engaged when Hillerman sent his people for us. Both of us survived the infection, obviously, and when we all escaped the whole group stayed together, moving from place to place. Eventually we all settled back here." He smiled at Annabelle. "She still wanted to get married, even after what we'd been through. I couldn't ask for anyone better in my life."

"I couldn't stop loving you because of that," Annabelle said, nudging him playfully with her elbow. I could tell she was tough, a fighter. "No matter what happened, we had to stick together."

"I stayed in Rebellion for a while," Lee continued. "It was nice living with the group, on our own. But then we realized our population kept growing. Hillerman was trying to make more like us. The strain he was working with was not the one he wanted, so he began disposing of the ones who weren't producing the results he wanted. We couldn't just remain where we were, living our quiet little lives, while our own people were being slaughtered. So we started sneaking them out of that place, the lab where you were. We'd gotten two hundred out when we realized that the lab in Philadelphia was not the only one creating Caitens. There's a lab in Madison, three times as big as the one in Philly. There's one in Atlanta, butchering our people like cattle. There are two in California, one near San Francisco and one in San Diego. There is also one on the plains northeast of Denver. In the past two years, there have been more than three thousand rescued Caitens. Now, there's fear that we will have to rescue thousands more." He nodded to us. "You two, Jeff, and Kost were the beginning of something huge, possibly even bigger than the Colician outbreak. We haven't begun rescues on the newest Caitens yet, but we know we'll have to soon. We can't leave them there for long. Security in the labs has gone up substantially since you left, but we can't use that as an excuse anymore. We can't leave our people behind to suffer."

"Does the world know about any of this yet?" I asked. "Do they know what scientists in the United States are doing? Do the people of the United States know what their government is doing?"

"Of course not," Lee scoffed. "We would be at war with the world if they knew. International tensions are already high because of the Colician outbreak. Our government created the original virus and it drastically changed the world; if any other country knew what was going on here now, they would put an end to us before things escalated even more."

"The government hasn't tried to get support from anyone else?" I asked. "If they're trying to find a cure for the original strain, wouldn't they—"

Lee startled me with a burst of laughter. "Do you really think that's what this is all about? That they're trying to *cure* the Colicians? The Colicians were the greatest scientific breakthrough in all of human history. There's no way they'd ever try to cure them. No, they want to remake the Colicians, just on a lesser scale."

Miriam and I stared at him, mortified. "Why?" Miriam whispered.

"So they can finish what they started. Learn from the Caitens what they couldn't from the Colicians. They want to know how the mind controls the abilities. They want super soldiers. They don't care about bringing the others back. They never did. You were turned for selfish reasons, not so you could be the answer to a cure."

"We were *told* they were making a cure," I protested. "It was brought up multiple times, by multiple people."

"They were lying," Annabelle replied. "They wanted you to believe that, in hopes that it might persuade you to stay with them. They wanted you to feel like you were important."

I now, if it was at all possible, hated Hillerman even more. "That bastard," I muttered. "That sick, twisted son-of-a-..."

"Why did you leave?" Miriam asked, cutting me off. "You said you liked living with the others. Why did things here change? What happened?"

"Perkins came into power," Annabelle explained. "He wasn't elected. He's former military, and he believed he was best suited to be in charge. He had an army of men ready to follow him. We knew he was delusional, and we couldn't have him in charge. The day he came into power, several of us tried to take him down. Perkins showed us just how powerful he really was. One by one, he drove each and every rebel over the edge, taking away their sanity." She glanced at Lee and then quickly looked away, shame in her eyes. "I was one of them. But I fought back. I wouldn't let him take me over. He couldn't take my sanity, so he took Lee's."

"I'm not as strong as you," Lee murmured. "I couldn't fight him. He took every bit of me and crushed me. I was so horrified by what I saw, what he showed me, that I ran. I ran and ran and didn't stop. I couldn't. I knew I couldn't go back, even with what I'd left behind." He squeezed Annabelle's hand again and gazed at me. "I'm sorry I lied to you about how I ended up this way. I haven't told that story to anyone until now."

I couldn't bring myself to speak.

"Anyway, I found myself in D.C. after a while and stayed there, working odd jobs until you found me. I didn't want to go back, but I knew I had to come get what I'd left behind. And I had to help those who are still here. It had been a year-and-a-half since I left."

"I wasn't the only one you left behind," Annabelle whispered, tears beginning to stream down her face. She stood up and took Lee's hand. "Come. There's someone you need to meet."

Even before she led Lee to Ingrid's School & Nursery, we all knew who it was Annabelle was taking Lee to meet. It was clear to us all.

When we entered the rundown building, a young woman, who I suspected was Ingrid, came up to greet us. "Hello, Annabelle. Can I help you?" Her eyes landed on Lee and they widened. "Oh. I'll get her." She rushed away into the next room.

I looked around at all the children. There were eight kids between the ages of five and twelve, and by the sound of the infants crying, I suspected there were many more in the next room. "Is she alone?" I asked, knowing that one person could not provide adequate care for so many children on her own.

"Yes," Annabelle said. "Our only other caretaker, Kathy, is also a nurse and can't work here every day. Perkins hasn't assigned any other women besides them to the school since it was established."

"Why women?" Miriam demanded. "Why can't he just assign anyone?"

"It's very old fashioned here," Annabelle said curtly, clearly not liking this fact. "Most of the men are soldiers or building the ship. All the women are assigned to lesser jobs, like this."

"They're building a ship?" I asked, but before anyone could answer, Ingrid came out with a toddler in her arms.

"Here you go." Ingrid passed the baby girl to Annabelle and rushed out again to attend to the crying infants.

The baby in Annabelle's arms had Annabelle's blue eyes, but she had Lee's blonde hair. "This is Penny," she said, handing the baby to Lee. "I was about three months along when you left. She's sixteen months old now."

Lee was so stunned that I thought he might drop his daughter. He stared at her, and she stared back at him. "Mine?" he whispered.

"Yes," Annabelle said, her voice cracking. "She's yours." She and Lee were both crying again, and the small family embraced.

~~*

After their brief reunion, Penny was left inside and we sat outside on the front steps, Annabelle now telling her story.

"After Lee left, Perkins had me thrown in Rebellion's jail and had me beaten. One man in particular, Trey Barnes, enjoyed raping me while his buddies watched. When they found out I was pregnant, the beating and raping stopped, but Perkins then told me that Trey Barnes was my husband, and Penny was his daughter."

That explained the nice apartment…

"There wasn't anything I could do. I couldn't leave; Barnes made sure of it. If I defy him or Perkins, if I don't do something they want me to do, they hurt Penny. I learned that quickly enough. I was planning to run away, find a way to escape, because I know if I don't get Penny out of here Barnes will start hurting her soon for no reason. And not just physically.

"I'm not the only woman Perkins has done this to. He assigns most unmarried women to one of his soldiers. Ingrid, the girl who takes care of the kids, she's assigned to one of the lower-ranked soldiers. Thankfully, he's not like the others. He's good to her, won't even touch her if she says no. Lois, the head physician, she's assigned to Perkins himself. She just had twins a few months ago, a boy and a girl. She can barely look at them after what Perkins did to her." Her voice dropped to a whisper. "I'm only telling you this because I know you're on my side. There's a group of us, mostly people who are mistreated by Perkins, who have organized to try to overthrow him. We have meetings every Wednesday. I hope to see you there tomorrow night."

"Where do we go?" I asked.

"I can't say," she replied. "None of us are allowed to say where the meetings are held. I'll take you there."

"What is this about a ship?" Miriam asked, bringing up what I'd been wanting to ask. "You're building a ship?"

"Perkins is making us build another ship," Lee said. "From the outside, it looks just like a New Age Cruise ship, so satellite imagery can't give away what it really is."

"What is it?" From Lee's earlier story, I thought maybe they were rebuilding the *Majesty*, to finally complete it, but that didn't really make sense. Then again, Perkins was a nut job, so who knew?

Lee and Annabelle exchanged looks. "Perkins named it the *Defiant*. It's a battleship."

"*A battleship?*" I repeated, flabbergasted. "Why the hell is he building a battleship?"

"We don't know," Annabelle said. "He only tells his top officers. Barnes doesn't even know. But whatever he's building it for, it can't be anything good."

If Perkins was building a battleship, then he was planning to use it for a fight. Would he attack the humans? The Colicians? Both? I didn't know any more than Lee or Annabelle, but I did know that we couldn't let Perkins carry out his plan.

"How long do we have left until the ship's completion?" I asked.

Annabelle shrugged. "A month? Maybe two. Not long, though. He's got most of Rebellion's population working on it."

"We need to figure out what he's planning to use that ship for and stop him," I said.

"No shit, Sherlock," Annabelle said. "What do you think we talk about in our meetings?"

"Then I'm coming tomorrow night," I said. "And we need to start having them more than once a week."

"Who died and made you king?" Annabelle snapped. "The only reason we don't have them more often is because Perkins and his army of numb nuts would notice if we did. Wednesday is the night they all go out to the bars and get shit-faced, so that's the night we can sneak around and not get caught."

"Well, Perkins and his pals are going to be going out to the bars more often."

"How do expect to convince him to allow that?"

I shrugged. "I don't know, but that's what's going to happen."

Annabelle stared at me, bewildered. "You're reaching a little too high for someone who walked through the gate less than an hour ago. You don't know shit about this place."

"Maybe that will help me," I said. "Look, I'm not going to sit here and fall into some stupid routine and pick my ass while a dictator is abusing my people. I don't care if I'm new and don't know squat about this place. I'm going to do something, and I'm going to start today."

Annabelle laughed scornfully. "Well I hope you've made your funeral plans, pal."

We sat in silence for a moment. Miriam was rocking James again, his car seat resting on a step. She absentmindedly gazed up the street. I looked back toward the front door of the school, another question pestering me. "Why are there Caiten children?" I asked. "I understand that babies have been born, but some of those kids were too old to have been born after the introduction of the Caiten Strain."

"Hillerman's not as nice as he seems," Annabelle muttered. "If he's going to make super soldiers, why not infect some children while he's at it, so they can grow up with their abilities and be better fighters when they're old enough?"

"Christ," I said, dropping my head in my hands.

Before Annabelle could add anything else, one of Perkins's white pickups squealed to a halt right in front of us, spraying us with dust and gravel. For a second I panicked, thinking we'd just been busted for talking rebellion. But I calmed when the dust cleared and I saw it was

Quinn. He rolled down his window and said, "Get in. I'm taking you to see Vincent."

I turned to Miriam, but she was already up and taking James inside the school. "Go," she told me. "I can't leave Ingrid to look after these kids alone. Go. Tell me how he is later."

I climbed into the passenger side and Quinn sped off.

~~*

When we arrived at the makeshift hospital, which was actually one of the nicer buildings in town, we went straight to Vincent's room and I sensed immediately that something was wrong. Vincent was different.

"What happened?" I demanded, glaring at him. "What did you do?"

He glanced away. "What I had to."

I looked at Lois, who was standing beside his bed. "How could you do it? How could you?"

"It was what he wanted," she replied quietly, her expression unchanging despite my outburst.

"You're an idiot," I said to Vincent. "You know that? You're a fucking idiot."

"Do you really think Perkins would have let him out alive as a human?" Lois asked me, her voice still calm. "This was his best shot at survival, and he asked me to change him."

"The only family I have left are Caitens," Vincent said defensively. "There wasn't any reason to stay human any longer."

"How did you even do it?"

"They have samples of the virus," Vincent said. "They stole some when they broke out."

"I hope your headache's a bitch," I said, and then stormed out. I didn't understand how Vincent could willingly accept something like this, even if what he said was true. Becoming a Caiten amidst a world of humans was not a gift, regardless of what Miriam and James were.

I couldn't face Miriam right now. I was too enraged to let myself be around her and our son. So I went to the only place I knew I could go to blow off steam: Chuck's Tavern. I went right up to the bar and selected a stool. The two other men at the bar and the bartender—Chuck?—were all older men with long, scraggly beards and hick outfits.

"New guy?" Chuck asked, bringing me a glass.

"Give me a shot of the strongest stuff you've got," I ordered without answering.

Chuck raised his eyebrows and looked as if he was going to ask if I was sure, but the expression on my face must have changed his mind. He shrugged and pulled a bottle of clear alcohol out from a cabinet below the counter. He poured me a shot and I downed it without even asking what it was. My rage prevented me from even feeling the burn as it went down. Chuck stared at me in shock when I held out my glass for another. "That's pretty strong. You shouldn't have another."

"Does it look like I give a shit?"

I guessed it didn't. He poured me another and put the bottle away. "I can't give you another," he said.

The first shot had cleared my head enough for me to choke on the second as it went down. I coughed and sputtered, making the two guys across the bar snicker at me as they drank their beers.

I guessed I should've listened to Chuck. My head was spinning and I couldn't see or think straight. I didn't even know Perkins had sat down beside me until he spoke. "First day and you're already drinking, eh?"

I turned to him, but it didn't make much of a difference. His face swam in front of me and the only way I knew it was him was because of his voice. "You'd be drinking too if you just found out that your girlfriend's brother turned himself into a freak," I muttered, my words barely distinguishable.

"Oh, yes," Perkins said, and I saw him smile. "Lois told me about him. Vincent, right? Well, he made the right decision. We're better changed."

I felt my anger beginning to take over again. I clenched my fists, trying to keep myself from vomiting up words that would get me in trouble.

"Hey, Chuck!" Perkins called. "Bring us two cold ones, will you?" Chuck brought us our beers and Perkins drank deeply from his. I didn't touch mine. "How old's your son now? James, right?"

I tried to think through the haze in my brain. "Like a week?" I said. It hadn't been easy keeping track of time lately.

"My twins are about three months now," Perkins told me. "A boy and a girl. Their names are Harvey and Jessica. You should start introducing your boy to my daughter soon. They're going to be husband and wife when they're older."

A burst of rage ripped through me. How dare he tell me who my son was going to marry! "My boy will marry who he wants to marry," I snapped. Had I been sober and not so angry, I would have just said, "Okay," but he caught me at a bad time and my lips were flapping again.

Perkins just chuckled, which both startled and relieved me. "I understand. You're new. Soon you'll start to see how this place works. Besides, you should be flattered. You and Miriam are both New Caitens, infected with a stronger strain. You are more powerful than any of the others here, save for me. I am the most powerful of all of you. Our children are good matches." He paused. "Are you and Miriam planning to marry?"

"Yes," I blurted. We hadn't discussed marriage, but I wasn't about to give Perkins a reason to pair her with some soldier. "We are."

"Excellent. I'll have the priest stop by your place tomorrow. You should plan to have it done this month." He finished his beer and stood up. "I would like to know, Austin, if you would like to be one of my top lieutenants?"

I was surprised, and through my haze I realized that I needed to take advantage of this moment. "Actually," I said. "I was hoping I could help with the ship's design."

Perkins blinked in surprise, and then his eyes flared angrily.

I thought quickly. "Lee told me about it because he knew about my past jobs. I used to be an accountant, and I'm very good with math. I could help with the engineering and planning. He knew I would be good for this position, which is why he told me. Please don't be angry with him; he was only thinking of Rebellion's best interest."

Perkins's expression softened, and he nodded thoughtfully. "That sounds like a great idea," he said. "Lee was right to tell you." He pointed at me. "You'll start Thursday. Quinn will take you where you need to go. Don't disappoint me."

"Sir?" I said as he started for the door. When he turned back to me, I said, "Vincent, Miriam's brother, used to be a soldier. He's very fierce and smart. He'll make an excellent addition to your...uh...military."

Perkins smiled his creepy, crooked smile. "Great. When the change is complete, I'll be sure to add him in. I've been needing a new top lieutenant for a while now. I finally have a *real* soldier!"

~~*

I gave Perkins thirty seconds to get lost before I ran out the door. I ran straight back to the hospital, a good half mile from the tavern. It was the largest building in town. The back of it was just yards from the sandy beach. About a mile south, I could see the port where the *Defiant* was being built.

Just before I reached the hospital, I paused. I looked out at the Atlantic, where the sky and water met on the horizon. It was beautiful. Looking out there, it was easy to forget everything that had happened. The lab. Kost. The Parallel Earth. Rebellion. Everything. It made me realize that there was still beauty in the world, even after all the horrible events of the past few months.

I continued on my way, entering the hospital and jogging to Vincent's room. When I entered this time, he was alone.

"Come back to chew me out some more?" he snapped, glaring at me.

"Listen, this may actually work to our advantage," I said, pulling up a chair and sitting next to him.

"Is that supposed to be an apology?"

"No," I replied. "I still think you're an idiot. *Listen.* Perkins is building a battleship. We don't know for what specifically, but it can't be good. He's going to make you one of his soldiers and you're going to infiltrate his operation to figure out what the hell's going on."

"What?" Vincent looked completely lost. "He's building a *battleship*?"

"I don't have time to explain it all right now." My words were slurring and I was out of breath. "When you're a freak like me, I'll let you read my mind."

"Are you drunk?" he asked me dubiously.

"A little," I said. My head was spinning and my breathing became heavier. "Maybe a lot. Oh…crap." I fell over and passed out, right after I puked all over myself.

~~*

I woke up in my new apartment. I knew that right away because of the smell. I blinked awake to a splitting headache, the pain searing my brain. It was so awful that I couldn't even sit up. I looked down at myself, seeing that I had clean clothes on. My breath was foul. The taste almost made me hurl again. With great effort, I rolled my head to the side. Miriam was in a chair next to the bed, her expression stony.

"Hey," I said, knowing what I was about to get.

"Feel like crap?" she asked curtly.

"Yeah," I replied.

"What the hell do you think you're doing?"

"Vincent let Lois change him."

"Yes, so I've heard. So you thought it would be a good idea to go get shit-faced?"

"I was pissed." I didn't understand why she was so angry with me. If anyone, she should be mad at her brother.

"That's not an excuse! Damn you, Austin!"

I looked around. "Where's James?"

"He's with Annabelle." She crossed her arms. "This isn't about him." She paused, thinking. "You know what, it is. You're a father, Austin! You can't act like a child when you have one! You can't have a tantrum and go get drunk! That's not how this works."

"Why are you yelling at me?" I snapped.

"Because you're juvenile!" she shouted, her face red. "I thought you'd grown up, but you're not any different than when we were in the study! You're immature and you do stupid things when you're angry! If you want to be a part of our son's life, and mine, then you need to grow up! *Now.*"

I couldn't believe it. Miriam was threatening to take James away from me. I wanted to retaliate, shout back at her, but she was right. And that just pissed me off even more. I pursed my lips and looked up at the ceiling, hating her and myself.

"Now," Miriam said, much more calmly. "I'm taking James, and I'm going to stay at the hospital tonight with Vincent. Get some rest and clean yourself up. I'll see you tomorrow." As she walked to the door, she called over her shoulder, "There're three water bottles on the counter. You're supposed to drink one an hour, to hydrate yourself. Don't drink the water out of the tap. Trust me." And then she was gone.

~~*

I slept on and off for hours. Miriam had placed a bucket next to the bed, and I was grateful for it. I wanted the water she left for me on the counter, but I was unable to reach it from where I lay. My throat was dry and the headache wasn't getting any better. Finally, when the sun was setting, I dozed off and didn't wake up until the sky was purple from daybreak. I felt a lot better, and I went to the counter, took one of the water bottles, and downed it. My stomach sloshed, but I drank half of another anyway. I went back to the bed and sat down, thinking of everything that had happened the day before.

I needed Miriam and James in my life. They were my family, and I loved them. I was willing to do anything it took to prove I was worthy of them.

Grabbing the half-empty water bottle, I went down to Annabelle's room and knocked loudly. I knew it was early and I was being rude, but I needed to do this and I needed to get it done before Miriam came back.

The door opened slowly, and I began. "Hey, Annabelle, I was wondering—"

It was not Annabelle who answered the door. It was a man with dark brown hair and sleepy brown eyes. He was taller than me by a few inches. His shoulders were broad and he seemed to be a fairly attractive guy. But I didn't see any of that. No, all I saw was Trey Barnes the rapist.

"Can I help you?" he asked, clearly annoyed. He yawned loudly, showing off his straight white teeth. Why did God make horrible people so perfect?

"I'm looking for Annabelle," I said through my teeth.

"Who are you?" Barnes demanded, sizing me up.

"A friend," I replied curtly. "Austin Rockwell."

"Oh," he said, smiling. "The new guy."

"Yeah," I said impatiently. "So is Annabelle here or not?"

"She's not," Barnes said, yawning again. "She works the night shifts at Chuck's on Tuesdays and Thursdays. Maybe I can help you?"

"I was wondering if I could borrow your cleaning supplies," I said. "Because my apartment smells like a rotting corpse."

He gazed back at me for a moment, a cocky sneer on his face. "Sure. Hold on." He went back inside and a minute later, he came back and handed me a gallon ice cream bucket full of supplies. "Here you go. Hope everything gets taken care of."

"Thanks," I muttered, taking it and turning to go. I stopped and turned back. "One more thing," I said, jabbing my finger at him. He sneered back at me, as if he knew what I wanted to say to him but also knew that I wouldn't say it. I was going to say, "Touch Annabelle again and I'll cut your nads off," but I thought back to what Miriam said. I couldn't get into trouble because of my anger, even if it was for something like this. I shook my head at him and stalked away.

Just before I was out of earshot, he called after me, "Tell your girl I think she's very pretty." I almost turned around to go practice a tae kwon do move on him I'd learned several years ago, but I made myself keep going.

~~*

I started with the kitchen. If my child and girlfriend were going to eat in here, they were not going to eat out of that filthy fridge and off that filthy counter. I scrubbed them both until my fingers bled and then I scrubbed some more. I scraped off mold, mopped up dust, and even got rid of the decomposing rat in one upper cabinet, which explained the smell of death. I didn't have the proper tools to fix the sink and get clean water flowing through it again, but I vowed to do so that day. I mopped the floor of the entire apartment three times, and then moved into the bathroom.

For four hours I cleaned. By the time Miriam brought James back, everything except the bed, kitchen sink, and bathroom sink had been taken care of.

"Austin," she said in amazement, staring at the clean room with an open mouth. She inhaled the smell of cleanliness, relief flooding her eyes. "What the hell?"

"Hey," I said. I grabbed the air freshener and sprayed some over the bed, inside the cabinet where I found the dead rat, and in the bathroom.

"What are you doing?" she asked, her surprise leaving her breathless.

"I've cleaned everything except the bed," I told her. "And both the sinks are broken. I didn't know where to get new sheets or tools for the sinks, so I figured we could go looking today. Oh, and we'll have to go grocery shopping too, as well as clothes shopping." I gestured around the skimpy apartment. "If anything isn't the way you want it, feel free to change it."

"Austin." She was staring at me with a strange look in her eyes. "Did you do this all by yourself?"

I nodded. "You were right. I need to grow up. If not for you, then for James. I figured this might be a good way to start."

Miriam set James down in his car seat and hugged me tightly. "Thank you," she whispered. "It looks great."

I smiled when she pulled away. "Can we be friends again?"

She offered me a smile in return, but I saw a devious glint in her eyes. "I'll think about it," she said, and we both laughed.

17

Rebellion's Rebels

I wasn't tired that day, surprisingly. Miriam and I went grocery shopping shortly after she came back; we left James at the nursery with Ingrid and the other childcare worker, Kathy, who was finally feeling better. We were given a small allowance that morning by Quinn to last us until we started working. We went to the grocery store and met the nice couple who owned it, Anne and Gary Evans. They helped us find everything we needed to last the next few days, and even offered us baby formula at half price.

Anne and Gary were in their sixties. They were friendly, but I saw the fear in their eyes that I saw in most of the Caitens of Rebellion. Anne had short, light brown hair that was graying, and peered at us through thick, square-framed glasses. She was short and folded her arms over her stomach a lot when she spoke, as if she were protecting herself from a possible blow. When she reached up to grab something off a shelf for us, her shirt pulled up slightly and I saw an enormous purple bruise. She must have mouthed off to one of our "superiors."

Gary had blonde hair that was graying and also had square-framed glasses. He was a little taller than Anne but still shorter than me. He stood close to his wife the whole time and didn't say much. I saw the anger in his body language, and knew that I would feel the same way if someone hurt Miriam the way Anne was hurt.

I wondered if this couple was an older version of Miriam and me.

We thanked them and asked them if they knew a good place to buy new sheets.

"There isn't anywhere in town you can buy sheets," Anne apologized. "But if you go to Ulysses's hardware store, he sells blankets in the back. You can take your old sheets to the Laundromat down the street. The woman who runs it uses a special home-made detergent to clean them, and it works wonders."

The news irritated me, but it seemed to be the best we could do.

Ulysses was short and stocky. He was in his forties or fifties and had no hair. His lower jaw hung down slightly as he watched us walk in, making him look like a piranha.

"Can I help you?" he asked, his serious face not shedding any friendliness. He stood behind a counter and looked to be mending a tool. He reminded me of a big bull, and I pictured him slamming through the counter and bulldozing right over us.

"Anne Evans told us this was a good place to buy new blankets," Miriam said, shifting uncomfortably. "We're new in town, so—"

"I know that, miss," Ulysses said. He took us both in, one at a time, studying our faces, our body language. "She told you correctly. Right this way."

We followed him down rows of tools and household items to the back of the store, where there were piles of blankets of all different colors and fabrics.

"Well, here you are." Ulysses waved his hand down the row. "Was there something specific you were looking for?"

"Um…" I looked at Miriam, since I wasn't really an expert on these things.

"Four," she told him. "Two small, two large. Soft, but not itchy. Color doesn't matter."

Ulysses sighed, as if this were a chore for him, went down the row, and selected four. The two large ones were red and the small ones were blue. They were all made from alpaca fiber, but had no designs on them. "Here." He handed them all to me. "Anything else?"

I started to say "No," but Miriam said, "Could we get some sandpaper too? Our baby's cradle has a few rough edges."

The stern, tough expression on Ulysses's face melted away with Miriam's words. "You have a child?"

"Yeah," Miriam said, looking at me uncertainly.

Ulysses disappeared around the corner for a few moments, and when he returned he had six sheets of unused sandpaper with him. He handed them to her.

"How much is this?" I asked him, hoping we still had enough.

"Nothing," he replied.

I hesitated. "Excuse me?"

"You keep it." Ulysses waved his hands at us. "You're trying to take care of your child. I'm not going to hinder your attempts. Keep it. Please."

I was going to argue, but the bizarre feeling I was getting from him kept me from doing so. "Thank you, sir."

"If you need any paint for the cradle or your apartment, please don't hesitate to ask." He walked us out.

"Thank you," Miriam said as we stepped outside, but he was already going back to his desk. We exchanged confused glances and went on our way.

"I guess he's got a soft spot for kids," I muttered.

~~*

Later that morning, when we got together with Annabelle and Lee in our apartment, Annabelle told us about Ulysses.

"The reason General Grant acts so stern," she said, "is because he's endured a world of heartache. It's his way of sheltering himself."

"General Grant?" I repeated.

"General Ulysses S. Grant?" Annabelle gazed at me expectantly. "He was the commanding general for the Union during the United States' Civil War. Mr. Ulysses Branson is a decorated general from the Army, so we all call him General Grant as a joke. Well, all of us who are..." She trailed off and looked away.

"He's one of the rebels, isn't he?" I asked.

"I'm not allowed to say who is and who isn't," she told me. "But what I tell you next should answer that question. His son and wife were both changed during the Colician outbreak. His wife was shot dead when a retrieval unit went to pick them up and she fought back. He doesn't know what happened to his son, but he never received any notification that the boy was alive, so he assumes he's dead. Ulysses's daughter fell in love with Anne and Gary's son after they were all changed. They were expecting a child."

"Hold on," I said, taking a step back. "Anne and Gary have a son?"

"I'm getting to that. When Perkins took control, Lilia Branson and Logan Evans were two others who fought back with me."

"So he drove them both nuts?"

Annabelle hesitated. I realized that this memory haunted her. "Not them. He made examples of those two. He killed them. Then he..." She swallowed so hard that she coughed. She was trying not to gag. "Then he cut out the unborn fetus in Lilia's womb and sent it to Ulysses in a box."

"Oh my God!" I covered my mouth with my hand and Miriam gagged slightly.

"Please tell me that didn't really happen," I said. The look she gave me told me it was the truth.

"Now you know why he is the way he is," Annabelle said. "In case he does something out of the blue that surprises you like he did this morning, you'll know why. He feels compassion for your baby because Perkins killed his daughter and his baby granddaughter. Many of us have lost a lot, but not many have sacrificed as much as Ulysses."

I felt a lot of pain for Ulysses, and I also felt guilt. I'd experienced so much grief over what I'd lost, but I couldn't imagine going through the mental agony that Ulysses had.

"I'm sorry," Annabelle said. "That was a pretty blunt way to say it."

"No," I said. "I mean, yes, it was, but I needed to hear it that way."

"We both did." Miriam's face was white. "It ensures our involvement in your movement. There's no way I will go about my life here like nothing's wrong. I wouldn't have before, but now I will make sure Perkins goes down no matter what happens to me."

"I'm sorry I left," Lee said suddenly. He was sitting in the armchair beside the bed, his guilt-stricken eyes on the floor.

"It's not your fault, Lee," Annabelle replied, going to him and kneeling in front of him. She took his hand. "I don't blame you for leaving. I never did."

"You hit me…" Lee whispered.

"I was angry," she told him, stroking his face. "But at myself, not you. It was never your fault. It was mine, for fighting back. If I hadn't fought, this wouldn't have happened to you." She hugged him tightly and kissed him hard on the mouth.

"I'm still sorry," Lee said. "I'm sorry for what happened to you after I left. I want to kill that man Barnes for hurting you. And I left you when you were with child…"

"You didn't know!" Annabelle sighed. "Lee, this was *all my fault,* and no amount of blame you put on yourself will change that. Don't punish yourself. Besides, it's over. You're back."

"Do you really think Perkins will just let me have you back?"

Annabelle laughed scornfully. "Do you think I give a damn what Perkins wants? You're mine, and I'm yours. I'll never belong to anyone else."

I had to smile at that. I took Miriam's hand and squeezed it, thinking the exact same thing applied to us. I could never belong to anyone else, no matter what.

"So Perkins is still making you stay with Barnes?" Miriam asked.

"Don't you remember?" Annabelle smiled bitterly. "He's my husband and Penny is his child."

Miriam's face twitched in anger and disgust. I was glad I hadn't mentioned my conversation with Perkins from yesterday, or my brief encounter with Barnes.

"So where are you staying, Lee?" I asked, before Miriam had a chance to blow up.

Lee shrugged. "Another apartment. On the other side of the block."

"Perkins put you there intentionally," Miriam said through her teeth.

"*Barnes* put him there intentionally," Annabelle corrected.

"This is such..." Miriam stopped herself from cursing, but I could feel the inevitable eruption coming.

"Miriam," I said warningly.

"No!" She stood up, letting her opinion be heard. "This is ridiculous! I haven't been here two days and I hate this place! I'd rather live with humans than in this godforsaken hell-hole!"

I took her hand and pulled her down. "Listen to me. I know this sucks, but we have to stay for now. We can't leave everyone else here. We have to help." I looked at Annabelle and Lee, our friends. "For them."

"What are we gonna do to make this place any better?" Miriam demanded, the fire still in her eyes.

I smiled. "I've got a job working on the ship."

Annabelle gasped. "You *what*? How?"

"How did you convince Perkins to let you in?" Lee asked skeptically.

"I guess I'm a better liar than I thought," I said. "Besides, he was already offering me a position in his ranks. I thought I could get better information if I'm actually on the ship. And Vincent's going to be one of Perkins's soldiers once he's totally changed."

"You convinced *Vincent* to work with *Perkins*?" Miriam asked, her disbelieving expression pretty amusing.

"Well..." I realized I never went back to explain the whole problem and solution to Vincent. "I told Perkins that Vincent was a soldier and he would be a good addition to the security team." I saw the anger flash onto Miriam's face again and tried to finish quickly. "I know that Vincent can figure out what's going on, what Perkins is planning."

"You signed Vincent up for something that dangerous and didn't even *ask* him?" Miriam demanded.

"I know Vincent can do this, and I know he'll *want* to do this. We need more people in deep, Miriam. I can find out important details where I'll be, but Vincent can get priceless intel working directly with Perkins. Trust me, Miriam. This will work."

Miriam's anger was fading, but she still looked irritated. "What am I supposed to do in the meantime? Do a job designated for a woman? Maybe I'll just stay here and make sandwiches for all the men during their lunch break."

"I know this eats away at your pride Miriam, and I'm sorry that it is this way, but if we want this to work, we have to play along. Can you do that? Please?"

With a huff, Miriam grumbled, "If Annabelle can do it, then so can I."

I kissed her forehead. "Thank you, baby. This will all work out. I promise."

~~*

Miriam decided to work in the nursery with Ingrid and Kathy. She felt that there were far too many kids for two girls to handle, so she insisted upon taking a position there. She started that afternoon

Since Annabelle had to get to work and Lee had to make sure he wasn't seen around her, I was alone that afternoon. For lack of anything better to do, I went to see Vincent so I could try to explain to him what his task would be during our time in Rebellion.

"So you want me to pretend to be an asshole so I can infiltrate security, so we can figure out what they're planning to attack with their enormous battleship?"

"That about sums it up," I said.

"Sounds like a piece of cake," Vincent said sarcastically. "Thanks for promoting me, buddy. So glad you're willing to speak for me."

"Look, dude, I'm trying to help the Caitens living here, which right now is you, me, and everyone we care about. If you don't want to live here forever, and believe me, you don't, then you really should do this. Besides, I thought you'd be happy to help."

"Oh, I am," Vincent said. "I just wish you'd talked to me before signing me up for something that could cost me my life."

"Yes, I know, and I'm sorry, but the opportunity was there so I seized it." I peered at him. "Has the headache started yet?"

He shook his head and shrugged. "Lois mentioned something about adding a compound in with the virus that acts as a painkiller. Haven't felt a twinge so far."

"I hate you," I told him.

I took a walk after visiting Vincent, through the town to check out every corner of it. The only shops were on the main street near the bar and grocery store. There were about half a dozen more we hadn't been to, almost all run by the women of Rebellion. I learned that the women who didn't work in the shops were nurses and interns at the hospital; Perkins allowed no women on the ship's construction team or in his military.

The rest of the town was made up of apartment blocks and a few other small maintenance buildings. Mostly it was just empty, wild animals and plants running the place. In part of the town I thought was abandoned, along the western perimeter fence, I found a small building with no sign that was leaning to one side. I shivered. Annabelle told me about this place; it was Rebellion's "Correctional Facility," otherwise known as the Rape Dungeon. That was where Annabelle was tortured and raped relentlessly. I wanted to go tear that place apart, knock down what was on the verge of falling anyway.

I averted my eyes from that horrible place and continued on. I never wanted to see that building again, unless it was to tear it apart piece by piece.

I walked back toward the main street, planning to go visit James and Miriam. I was still pretty far away when I started hearing the voice in my head. At first, I didn't realize it was in my head. I thought it was someone in town yelling my name, but then I recognized the voice as it grew louder and more distinct.

Austin! Austin! Can you hear me? Hello? Austin?

Jeff! I cried, almost shouting it out loud. *You're alive! How are you?*

Much better, he replied. *Dr. Perry said I should be fine from here on out. What about you and the others? How is everyone?*

I started running toward the nursery, excited to tell Miriam the good news. *It's not so great over here, my friend. The man in charge, a soldier called Perkins, has everyone under his thumb. Don't come here, man. Stay where you are. We could use your help from over there.*

I'm not going to leave you there if you're in danger! Has anyone been hurt?

No. Well, he killed a Colician, but so far none of us have been hurt. Vincent and I are going to begin infiltrating Perkins's command structure tomorrow with new jobs. We'll relay information to you. Can you and the Colicians help us figure out what's going on here?

Sure. If I can't help you there, I'm going to help you here.

Thanks. Are they treating you well over there?

Of course. Why wouldn't they?

Just making sure. Talk to Walter for me. Tell him he was right.

How big is the town?

There are a few thousand people here. The town is called Rebellion. Hillerman's still making more of us, and in more locations than just Philadelphia. This is going to get out of hand.

No kidding. How's James?

He's good. He's growing. Miriam's working in the nursery where he goes during the day.

What are you going to do for your job?

I paused. *That's a bit of a story. I'll have to tell you—*

"Stop!"

I'd just reached the main street when I heard the shout. I stopped in my tracks, startled, and stared as five men in military attire came rushing at me from all directions. Jeff was shouting at me in my head, asking what was happening, but for some reason I felt myself unable to answer.

As the men approached, they all drew out their weapons: some handguns, some rifles, and one AK-47. I raised my hands instinctively, not sure what I'd done.

"Get on the ground!" one man yelled, and I realized it was Barnes.

I didn't have time to lower myself to the ground; I simply fell. I couldn't move, and as I was cuffed and carried off by the soldiers I understood that they were all suppressing my ability to function. I couldn't fight back, I couldn't even speak. The last thing I remember was Jeff saying, *Jesus, Austin. You need to get out of there!*

~~*

Barnes doused me with a bucket of water to wake me up. I shook my head and sputtered, blinking the water out of my eyes. I heard snide laughter around me, and I saw that there were six men with me in a small concrete room. Five were the men who'd rendered me helpless and then hauled me off, and the sixth was Perkins. He sat in a chair in front of me, looking none too happy. I was sitting in another chair with wobbly legs, my wrists cuffed behind me. I knew exactly where I was: The Rape Dungeon.

Barnes and his buddies were cracking jokes about me as they stood off to the side of the cell, allowing Perkins to have the first go at me. "You're in a hell of a lot of trouble, boy," he growled.

The cell was cramped, smelled of mold, and had no windows. A single dull bulb hung overhead, casting eerie shadows around the room. It was also surprisingly cold, causing me to shiver in my soaked clothes.

"Why?" I asked, still confused as to what I had done.

Perkins looked to Barnes, and Barnes explained, "You were projecting a message to someone not in Rebellion." He stepped forward and punched me in the side of the nose. "That's illegal."

My nose throbbed and I felt a little blood starting to drip out of one nostril. "Jesus, asshole!" I snapped. "You didn't have to hit me!"

He hit me again. "Don't cuss, shit head."

His buddies laughed at that one.

"Leave him alone, Barnes," Perkins ordered as I wiped my bloody nose and lip on my shoulder. "I'm sure he has a perfectly good explanation for what he did."

"Yeah, I do." I glared at Barnes. "I was speaking to Jeff Robinson."

The other soldiers went silent.

"Is he well?" Perkins asked eagerly.

"No," I lied. "He's still sick, but getting better. And after hearing your minions attack me in the street, he says he doesn't even want to come here anymore. He said he'd rather stay with the Colicians if this is how things are run here." I flinched slightly, worried about what kind of retaliation I might receive from that comment, but also hoping that Perkins would get the message.

Perkins's expression was angry for a moment, but then it changed to concern for his image. "Please accept my apology, and relay that apology to your friend. I'm very sorry for what happened."

"It *is* illegal," Barnes pointed out, sneering at me.

"Well," I said, scowling back at him, "maybe next time you'll remember to tell newcomers the laws in this town before you beat the crap out of them!"

"Why were you telling him the town's population?" Barnes asked.

"He was curious," I said, relieved that was all he had heard of our conversation. "He wanted to know how many of us were living together."

"He doesn't plan to relay any information to the Colicians, does he?" Barnes asked suspiciously.

"No," I lied again. "He's not like that. That information was for him and him only." I suddenly had a burst of fear. We were all Caitens; we could all read each other's minds. How come none of them had caught me in the act of lying yet? Was no one actually *using* the abilities they were given? I'd already told Perkins several lies, and not just today. If he was so powerful, why wasn't he using his power to his advantage? More questions for Annabelle.

"Well, you're free to go then," Perkins said, and one of the other soldiers uncuffed me. "Sorry for the confusion. And don't do it again."

"Now that I know it's illegal, I'll be sure not to do it again." I glared at Barnes again as he walked out.

"Oh, Rockwell." Barnes sneered back at me. "Tell your friend Stewart to stay away from my girl."

"She's not your girl!" I started to snap, but I stopped myself.

"He's right, Austin," Perkins said. "Lee chose to leave, and Annabelle was paired with Barnes. That's how it works here."

"Whatever," I muttered, and quickly went home and locked myself in my apartment.

~~*

I slept for about an hour, despite my pounding heart. When I woke, I saw a bloody circle on the pillow where my face had been; my nose had started bleeding again. I went into the bathroom and cleaned the crusty blood off my face. There was a large bruise on the left side of my face where I'd been punched. I gently touched it and winced. I tested my facial muscles and found that simply smiling caused a burst of searing pain.

"Crap," I muttered. I'd better go to Lois to make sure nothing was broken, but first I had to talk to Annabelle.

"What the hell happened to your face?" Annabelle gasped when I entered the tavern and took a seat at the bar.

"Your husband's quite a catch," I replied, offering a sarcastic smile and then wincing.

"You didn't pick a fight with him, did you?" she demanded in a whisper.

"Why are you whispering?" I asked. We were the only two in the tavern. Chuck wasn't even around.

"Because if the wrong person finds me talking to you, it's my ass that will get in trouble!"

This news startled me. "You'll get in trouble for talking to me?"

"After the uprising, if I'm seen talking with any non-soldier by myself, especially a guy, people get suspicious. Barnes especially."

"I'll have a beer then," I said. When she brought me one, I dumped it all out on the counter in front of me. "Oops. Sorry. I guess you now have a legit excuse to be over here talking to me."

Annabelle gave me a dirty look and grabbed a couple rags. She brought me another beer and began to slowly mop up the mess. "So what exactly happened?" she asked, her voice still low.

"Jeff contacted me," I explained. "He's still on the Parallel Earth, and in the middle of our conversation Barnes and a few others attacked me and dragged me off to some cell. Perkins was there, and then Barnes started hitting me, telling me I was 'projecting a message' and that it's illegal."

"It *is*," Annabelle pointed out.

"Nobody told me this!" I snapped. "No one tells me anything until I start asking questions! I don't even know this town's laws until I get beaten for breaking them!"

"Welcome to Rebellion, Austin," Annabelle said flatly. She was clearly not in the best mood. "It sucks. Get used to it."

I stared at her, but she wasn't making eye contact. She continued to mop up the spilled beer, a dark expression on her face. "Are you okay?" I asked.

"No, I'm not okay." She tossed the soaked rag over her shoulder and glared at me. "I'm in a forced abusive relationship, I'm now threatened if I have anything to do with the man I really love, and I'm stuck working this shitty job because the man in charge of this shit town is a psycho sexist! My life sucks, Austin! At least you get to stay with the person you love. I get beaten and I can't even be with Lee." She looked away, her eyes misty.

"I'm sorry," I muttered.

"Don't be." She grabbed another rag to finish cleaning up. "There's nothing you can do for me."

I knew that there was, but it would take time. We were going to overthrow this dictatorship, no matter what.

"I was wondering," I said, remembering the actual reason I'd come. "I was lying to Perkins's face with five other guys ready to knock my teeth in, and none of them caught me. This isn't the first time either. If he's so powerful, why isn't he using his ability?"

"He's projecting his mind around the whole town," Annabelle said. "Kind of like a force field, but it's to keep things in rather than out. He doesn't want other Caitens to use their abilities, so he projects a dampening field over everyone. You can still use your abilities, but what he does makes you sort of forget that you can. You've probably noticed that *you* haven't been using your ability much either."

I hadn't, but now I did.

"Anyway, since he's dedicating so much energy to that, he has trouble using his mind reading and mind controlling abilities. His force field thing is also why the other soldiers can't read your mind. You can lie to their faces and they'll never catch you."

"Then how did they catch me projecting my message to Jeff?"

"That was Perkins. Since it's *his* dampening field, he can sense if someone breaks through it. He sent those guys after you when he felt you break through."

"Wow," I said. "How do you know all this?"

"I read his mind," she replied, shrugging. "When I found out, it became easier and easier to use my ability. The same should go for you too."

"Is that how you managed to rebel?"

"Yeah," she muttered. "That's what happened."

I put my hand on hers, stopping her as she furiously cleaned the counter. "I promise you that things will get better. You just have to stick it out for a while longer."

Annabelle sighed, and she suddenly looked very tired. "It's not as easy as you think."

Someone behind me cleared his throat and startled us both. I snatched my hand away and Annabelle started cleaning again. I turned and saw Perkins standing behind us, his hands in his pockets. Crap. How much had he heard?

"Annabelle, have you made sure the spiced rum and whiskey have been thoroughly stocked for tonight?" he asked.

"Yes, sir," she muttered, turning her back on him.

I relaxed a little. If he'd heard anything threatening, he wouldn't be acting like this.

"Austin," Perkins said, gesturing for me to come with him. "Let's take a walk."

Seeing that it wasn't a request, I left with him. For a while we walked slowly down the main street. I kept waiting for him to speak, but for the longest time he didn't. Finally, he said, "So Annabelle is a friend of yours?"

"Yes," I said. "She's helped Miriam and I get settled in."

"Do you know of her past crimes?"

My stomach churned at the thought of what she went through, all because she wanted the chance to live free. "Yes," I said through my teeth.

"Then you should be careful who sees you with her," Perkins told me.

"Meaning you?" I stopped, facing him defiantly.

"Precisely." Perkins imitated my stance. "I don't want men who work for me to associate with criminals."

"I wasn't aware I worked for you."

"Who do you think you're working for?"

"The town of Rebellion."

Perkins laughed. "You're funny, Austin." He slapped my shoulder. "If you're working for Rebellion, you're working for me. It's as simple as that."

It was my turn to laugh. I was amazed by this man's stupidity. "Why does it matter who I associate with? I'm a Caiten. This town is the only haven for Caitens. Do you really think I would betray it?"

Perkins looked darkly at me. "I didn't think Annabelle would betray it."

We stood in silence, staring each other down, neither of our gazes faltering.

"Anyway," Perkins eventually said, clearing his throat. "The main reason I wished to speak with you was because I wanted to apologize again for what happened today. I am truly sorry."

"You don't have to apologize," I grumbled. "If anyone, it should be Barnes."

"And," Perkins added sharply, "I wanted to invite you to have drinks with my soldiers and myself tonight at the tavern, as a more informal apology. Drinks are on me."

I started to consent, but then I remembered what day it was: Wednesday. "I would," I said, "but I can't. Miriam and I still want to fix up our apartment, and then spend some time together as a family. Maybe next time. Thanks anyway."

Perkins nodded respectfully. "And I have no desire to get between a man and his family."

I almost laughed sarcastically, thinking of Lee, Annabelle, and Penny, but I stopped myself for their sake.

"Enjoy your evening then. And you should take care of that." Perkins pointed to the bruises on my face. "Tell the girl at the desk that I sent you. She'll get you right in to see Lois." He turned to leave, and as he walked away, he called back, "And I would like you to seriously consider what we talked about. About Annabelle."

I gritted my teeth, refusing to answer. Tonight couldn't come fast enough.

~~*

"Did you get hit by a car?" Lois asked when she saw me.

"Barnes, actually," I said.

"Wonderful," she muttered, peering at my face. "I thought I was going to see a soldier in here. Usually they're the only ones who get a cut-in-line pass from Perkins."

"Oh," I said, feeling guilty. "Were there people ahead of me?"

"Yes," Lois said, but she didn't elaborate.

"Well," I replied, feeling awkward and even more guilty. "Don't take too much time with me. I'll be fine."

She didn't respond. She studied my bruises carefully, gently prodding each one to see if she could feel anything broken. I winced each time she touched me, but I forced myself to hold still. My cheek was what hurt the worst, a sharp stab of pain shooting through my face with every move I made.

"Well," Lois said. "Your nose isn't broken, just seriously bruised. You have a minor fracture in your cheek, from what I can tell. There's nothing I can do for it, so just ice it a few times a day and refrain from any more fighting."

"I wasn't fighting!" I protested, but she was up and out before I got the words out of my mouth.

~~*

I was so relieved when Miriam finally came home. "Oh my God!" she said, her mouth falling open as she laid James down in his cradle. "What happened?"

"I committed a crime," I replied grimly. "I didn't *know* it was a crime, but I paid for it."

"What did you do?" I saw her anger returning.

"I talked to Jeff," I said. "He's okay, but I told him to stay with the Colicians. I told Perkins that he's still sick. And apparently it's illegal to project messages beyond the perimeter of Rebellion, just so you don't make that mistake, too."

"So they beat you?" Miriam demanded, her voice rising.

"Just forget about it," I begged. "It's over and done."

Miriam huffed, but she knew that we couldn't make a scene about these sorts of things without wrecking our master plan in the process.

"We should probably eat," I said, seeing the first shadows of sunset. "I'm not sure what time Annabelle's going to arrive to take us to the meeting." I went over to James's cradle and smiled down at him. "How's my little man?"

"Hungry," Miriam muttered. "I've nursed him almost nonstop all day."

"Hungry?" I said, picking up my baby and making a silly face at him while he laid in my arms. "Is my little man hungry?"

James scrunched up his face and smiled at me in return.

"He's probably just growing, and fast," I told her. "We really can't know what to expect with his development."

Miriam only shrugged in response and laid down.

For the next hour and a half, Miriam napped and I took care of James while making a small dinner. It was a quiet evening, and it was nice. This, I felt, is what family was all about: being able to do nothing with them and still enjoy their company.

Around 9:00, we dressed ourselves appropriately and waited for Annabelle to come get us. We told each other about our day, nothing exciting to note that hadn't already been said.

Annabelle came around 9:30, Penny sitting on her hip and clinging to her.

"Is there somewhere we should take James?" I asked.

"Bring him," Annabelle instructed. "We all take turns looking after the kids."

I could tell Miriam was hesitant about bringing James, and so was I, but what could we do? He should be sleeping, but we couldn't leave him here alone.

We left the building, Annabelle carefully scanning the area for potential problems. There were people in the street, but they didn't seem to be a threat because Annabelle didn't slow for them. We passed the bar, where there was hooting and hollering and a hell of a commotion going on inside. I glanced inside, but Annabelle told me to keep my eyes forward. Somehow I wasn't surprised when we went right up to the front door of Ulysses's Hardware & Home Maintenance and went right in.

Ulysses was seated behind his desk, reading a magazine that looked like it had gone through a shredder. Were we seriously not allowed to read anything up-to-date? Ulysses looked over the top of his magazine at us, taking in each of us individually, his gaze lingering over James and Penny. His gaze went back to Annabelle and he asked, "How was your day, Annabelle?"

Annabelle shrugged. "Pretty shittastic. Yours?"

"Same," he replied, looking over Miriam and I again. "What about them?"

"Their days were just as bad," Annabelle told him, and I had the odd feeling that she was reassuring him.

Ulysses nodded and waved toward the back, going back to his magazine.

Annabelle led us down the packed aisles to a door in the back, which she opened before starting down a dark set of stairs. "Be sure to close it behind you," she called back.

I bumped into Annabelle at the bottom, and Miriam bumped into me. Annabelle knocked six times in a rhythmic pattern on a wooden door. A few moments later it opened. A large man with whom I was not yet acquainted looked us over, his eyes narrowing.

"Relax, Pete," Annabelle said flatly, pushing past him and gesturing for us to follow. We walked down a long hallway and came to another door, which Annabelle opened on her own. This door was steel and heavy, and as it swung open, I jumped as I was greeted by an explosion of noise. James jumped in my arms and turned his head several times to see where we were, his mouth in the shape of an O.

Off to the side, in one of the corners, four adults were looking after a dozen or so infants and toddlers, and that was where Annabelle was heading to drop off Penny. In the other three corners, there were small groups of people arguing around small tables, and in the center, there was an enormous table, around which were dozens of men and women, all shouting at the head of the table, where Lois was standing. The expression on her face was like nothing I'd seen before. The anger, ferocity, and authority on her face scared me. She was shouting back at them, her face the color of a ripe tomato and the veins in her neck bulging out. After seeing the withdrawn, obedient woman Lois seemed to be, it was very startling to see her like this, in charge and furious.

It only took a few moments for the rebels to notice us, and when they did, the entire room went silent, apart from the kiddy corner. Some stared at us with amusement, some with disbelief, and others with anger or irritation.

The silence allowed Lois to catch her breath, and when she did she said, much softer than her previous words, "Austin, Miriam. Come join us."

The commotion began again, starting out soft but then rising to its earlier volume and intensity. I dropped James off with Gary, who was one of the people looking after the kids, and then went with Miriam to a corner of the large table, where we had to squeeze in between the others.

I didn't recognize a lot of the people around the table. I did see Anne across from us, and Quinn next to Lois, and I saw Ingrid with a young man who was in a soldier's uniform. I panicked at first, wondering why in the hell there would be a soldier here, but then I recalled what Annabelle told me about Ingrid's husband: "*He's good to her, won't even touch her if she says no.*" I guessed that meant he wasn't just kinder than the others; he had actually switched sides.

Now that we were closer to the action, I could actually make out some of the argument:

"We need to *do* something!" a man shouted at Lois, waving his hands in the air dramatically. "We've been having these meetings for nearly two years but we haven't actually *done* anything!"

"I agree," another man said. "How are we supposed to accomplish anything when all we do is talk?"

"We don't have enough people on the inside to pull off an effective offensive strike," Lois replied in exasperation, as if she'd been telling them this over and over again. "Anything we do will be uncoordinated and will result in calamity for us. Think of your children. We try anything with what we have now, they'll be killed or left as orphans."

"But what about our numbers?" the first man demanded. "We have well over two thousand people on our side. Does that really count for nothing?"

"Yes, Les!" Lois snapped. "It does count for nothing! In how many different ways do I have to explain this? We don't know how to strike or where to strike until we have someone close to Perkins—"

"We *do* have someone close to Perkins!" a woman shouted, pointing an accusing finger at her. "How come you can't tell us anything?"

Several others shouted in agreement, but Lois was quick to defend herself. "Do you really think he'll tell me anything? He knows I hate him. We need someone close to him *in rank*."

"I think I can help with that," I called over the noise.

Everyone's eyes turned to me and I heard several annoyed groans. "What would you know?" the man called Les demanded. "You just got here!"

Les was a big man: broad shouldered, beefy, tall. His dark eyes were serious, impatient with my interjection. His shaved head and many tattoos, which ran down his arms and around his neck, made him all the more intimidating.

"Yes," I agreed, "I did. But I came here with a few advantages."

"What advantages are those, Austin?" Lois asked, sighing and rubbing her forehead.

"Well, for starters, I have the Colicians on my side."

This caused another uproar.

"The Colicians don't care about us!"

"They're too far away to help!"

"Why would they have any interest in us?"

Above all the voices, another voice rose up and bellowed, "Let him speak!"

The room went silent, and I saw that the man who rose to my defense was Ingrid's husband. He gazed across the table at me. "Please explain."

"The Colicians *are* interested in helping us," I told them all defiantly. "Walter Reifert has already saved my life several times on my journey to get here. I have a friend working with them on the Parallel Earth, a Caiten, and as soon as I can start relaying information to them, they're going to start helping us. I trust Walter. He'll help us."

"But so far away?" Les asked, his voice lower but his body still tense and impatient. "What are they supposed to do for us over there?"

"They've been traveling back and forth through the rift ever since it was created," I said. "They're here all the time."

"But like I was saying, Austin," Lois interjected. "We don't have anyone close enough to Perkins to give us enough of an advantage in an uprising."

I grinned. "Yes, we do."

18

Double Agents

Miriam and I got a lot accomplished that first night with the rebels. We told them about Vincent, and how Perkins was planning to add him to his top ranks. I also told them about my new position as a ship designer. They weren't as excited about my position, because they had a few other ship designers on their side and hadn't learned much of importance from them, but they were ecstatic when they heard about Vincent. Very few soldiers were on our side, and those who were were of lower rank. We had Ingrid's husband, Olson, and four others who weren't present that night. To have a top lieutenant on our side would be a huge leap forward. We could hopefully get all the information we needed to coordinate an effective offensive strike. I hoped we were looking at two months, three months tops, until we could make our move against Perkins. Apparently, this was the biggest leap forward the rebels had seen.

I tried to convince Lois to have meetings more than once a week, but she said it was way too risky. If something important happened that required an emergency meeting, every apartment would have a flier slipped under the front door announcing a sale at Ulysses's store. That meant there was an emergency meeting at nine p.m., and to everyone who wasn't involved with us, it was simply an advertisement. Assuming everything went according to plan, we would continue to have meetings on Wednesday so I could give updates on everything Vincent and I had learned, and in one month we would start having longer meetings to start finalizing our plans for a coup. Vincent would be unable to attend meetings; as one of Perkins's top lieutenants, he had to play the part. Getting drunk on Wednesday nights was part of his new job description. If he didn't show up, Perkins would start to wonder.

We really needed to have a more coordinated way to communicate. We needed to have a way for everyone to be updated every day on events, but in a way that would be invisible and undetectable to Perkins and his soldiers. Les suggested a type of message board, something we could all access with our minds. One of us could have this message board in his or her head, with all the updated information listed for us to see. Whoever created the message board could set up a block for people in Rebellion who weren't invited to see it, such as the soldiers. It was a weird concept to grasp, especially for those who hadn't been using their abilities due to the block Perkins had over the town. But everyone agreed it was the best way for everyone to stay informed. Lois asked for a single change in the plan: to have three of us hold the message board in our minds. If only one person had it and something happened to him or her, then our information would be lost. So we agreed to have three people hold the message board. Les immediately volunteered to be one, and then Olson volunteered for the second position. I was about to offer myself as the third, but Miriam beat me to it. She looked at me after she spoke, her gaze hard, and I understood. She felt diminished after Perkins put her in a "woman's position," and being one of the message board holders would allow her to feel more useful, more independent.

"Okay," Lois said at the end of the long meeting. Most of the children were asleep in the corner, those still awake lethargic. "Les, Olson, and Miriam are going to hold the message board. That means we're entrusting the three of them to figure out together how to coordinate it. They'll be creating it and posting the news however they choose. The first time anyone tries to view it, you'll have to request access to the three of them. Once they give you access, you'll be able to get in anytime to view it. We're also entrusting the three of them to keep out anyone who's not a part of our organization. Miriam, I'll have to give you the mental roster so you know who's a friend and who's not. If anyone has news, mentally contact one of them so they can post it and relay it to the other two. We've never tried anything like this before, so it may take a while for us to get the hang of it. Let's hope this works. Dismissed."

On the way back, Annabelle told us that if we wanted to get into the meetings, Ulysses would stop us at the front of the store and ask us how our day was. If we weren't followed, we would say it was terrible and go down to the meeting. If we were followed, we would say our day was great and look around the store for a while before leaving, and then we could come back and try again once we lost our tail.

"Why didn't Lee come?" I asked her as we reached our apartment block.

"We're both being watched to ensure we stay away from each other. He couldn't shake his tail. Barnes made sure of that. It was risky enough for me to try to go to the meeting tonight."

I felt a moment of anger toward her for putting myself and my family at risk, but it soon faded. Everything we did was a risk here.

We bid each other good night and Miriam and I headed up to our apartment. James was sound asleep, his little tongue poking out of his mouth as he slept, and I carefully set him down in his cradle so he wouldn't wake.

"So what now?" Miriam whispered, climbing into bed.

"Now," I told her, "we are double agents. We pretend to do whatever Perkins wants us to do, but in reality we're gathering intel for Rebellion's rebels."

"Rebellion's rebels," Miriam repeated. "That's catchy."

"I know, right?"

"Do you have to work tomorrow?"

"Yep. First day. I have no idea when I start or what I'll be doing, but at least I'll be getting started on cracking Perkins's plan wide open. I'm not sure how much longer I can tolerate being here."

"Me neither," Miriam muttered, and we turned off the light and slept.

~~*

I was awakened at seven to someone rapping at the door. I blinked several times to clear the fog from my eyes. James started fussing in his crib from the noise, and Miriam grumbled angrily, "Who *is* that?"

I mumbled something inaudible in reply and got up, going to the door and opening it. "Hello?"

A man in black robes with a white collar, a cross hanging around his neck, and a Bible clutched in his hands stood in my doorway, peering at me uncertainly. And then it hit me. I was standing in front of a priest in my underwear.

"Hi," the Priest said, extending a hand and offering a warm smile. "I'm Father Parker. You're Austin Rockwell?"

"I am," I said, still trying to understand why the hell there was a priest at my door. "Can I help you, Father?"

"Who is it?" Miriam got up and came to join me. At least she had the sense to wrap one of the alpaca blankets around herself.

"Hello, ma'am," Father Parker said, smiling at her and shaking her hand. "Father Parker. Are you Miriam Lobner?"

"Yes," she said. "What can we do for you?"

"I tried stopping by a few times yesterday, but you were out each time," he explained.

"Yeah," I said. "We were shopping for supplies for our apartment."

"Which is why I came by early today," Father Parker said. "Captain Perkins spoke to me about the two of you getting married. Is that what the two of you were planning?"

Crap. I completely forgot that Perkins told me he would send a priest over.

"Uh…" I couldn't think of anything to say. I knew Miriam was going to explode. To my surprise, she did the complete opposite.

"Yes," she said. "That was the plan. Was there a certain time he wanted us to have the wedding?"

"If you're fully prepared, we could have the ceremony next weekend," Father Parker replied, pulling a small notepad and a pen out of his robe pocket and scribbling something down. "Do you have a preference to as to what day it is?"

"What do think?" Miriam asked, turning to me. She had a surprisingly calm expression on her face. "Do you want to do Friday night? We could have the ceremony and get a drink at the bar afterwards."

I was speechless, so I simply nodded in agreement.

"Friday night, then," Miriam said, turning back to the priest. "Does eight o'clock work?"

"Eight o'clock works just fine," he said, scribbling more information down. "Do you have any preferences for the ceremony?"

"Oh, we just wanted something simple. A quick ceremony." Miriam turned to me again. "Does that work, or were you thinking of something different? I'm fine with whatever."

"Uh…" I said, and managed to spit out a few words. "That's fine."

"Okay," Miriam said, turning back to the priest.

"Who would you like as your witness?" Father Parker asked her.

"Annabelle Lawrence," she said immediately. "And Lee Stewart, if Perkins will allow it. They're both good friends."

"I will speak with him and see what he says." Father Parker scribbled a few more things down, snapped his book closed, and slipped it and his pen into his pocket. He smiled at us. "All right. I'll see you at the church at seven-thirty next Friday. Have a great day."

"Thank you," Miriam said, and closed the door.

"There's a church here?" I asked dubiously as she went to James's crib and scooped him up.

"Apparently," Miriam replied, slipping her arm out of her shirt to breast-feed James.

"I'm sorry," I said, hoping to explain everything before she exploded. "I didn't want to consent to anything without talking to you, but Perkins was going to—"

"I know this wasn't your doing," Miriam assured me, turning to me while James had his breakfast. "I know you wouldn't have agreed to this without talking to me unless Perkins was threatening to pull us apart."

"So you're not mad?" I asked uncertainly.

She shook her head.

"Are you okay with getting married?"

She shrugged. "You're my man, and I'm your girl. I can't see myself marrying anyone else. I love you."

I smiled. "I love you too. I'm sorry this has to happen this way. It's so sudden, and I don't want you to feel like you're being forced into anything."

"I wouldn't have agreed to it if I wasn't sure."

"I know…" I sighed. "I just wish it could have happened on our own terms."

She shrugged again. "I never cared much for weddings anyway." She looked at the clock on the stove. "When do you have to be at work?"

"I still don't know," I said. "You?"

"One. I guess I'm not supposed to work full time until James is a certain age."

"That's nice. What are you going to do until then?"

"I don't know." She paused to think. "I'll probably see if Annabelle and Penny want to go for a long walk with us. I'll have to see if I can find a stroller."

"I don't agree with Perkins," I told her, "but he's been telling me that I'm spending too much time with her. He's probably going to bring the same thing up to you. After her involvement with the first uprising, everyone's keeping close tabs on her. Anyone who spends time with her is watched. You could put yourself in danger if you spend too much time with her."

"She's the only friend I have, Austin," Miriam said quietly. "And I'm the only friend she has. I can't just abandon her."

I wanted to argue with her, explain to her that it wasn't just herself she was putting at risk, but I understood where she was coming from.

For a while, back at the study, Miriam was my only friend. I knew how hard it would be to lose one's only friend.

"What's wrong?" Miriam asked, her face concerned.

I realized I'd been silent for a while and was staring at the floor. "I was just thinking about the study," I said. "And Kost and Jeff. I miss them."

"Don't think about them." Miriam set James down in his crib and came to me. She hugged me tightly. "Don't think about them. Kost is gone. We can be with Jeff again, but not for a little while. Just don't think about them."

"It feels like so long ago…" I said, realizing that our escape from the study was only a few months ago. It felt like years had passed.

"Don't think about it," she whispered. She pulled away slightly so she could see my face. She peered into my eyes for some time. I could swear that if we looked into each other's eyes long enough, we could see each other's souls. And hers was beautiful. It was dark purple and blue, with a hint of pink at the center. The edges swirled and melted together forming a shape that could only be described as unique. Everyone's soul had its own unique shape.

My soul suddenly sprang forth, reaching for hers. It was red and orange, sprinkled with a deep green and jade around the edges. My soul was more jagged than hers, its edges sharp and threatening. But when it touched Miriam's, the sharp edges disappeared. It molded perfectly with hers, and our souls swirled and danced around us. Caitens may not bond the same way Colicians did, but I knew from the way I felt about her and the way our souls fit together flawlessly, that we were soul mates.

I didn't remember our clothes coming off or getting into bed, but we were suddenly making love with a rhythmic precision that I couldn't describe. Our souls weren't the only things that fit together perfectly.

For an hour, we both forgot the world. We forgot about Perkins and the battleship. We forgot Rebellion and all its people. We forgot we were no longer humans. We forgot the study and Hillerman. We forgot Jeff and Kost. We forgot about Walter Reifert and the Colicians. We even forgot our son snoozing in the crib beside us. We lost ourselves in each other.

When we finally pulled away from each other, we were both exhausted yet refreshed. Our souls unwound and pulled back into ourselves. We laid side by side, eyes closed, holding hands. Our breathing synchronized.

"I feel so alive with you," I whispered.

"Did you see that?" she asked me, and I knew she was talking about our souls.

"Yeah," I said. "That was…different."

"It was beautiful."

We were silent for a moment. "Can you believe this is the first time we've done that since James was conceived? Only our second time, and it's amazing. You're amazing."

"I guess soul mates exist outside the Colician reality," Miriam said.

We laid together for a while longer, until we received another rap at the door. "Who is it?" I called.

"It's Quinn. I was sent to escort you to your duties."

I sighed. I didn't want to leave Miriam, but if we ever wanted a life together without being oppressed, I'd have to. "I'll be out in a few minutes." I kissed Miriam. "I love you," I told her.

"I love you," she replied.

~~*

Quinn wasn't sent just to take me to work; he was also sent to lay out all the dos and don'ts of my job.

"Don't speak of your job to anyone outside of the design team. Don't speak to the design team about the job unless you're on the ship. Don't ask questions about the purpose of your work unless the answer will directly affect—"

"I got it, I got it!" I snapped. "Don't talk about it. I understand."

"I have to give this speech to everyone who works with the ship," Quinn explained apologetically. "If someone steps out of line, it's *my* ass that pays for it."

"So what's the deal with the ship anyway?" I asked, thinking aloud. It was pretty obvious he didn't know anything; after all, he was Lois's twin. He *had* to be a rebel. If he knew anything, we would already know about it. "Who are they planning to use it against?"

He gave me a "you can't be serious" look. "Did you hear anything I just said?" He shook his head and sighed. "Do you really think they'd tell *me* anything about that?"

It made sense; if I was in his position and *my* sister was in a forced marriage with Perkins, I'd use every opportunity I had to bring Perkins down. Despite Perkins's beliefs that his methods were right and just, he seemed to realize that they still pissed a lot of people off.

I shrugged. "It was worth a shot."

He drove me the mile or so down the beach to the shipyard. The massiveness of the vessel caught me off guard. The ships looked huge on television, but media could never quite capture just how magnificent something of this size was. It rose at least a dozen stories above the surface. The ship was painted navy blue, as all New Age cruise liners were, and along the side of the ship in bold black letters was its name: NEW AGE *DEFIANT*.

Rebellion and Defiant. There seemed to be a running theme with these names.

The sky was very gray today, and its gloominess was reflected in the water below as it gently lapped along the edge of the slip. After the rundown, Quinn didn't speak again and I didn't feel like making conversation. As we neared the ship, I noticed a small building, which sat in front of a tall, winding ramp that allowed access to the middle levels of the ship. The building was a single story and resembled a small warehouse. It had dark grey paint on the sides that was flaking off in the breeze. The roof was not going to remain attached for long; a small portion of it flapped in the wind, banging against the supports.

"Go right in there," Quinn said as he pulled to a stop in front of the little building. "You'll be directed where to go from there."

I got out and jogged to the door at the front of the building. It was just as warm near the ocean as it was back in town, but the wind was making me shiver. There weren't any large waves forming in the ocean because of the wind, but my stomach churned at the sight of the dark clouds on the horizon. Something bad was coming: a storm. I shrugged off the feeling of dread and continued to the building.

Once inside, I was greeted by a cacophony of noise. Dozens of men were crammed into the small space, many of them trying to run back and forth between the tables set up around the perimeter. There were seven tables in all, six long rectangular ones on the sides and one extra large circular table in the middle. The men were pouring over blueprints and diagrams, furiously scrambling back and forth between tables and papers, yelling at each other over the smallest things. They all wore brown t-shirts under fluorescent orange vests, and torn blue jeans. Old boots with holes at the toes covered their feet and yellow hard hats covered their heads. This was apparently the construction team.

I spotted one of the men from last night, Les, yelling at the men at the table closest to me. His face was bright red, and I thought he was going to pass out if he didn't stop to take a breath. When he saw me, he paused and gestured for me to come over. I obeyed, slipping through the narrow path the men made for me.

"Austin!" Les yelled over the noise. "How are you?"

"Fine, thanks," I yelled back. "What's going on?"

"There's a hurricane coming!" he told me. "It's coming right at us, and right now we can't protect the ship from the waves. We're trying to come up with something in the little time we have left."

A hurricane. Wow. With everything that had happened, I completely forgot nature was also capable of packing a punch. "When's it going to hit?" I asked, now understanding why it was so gloomy outside.

"Two days until the worst of it," Les replied. "The wind is only going to get worse. We're all going to be trapped in our homes for a while. Hurricane Jackson is supposed to be the worst storm to hit the United States in years!"

"Is there something I can do to help?" I asked.

"No, thanks. We've got it covered. They need you on weapons design."

"Weapons design?" I repeated skeptically.

"That's been going around like high school gossip," Les told me with half a grin. "Austin Rockwell, the new Defiant weapons designer. Seriously? No one told you that?"

"Do I look like someone's told me?" I was still trying to let it sink in. I was going to design weapons of mass destruction for Perkins, who was planning to use them for God knew what. Would I be the reason for mass deaths? I sure hoped we could lead an offensive strike against him before this ship became operational.

"I guess not," Les said. He turned and whistled at someone, and gestured wildly for that someone to come to us. A man started pushing his way through the crowd toward us; he was too short for me to see his face, so all I saw was his hard hat bobbing around. "This is Kevin, Austin," Les said, and I realized Kevin wasn't a man at all; he was a boy. He couldn't have been older than sixteen. Freckles covered his boyish face. His eyes were hazel—at least, the eye that I could see was; his right eye was covered by brown hair that swept across his forehead to that side. "He's supposed to coordinate with your team today. He'll take you where you need to go."

"Hi," Kevin said shyly, offering his hand.

"How's it going," I replied, shaking.

Kevin led me to a back door, yelling at everyone to get out of the way. For someone who seemed so shy at first, he sure had a voice. Once we escaped the crowd, he led me across the sand to the ramp. I was grateful for the quiet out here. I breathed in the salty breeze, and then shivered again. Although the wind was warm and humid, the coming storm was bringing with it a sense of foreboding.

"So how old are you?" I asked him.

"Fifteen," he replied. "I'll be sixteen in November." Kevin had a thick southern accent.

"Jesus," I said. "Why are you working here?"

"No offense to Ingrid and Kathy, but they're not the greatest teachers. Especially when they've got the babies to look after. This job gives me more opportunities."

"How did you end up as a Caiten?"

"I joined the Atlanta study when I was fourteen. My dad and older brother are both Colicians. My mom was killed a few months later during a home invasion. I dropped out of school and joined so I could support my little sister."

"Where is she now?"

"I don't know." Kevin shrugged. "Haven't had contact with her since I was infected. I can only hope the labs didn't take her, too. She was also A negative."

I felt bad for the kid, but I was also stunned by his lack of emotion. This was his little sister he was talking about! I was devastated when I lost mine; how could he barely seem affected by not knowing whether his sister was in captivity, or even alive?

Kevin glanced at me, offering a weak smile. "My name's Kevin Garber, by the way. I know you know my first name, but I figured you might as well know my full name."

"I'm Austin Rockwell," I told him.

"I know," Kevin said. "Most people working on the ship know who you are."

"How did news spread so fast?" I asked. "I didn't even find out about this until a minute ago!"

"News travels fast here," he said. "Everyone knows when Perkins starts taking a liking to someone. He's also bad about letting people know their duties until they have to do them."

"So Perkins likes me, huh?" I thought this really ironic, considering what I was planning.

"You're new and you got a job designing weapons. Perkins hasn't added a new weapons designer since the beginning of construction. Yeah, my guess is he likes you."

"Wow," I said. That was really all I could say. I didn't understand why Perkins put *me* in this position. He didn't know me; he had no reason to trust me. This made me all-the-more suspicious; it was out of character for Perkins to make a decision like this. Perhaps he had an alternate agenda he wasn't telling me about.

I knew that Kevin wouldn't know any of this, so I decided to just make conversation with him while we ascended this ridiculously long ramp. "So are you from Atlanta originally?"

"Yeah," Kevin said. "You?"

"Manhattan."

"How did you end up a Caiten?"

"After my dad and sister were taken by the Colician Strain, I got into some bad business. The Feds offered me the Philadelphia study or prison."

"Yikes. What kind of business were you in?"

I hesitated. Kevin seemed like a nice kid who wouldn't judge, but I didn't want to risk ruining our first encounter with my dirty past. "Drug dealing. I didn't do the dealing; I just did the math."

Instead of tensing up or giving me a weird look, Kevin just nodded. "I totally get you. I got into that shit after my family was taken, too. I was actually dealing though. It brings in good money."

"Yeah," I muttered, "it does."

"But this new strain has really helped me. I feel like it gave me a second chance at life, even though things haven't been working out so great yet." He looked around a few times, and then lowered his voice as he asked, "Rumor has it you and the others you came with are going to help us overthrow Perkins. Is that true?"

"That's business that shouldn't be discussed right now," I told him. "But yes. That's the plan anyway."

Kevin beamed up at me, as if I was suddenly his idol. "I hope your plan works. I'll help in any way I can."

"Start coming to the meetings, kid," I replied, clapping him on the back like a big brother would do to a little brother.

We were quiet for a minute. As we rounded the final turn of the ramp, Kevin asked, "You have a baby, right?"

"I do," I said.

"Can I come see him sometime?" He quickly added, "I'm good at building things. I can make him toys and stuff to help him learn and walk and talk."

I smiled. "Sure. We wouldn't mind having the company."

We reached the top and entered the *Defiant*.

Where we entered, it was mostly bare and the only things around were construction equipment. The walls were bare and metallic. I couldn't tell what material the floor was made out of, but my shoes made a loud *clunk* with each step. We rounded a corner after several feet and came to a checkpoint. Barnes and another soldier I didn't recognize were standing along either side of the narrow walkway, rifles shouldered and posture slacked. The second soldier straightened up as we turned the corner, and he ordered, "Stop."

Kevin pulled out two badges from his back pocket. He handed one to me and offered the soldier his own. "We're supposed to—"

"Yeah, yeah, shut it!" the soldier, whose name appeared to be R. Finley by the inscription on his jacket, snapped. "Go on and get outta here before I get annoyed and hit you."

Kevin hurried past them.

I looked at the badge he gave me. It had my full name, job title, and a photograph of me. I recognized it as my senior yearbook photo, but how the hell did they get it?

"Any day now!" Finley snapped, gesturing for me to give him my badge.

"Take it easy, Fin. This here's the new guy." Barnes sneered at me from his spot along the wall. He hadn't moved since we got here, and he didn't make any attempt now.

Finley took my badge, glanced at it, and nodded. "Austin Rockwell. So you're Captain Perkins's new favorite?"

"Seems that way," I said. "I sure hope you were never one of his favorites. I was just starting to believe he had good taste."

Finley's jaw tensed and he started to make a move toward me, but Barnes cleared his throat and shook his head at his comrade. Finley reluctantly settled back along the wall after giving my badge back. "You ought to watch your mouth before someone comes along and makes you pay for it."

"I've been told that before," I said, knowing I should just shut up and be on my way. "It's funny how it's always the dipshit security guards who tell me that."

Again, Barnes stopped Finley from advancing on me. "Why don't you be on your way, Austin," he said. "The captain wouldn't appreciate you being late on your first day."

I walked past them. As I was about to turn a corner to join Kevin, Barnes called, "Have a nice day, Austin."

"You too, Barney," I called back. After I rounded the corner, I wished I'd at least looked back to see Barnes's reaction.

Kevin was waiting for me a few feet down the next turn, bracing himself against the wall and breathing hard. "They're the worst part of this ship," he said, his voice breathless and wheezy. A moment later, he pulled out an inhaler and took a hit. "I hate them."

"They're a bunch of losers," I replied, taking him by the arm and helping him to keep going. "Don't act afraid in front of them. That's what they want. They're nothing without intimidation."

"And you called him Barney!" Kevin said, staring at me in disbelief and awe. "You have balls of steel, man!"

"I have a habit for creating degrading nicknames for people I hate," I said. "You can help me come up with one for Finley."

"I wish I was as tough as you," Kevin muttered.

I looked down at Kevin and felt that big brother/little brother bond again. It was already clear that I was going to take this kid under my wing. "I'm not tough. I'm provocative. Huge difference. Gets me in trouble a lot too." I paused. "Finley hasn't actually hit you, has he?"

Kevin nodded, giving me a look that suggested the answer should have been obvious. "All the time. He probably didn't this time because you were there. Whether I come in alone or with my team, he always hits me."

I leaned down and whispered in his ear, "When this is all over, you'll get the final swing at him."

Kevin grinned.

The narrow walkway led us to a small square-shaped room with other walkways breaking off from it. There were four elevators, two built into each of the two side walls. Kevin pushed an arrow imbedded in one wall and it lit up. I could hear the hissing sound made by the elevator as it approached us. It gave a *ding* and the doors slid open. Inside, it looked like any elevator would in a fancy hotel. Red and green patterned carpet, shiny mirror-like walls, and soft jazz playing on a speaker I couldn't locate. Kevin pushed a button as we entered, and a robotic voice chimed, "Deck 7: Lodging."

"Lodging?" I repeated as we began our ascent.

"It's supposed to look exactly like a cruise ship," Kevin explained. "On the outside *and* the inside."

We stepped out when the doors opened, and what I saw left my mouth hanging open. It looked like the inside of a cruise ship, not a battleship. To our left was a staircase leading both up and down, and to our right was a corridor that led to two other hallways behind each set of elevators. The carpet was the same green and red pattern from inside the elevator. The walls were made from beautiful oak and the railings of the staircase were painted gold. At the first landing up the stairs, there were abstract paintings of people, in various shades of purple and blue used to represent the artist's inner eye. The place was...fancy. Nice. For a moment I forgot I was on a battleship.

"Pretty convincing, huh?" Kevin said.

"No kidding," I replied. "How long has Perkins been working on this again?"

"No idea." Kevin gestured for me to follow him.

"How much is this thing going to cost?" I asked as we headed down the right corridor.

"I don't pay the bills," Kevin said. "I just work here."

The hallway we were now in had door after door, room number after room number, stretching on for as far as I could see in both directions. The rooms toward the center of the ship were all closed and silent, but the rooms along the outer hull all had their doors open. Inside them I could hear drilling, sawing, yelling, and hammering.

"Eldritch said the morning meeting was to be in Room 765," Kevin yelled, his voice barely audible over the noise. "It'll be that way." He pointed to our left. "Your team will be meeting in there. I have to stay here and work with the construction team for a while." Without another word, he started walking away and disappeared into one of the outer rooms.

I started down the corridor, counting down the numbered doors until I reached 765, which was actually only a few doors down. It was one of the outer rooms, and the door was closed. I opened it and stepped inside.

"Ah, Rockwell. Nice of you to join us." An old, gruff man stood at the back of the room by the window with several large pieces of paper in his hands. The man was short and pudgy, with wild gray hair and a thick beard. He glared at me through old spectacles that looked like they were about to fall off his face. "I'm afraid you're a little late for introductions, so I'll just give you the ones you need to know. I'm Phil Eldritch, head weapons designer." He looked around at the men crowded into the small room, and pointed to two I couldn't see. "This here's Blake Conover and Roy Burma. They're your small group. They'll explain when we break off." He began addressing the entire group again. "As I was saying, Perkins wants these guns in by…"

I tuned him out for a moment so I could take in my team. There were ten of us in total, counting myself and Eldritch. Two were African American, one was a Pacific Islander, one was Hispanic, and the rest of us were white. It was hard to think of us as separate races, like humans did. We were all one race now, and if we wanted to survive, that's how it would have to remain. As I looked over their faces—the ones I could see, at least—I realized that I didn't recognize any of them. None of them were rebels. No wonder Lois and the others were so thrilled when they learned of my new position. I squeezed in closer and closed the door behind me. The room was surprisingly quiet once the door was closed, considering all the noise going on around us. I slowly moved around until I was able to see the rest of the faces. The two guys Eldritch pointed out were sitting crossed-legged on a bed that was set up in the corner, since there wasn't enough space for everyone to stand. The one on the left was African American, very skinny, and looked to be in his forties. He had a thin beard and mustache, black-framed glasses, and looked to be quite ill. His eyes were moist and dull, and he kept sniffling and shivering. The second guy couldn't have been more than a few years older than me. He was maybe twenty-four, twenty-five tops. He had sandy-brown hair and a blank expression. He looked bored, honestly. He had a stocky build and looked like he would be about my height if he stood up.

He must have sensed me staring, because he turned his head and looked right at me. I lost the ability to breathe for a moment. His eyes were gray, a cold, icy gray like the sky and ocean outside. I knew those eyes all too well, and I had hoped I'd never have to meet their owner.

It was the man from my dream, my vision. The man who killed me.

It *was* him, but much younger. I recalled that my dream was futuristic, and that we were both much older when he shot me. Would this actually happen in our future? I hadn't been sure whether or not the dream was a vision before, but now that I was looking at the guy, the possibility seemed much greater.

So who was this guy? Why was he here? Was he really a Caiten? How else could he have gotten this far? He couldn't be a Colician, because Perkins and Company could identify them; besides, why would a Colician destroy his own people like in my dream? He couldn't be a human. There was no way.

All the while I considered the possibilities, Gray Eyes's expression remained unchanged. His eyes had narrowed slightly, watching me carefully. He could tell that I knew something the others didn't. His eyes then gave me a warning look, to keep my mouth shut or I'd regret it. I wasn't planning on saying anything. Yet. I had my own questions that needed answering. Like why the hell did he kill me in my dream?

"So get to it," Eldritch said, and the guy beside me was suddenly pushing me back out the door. I scrambled to get it open, momentarily disoriented after losing myself so deep in thought. I stepped back out into the corridor of sound, moving aside so the other men could get out as well. The other men went off in the opposite direction, leaving me alone with Gray Eyes and our other team member.

Gray Eyes *was* my height. He looked harmless at first glance, but my instincts told me to beware. He eyed me for a moment, and then said, "Looks like you got stuck with both new guys today, Blake."

"Yeah," the other guy—Blake—agreed, his voice nasal. "Hell of a time, too." He sneezed.

"Bless you," Gray Eyes said. His voice was silky, in a way that creeped me out yet drew me in.

Blake pulled some torn tissues out of his pocket and blew his nose. "Thanks." He gestured to the both of us. "Austin Rockwell, Roy Burma."

Gray Eyes (I refused to call him Roy, because I knew that wasn't his name) turned to me, eyeing me again, and then gave me a small smile. "Austin," he said, holding out his hand.

"Nice to meet you," I replied, shaking his hand, which was surprisingly warm given the coldness of his eyes. This guy's eyes were so bizarre! I felt like I was in a trance when I looked into them. "I thought I was the only new guy. I was told there haven't been any new additions to this team for a while."

Gray Eyes shrugged, never taking his eyes off mine. "I guess they made an exception for us."

"It's kinda funny, isn't it?"

He raised his eyebrows, and I saw half a smirk form on his lips. "What's funny, Austin?"

"It's just kind of a coincidence, don't you think?" I watched as his smirk grew bigger. "Two of us suddenly getting such an untouchable position at the exact same time."

Gray Eyes looked as if he was about to start laughing. "That is kind of funny, isn't it?" he said. He turned back to Blake, who was still scrubbing at his nose. "Are you sure you don't want to go home?"

"I'm fine," Blake said, letting out a few rattled coughs. "Besides, I can't leave the new guys on their own to mess things up."

"No." Gray Eyes glanced my way again. "We wouldn't want that, would we?"

I shivered. This guy was seriously creepy.

We followed Blake to the end of the hall. Our room looked identical to the meeting room, and the three of us were forced to crunch inside together to do our work.

"This is tight," I said as Blake spread blueprints and blank paper on one of the beds.

Snickering, Blake replied, "You should see it when both bunks are down."

I looked up. In the ceiling, there were cracks forming a rectangle over both beds. The bunks must drop down from the ceiling. How in the hell did four people fit comfortably in here?

"Sorry I was late," I told Blake. "We had a problem with the guys out front. What exactly are we doing here?"

"We're designing weapons to fire out of the windows," Blake explained. "For now we're mapping out the rooms to figure out the dimensions of the long-range missile launchers."

"What?" I said, at the exact same time that Gray Eyes said, "Long-range missile launchers?"

"That's what our small group is working on," Blake said, as if the fact that we were about to start designing long-range missile launchers wasn't concerning at all. "We get the missile launchers, and the other two groups get the large-caliber guns."

"Why are two groups working on the guns and only one on the long-range missiles?" Gray Eyes inquired, peering back at Blake with narrowed eyes.

I stared at him. "Seriously? I think the question you should be asking is who is Perkins planning to use them against?"

Blake crossed his arms and glared at the both of us. "Your escorts *did* clue you in to how things work here, right? No questions, remember?"

I started to protest, but Gray Eyes caught my gaze. He gave a small, subtle shake of his head, and then turned back to Blake. "We remember. Our apologies. We were just taken by surprise."

Blake grumbled under his breath and started organizing his blueprints.

While his back was to us, Gray Eyes and I met each other's gazes again. I tried to listen to his thoughts, to see what he was thinking. I wished I'd done that sooner; with the mental block Perkins had established throughout the town, I found myself time and time again suddenly remembering that I *had* an ability. But when I tried looking into Gray Eyes's mind, I heard nothing. There wasn't a block in place; there just wasn't anything to hear. He wasn't thinking anything. How in the hell could he do that?

~~*

For the first three hours on the job, we carefully mapped out the entire room. I didn't understand why no one had done this before, or had marked down the dimensions somewhere while building the ship. Even though the ship appeared very convincing, the little things were sloppily done. Since the rooms on this deck were all identical, we only had to do this once (thank God). I was bored from the moment we started. My back was killing me from bending over repeatedly. When the three hour mark hit, we were allowed a thirty minute break for lunch and the bathroom. I heaved a sigh and sat down on one of the beds, cracking my stiff back. Gray Eyes leaned casually against the door and munched on a stalk of celery he'd brought with him. Blake retreated to the bathroom, his hacking and sneezing having gotten much worse. While he coughed his raggedy cough and sneezed repeatedly, I called, concerned, "Are you sure you don't want to just call it a day? You really sound awful."

"I'm fine," Blake replied, and then started coughing all over again.

"You sound like you have bronchitis," Gray Eyes said in his calm voice. "You should go to the hospital and get checked out."

"I don't have bronchitis," Blake snapped, stepping out of the bathroom and going to sit on the bed opposite me.

By the sound of his labored, rattling breaths, I was ready to stand by Gray Eyes' diagnosis. "You do sound pretty bad, though," I said. "You should at least take the rest of the day off so it isn't worse tomorrow."

"I can't just leave!" Blake protested. "You're both new and I can't leave you working on your own the first day!"

"Hold on." Gray Eyes came over to Blake and put a hand on his chest. "Take a deep breath."

Blake did, and in the middle of it he had another coughing fit.

"Yes," Gray Eyes said matter-of-factly. "That's bronchitis, if not worse. You need to go get checked out."

Sighing in frustration, Blake started, "I can't—"

"If you don't get antibiotics, you'll have pneumonia by the weekend," Gray Eyes insisted, raising his eyebrows. "I can guarantee you that, and then who will supervise us?"

I thought Blake was going to protest again, but he actually paused to think this information over. He sighed again. "Okay," he said. "What are you going to do?"

"We'll stay here and finish our break," Gray Eyes said. "Once we're finished, we'll find Eldritch and explain what happened with you and get our new instructions for the day from him. We're grown men, Blake. We can handle ourselves."

Nodding, Blake said, "I guess you are. Okay. I'm going to the hospital. Keep out of trouble."

"We will," I promised, standing up and going to open the door for him. "You just take care of yourself." Blake left, coughing and sneezing as he went down the hall. As I closed the door, I asked Gray Eyes, "What are you, a doctor?" I turned around when he didn't reply, only to be answered with a pistol in my face.

"Make a sound," Gray Eyes said calmly as I opened my mouth, "and I'll blow your head off."

Unsure of what else to do, I slowly raised my hands.

He gestured to the bed. "Sit."

I did what he said. He kept the gun trained on me and when I was seated, he went to the door and clicked the lock shut. He turned back to me. "Who were you planning to tell?"

"About what?" I asked, making sure to keep my voice down so he wouldn't shoot me.

"About me. Who were you planning to tell?"

"I wasn't…I don't even know who you are!"

Gray Eyes smirked. He sat down on the bed opposite me but didn't put the gun away. "Then I guess some introductions are in order. Who are you?"

"Exactly who I said I was," I snapped. "Austin Rockwell."

He made a face. "That's not very smart. Doing what you're doing under your own name."

"And what am I doing?" I demanded.

"The same thing I'm doing. Trying to figure out what's going on."

"Who are you?" I asked. "What species are you?"

"Well," Gray Eyes said, actually smiling instead of smirking. "You are smart, aren't you?"

"I'm all right," I replied. "Are you going to answer or not?"

"My name's Jackson Odau," he said. "And I'm human. But that's still a secret, so don't tell anyone."

"How the hell did you get into Rebellion?"

"That's my little secret."

"Do they know you're human?"

Jackson shook his head. "You're the only one who's figured me out so far. How did you do that?"

"I think I'm going to keep asking the questions right now," I said sharply.

"Let's just remember which one of us is holding the gun," Jackson replied, waving the gun and smirking.

I set my jaw. This guy wasn't going to budge while he was in control. I just had to go along with him until I got the gun away from him. "I had a dream about you," I told him.

The smirk only got bigger. "Really?"

"Yeah," I said, feeling my face grow hot. I realized just how awkward that statement really was. "I guess it was a vision, because here you are."

"So what exactly happened in your dream?" he asked.

I definitely wasn't comfortable sharing that information. At least not all of it. "We were both older," I said. "I'm not sure how old, but several decades at least. We were standing on a building on the Parallel Earth. I asked who you were and you said that I should know."

"Hmm," Jackson said thoughtfully. "That's it?"

"Yeah," I lied.

He chuckled. "I can tell when you're lying, you know."

This guy was really creepy. From what I was observing, he seemed like he was a very powerful Caiten. I was the only person who knew he was a fraud. Now he was acting like he could read my mind. *Beyond creepy.*

"But that's fine," he continued. "I'm not nearly as interested in your dream as I am in this ship." He stood up and went to the window, looking out at the brewing storm.

"You know," I said, "the hurricane's name is Jackson."

"Really," he replied, nodding. "Well, there is indeed a storm coming. I don't think it's the hurricane we should be worried about."

"Who are you?" I demanded again.

He smirked again, still staring out the window. "I already told you." He sighed and returned to his spot on the bed. The gun was still in his hand, but it was no longer pointed at me. "I'm a soldier. Sort of. I was deployed in New York during the Colician outbreak. I rounded up Colicians and shipped them off to labs."

"Did you kill any?" I asked, suddenly angry.

Jackson's expression didn't waver. "One does what he has to do." He looked toward the door when a loud series of bangs and shouts erupted right outside, but then he looked back to me. "In 2019, my unit was dishonorably discharged for various reasons. I've always been quite intelligent, and the government didn't want to simply throw me away. They have me studying in medical school at New Harvard, my main focus on genetics and the Colician Strain."

"Why the hell are you down here then?" I asked, confused. New Harvard was in Baltimore; I couldn't see how he was keeping up with his studies while playing undercover in Miami.

"I'm not exactly supposed to be here," Jackson said.

"No shit," I replied.

"As someone who works for the government, I…hear things. I heard about this itty-bitty town in Miami built by escaped lab inmates, and how they were building a New Age cruise ship. We may be humans, but we're not idiots. We knew this wasn't a cruise ship from the beginning. So I came down here to investigate, because I knew I was the only one who could get in and out unscathed."

"What makes you so confident?"

He raised his eyebrows at me. "It's worked so far, hasn't it?"

His cockiness was almost up to Barnes's level, and it was irritating me. But since he still had a gun in his hand, I didn't want to make a remark I'd regret. "If you humans know we're down here, why haven't you tried anything yet?"

"This town is untouchable. We can't even get near it. The telepathic abilities of the guy in charge are unmatched. That's why I decided I had to get inside, to find out for myself what's going on."

"If no one can get near it, then how did *you* manage to get in?"

"Again, that's my own little secret."

"Why haven't you tried nuking it?" I asked, knowing Perkins couldn't telepathically stop a nuke.

"Don't know," Jackson said. "I'm not in charge."

"So you were sent here to investigate. Sounds exciting."

"I wasn't exactly *sent*," Jackson corrected. "I submitted my request to be posted here, and it was denied, so I just went on my own."

I nodded. "Defying the United States government. You've got some big balls, man. Have you found anything worth your while?"

"What makes you so curious?" Jackson asked, eyeing me.

"Like you said, we're here for the same reasons. We both want to know what's going on."

Jackson continued scrutinizing me and nodded. "I guess you're right." His smirk suddenly came back. "Maybe we can work together. Each help the other connect the dots. What do you say? I suppose it would give you a reason to stop contemplating when to get the gun out of my hand."

Once again, he startled me. Getting the gun away from him wasn't my top priority anymore, but the thought was still in the back of my mind. I was seriously wondering whether this crazy human could actually read my mind.

He shook his head. "I can't read your mind. I just know how people think."

I nodded, still irked.

"So what do you say?" he asked, still smirking. "Want to be partners?"

"You want to join our...rebel force?" I asked, realizing we didn't really have a name.

He laughed, loudly and scornfully. "No. I have my own agenda. I don't care about yours, nor should you mine. But since we're both moving toward a common goal, I thought we could help each other get there. Just the two of us. You can use this information to help your friends, of course, but leave me out of it. What do you say?"

"If I say hell no, will you shoot me?" I asked.

He smiled. "Yes."

I rolled my eyes. "I guess I don't really have a choice then, do I?" I stood up. "I guess the human and the Caiten are working together now."

"It looks that way," Jackson agreed. He looked back at the door. "I guess we should go find out what our next job is."

~~*

We ended up being sent home. Eldritch didn't want us working without Blake's instruction, and he said our current calculations would cut it for the day. We were all going to be out of work in a few days anyway once the hurricane hit, so apparently one extra day of delay wasn't a problem for them.

That night, once she got off work, I really wanted to tell Miriam about Jackson Odau, but I was sworn to secrecy. At least Vincent came by to debrief us on his first day on the job, so I could think about something else.

"I didn't even realize you were out of the hospital," I muttered, trying to ignore James squirming in my arms.

"It was a spur of the moment thing," Vincent said, keeping his eyes on the floor. He kept making this weird expression, where his eyes would cross and then one eye would get really wide while the other reduced to a slit. It was starting to freak me out. "I was feeling fine and Perkins was short a man, so he had me go in."

"Well, the sooner the better, I guess," I replied, handing James to Miriam when his squirming almost caused me to drop him. "What's going on with him?" I asked her.

"I don't know," Miriam replied, seeming frustrated. She put James in his crib when he wouldn't stop squirming for her either. "He's been like this all day. All the babies at the school were, too. It's like they can sense something. It's really creepy."

"It's probably the storm." I glanced at Vincent just in time to catch him making the face again. "Dude, seriously. What the hell is wrong with you?"

279

"I'm sorry," Vincent said, but he didn't seem able to stop. "I'm just trying to adjust to this ability. I can't help it, I swear. It's freaking me out too."

"You want me to slap you?" I asked jokingly. "See if that stops it?"

"Yeah," he muttered. "No thanks. Do you want to hear what happened today? I think it might interest you."

"Yeah, spill it!" I said, gesturing for him to sit down on the bed next to Miriam. I was worried he was going to fall over from crossing his eyes so many times.

He gladly sat and rubbed his forehead. "I don't even know how I managed to hear it. My ability flares up randomly; I can't control it yet. It had just flared up again when I heard something in Perkins's head."

"What was it?" I sat down in our armchair, but ended up jumping to my feet again because I was too worked up to sit.

"I've heard from the other guys that nobody can get inside Perkins's head, because he's so powerful or whatever. He must have let his guard down for a moment. I heard him think something about D.C."

"Oh, goody," Miriam said.

I hadn't told anyone about my new job yet, and I figured now was a perfect time as ever. "Did he think anything about attacking D.C.?"

"No," Vincent replied.

"I was assigned to weapons design today," I explained. "It's apparently one of the hardest jobs to get here." I paused, thinking about Jackson, but went around him. "We're designing big guns and long-range missile launchers."

"Great," Miriam muttered, and picked up James despite his fussing.

"You're sure he didn't say anything about attacking the capital?"

Vincent threw up his arms helplessly. "I can't control my ability! As soon as I start trying to listen, I lose it. All I heard was something about our people and D.C. I didn't hear anything about an attack."

"Washington has to be his target," I said, mostly to myself, finally willing myself to sit down and stay down. I thought for a while. "He's building a battleship! He's going to attack something. D.C. makes perfect sense."

"It didn't sound like that to me," Vincent said. "The way it sounded made it seem like we had people *there*. Honestly, I think he might be planning a rescue mission."

I sighed. I didn't want to tell Vincent he was wrong.

"Whatever it is, I'll figure it out." Vincent stood up. "If Perkins let his guard down once, he's bound to do so again. I just have to give this ability some practice." He turned to go.

"You're leaving?" Miriam asked, disappointed.

"I have another shift starting soon," he explained. His expression then grew disgusted. "Perkins also wants to pick a woman for me. His words, not mine. I'll see you soon." He shook his head. "This place is disgusting." He left without saying goodbye.

~~*

Miriam and I were both worried about the news Vincent left us with, so we spent the next hour figuring out how to set up Miriam's message board and post new information to it. It was tricky, but it worked itself out. Soon enough we had her message board up and running and the two of us were posting every bit of information we had on Perkins and Rebellion. I made sure to post the information about the missiles and guns right away. Now we just had to wait for the others to start requesting access to it.

"So how was work for you today?" I asked her as we lay beside each other on the bed.

"Stressful," she said. "There's three of us looking after nearly three dozen kids. We need three more people at the very least."

"Well, hopefully we won't be here for very long," I replied, closing my eyes as fatigue found me.

"A few months feels like a long time to me," Miriam grumbled.

"Well, compared to what it could be—"

"Hold on," Miriam interrupted. "A few people are trying to get in."

It took me a moment to realize she was talking about the message board. I waited as her eyes clouded over and her lips moved silently while she granted access to those requesting it. After a minute or so she blinked and looked at me. "Who was it?" I asked.

"Les and Olson," she said. "The other message board holders. They've had theirs up for a couple hours. They said others should be requesting access soon. Speaking of which..." Her eyes blurred out again, and this time, even after several minutes, she didn't come back to me. I decided to get some sleep while she figured everything out.

~~*

I didn't know how much time had passed when I was awakened by a screeching inside my head. I sat straight up and my head collided with Miriam's, who was shaking my shoulder. We both clutched our heads, and by the look on Miriam's face she seemed to be experiencing the same phenomenon. James screamed in his cradle; was this happening to everyone? The intensity of the screeching increased for several seconds before it suddenly ceased and Walter Reifert's voice was in my head.

Stop, he said. *Stop what you're doing. We know everything.*

I looked to Miriam, wide-eyed, and she responded with the same look.

We know what you're building. We know what you're planning to do. We know what you're doing to your own people. Stop now, or we will be forced to interfere.

The screeching started up as soon as his voice vanished from our minds, but it wasn't as loud and it quickly faded away to nothing.

Miriam and I looked at each other. "Did you...?" she asked.

"Yeah," I said.

James was still wailing, so I scooped him out of his cradle to rock him. Even after I picked him up, he refused to calm. The agitation extended beyond him. In adjacent rooms, above us, below us, and on our sides, I heard shouts and cries of fear and confusion. Everyone knew Walter's voice from his Declaration of Independence speech three years ago, and those who didn't know how kind Walter was would certainly find his message terrifying. I had to admit it frightened me a little.

I heard pounding footsteps in the hall, a crash, and a scream. I opened the door to try and calm people down, but instead I was greeted with Barnes's pistol in my face.

"Dude!" I shouted, turning away despite the threat. I didn't want James to get caught up in anything. "Take him," I told Miriam, and she quickly took the baby from me.

Barnes grabbed the back of my shirt and yanked me into the hall. He shoved me against the wall and grabbed my throat, still pointing the pistol at my face. "You son-of-a-bitch!" he yelled, spit flying out of his mouth. Someone came out of a room a few doors down, saw the situation, and immediately went back inside. "You conniving, treacherous little shit!"

"That's real mature, man," I snapped, finding that statement coming out of my mouth ironic.

He punched me in the stomach and I doubled over. I could hear Miriam crying inside, trying to shush James. "I don't know what I did," I told him, still doubled over, "but can you not do this in front of my family?"

Grabbing me by the shirt, he dragged me down the hall and threw me down the stairs. I rolled to the bottom, banging my head, ribs, and knees. I laid at the bottom, trying to catch my breath, waiting for Barnes as he came down the stairs after me. I didn't pull my knees up fast enough and he kicked me square in the balls. Just like the last time, I couldn't help it; I puked all over his shoes. Barnes let out a cry of disgust and tried to kick me again, but three gunshots echoed through the building before he could. He jerked backwards with every shot, and he dropped down onto the bottom few steps, his blank eyes staring at the ceiling.

I rolled over to see who saved me. The first person I saw was Annabelle, and fear shot through my body at the thought of what would happen to her for killing Barnes. But she had the same shocked expression that I had. It was then that I saw Jackson standing a few feet behind her, gun raised. Annabelle looked behind her, saw Jackson with the gun, and then rushed to my aid. "Are you okay?" she asked. "I'm so sorry!"

"Thanks, man," I croaked, nodding to Jackson as Annabelle helped me sit up.

"Don't worry about it," he replied, coming over to us. "Just a friend helping out a friend."

"No, seriously," Annabelle said, looking up at him. "*Thank you.*"

~~*

Fifteen minutes later, the three of us were in an interrogation room. It appeared to be the same one where Perkins and Barnes questioned me the other day.

We were alone for about ten seconds while Perkins dealt with a commotion outside the door. Annabelle looked at us intently. "Let me do the talking," she insisted.

"I'm not sure he's going to allow that," Jackson began, but he was cut off when Perkins burst inside.

"Somebody better explain what just happened!" he shouted, his face bright red. I hadn't seen him this pissed since the Colicians dropped us off. I swore he was going to start shooting lasers from his eyes at us.

"Sir, Barnes went crazy after the Colician contacted us!" Annabelle burst out. "He was yelling that he was going to kill Austin—"

Perkins silenced her with a hard slap to the face, striking her with such force that her neck snapped to the side. She gasped and clutched her cheek, hiding her face from the rest of us.

"Excuse me," Jackson said sharply, "but the lady is correct. I was there. I suggest you listen instead of striking an innocent woman!"

I was so sure Perkins was going to hit him too, but he just glared at Jackson, fists balled at his sides. His face was so red I was certain his head would pop right off his shoulders and shoot through the ceiling, but he let out his breath and looked down at Annabelle. "Speak, woman."

She lifted her head but still clutched her cheek. Tears ran down her face. I wasn't sure if she would be able to talk after a blow like that, but she sniffed once and began. "After the Colician said he knew what we were doing, Barnes freaked out. Even before the message was over, he smashed our window and put his foot through the wall. He was yelling that he was going to kill Austin and then his family. I found him beating Austin at the bottom of a flight of stairs." When Perkins only stared at her, she cried, "He was going to kill them!"

"Was he?" Perkins asked, sounding uninterested.

"It's true," Jackson piped in. "I heard the noise and went to investigate. The man had his gun on Austin."

"She just said he was beating him!" Perkins shouted, the redness returning to his face.

"He was," Jackson said. "He was kicking Austin, but he was also pulling his gun out. That's why I shot him. Trust me, I wouldn't have shot the man if I didn't think it was necessary."

Perkins let out a loud breath and finally turned his eyes on me. "Well? Is this the truth?"

"I don't know," I said, shrugging helplessly. "He just attacked me and threw me down the stairs."

"Was he going to shoot you?"

I could feel Jackson's eyes on me. Barnes didn't have his gun on me when Jackson shot him, but who knew what the nut was going to do.

"Yes," I said. "Jack—I mean Roy showed up just in time. I thought I was screwed for sure."

Knowing this seemed to calm Perkins down some. He turned to Annabelle again, his eyes softer. "Do you know why he wanted to kill Austin?"

She shook her head, finally removing her hand from her face. Her eye was nearly swollen shut and she had a large welt on her cheekbone. "He didn't say. He just went crazy! I think the Colician made him do it. He made my husband go crazy!"

He stood for a while, thinking this over. He scratched at his beard. "Well, he wasn't the first case. Others got into fights after the message, but Barnes was the only fatality. That was why I was so upset. He was one of my best men. I apologize for what happened to your husband, Annabelle. You are all dismissed." He went and opened the door, ushering us out. He called after us, "And Mr. Burma, try to not commit any more vigilante acts, understand?"

On our walk back home, none of us dared speak. We were all in too much shock over what just happened to say a word. I think we were also too busy staring at the ominous clouds above us and the violent waves crashing onto the beach. A tempest named Jackson was coming, and its full fury would soon be unleashed against us.

When we were about halfway back, it started sprinkling. The drops were fat and warm, yet they made me shiver. About a minute later it started to pour, and with the rain came the wind. Thankfully it was blowing into our backs so it merely propelled us home faster. Once safely inside our building, it took all three of us to close the door against the wind.

"Do you live here?" I asked Jackson.

Wiping his shaggy hair out of his face, he pointed to a room just a few doors down.

"We're practically neighbors," I muttered.

"I need to talk to you both," Annabelle said, leading us to her room. When we were inside, she let me lay down on her bed. Then, she turned and threw her arms around Jackson's neck. He looked surprised, but he accepted it, patting her awkwardly on the back.

"Thank you so much," she said, her voice catching in her throat. "You have no idea how long I've been wishing for that."

Confused, he glanced in her direction. "I thought you two were married?"

"She was forced into it," I quickly said before Annabelle could react.

"Oh. Well, then, you're welcome."

"And thank you, Austin," Annabelle said, turning to me and smiling. "I'm sorry he beat the shit out of you, but at the same time I'm glad he did."

"Glad to be of service," I grumbled.

"I lied, you know," she told me. "About knowing why he wanted to kill you. When he was freaking out in here, I listened to his thoughts to figure out what was wrong. He thought you told the Colicians about the ship."

"That's it?" I asked, but I guessed that was a huge deal to the soldiers. Secrecy was going to be one of their biggest assets when they decided to attack.

"Did you?" Jackson asked.

"No," I said. "I told Jeff about the town, but I didn't have a chance to say anything about the battleship."

"Who's Jeff?"

"Who are *you*?" Annabelle turned on Jackson, her gratitude turning to suspicion. "Caitens can't even get in here without us knowing! How the hell does a human get in here?"

Jackson turned his icy gaze on me.

"I swear to high heaven I didn't say a word to her!" I said.

"No, I figured it out for myself. You might have those brainless idiots fooled, but I know how to work around Perkins's net." Annabelle crossed her arms. "So who are you? I'm not going to tell anyone, especially after what you just did for me. I just want to know."

Jackson glanced at me, asking with his eyes if she could be trusted. I nodded. "My name is Jackson Odau. I came on behalf of the United States government to find out what is going on here."

"What are you planning to do once you find out?" Annabelle asked angrily.

"Report back." Jackson shrugged. "I have no quarrel with your people. I have no intention of hurting anyone. Your husband was just a...an accident."

"A *good* accident," Annabelle corrected. She yawned. "Well, nice meeting you. Thanks again. Figure out what Perkins is up to so we can put an end to it. Our people want to be rid of him just as much as yours do. I have to go pick up Penny."

"Where is she?" I asked.

"I left her with my neighbor when Barnes ran out of here, and Lee picked her up from there." She went to her door and gestured for everyone to leave with her.

"I hope I don't have to lay out the consequences of sharing what you know about me," Jackson said coldly.

Annabelle waved her hands at him. "I don't care, honestly. Just watch out for Perkins."

We said goodbye and she left to get Penny. I turned to Jackson. "Thanks," I said again. "Who knows what could've happened if you weren't there?"

"I think we all know what would have happened," Jackson replied.

"Yeah," I said grimly. "How did you know I needed help?"

"I didn't. I was coming to find you to ask you what you knew about Reifert's message. I was just in the right place at the right time, I guess."

"Oh. Well, I don't know how they found out. I guess Walter figured a way to get in here mentally."

"Perkins has the most powerful mind I've ever seen," Jackson said.

"Walter's stronger," I insisted. "That must have been what the screeching was: Walter and Perkins fighting over telepathic control." I thought about what Annabelle said, about Perkins's telepathic net being the reason others couldn't detect Jackson's true identity. "Annabelle and I aren't the only ones who are working around Perkins's block. If we both figured you out on the same day, how many more of us do you think know about you?"

Jackson shrugged. "You're the only two who have approached me so far, and I'm still here, so I guess not many."

"So are you going to reconsider coming to our meetings?" I asked, thinking it would be safer if he did before the wrong person found out about him at the wrong time.

He paused. "No. If more anomalies like you and your friend pop up, then I won't have a choice. What was her name, by the way?"

"Annabelle Lawrence."

"I like her," he said. "She's very...feisty. Well, I don't know about you, but I'm tired so I'm going to hit the sack. See you at work."

"See you at work," I replied as he headed downstairs.

19

The Storm

About an hour later, after I explained to Miriam what happened and assured her that I was all right, the town of Rebellion received another telepathic message. It was Perkins, telling us that the Colicians were bluffing. He said we were safe and should remain calm until we were alerted by him that something was wrong. A few minutes later we received yet another telepathic message, this time from someone whose voice I didn't recognize.

Due to the incoming storm, all work shifts except security have been cancelled until further notice. Current weather conditions are not safe for outdoor travel as of seven p.m. tonight. Please remain indoors. Supplies will be brought to your living quarters. Please wait for further instructions. All construction personnel report to the port immediately.

After that message, I heard several doors opening and closing and hurried footsteps in the halls.

"I guess it's here," I said to Miriam.

"I guess so," she replied, rocking James. He wouldn't stop wailing, no matter what we did. I could hear another baby screaming somewhere else in the building. The storm must really be bothering them.

"Do you think he's okay?" I asked, worried that if he was crying this much, the storm might actually be hurting him.

"I think so," Miriam said, setting James in his crib since nothing we did was working. "I think he can just sense the storm and he's scared. You know how some animals can sense when weather's bad? Maybe our babies can, too."

"Well, I hope he calms down soon." I laid down on the bed, exhausted. "I love him, but he's making my brain hurt."

"Ditto," Miriam muttered, turning off the light and getting into bed.

He didn't stop, and Miriam and I couldn't sleep. All night, the poor kid wailed and wailed. Nothing we did made it better. He screamed until his throat grew raw and then he kept on screaming. He screamed until he threw up and started screaming all over again. I took care of him for as long as I could, letting Miriam try to get a few winks. I did everything I could think of to calm my son, but to no avail. If anything, the contact between us only made him scream louder. When I couldn't keep my eyes open for one more minute, I woke Miriam and she took over. I was certain that sleep was impossible while my eardrums shrieked with pain, but the next thing I knew I was being roused by Miriam. When I blinked myself awake, I saw she was crying. "What's wrong?" I asked, worried something had happened to James.

Between sobs she said, "I can't take it anymore!"

Not knowing what else to do, I got up and went to get help. Once in the hall, I heard infants crying above and below me; all the babies in Rebellion must have been keeping their parents up all night.

I went down a floor to Annabelle's room and realized that her baby was the one I could hear. I knocked on the door, and Annabelle answered before I even rapped twice. She looked exhausted yet relieved. "James, too?" she asked, brushing her black bangs out of her face.

I nodded. "What the hell's going on?"

She shrugged, beckoning for me to come in. Penny was laying in the middle of the bed, her little hands curled into fists and her face scrunched up as she screeched. "I don't know. The storm? Penny's never been like this, and nothing I do will calm her."

"We have the same problem." I sighed, exhausted. "We have to make them stop though! This much crying can't be good. Can't be healthy, I mean."

"Come on," Annabelle said, scooping up Penny from the bed and leaving the room. "Let's see if we can figure something out together."

We mounted the stairs and sluggishly hiked up to my apartment. At the top, I saw that the door was ajar, and I could hear someone yelling inside. I quickly ran in to find a man pointing an accusative finger at Miriam, who was cowering on the bed with tears spilling down her face as she shielded James. I grabbed the man, who was in his fifties with graying hair and a slight hunchback, and dragged him out. I slammed him up against the wall in the hall. "Can I help you?" I asked, my voice surprisingly pleasant.

The man looked terrified, but he still had the audacity to yell in my face. "Your damn baby's been screaming all night and my wife and I can't sleep! And now you brought another one up here!" He waved his hand at Penny.

I brought my face close to his. "You ever come near my family again, I'll make sure you can sleep so well you'll never wake up again.

Understand?" I released him and gave him a shove. He quickly hurried away, muttering under his breath.

I took Annabelle and Penny inside, where Miriam was rocking James and sobbing uncontrollably. "Are you okay?" I asked her above the screaming. She didn't answer. I was about to ask again, but the babies both simultaneously stopped crying. They looked at each other, reaching their little hands out to one another, and then started crying again.

"What was that?" Annabelle asked, looking between Penny and James. The babies were still reaching out toward each other, so she walked over to Miriam and sat down beside her. The babies grasped hands, as well as they could, and their cries reduced to whimpers. After a minute or so, they were both dozing off, still holding hands. Annabelle and Miriam stared at each other, and then turned their eyes on me.

"Don't look at me," I said. "I have no idea what just happened."

None of us knew why the babies stopped crying, nor why they had to hold hands to stay calm, but we were too exhausted to question it. We set the babies in James's crib to sleep together, and then I let Annabelle take my spot on the bed next to Miriam while I slept on the floor.

Just before I passed out, I heard the wind howling outside, and the windows began to rattle.

~~*

I didn't know what it was about Rebellion citizens waking each other in the early morning hours, but once again I awakened to an urgent knocking at the door. As I forced myself to rise, I heard Annabelle stirring and muttering, "What's that?"

"Go back to sleep," I said, having no idea what time it was. I stumbled to the door in the dark and opened it, shielding my eyes from the light in the hallway. "What?" I asked sleepily.

"Austin, right?" A man in his thirties stood outside, wringing his hands. He looked like he'd gotten less sleep than I had.

"Yeah," I said, rubbing my eyes. "What's up?"

"People are saying you figured out how to make your baby stop crying."

I took a good long look at the man. Brown hair, brown eyes, high cheekbones, thin frame, and a desperate, helpless expression. I realized that I recognized him. I couldn't remember where, but I'd definitely seen him around Rebellion before. "You have a baby too?"

"Yes," he said. He held out his hand. We shook. "I'm Jay. My wife Amy is upstairs with our daughter Ella. We can't get her to stop crying, and people were saying you found a way to quiet your son…"

"Bring her down here," I said. "She has to be down here for me to help."

Jay nodded and immediately ran upstairs. Regretfully, I turned on the overhead light. Miriam and Annabelle mumbled protests and covered their eyes with their arms as I walked back into the room. The babies didn't stir; they still snuggled together in James's crib, holding hands. Miriam rolled onto her stomach and buried her face in the pillow. Annabelle blinked her eyes open and glared at me. "The hell are you doin'?" she snapped.

"Another couple has a baby that won't stop screaming," I told her. "So they're gonna come down and put her with ours. I'm guessing she'll quiet right down like these two did."

She nodded. "Well, turn off the light soon."

Jay knocked a moment later, and I went to let him and his family in. "As soon as we put James and Penny together, they stopped crying," I explained as Jay tried to fit Ella among James and Penny. The baby looked to be about eight months old, and her cries had died down as soon as she entered the room. When Jay set her down, she stopped fussing altogether. She took James's free hand and closed her eyes. In a minute her snores were synchronized with theirs.

Jay and Amy breathed a sigh of relief. "Thank you," Amy whispered. She was a blonde-haired, blue-eyed woman who looked several years older that Jay. "I don't know why this works, but…"

"We didn't know what else to do," Jay finished as Amy started weeping. He put his arm around her. "How long do you think they need to stay like this?"

"My guess is until the storm's over," I told him. "It seems to be the storm that upset them, so I wouldn't risk pulling them apart until it's over."

"Ladies trying to sleep here!" Annabelle grumbled from the bed.

"Right," Jay said, pushing Amy to the door. "We'll get out of your hair."

"What about Ella?" Amy asked. "Shouldn't we stay with her?"

"I'll stay," Jay replied. "You go be with Elliot."

Amy nodded and left. Jay turned to me and asked, "Is it okay if I stay?"

"Of course," I said. "I'm sorry, but you'll have to sleep on the floor by me and we don't have any spare blankets..."

"Don't worry about it," Jay said. "I'll be fine."

The two of us slept beside each other on the floor, and when we were awakened by the howling of the wind later that morning, it felt like we'd gotten several good hours. I felt refreshed, something I wouldn't have believed possible when we went to bed the night before. Rolling over, I looked at Jay, who was laying on his back and looking up at the ceiling with his hands behind his head. He glanced at me. "Morning," he said.

"Sleep okay?" I asked.

"Surprisingly. Your wife and her friend left a little while ago. Food was delivered at the front doors of each apartment block, so we won't run out while we wait out the storm. They went to pick up their shares."

"Who the hell's outside *delivering* the food?" I muttered, mainly to myself. "And she's not my wife. Not yet, anyway."

"I would have gone with them," Jay continued, "but I didn't want to leave Ella. No offense."

"None taken," I replied. "I don't exactly like leaving my kid with strangers either."

"The eye is going to hit us tomorrow in the early morning. The storm is moving so slowly we have about three more days of this."

"How do you know?"

"They left notes under everyone's doors this morning," Jay said, holding up a slip of paper. "Gave us all the information they know so far."

"Why didn't they just send out a mass telepathic message?" I asked, puzzled.

He shrugged. "Maybe the storm interferes with it? I wouldn't know."

I tested out Jay's theory. I tried to contact Miriam with my mind, but found myself unable to. I couldn't hear anybody's thoughts, not even Jay's, and he was sitting right next to me. "Looks like you're right," I grumbled.

"Not working?"

"Can't even hear you."

Miriam came back a few minutes later with a plastic tub full of food. She had a small smile on her face, which was nice to see. "Hey, babe," I said, getting up to help her.

"Hey," she replied, giving me a light kiss. "This should last us through the storm."

"Great. Where's Annabelle?"

"Downstairs, putting her food away. She'll be back soon." Miriam looked at Jay, who was now getting up. "Hi," she said. "I haven't had a chance to meet you yet. I'm Miriam."

"Jay. Nice to meet you."

"You have a beautiful daughter."

"Thank you. Her name is Ella. And your son is…?"

"James," I said. "Where you off to?"

He was heading toward the door. "I need to get food for my family before they run out. I'll send Amy down in a minute."

"You know, we don't mind watching her for a little while," I said, but he left before I finished my sentence. I glanced at Miriam. "I don't think he trusts me."

Miriam snorted. "Who would trust *you* with their kid?"

"Hey!" I protested, grabbing her in a bear hug and kissing her head.

She laughed and hugged me. "Why do you think the babies stopped crying as soon as we put them together?"

"I don't know," I said. "We can't exactly ask them, so I guess we'll never know."

Annabelle came back a minute later while we were putting stuff away, and after another minute someone knocked on the door. I assumed it was Amy, but when I opened the door a boy who looked about twelve stood in the doorway. "Hi," he said.

"Can I help you?" I asked.

"I'm Elliot," the boy said. "Ella's my sister. Jay told me to come watch her. My mom's not feeling good."

"Oh. Sure. Come in." He followed me inside and went straight to the crib. He stood there, looking down at the babies, and didn't say a thing. Annabelle and Miriam looked at me questioningly.

"This is Elliot," I told them. "Jay's son."

"Jay's not my dad," Elliot said quickly. "My dad's dead. My mom and Jay got married after we got changed."

"Oh," I said. "Sorry." I looked at Miriam and shrugged.

After we put everything away, we sat on the bed and chatted with Annabelle, until we got another knock. This time, it was Jay, accompanied by Lois.

"How's it going?" I asked upon seeing Lois.

"I hear your infants are anxious," she said. "I have something to help."

"It's a mild sedative," she explained to us all as we gathered around the crib. "Give them two drops every six hours and they should be calm throughout the rest of the storm."

"It won't hurt them?" Annabelle asked, uncertain.

Lois glanced at her. "Do you really think I'd give them anything that would?"

"Will they be okay separated now?" Jay asked.

"They should be. Let's find out." Lois had three vials of a translucent liquid, and she handed one to Jay, one to Annabelle, and one to Miriam. Each of them took the pipette out of the vial and squeezed two drops into the babies' mouths. To test it, Annabelle took Penny out into the hall.

"She's fine!" she called. "I'm going to go home, then."

We said goodbye and thanked Lois for the help. "No problem," she said. "If you'll excuse me, I have to get to the other infants so the parents can get some sleep. Stay safe."

"Bye," I said. I turned to Jay, who was holding his daughter. "Well, it was nice meeting you."

"And you," he replied, heading for the door with Elliot in tow. "I'll see you Wednesday." They left.

I suddenly realized why I recognized him. He was at the meeting on Wednesday, with the other rebels.

The next few days passed slowly. We got relief from the howling wind early the next morning, while the eye passed over us. During the days the storm was upon us, we gave James the sedative, and he gave us no grief. He slept a lot and when he was awake his eyes were clouded over and he could barely nurse. We were relieved when we received the all clear and could stop giving James the drug.

"That was insane!" Annabelle said when she met us in our apartment for lunch the day after the storm ended. "The days felt never-ending, and the wind was driving me mad!" She set Penny in the crib with James; the two babies seemed to have developed a friendship because of their time together during the storm. They smiled, giggled, and cooed at each other.

Annabelle lowered her voice. "I thought just being in this place was like being in purgatory, but that storm took everything to a whole new level!"

"The word *hell* comes to mind," I muttered, making sandwiches for the ladies. "Especially when we couldn't get the kids to stop crying."

Annabelle grunted in agreement, and smiled at the babies. "They're so cute together! I think we have a pair of best friends on our hands."

Looking at Penny and James talking baby talk to each other, I thought back to something Perkins said to me on our first day here. "Perkins told me he wants James to marry his baby girl. It's disgusting to think that my son's marriage plans were made just after his birth."

"He said that?" Miriam asked, staring at me, and I realized I'd forgotten to tell her this.

"Yes. I'm sorry I didn't tell you, but that's not going to happen. Perkins will be long gone by that point. No psycho military dictator can decide my son's future."

"If you don't want that to happen," Annabelle said, giving me a look, "you'd better start getting more information on that ship. And how to get us out of here."

I completely agreed with her; today was Wednesday, and since the businesses on the street were open, and the soldiers were going to be celebrating the end of the storm in the bar tonight, our meeting was still on. Rebellion's rebels were still in operation, at least for one more night.

~~*

S"Long-range missiles!" was the greeting I received when Miriam, Annabelle, and I arrived at the meeting that night. I was then bombarded with questions, none of which I could hear because they were all being shouted at once.

"Let him get settled, ladies and gentlemen!" Lois yelled, and whistled shrilly to get everyone's attention. She gestured for me to join her at the head of the table. "Austin, everyone is very eager to hear more about these weapons. Please tell us more."

Miriam and Annabelle squeezed in among the crowd as I maneuvered to meet Lois. There were a lot more people here than last week. Mothers and fathers had to hold their children because no one wanted to miss out by being the babysitter. The information on the message board had obviously been getting people's attention. I even saw Ulysses among the sea of people; he hadn't been upstairs to greet us, so he must have been just as curious, or as apprehensive, as everyone else.

People hushed each other, anxiously awaiting my explanation. I looked at Lois, intimidated by all these people looking to me for answers. I wasn't much of a leader. I couldn't even get along with many people. Lois nodded at me to speak.

"Well, as you all know, Perkins is building a battleship." I licked my lips, which were very dry, and I moved my eyes across the crowd, searching for Miriam's face. "I've been assigned to the weapons design team, and I was informed the other day that we were to begin designs on long-range missiles and guns."

The questions and shouting started up again.

"But why?"

"What is the target?"

"When is he planning the attack?"

"What's the range of the missiles?"

"People, people!" I heard Annabelle somewhere in the crowd, snapping at people to get out of her way. She emerged a few feet down from me, Penny resting on her hip. "We need to be more organized than this! We can't answer anyone's questions if you're all shouting over each other. Raise your hand, just like in school."

Just about everyone's hands shot up.

"Now hold on," Lois interjected. "Let's let Austin explain a little more before we start asking questions. Austin?"

I cleared my throat. "I didn't learn a whole lot because I've only worked for part of one day, but I'll tell you what I know and what I think. Our team is currently designing big guns and long-range missiles, meaning that he intends to fire on distant *and* close targets. He may be targeting somewhere inland, planning to bring the ship as close to shore as possible, or he may be planning to fire on the coastline while keeping the ship farther out to sea, so it will take longer for a response team to reach the ship. I don't know the target, nor do I know how far the missiles can go. As soon as I know more I'll post it to the message board with as much detail as possible. As for right now, I think we should start brainstorming potential targets." I saw a small chalkboard on a stand over in the kid corner, so I went and snatched it. I set it on the table to my right and picked up a piece of chalk. "Places Perkins is likely to target, most likely along the East Coast, probably not too far inland."

"D.C.!" someone shouted right away. I wrote that down.

"Atlanta!"

"What's the point?" a woman replied. "Florida's done that already."

This comment received several laughs, but people quickly continued shouting out possibilities.

"Baltimore!"

"Charleston!"

"New York City!"

"Norfolk!"

I paused and looked up, confused. "Where the hell is Norfolk?"

Just about everyone gave me a look suggesting that I should definitely know where Norfolk is.

"It's the United States Naval Base," Annabelle said, staring at me incredulously. "Like, *the main* Naval Base."

"Okay, sorry!" I grumbled. "Norfolk. Where is that?"

"Virginia."

I wrote Norfolk down, and took more suggestions.

"Boston."

"Orlando."

I shook my head. "Too close. If he wanted to attack Orlando he wouldn't have to build a ship to do so. Any other ideas?"

"Philadelphia."

We all paused at that. None of us had considered Philadelphia as the target. I wrote it down. "Okay. I think these would be the most likely targets along the East Coast. On the off chance that Perkins decides to hit somewhere along the Gulf, let's make a list of potential targets in that area."

We came up with seven possibilities, but only five were taken seriously: Pensacola, Mobile, Houston, Baton Rouge, and Galveston. Tampa Bay was taken off the list like Orlando was because it was too close, and most of New Orleans was under water, so there was no strategic value in attacking it. Lois volunteered to put a map up on the wall and on the message boards to pinpoint each potential target. If anyone learned anything more, they could pinpoint a new target. We agreed to narrow down our target list next week by researching reasons Perkins would be interested in attacking each city. The research would be difficult, but necessary. Right now we had other matters to discuss.

"While the details of the attack are important, so is our freedom," Lois said. "We need to start planning an offensive strike against Perkins. In order to do so, we need to know how many people are on either side. We'll start a census on the message boards. Spread the word to those who haven't yet been granted access so we'll know who's with us.

Miriam, can you get your brother to get us a census of the town from Perkins? I know only Perkins and his top officers have access to it. With that, we'll know how many we'll be up against."

Miriam nodded. "Sure thing."

"Good. Well, that concludes this evening's meeting. We'll talk more about the ship and our offensive strike next week. Take care and remember to trickle out so we don't draw attention to this place. Good night everyone."

A group of us waited a half hour for the others to clear out. There were twelve of us left, not including James and Penny, when I realized that everybody was staring at me. "What?" I asked, feeling a bit self-conscious.

"You realize that a lot of responsibility has just fallen on you, don't you, Austin?" Lois asked me, looking rather doubtful.

"Sure," I said. "I guess so."

"You're our inside man here," Les said.

"We need to be able to count on you," Olson told me, looking just as doubtful as Lois. "What happens over the next several weeks will define the rest of our lives. Everyone in this town is relying on you."

My anger flared up again. "Why does everyone think I can't do this? Believe it or not, I'm very smart! If this town is depending on me, I'm going to do whatever it takes to ensure its freedom and safety. Now if you'll excuse me, I'm going to leave before I hit someone."

James was beginning to fuss, anxious about my raised voice. I gestured to Miriam and Annabelle to come with me, but I was stopped by Lois.

"Austin, wait," she said. "We weren't trying to insult your intelligence. We weren't suggesting that you're the wrong person for the job. We just want you to understand the position you're in."

"I do," I snapped.

"You're a leader now. You're going to help save us, and people are going to start looking up to you. You're young. Are you ready for that?"

"Walter Reifert became president of an entire world at eighteen years old," I said. "If he can do *that*, then I can do *this*."

Lois nodded. "Okay. Thank you. And one more thing: we need you to get in contact with your friend on the Parallel Earth. Jeff, right?"

"The last time I spoke with Jeff, I was beaten for projecting my mind out of the town. Remember that?"

"Go to the outskirts," she instructed. "Along the fence. Perkins can't hear you that far away because of the toll maintaining the shield takes on him, and the soldiers won't be able to catch you if you're away from the town. Trust me, I've done it before."

I nodded. "Okay. What do you want me to tell him?"

"Ask him if the Colicians can give us any information on the cities we identified today. We need as much as we can get in order to pinpoint which city he's targeting."

"Why don't I just ask the Colicians to blow up the damn ship?"

Lois laughed. "They wouldn't be able to. That ship cannot be destroyed from the outside. Someone tried that already."

"Seriously?" I hadn't heard this story yet. "How?"

There was a pause around the room. Lois looked to Ulysses, who answered, "My daughter and son-in-law tried to detonate explosives on the hull of the ship after the initial structure was completed. The exoskeleton of the ship was fabricated with some sort of Colician technology. I guess *force field* is the best term for it. Nothing can penetrate that ship. It has to be taken down from the inside."

I hadn't heard this part of the story before.

"And there's no way the Colicians will get inside that ship," Les added. "You remember what happened to your friends who dropped you off? Perkins is on the lookout for any non-A Negatives. This is our fight. They can't help us. Not physically, anyway."

If Perkins was keeping a lookout for non-A Negatives, then how had Jackson not been caught yet? There must have been something more to his deception than Perkins's dampening field.

"That's why we need their help getting information," Lois said. "They're our only allies on the outside. So please ask Jeff if they'll get us information on the cities."

"Sure," I said. "Anything else you need me to do?"

"Find out more about those missiles." Lois turned to Annabelle. "I need to speak to Lee as soon as possible. Could you tell him that?"

"Absolutely." Annabelle shifted Penny to her other hip.

Lois heaved a sigh. "That should be it. Anyone have anything else to add?"

Nobody replied.

"Then let's go home," she said, and we went our separate ways to our apartments.

"Where has Lee been, anyway?" I asked as we walked.

Annabelle shrugged. "We thought it would be better to stay separated for a while, so Perkins won't suspect Barnes's death was anything but an accident."

"Good idea," Miriam muttered.

As we approached the bar, four drunk soldiers stumbled out, laughing, drinks in hand. They didn't notice us passing at first, but then one of them spotted us. "Hey," he called, swaying as he stepped in front of us. "Where you headed?"

"Home," I said, rolling my eyes and trying to step around him.

"Oh really?" The soldier grabbed the front of my shirt and pulled me up close to him. "I don't believe you."

I glanced over at the three others, who were chuckling and eyeing up the women. I turned back to the one holding me. I wanted to fight, but not with my family in the middle of it. "We're just going home, man."

"Oh yeah?" The soldier's breath was foul and I leaned my head away to try to get away from the smell. "Where were you coming from?"

"We were just on a walk, okay!" I tried to push him off of me, and instead he shoved me to the ground.

"Don't you dare push me!" he screamed, spittle flying from his mouth.

I took a good look at the guy and realized he was younger than me by several years. He looked barely seventeen. What the hell was wrong with this place?

Miriam screamed as one of the other soldiers tried to snatch James out of her arms. I tried to get to my feet, but the young soldier kicked me hard, right under the chin, causing my neck to snap back. My vision went red and I fell back to the ground, gasping. I had a moment of panic, certain he'd broken my neck.

"HEY!"

I'd never heard such a loud, furious scream before. My vision went back to normal just in time for me to see Vincent, still in full uniform, beating the living shit out of the kid who kicked me. He only ended it because Miriam was crying for him to stop. He stood up, red in the face, breathing hard, looking twice as big as normal. He stared at the kid, who was lying on the ground, barely conscious. "You leave him alone!" he growled. "He works for Perkins, and he's part of my family. You never lay a hand on my family! And you…" He turned to the soldier who'd tried to grab James from Miriam. "You touch my nephew again, I'll kill you with my bare hands. Understand? Now go home!"

He nodded quickly, and he and the other two helped their injured friend to his feet and hurried off.

Vincent bent down to help me up. "You okay, bro?"

"Don't move me!" I said. "He hurt my neck…"

"What happened?" Lois came running up to us, her expression worried.

"A soldier attacked him," Vincent explained.

"He kicked Austin in the face and his neck snapped back," Annabelle elaborated, trying to comfort Miriam. Miriam was hysterical and so was James, both crying loudly.

Lois kneeled down beside me and gently massaged the vertebrae of my neck. I was relieved when her touch didn't hurt. "I don't think anything's broken," Lois said, "but I'll have to do an MRI to confirm it. Don't move, Austin. I'm going inside to call an ambulance."

As she ran into the tavern, I said to Annabelle, "Annabelle, take my family home, please."

She nodded and led Miriam, who was still hysterical, onward to our apartment. Vincent knelt down in the dirt beside me and took my hand in his. "You'll be okay, brother," he told me quietly. "You'll be okay."

It only took a few minutes for the ambulance to reach us from the hospital. Lois and three other medics carefully loaded me onto a stretcher and strapped me in place so I couldn't move and further injure myself. Perkins, along with others in the bar, came out to watch the scene. That was all. He just watched. Didn't even come over to see if I was okay. Prick.

On the short ride to the hospital, I became increasingly drowsy. I was scared out of my mind that something was seriously wrong, and knew that if there was it would not only affect me but also my family.

As soon as we were inside the emergency room, Lois had me wiggle my toes and fingers, and also pressed on several places across my body to make sure I still had feeling. I did, and I was able to move all of my toes and fingers, but Lois still wanted to do the MRI. It was the longest half hour of my life, laying in that tube wondering if my life was going to be seriously affected by some cocky kid.

When Lois finally came back into the room and pulled me out of the tube, she was smiling. "I've got good news and bad news."

"Is my neck broken?" I asked.

"No. You have severe whiplash. Probably pinched a nerve. But you should be fine."

"I take it that's the good news?"

Lois nodded, still smiling. "Yep."

"And the bad news?"

She held up a neck brace. "You get to wear this for a week."

"Aw, come on!" I cried, almost sitting up. I then remembered, "I'm getting married on Friday!"

She carefully helped me sit up and put the dorky thing on. "You can take it off for your wedding, but as soon as it's over this needs to go back on. Seriously, Austin. I know it looks stupid, but you'll heal faster with this. Neglect to wear it and you will only make things worse."

I sighed. "Whatever. I just wanna go home. Do I have to wear it while I sleep?"

She nodded. "And you have to sleep on your back. No rolling."

I shook my head, but because of the brace I pretty much shook my whole body side to side. "Awesome. Thank you, though. Really."

"You're welcome," she said. "Vincent will drive you home."

When Vincent parked his jeep—a gift from Perkins in exchange for his services—beside our apartment complex, he turned to me. "There's something you need to know."

"Your friends are assholes. I already figured that out, dude."

"This is serious!" Vincent looked really tense, anxious. "I overheard Perkins talking to a guy called Trent. I think we're in trouble, Austin."

"What do you mean?" I asked, afraid.

"You have a mole."

"What are you talking about?"

"Among the rebels! There's a *mole*! You're being infiltrated!"

I thought I was going to crap out my insides. "Perkins knows?"

Vincent nodded. "He knows about the rebels, but he has no names yet. It's only a matter of time before he does, though."

~~*

Vincent gave me a lot to think about. After he dropped me off in front of my building, I trudged up to my apartment, worrying about how I would tell Miriam. Should I even tell Miriam? After what she saw tonight, I didn't think she needed anything else to worry about.

I let myself in quietly, knowing that Miriam and James were probably asleep. I'd been gone awhile and it was late, so I really hoped they were. The lights were off, and I heard their soft, synchronized breathing.

Good, I thought, closing the door gently behind me and going into the bathroom to clean myself off despite my fatigue. As soon as I entered, a gentle rap sounded at the apartment door. I crossed the floor quickly, opening the door before my visitor could knock again and wake someone. Miriam moaned softly in her sleep, but that was all. I sighed, relieved, but my relief vanished when my eyes landed on my visitor.

It took all of my self-restraint not to scream when I saw Gorilla Man on the other side of my door. It had been so long that I assumed he was gone for good. My heart pounding, I stared at the furry ape face, confused and horrified. What would it take for these hallucinations to stop? I'd already found Lee and prevented my death at the safe house. Why was I still seeing this stupid thing?

I closed the door as quickly as I opened it, a loud thud echoing through the apartment. Still, Miriam and James slept, and I joined Miriam in bed, completely forgetting about my plan to clean my face. My heart was still pounding and I was too terrified to do anything but lay in bed, my eyes wide and darting about the room for any sign of my furry nightmare.

For a long time, I waited for another knock at the door, for Gorilla Man to stir my nerves even more. But he must have left, because I didn't hear anything the rest of the night.

I visited him in the middle of the night again, without waking my wife this time. My son and his wife and daughter were sleeping in the two guest rooms, but I managed to creep by without alerting them to my restlessness. As I passed by my granddaughter's room on my way back to bed, I heard her giggling, talking to a boy on her holophone. The conversation had been underway when I first passed by to get to the powder room, and it didn't seem like she was planning to end it anytime soon. I wanted to knock and tell her she was up too late, and shouldn't be talking to boys at such an hour, but I didn't want to alert her to my late night activity. I passed by and quietly returned to my bedroom, slipping into bed beside my wife.

This last time hadn't gone so well. I planned on saying a few words to him when he opened his door, just a few words to help him understand why I was there—while still not giving away too much—but he slammed the door in my face before I could say anything. I didn't blame him. The sight of anyone in that costume was terrifying, especially when it came out of nowhere in the middle of the night. But I needed him to understand my warning. If he didn't, he would have no chance of saving his friends.

20

Unity

I couldn't sleep that night, half from discomfort, half from worrying that Perkins was going to come barging through the door and kill my family. My fears had eventually shifted from Gorilla Man to Perkins, and Perkins seemed to be much more of a threat at the moment. He had to know I was involved with the rebels. It was obvious that Annabelle was involved, and by the amount of time my family spent with her, it was pretty obvious that we were involved too. But no one came for us. The town was silent.

What was Perkins waiting for?

I waited for Miriam to wake up before I got out of bed, partly because I needed her help to do so but also because I didn't want to leave her alone after what happened last night. She slept in, only waking up when James began whining for his breakfast.

She reached her hand behind her to feel if I was beside her, and when she grabbed my leg she quickly rolled over and hugged me. "Did he break your neck?" she asked when she saw the brace. Her bottom lip was quivering and her eyes were tearing up as she waited for my answer.

"No," I answered. "It's just whiplash and maybe a pinched nerve. Lois said I have to wear this thing for a week."

Miriam started crying quietly and she hugged me again. "I wanted to do something but I didn't know what to do!"

"Don't cry," I begged. "I hate seeing you cry."

"I hate seeing you like this!" Miriam said, gesturing to my damaged body. "I swear, every other day you get into a fight or get beaten up! I cry because you're a disaster magnet! What am I going to tell James if one day something like this happens and you don't come back from the hospital? What the hell am I supposed to tell him!"

I sighed, completely agreeing with her. I had a family now, and I had to make a choice. "Well, I'm not going to fight anymore. I promise."

Miriam sniffed. "Really?"

I nodded. "Unless it's to protect you or James, I'll swallow my pride. I don't want our son growing up without a father."

"Thank you," she whispered, kissing me. She pulled back, a slightly disgusted expression on her face. "You really need a shower."

I grinned. "Maybe you should give me a sponge bath."

She slapped my arm playfully. "Men." She shook her head and got up to feed James.

~~*

I decided not to tell her about the mole. I would have to eventually, but not yet. No, I would wait for a better time.

That "better time" came at about ten in the morning, when an argument broke out on the message boards.

Good going, Vincent, I thought to myself, rolling my eyes. Vincent was demanding that we shut down the message boards immediately because they were giving the mole access to everything Perkins needed. People were freaking out, pulling themselves out of the message boards so their names would no longer show up. Some were posting blind threats to whoever the mole was. Others were demanding why they weren't told about this sooner.

"Did you know about this?" Miriam demanded, turning on me.

"Yes," I replied. "Vincent told me last night."

"And why didn't you tell me?"

"Why do you think? You think I was going to add more stress to your life right after you watched me nearly get my neck broken?"

Miriam looked guilty for being angry at me, and didn't bring it up again. We watched the argument play out for an hour, up until Lois declared that we would not be closing the message boards.

We're not all going to give up because one of us did! she posted, her tone full of venom. *To whoever has decided to betray us, I simply hope that your treachery was worth it. To everyone else, we will continue as planned. We're stronger than this. We will not give up!*

"Your brother's an idiot," I told Miriam. Right after I finished saying that, Vincent opened the door and rushed inside, breathless. "Oh, right on time!"

"We all had a right to know, Austin," Miriam said, keeping a firm grip on my arm when I tried to get up off the bed.

Vincent stared at me, confused. "You're mad?"

"No shit, Sherlock!" I shot back. "What the hell were you thinking? Are you *trying* to cause a panic?"

"Was I not supposed to tell anyone?" Vincent demanded. "Were we just supposed to keep this a secret until Perkins comes for us? Everyone needs to know what we're up against!"

"Everyone already knows what we're up against, Vincent!" I shouted. "We're all living here!" I lowered my voice. "You should have told Lois and let her make a decision."

"Are we supposed to go to her for everything? You gonna ask her if it's okay to wipe your butt every time you take a dump? For Christ's sake, Austin! This is how dictators rise in the first place! Everyone bows down to one person and lets him make *every single decision!*"

"Regardless, we need a leader, Vincent! She's about as good as it gets."

Vincent shook his head, furious. "I have no regrets, Austin." He turned and stomped out.

~~*

Miriam didn't talk to me for the rest of the day. I could tell she was mad about my fight with Vincent. I hoped she wasn't just angry with me, because her brother was just as much at fault as I. She left with James shortly after the fight, most likely to vent to Annabelle, so I used my time alone to go to the outskirts of town to talk to Jeff like Lois asked. Whether or not Vincent liked her, I trusted this woman with my life and would do whatever she asked me. She took this situation more seriously than anyone else.

I felt so stupid walking down the street with the neck brace on. Occasionally passersby glanced curiously in my direction, but there wasn't gawking like I expected. Still, the quick glances made me self-conscious.

"Austin!"

I was just past the final set of buildings on the street when I heard the shout. I turned and barely managed to keep myself from rolling my eyes. Perkins was strolling toward me from the bar, his hands in his pockets and expression passive.

"Can I help you, sir?" I asked when he reached me. I became self-conscious about the neck brace again.

"I wanted to make sure you're okay," he said. "You looked pretty bad last night."

"I'm all right," I said. "We weren't sure if my neck was broken, which is why the scene was so dramatic."

"But it's not broken."

"No, sir. Just whiplash. Lois—I mean your wife—said I need to wear this thing for a week."

"Do you know when you'll be getting back to work?"

I realized that he didn't care at all about whether or not I was okay. He only wanted to make sure I could still perform properly. "I was instructed to take a few days off, so I should be back Monday."

He nodded. "Good. If we can get back on track quickly, we should be able to finish two to three weeks early. But we need everyone."

"Really?" I was suddenly interested in where this conversation was going. "So when are you thinking it will be finished? How many months?"

"Two and a half if we can get going quickly. It's looking good." He narrowed his eyes at me. "Where exactly are you going, if you can't be working?"

"Oh." I shrugged, trying to play it cool. "Just for a walk. I've been inside too long, with the storm and everything. I just needed to get out for a bit."

He nodded again. "As long as you don't hurt yourself again. I'm sorry that you keep having run-ins with my men. Let's try to stay out of trouble from now on, huh?"

"That's the plan," I replied. "Have a good day, sir."

"And you," Perkins said, turning and walking back toward the bar.

Did he live there?

I continued on my way, running over the new information I'd just received. We were leaving early. That gave us even less time to make our move! I waited until I reached the perimeter fence twenty minutes later to put this information on the message boards: *Perkins is planning on having the ship finished early. Departure should be in about ten weeks.*

I knew this was going to cause another argument among those who were still on the message boards. The number of participants had been reduced by more than half since this morning, and I was worried we wouldn't have enough people to pull this off if no one who left came back. *Just give them time,* I told myself. *They're scared. Some of them will come back. Hopefully…*

Now, I let my mind reach beyond this awful place, to a place I knew was much better. I searched for the friend I was missing, to the only one of my kind outside this fence who would help us. Who *could* help us.

Jeff, I called. *Hey man, you there? I need to talk to you.*

No answer.

I tried again. *Jeff! Please answer me! We need your help!*

I waited for a minute, but there was still no answer. I decided to try one more time.

Jeff! Hello? This is really important! Please talk to me!

"What are you doing?"

I whipped around, startled. I was afraid it was Perkins or one of his soldiers, but it was Jackson. "What's it to you?" I demanded.

He ran his eyes over my neck brace. "You shouldn't be out here, alone, in your condition."

I rolled my eyes. "Okay, Doc. Whatever you say."

"What are you doing?" he repeated, his eyes pressing.

"Trying to talk to my friend," I replied. I looked him up and down. "Why? What are *you* doing?"

"I hear you have a mole," Jackson said, leaning against the fence.

I glared at him suspiciously. "How would you know that?"

He shrugged. "Small town. What are you going to do now that your little... *operation* is compromised?"

"Same as what we've been doing." I folded my arms. "We're not going to give up because of one person."

"One person can make a huge difference," Jackson pointed out, raising his eyebrows matter-of-factly.

"Well, we're not going to let that person intimidate us. We have to get out of here."

Jackson nodded. "You're brave. Or you're a fool. I haven't figured out which yet."

"I'm a fool for fighting for my rights?" I snapped defensively. "For my family's rights?"

"Not at all," Jackson replied, still as calm as ever. "You're a fool for thinking this will end well for everyone. Nothing like this ever ends well for everyone."

"What do you want?" I demanded. "I'm a little busy, if you hadn't noticed."

Smirking, Jackson said, "Of course. I was just out for a stroll and saw you, and wanted to see what you were up to, that's all."

"Well, now you know," I replied dismissively, turning away from him.

Jackson snickered. "Ignoring me won't do you any good, Austin. The mole is someone close to you."

I whipped around. "You know who it is?"

"Of course not. But from what I've heard, this person knows a lot, more than any old snoop would. This person's in deep with you. Watch your back." He nodded to me. "Enjoy your day." He turned and strolled away, toward the beach.

I watched him go, surprised and anxious about this new information. Was Jackson telling the truth, or was he just trying to stir me up? It was hard to tell with him.

Austin! Austin!

I started at the sound of Jeff's voice in my head. "Jeff!" I cried, and then shook my head, feeling stupid. *Jeff! Where have you been? I was calling for you!*

It's the middle of the night where I am.

Oh. Sorry. How are you?

Doing well. Still on the Parallel Earth.

Good. That's as good a place as you can be right now.

There was a pause. *What about you?* he asked. *How are you and Miriam?*

We're surviving. Listen, shit's getting hairy down here. We need your help.

Of course. What can I do?

The guy in charge here is building a battleship. Walter's probably already told you about it. He's planning to attack somewhere, but we don't know where. We think it's going to be somewhere along the East Coast, but it may be along the Gulf Coast. We have a list of cities as potential targets... I gave him the list. *Can you do research on each for me so we can get a better idea of what he's planning to do?*

Sure. I feel like D.C. and Philadelphia would be the most likely, but I don't know his motives so I can't say for sure.

Same here. I was thinking those two, but you never know what's going through this man's head.

Sure. Anything else?

Yeah. Don't contact me when you get your results. I'll be in serious trouble if you contact me at the wrong time. I'll get back to you, probably on Sunday.

Are you guys going to be okay down there? Should we just come get you?

You'd only be able to get a few of us out, and I can't leave everyone else behind. This is an inside job, Jeff. You'd understand if you were here.

What's your plan, Austin? If this guy's so powerful, how do you plan to get everyone out alive?

We're still working on that. I gotta go. If I'm gone too long people will notice. I'll let you know more on Sunday. Take care of yourself over there.

Take care of everyone else, man.

~~*

The next morning, while we were all asleep, our door burst open and our lights flashed on. Temporarily blinded, I couldn't see who it was that came running into our room. I was terrified, thinking that Perkins had come for us, but instead there was a cacophony of voices screaming, "SURPRISE!"

James started crying from the sudden noise, and Miriam and I were both on our feet in a flash. Miriam scooped up James and I was prepared to fight.

The people who'd entered our room—who were all women I knew or recognized—burst out laughing, and I heard Annabelle shout, "Happy wedding day, bitches!"

I breathed a sigh of relief, and then grew irritated. "Did you really need to scare us half to death?" I demanded as Lee came and clapped me on the back.

"It's Rebellion tradition," Ingrid said, smiling. "Some traditions here are actually a lot of fun. Now get out of here, Austin! We have to make your future wife all pretty!"

Miriam and I looked at each other. We still hadn't talked since the fight between me and Vincent. I didn't even know if she still wanted to go through with this. "Can you give us a minute?" I said as Annabelle started pushing me out.

"Absolutely not!" she said. "The groom can't see the bride before the wedding!"

"I don't even have pants on!" I protested, but I was already in the hallway, where several guys were waiting for me, clapping and whooping. "What is going on?" I cried, still waking up.

"Bachelor party!" Vincent said, giving me a big bear hug. While we embraced he whispered in my ear, "No hard feelings, man."

I was glad Vincent had forgiven me, but I was still unsure about Miriam's feelings. I didn't want to get married while she was angry at me.

I looked around at all the guys. There were eight: Vincent, Lee, Les, Kevin, Ulysses, Gary, Olson, and Quinn. They were all in casual clothes and looked like they had some serious shit planned for me today.

Les gave me a hard shove and I stumbled into the wall. "Ready to get messed up?" he asked, grinning evilly and tossing me a fresh pair of pants.

~~*

We got messed up. We got *really* messed up. I was surprised we didn't get arrested. I guess having Olson and Vincent, two soldiers, with us gave us serious leeway. People barely even looked twice at us, even when causing mischief. I wondered if the town was warned the day before a wedding so they wouldn't be caught off guard with the shenanigans of the bachelor party.

We started at the tavern, playing beer pong and flip cup until we were all considerably drunk. Then it was Quinn's brilliant idea to make a game out of chugging baby bottles full of beer, a tribute to my son; whoever finished first didn't have to chug another. Whoever won the second round didn't have to drink any more, and so on. I ended up coming in fourth place, having to chug four whole baby bottles of beer. Poor Kevin came in last place, and he was falling over by the end.

"Should he even be drinking?" I asked, feeling pretty dizzy myself.

"If you can work, you can drink," Gary said, swaying after his seven bottles.

After that game, I was sure the drinking was done. I was so wrong.

The President of the United States was making an address today, and Ulysses decided to make another game out of that.

"You know, I'm getting married tonight," I reminded them. "I'd like to be sober for that."

Kevin tried to get over to me, and ended up falling on my lap and hugging me around the waist. "We're Caitens, and alcohol gets out of our system faster. You'll be sober by tonight."

"If you say so," I muttered.

"Here's how it works," Ulysses said, raising his half finished beer and wiping his lips on his sleeve. "If he says Colicians, take a drink. If he

312

mentions the tensions between us and the U.K., take a drink. If he mentions the civil war in Cuba, take a drink." He paused, staring into space. "Oh yeah. And if he makes an excuse, take a drink."

"You're asking for a vomit-stained floor," I said, laughing with all the others.

"You could get drunk just by drinking when he makes an excuse!" Vincent said.

"What a dumb-dumb," Kevin giggled as he slid off my lap and onto the floor.

"He's worse than Ashton," Ulysses added as he plopped down in a cushioned chair beside me.

Oliver Kingsley was inaugurated at the start of this year after Richard Ashton declined to run for a second term. Ashton had died just two weeks after Kingsley took office; the presidency and the stress that came with it were clearly too much for him. Or perhaps the decisions he made during his term were what caused the heart attack. Regardless, America voted this guy Kingsley into office, who was a forty-two-year-old Kentucky native and one of the most incompetent idiots to ever be sworn in. As Ulysses pointed out, rather than doing something worthwhile, the man made excuses for why he never did anything. He also brought up the Colician outbreak a lot, referencing Ashton's mistakes to make himself look better.

"Hey, General Grant," Kevin said, managing to pull himself up into a chair in front of the TV. "We should drink if he mentions the nukes in Vatican City!"

"Do what you want," Ulysses replied as he clicked on the TV.

I ended up drinking several more beers over that hour-long speech. Wow, that man was predictable. But thankfully, after that, the drinking was over. I wasn't sure I could take anymore anyway.

"On to the next game!" Gary announced, leading us outside.

Out in the street, already set up for us, was a baseball diamond.

"I'm *waaaaaay* too drunk to play," Kevin said as I helped him walk to home plate.

"Same here," I agreed, and we both fell down in the dirt.

"That's the point," Olson said as he and Les helped us up. "Drunk baseball. The *real* American pastime."

"Are we still Americans?" I asked, not sure that we qualified as Americans anymore. We certainly didn't qualify as humans.

"Who cares?" Gary said, picking up a bat and taking a practice swing.

"We were all born Americans."

"I'm still not sure," I said, my neck having been sore all day. "Do you think it's okay for me to play with this on?"

"Quit making excuses!" Les ordered. "Now let's play!"

I played on Gary's team along with Quinn, Vincent, and Kevin. The teams were uneven, but Kevin was so uncoordinated and I was so useless in my brace that it balanced out. Besides, Les had a mean swing, getting a home run every time he went up to bat. He also blew out two windows, one of them an apartment window and the other one the front window of Ulysses's shop. Each time, we all froze, and then burst out laughing.

"How dare you!" Ulysses shouted when his shop was hit, but couldn't manage to keep a straight face.

"Are we going to get in trouble for this?" Vincent asked, doubled over laughing.

"Not a chance," Olson said. "This stuff always happens the day of a wedding."

For that whole day, I forgot where we were. I forgot that we were in Rebellion, our haven and our prison. I forgot about the world and everything bad that came with it. I had a wonderful time with my friends.

After the baseball game, we went back into the bar, where an ancient model of Guitar Hero was hooked up to the TV. We took turns for thirty minutes, after which we switched to an even older version of DDR. I had no idea Gary could dance until he whooped my butt at it.

Chuck the bartender fed us lunch, some kind of mushroom soup and grilled cheese. Once lunch was finished, we were all feeling a little more coherent, so we decided to go swimming. We ran to the beach, hollering the whole way and stripping off our clothes once we hit the sand. I shed my neck brace, disregarding Lois's instructions. Nobody had planned for this, so we all went swimming in our boxers.

The water was refreshing. We swam and splashed each other, soaking away all our sorrows in the salty surf. Ulysses was the one to call off the fun.

"Guys!" he called from the beach, his shirt sticking to his big wet belly as he slipped it on. "It's time!"

Everyone immediately stopped what they were doing and headed for the beach, making sure they got all their clothes. "Time for what?" I asked as I put my brace back on.

"Time to get you ready," Quinn declared.

"Time to get to the bachelor pad!" Olson yelled, pumping his fists and running back toward town without a shirt.

"You got a pad?" I asked, excited.

The other guys chuckled. "*Pad*," Ulysses said, putting air quotes around the word.

I understood why as soon as I saw it. It was a little shack built behind Gary's store. The structure was falling apart, paint chipping off the wooden boards. I was prepared for the worst when they ushered me inside, but to my surprise it was fairly nice in there. Posters of *Star Wars* and half-naked women covered the walls, hiding the cracks and holes. Two old sofas took up most of the space, and most of the guys immediately plopped down. Quinn pushed me toward the other side of the shack, where I realized part of the wall was actually a door that led into another small room. "Clean yourself up," he told me. "Everything you need should already be in there. We'll have your tux ready when you're done."

"Why are you guys doing this for me?" I blurted, overwhelmed by the kindness they were showing me.

Quinn gave me a dubious look. "Because we're your friends." He pushed me inside and shut the door. The guys quickly resumed their own party in the main room.

I flipped on the light. I was in a spacious bathroom; there was a nice shower with a variety of soaps and shampoos, and a wash basin area with a brand new toothbrush, toothpaste, and bottles of stuff to style my hair and make the rest of me smell awesome. I looked around at all the fancy towels and accessories I didn't think were available in this town. Weddings must be a big deal here, or else these guys had gone *way* out of their way to get this stuff for me.

I stripped off my boxers and neck brace and climbed in the shower, drawing the curtain closed. I braced myself for a stream of cold water when I turned it on, but was surprised by the nice hot shower I received instead. I carefully scrubbed the salt off my body and out of my hair, making sure every part of me was squeaky clean. While in there, I remembered to enjoy the hot water as much as possible; the shower in our apartment was freezing and when I asked about it, the reply I got was a shrug of the shoulders.

I hadn't heard anyone come in while I showered, but when I got out I saw a brand new black tuxedo, still on its hanger and in its plastic wrapping, hanging on the door. A fresh pair of socks and boxers were also waiting for me on the small wooden bench just inside the door.

Still in my towel, I observed the items available to me. On the counter beside the basin I saw the toothbrush and toothpaste, three different types of hair gel and deodorant, body spray, combs and brushes, and…

"Thank God," I breathed, grabbing the razor. I was beyond scruffy; I hadn't shaved since the Parallel Earth. I carefully shaved, not wanting to knick myself. I wanted tonight to be perfect. "Work of art," I said when I was finished and didn't have a single mark or stray hair. I put a good amount of deodorant on, because I knew I was going to sweat from nervousness, and hosed myself down with a body spray that smelled light and musky. "I feel fabulous," I said to myself. I wondered if Miriam would like the smell.

Miriam…

I still hadn't gotten to talk to her about yesterday. I hoped she didn't feel pushed into this, because if she didn't want to go through with it then neither did I. Sighing, I continued to get ready. I slipped on the boxers and socks and maneuvered my way into the tux. It fit perfectly, and I was pleased to see it came with a legit tie instead of one of those bowties. I hated bowties.

The tie was a pleasing deep blue color, as was the pocket square. Once the tux was on and my tie was tied, I looked in the mirror and almost gasped. It looked great on me and was exactly what I would have wanted. It was perfect. How did they know?

One of the guys pounded on the door. "Hey, hurry up! Wedding's in less than two hours and we still got stuff to do!"

"Almost finished," I called back, taking a whiff of each of the hair gels and selecting the one that smelled faintly of sea spray. Styling my hair wasn't something I was a pro at, but I was going to at least put in a decent effort. I ran the gel through my hair and used a comb to slick my bangs to one side. I looked at myself and snorted. "I look like a tween," I said. I opened the door. "Hey, I need help with my hair, guys."

The guys were all sitting around the room, cleanly shaven and dressed in formal suits. They took one look at me and burst out laughing. "Yeah," Kevin said. "You do." He took the comb and stood on his toes. He slicked my hair back, and I felt him starting to part it.

"I don't part my hair, dude," I said firmly.

"Trust me," Kevin replied, continuing with his work.

"Kevin's a hair genius!" Olson insisted. "He's never let a fellow dude down!"

I was still hesitant about parting my hair, but I let Kevin have his fun. When he was finished, he smiled. "Much better. You actually look five years older now instead of five years younger!"

"What do you guys think?" I asked uncertainly, spinning around for them to see.

They whistled and clapped. "Damn!" Vincent said. "You clean up *awesome*!"

"Don't go getting a man crush on me now," I replied, punching him in the arm. "I'm marrying your sister, after all."

"Speaking of which," he said, his tone suddenly changing. He gazed at me sternly. "I have something important I need to tell you."

I had a feeling about what was coming. "Can you hold on one sec? I just want to take a peek in the mirror." I went back into the bathroom to check out my hair. It looked great, and I did look several years older. My hair was slicked back and to the side, and parted on the other side. The part looked very natural yet formal, and I was pleased. "Great job, Kevin," I said as I went out and sat across from Vincent. "You'll have to teach that to me." I gazed back into Vincent's awaiting scowl. "Yes, sir?"

He pointed a finger at me. "If you ever, *ever* hurt my sister, mentally, or physically, or do anything to put her or my nephew in danger, so help me God..." He leaned forward and smiled, a disturbing sight given what he was saying. "You will die." He sat back and crossed his legs. "Need I say more?"

I raised my hands. "I think you were perfectly clear without saying anything at all."

He nodded and smiled again. "Good. Now we can get back to the fun."

"What fun?" I asked, right before Les pulled a bag over my head.

~~*

I had no idea where we were going, and was frankly a little nervous, but the guys were laughing and joking with each other and it was *my* wedding, so how bad could it be?

We didn't go very far; we went around the store and were somewhere on the main street I heard a chair being dragged across the ground and I was pushed into it. There was shuffling and the sounds of more chairs being dragged across the ground before my hood was finally taken off.

"Surprise!" the guys yelled. My mouth actually fell open. We were all seated around a rectangular table, myself at the head, and in front of us was my favorite meal in the entire world: lobster tail with seafood pasta. I looked closely at the pasta and saw that it had everything I liked in it: shrimp, calamari, clams, and mussels still in their shells. My mom used to make this all the time when I was a kid. She'd get fresh seafood from right off the boats and make this on the first of every month. It had been my favorite childhood meal, and I never thought I'd have it again after she died. The plate full of food in front of me was a wonderful tribute to my mom and her memory. Tears welled up in my eyes.

The table was lined with a beautiful white tablecloth, and the dishes were old-fashioned China with silverware made of real silver. Crystal glasses of champagne rested behind our plates.

The guys clinked their spoons on their glasses, and Ulysses stood up. "Our wedding traditions are different than the humans'. You've probably figured that out by now. The bride and groom are awakened and separated. Each of them is treated to fun and games and their own party. Trust me, Miriam's been having just as good a time as you. Before the wedding, the bachelor and bachelorette parties help the bride and groom get ready, and then treat them to their favorite dinners. After the wedding, we'll have the dessert and after-party, which is where the clinking of glasses and toasts and kissing will commence. But now, right here, we're going to have our own toast." He raised his glass to me, and so did the others. "To Austin, a hard-headed yet extremely kind individual. We hope your marriage brings you the happiness you deserve."

The other guys laughed at me when I blushed. What did they expect? These guys—and the women that were with Miriam—went out of their way to make this day beautiful for us. I was planning on just having a simple wedding, with a boring ceremony followed by a drink at the tavern. These people made it so much more than that.

"To Austin!" the rest of the guys said. We drank deeply and dug in.

The bag over my head messed up my hair, so Kevin fixed it before we entered the chapel. This was a building I'd never seen before. It was located near where we entered Rebellion for the first time, close to the ocean. Its windows were still boarded up from the hurricane, and the air inside was damp and warm. We were the first to arrive. I went up and stood at the altar, already sweating and bouncing on my heels. As the other guys sat down in the pews, Les came up and slapped me on the back. "Relax, punk," he said. "All you have to do is stand here and repeat after old Father Parker."

The actual ceremony wasn't what I was anxious about. I was anxious to see Miriam. I didn't know how she was feeling about us, and I wanted us to be okay before we made this final commitment. I was also just anxious to see her. I was completely transformed; I wondered if she was too.

While I waited for the ceremony to commence, I looked around to take in the scene. The pew area wasn't decorated, but the area where I stood was. Dozens of candles were lit, illuminating the velvet strips that flowed off the altar. The velvet was white and blue, the same blue as my tie and pocket square. In decorated pots, white lilies bloomed and filled the air with their scent. It was simple, but beautiful.

Father Parker and I waited at the altar for several minutes before we heard the main doors open and women's voices filter in. Seven women, all in beautiful, colorful dresses, hurried in and sat in the pews on the opposite side of the aisle as the men. They all spoke to each other in hushed giggles. I looked at each face to see who had treated Miriam today: Annabelle, Ingrid, Anne, Kathy, and three other women with whom I wasn't acquainted but recognized. I wondered where Lois was, because I'd seen her this morning but didn't see her now. Also, where was James?

Music began playing, and I looked behind me, startled to see an organist. The women shushed each other. Penny came from around the corner and entered the sanctuary, carrying a little white woven basket full of flower petals. The women were smitten with her little pink dress and how cute she looked walking down the aisle on her little legs. She met my eyes and grinned, tossing petals in the air as she walked to meet me. I smiled back at her. Our flower girl was absolutely precious.

Next came our ring bearer. Lois entered, carrying James, who had a little blue velvet pillow tied to his arm. The pillow was the same blue as my tie, and held the rings. When my baby boy saw me, his face broke into a smile and he started squealing, holding his arms out to me. Everyone in the chapel laughed.

Once Penny, Lois, and James made it to the front, Lois handed the priest the pillow and sat in the front pew with the children. Then, the moment I was so anxious for arrived. "Here Comes the Bride" began on the organ and Miriam rounded the corner into the sanctuary.

She took my breath away. She had never been more beautiful. Her long hair was braided and tied up on her head, silver glitter shining in it. Her headpiece was a chain of diamonds that wrapped around her head and left a large diamond heart at the center of her forehead. Her jewelry was also eye-catching. She wore earrings made up of many tiny diamonds dangling from their spade-shaped frame. Her necklace was made of pearls, with one large pearl at the center resting on her chest. There was no veil covering her face, and I was glad for it. She beamed, self-conscious yet happy, her makeup light but emphasizing her face and bringing out her brown eyes to make them look like gems. Her perfectly powdered face was flawless, and her teeth gleamed in the light as she smiled and made her way up the aisle.

And the dress...wow. It fit her body perfectly, emphasizing curves while flattering her small size. It was strapless, clinging to her from her breasts to her knees, where it billowed out in a sea of ruffles, falling behind her as a train. Her bare shoulders were sprinkled with the silver glitter that was in her hair.

She looked perfect. This wedding was perfect. Even in the awful place we were living in, our friends managed to make one night for us exactly how we wanted it.

Before I knew it, Miriam was standing beside me at the altar, and we turned to face each other. "Wow," I said, looking her up and down again. "You look amazing. Well, amazing's an understatement. I just don't know another word to describe it—I mean you."

"Stunning?" she offered. "Breathtaking? Sexy?"

"All of those," I said, grinning.

"You do too," she replied, taking my hands in hers.

Father Parker began the ceremony, addressing the audience and us. I didn't hear a word he said. I was too focused on my beautiful bride.

You're supposed to be listening, Miriam teased when I couldn't stop staring at her.

I've heard it all before, and I'll hear it again. I only get to see this once.

You get to see me all the time. Just don't expect me to dress up this nice every day.

I almost laughed out loud, and then remembered this was a private conversation. *I meant to apologize for yesterday,* I said, wanting to get this out before we spoke our vows. *You know me. I avoided it until it was too late. I really am sorry though.*

That's okay. The two of you didn't need to work it out with your fists, which is good. I'm proud of both of you for that.

So you're sure you still want to do this?

She raised an eyebrow. *For better or for worse, right?*

I got to say my vows first, after a few minutes of Father Parker talking. "I, Austin Dean Rockwell," I began, unable to stop grinning as I said these words, "take you, Miriam Andrea Lobner, to be my lawfully wedded wife, to have and to hold, from this day forward, for better, for worse, for richer, for poorer, in sickness and in health, until death do us part."

Miriam grinned, and then it was her turn: "I, Miriam Andrea Lobner, take you, Austin Dean Rockwell, to be my lawfully wedded husband, to have and to hold, from this day forward, for better, for worse, for richer, for poorer, in sickness and in health, until death do us part."

We both said our "I do's" quickly, excited that this was finally happening. After everything else was taken care of, Father Parker paused, and I was dying with anticipation. Then, he finally said the two lines I was waiting for.

"I hereby pronounce you husband and wife. You may kiss the bride."

Everybody cheered and screamed as I grabbed Miriam around the waist, dipped her, and gave her a long, passionate kiss. Lois brought James over and handed him to me. I cradled him with one hand and with the other I took Miriam's hand and led our family down the aisle. As we skipped down the aisle, everyone threw flower petals over our heads. And that wasn't the last surprise. There was another waiting for us outside.

"Horses?" Miriam said, and laughed ecstatically. Right outside the entrance was a carriage headed by two large horses, one black and one white; one for the bride and one for the groom. Ulysses had slipped out unnoticed and now sat in the carriage, reins in hand.

We climbed in and Ulysses clicked his tongue. The horses snorted and pulled us back into town.

The carriage was old and shaky, but there were pillows on the wooden seats that kept us comfortable for the ride. We settled in beside each other, and Miriam took James from me. Our son was smiling and laughing, as if he knew just what a happy time this was. "Who's my baby boy?" Miriam said to him, rubbing her nose up against his.

"Do you guys do this every time there's a wedding?" I called to Ulysses, bewildered. Our wedding party was trotting along behind the carriage, cheering and making a lot of noise.

Ulysses turned his head to the side, and I strained to hear him. "It's different with every couple, but yes."

"How did you guys know to make it so perfect?" I asked, still amazed.

"The people closest to you go into your minds and pull out your favorite things, and your thoughts of what would be the perfect wedding for you. So before you thank anyone, thank Vincent and Annabelle. They told me everything you wanted."

"So Perkins lets people go through all this trouble every time there's a wedding?"

"That's correct."

"*Why?*"

Ulysses swiveled around in his seat to face me. "Life isn't about getting what you want. That's fantasy. But for one day, this one day, we believe everyone deserves to have exactly what they want. So Perkins makes it happen. Every time there's a wedding, he makes sure the couple has exactly what they want."

I was amazed. For a moment, just for a moment, my feelings toward Perkins shifted. Could he really be such a bad person?

"Does he pay for the honeymoon, too?" I joked.

He laughed. "Do you really think he allows a honeymoon?" He gave the reins a snap to make the horses pick up the pace. "You'll be staying here."

"Well, thank you for helping out. We really appreciate it. We've had a wonderful time."

"Absolutely wonderful!" Miriam called to him, smiling boldly and laughing.

"More to come," was all Ulysses said.

As we approached the main street, I saw an orange glow lining it. I squinted, and thought there were several torches illuminating the street. As we got closer, I saw that the entire town was outside, clapping for us. Then, in an act the startled all three of us, a firework was launched from the center of the street and it exploded into a pink heart.

"Happy after-party!" Ulysses yelled to us.

We were dropped off in front of the tavern, where there were three huge tables waiting for us in the middle of the street. On the center table was our cake, a red velvet beauty with vanilla frosting, decorated with red roses. On the left table were other treats, cookies and fudge and ice cream. On the right table were drinks: water, punch, Kool-Aid, champagne, and wine. Miriam and I were ushered to the cake table, where Lois took James so we could eat our first piece of wedding cake. We were handed our plates, and Miriam was quick to get me. I hadn't even opened my mouth before she shoved the piece in my face. I managed to get some of it in my mouth, and it was delicious. While I enjoyed the tasty treat, Miriam smeared the frosting all over my face, even on my ears! Everyone was laughing hysterically. Someone snapped a picture, and when Miriam glanced behind her to see where the flash came from, I took my piece and shoved it in her face. We were both messes when it was all over, with frosting on my jacket and Miriam's dress. It took about half a dozen napkins for each of us to get cleaned up, and then we were given new pieces to actually enjoy.

Other people picked up plates and selected their dessert while Miriam and I went to one of the many tables set up. We sat down to enjoy our cake, and we were brought tall glasses of champagne. "We can't take care of James if we're drinking," Miriam told me worriedly.

"Don't worry about that," Lois said, coming up to our table empty handed. "We always set up a sitter ahead of time for children so the newlyweds can have their night all to themselves. Don't worry about a thing. You two just have fun!"

She left us and, not knowing what else to do, Miriam and I went back to our cake. We had no reason not to trust Lois; other than Vincent, Annabelle, and Lee, Lois was the most trustworthy person here.

The mole is someone close to you...

I found myself repeating Jackson Odau's message in my head, and my stomach became uneasy. What if he was right? I had absolutely no reason to believe him, but what if, just what if, he was actually telling the truth? It could be any one of the people I trusted most.

Forcing myself to push these thoughts aside, I focused on my cake and my wife. My wife...I liked that word. I was glad to be able to call Miriam my wife.

"You okay?" Miriam asked, looking at me curiously.

"Yeah, sorry," I said, sitting up straighter and focusing my attention on her. I smiled. "My thoughts just got carried away. I'm fine. What do you want to do when we're done eating?"

Miriam grinned. "I thought we could dance for a while before slipping away."

"There's no music," I pointed out.

"Who says we need music?" She pulled me to my feet and led me to the center of the street, where people were milling about and chitchatting. She put her arms on my shoulders and I slipped mine around her waist. We swayed back and forth to an imaginary beat, gazing into each other's eyes and smiling. "This is the happiest day of my life," she whispered.

"Mine, too," I replied, overcome with joy.

There was suddenly a chorus of clinking glasses, and all eyes were on us as everyone cheered. "Shall we?" I asked.

"Pucker up." Miriam stood on her toes and we kissed for our audience, who cheered their approval. As soon as the scene was over, festive music started blaring out of speakers set up on the roof of the tavern.

"Yay!" I said. "Now we have a real beat."

Miriam looked past me, grinning. "We're not the only ones who have a beat."

I turned and saw Vincent dancing with Kathy, the other woman who worked at the daycare with Miriam and Ingrid. She had short blonde hair and was at least a foot shorter than Vincent. Her purple dress, I realized, matched Vincent's own tie and pocket square. They were dancing slowly, smiling at each other in the way Miriam and I were smiling at each other. While we watched, Vincent leaned down and kissed her lips lightly.

"I'm so glad he's found someone," Miriam said, smiling at her brother.

"What's she like?" I asked. "I don't know anything about her."

"She's around his age. She's from Nebraska. She had a son as a teenager, and he was accidentally killed by a Colician trying to escape from a retrieval team."

"That's awful," I said. "Well, I hope her life's at least getting a little better with Vincent. Although it's hard to tell with his mood swings…"

"Cut it out!" Miriam playfully punched me in the ribs. "It's cute! Let's be nice to them."

"Never said I wouldn't be." I looked at them again. "I'm happy for him. For both of them."

We danced for a while, and eventually got tired of all the people. It was our time to be alone. Taking Miriam's hand, I led her through the crowd of dancing people toward our apartment.

Annabelle, who was dancing closely with Lee, touched Miriam's arm as we passed. "Have fun, you!" she told her, winking at me.

"You too!" Miriam replied, gesturing to her and Lee. We were happy for them, too. With Barnes gone, they might actually have a chance together.

Half of my outfit was off before we even got to our door. Everyone was outside enjoying the party, so we didn't have to worry about bumping into anyone.

"I love you," Miriam said breathlessly, the longing—the needing—clear in her voice and eyes.

"I love you." I pushed our door open, scooped Miriam up, and carried her inside. We found candles lit around the room, giving off the scent of pine. Our bed was made, with chocolates and rose petals sprinkled on the comforter. "How romantic," I said, and Miriam giggled. I set her down on the bed and started taking off the rest of my clothes.

"Are you sure these walls are soundproof?" Miriam asked, raising her eyebrows and unzipping her dress.

"Let's just hope everyone passes out drunk," I said with a laugh.

And so we ended our perfect day with a perfect night, losing ourselves in each other's bodies, forgetting that today was simply an anomaly. No day after this was going to feel this good, or even come close. Not while we were still trapped in Rebellion.

21

Overpopulation

Two months passed, slowly, but I felt better knowing Miriam was formally by my side. She hadn't taken my last name, but I was okay with that.

Nothing changed much after the wedding. The rebels didn't find out anything new; I didn't even hear any information useful to our cause in my new job. I wasn't told very much, except for the distance they wanted the long-range missiles to travel. Jeff and the Colicians hadn't found out anything specific about where Perkins was planning to attack. Even after I'd sent him the firing range of the missiles, they couldn't figure it out. There were plenty of places he could attack, but we needed a motive. From what we had so far, Washington, D.C. and Philadelphia were the most likely targets.

Perkins hadn't exterminated the rebels yet, and we couldn't figure out why. If there really was a mole, why hadn't they given Perkins the information he wanted? We were all dying of boredom here, living repetitive, monotonous lives. We seriously needed to get our butts in gear or we were all going to die of old age before we ever got out of here.

James was huge. He was already eighteen pounds and looked like he would be crawling soon. He stayed a healthy, happy baby despite our situation, and I was glad for that. I was glad he wouldn't be able to remember this place when he got older.

Miriam and I worked endlessly, only seeing each other at night, usually too tired to talk to each other. But today was Sunday, so we didn't have to worry about getting up early for work.

When I woke up, Miriam was still asleep. She looked so beautiful, so happy, sleeping there with a smile on her face. I couldn't stand to wake her, so I decided to go for a walk on the beach. I pulled on some clothes and tiptoed to the door. I made it down one flight before Annabelle burst out of her room, breathless. Unfortunately, she came out before she'd wrapped her robe all the way around her and I saw her completely naked.

"Whoa!" I cried, putting my hands in front of me and closing my eyes. "That's an image I won't be able to get out of my head."

"You're welcome," Annabelle replied, grinning. "I have some great news for you!"

"As long as it doesn't involve seeing you naked again."

Lee poked his head out from behind Annabelle before stepping out to greet me. A sheet was wrapped around his waist. "Hey, Austin! How was your night?"

I recalled the events that took place in my bed the previous night, something that rarely happened nowadays. "My guess is we all did the same thing," I answered, giving them both a look.

"That's the news," Annabelle said excitedly. "Perkins is letting us get married!"

Despite the awkward situation, I was so excited for them. "You're kidding me. Congratulations!"

"Since Barnes is gone, and since Lee is Penny's actual father, Perkins agreed that marriage is the best thing for all three of us." She looked so happy, and after what she'd been through, I completely understood.

"Well, I'm very happy for you," I told them. "Maybe now Miriam and I can return the favor for the wonderful wedding you gave us."

"We already decided that you two will be the best man and matron of honor," Lee said. "That is, if you'll accept." He rubbed his wrists together nervously.

"Of course! I'd love to, and I know Miriam will, too."

Annabelle sighed happily. "Well, I heard you coming and wanted to tell you. You have a good day now."

"Thanks. I'll let the two of you get back to your business."

Annabelle giggled and they both disappeared back inside.

I continued on my way, and was nearly knocked off my feet when I opened the door. A hard, cold wind was blowing in from the Atlantic. I hoped another hurricane wasn't on its way. I shivered, wishing I had brought a jacket. Slipping my hands into my pockets, I sucked in a breath and walked through the cold.

It had to be, at most, sixty degrees Fahrenheit. I never imagined Florida being this cold at this time of year, but the drastic weather changes the world had been experiencing over the last few years had changed everything. Goose bumps covered my arms and neck, and all the hairs on my arms were standing straight up. To warm up a bit, I slipped my arms into my shirt and rubbed them to get the blood flowing. I walked quicker, hoping to generate a little more heat.

I was at the beach in about five minutes. Waves slammed loudly onto the sand, throwing sea spray into the air. The sky was gray and the water fierce. Once again, like when I'd looked out to sea before the hurricane hit, I had an ominous feeling in my gut. Something was coming, only this time I was pretty sure it wouldn't be something sent by mother nature. I felt like I got close to an answer when I looked toward the battleship and saw another, smaller ship coming in. It was just pulling up to the dock, sounding its horn to announce its arrival.

"Where did that come from?" I wondered aloud. I squinted to get a better look. I began jogging quickly down the beach toward the dock. By the time I arrived, the several hundred occupants had already disembarked. Each of them wore a white uniform, making them all look like asylum inmates. Then I remembered: I'd worn that same outfit for the few weeks I'd been imprisoned by Hillerman.

The new arrivals were all standing together, most looking nervous, but many also looking relieved. Quinn was standing in front of them, yelling out greetings and instructions through a megaphone. Perkins stood beside Quinn, and took the megaphone so he, too, could speak to the crowd. I spotted Vincent in uniform on the edge of the perimeter, and I jogged over to him. "What's going on?" I asked him. "Who are all these people?"

"Refugees," Vincent replied through his teeth.

"From where?"

"The Philadelphia lab."

I was stunned. There had to be at least six hundred people standing on the beach. "How did Perkins rescue so many of us? Are the labs not guarded at all?"

"I don't know," Vincent grumbled. "He didn't tell me."

I glanced at him. "Who pooped in your Corn Flakes?"

His face was stony, and he was glaring at the crowd. "Look who Perkins rescued."

I looked back to the crowd, looking for the source of Vincent's anger. I did a double take when I saw Anders. "Oh, great," I muttered. Next to Anders was Diereks, and next to Diereks was the blonde guy, Tyler, who'd broken my arm in the lab. And next to Tyler was —

"*Hell* no!" I shouted. A few of Perkins's soldiers who were nearby shot me dirty looks, but most people couldn't hear me over the surf and the megaphone.

"I'm going to kill him," Vincent said.

"Get in line," I snapped.

Sergeant Jaeger was among the crowd, along with the rest of the Philadelphia lab's security staff. But unlike Anders, Diereks, Tyler, and the others, Jaeger wasn't wearing his original uniform; he was wearing the same white uniform as the other refugees. That could only mean one thing: Jaeger had, sometime in the past few months, become one of Hillerman's prisoners. Something had changed about him, and it wasn't just the outfit. His face was softer, defeated. He didn't look so tough anymore. Still, I felt no sympathy.

"We have to tell Perkins," I said.

"He brought him here because he's a soldier," Vincent snapped. "He doesn't care what either of us has to say."

"He doesn't care that Jaeger's a damn traitor?" I demanded. "He tried to kill us! After we gave him a second chance! He'll turn on us again—"

Vincent grabbed me by the back of the neck and pulled me away from the group. "Perkins doesn't care about what Jaeger did in the past. Until he tries to kill people inside Rebellion's walls, he has a refuge here. End of story."

"This is...such...*bullshit!*" I hadn't been cussing as much the past few months, having tried to clean up my mouth for my son's sake. But now, in this moment, I couldn't contain the outburst. I was so angry. "So are we supposed to just let him walk free among us until he starts bombing us or shooting us again?"

Vincent snorted. "Hell, no. I think the two of us owe Jaeger a greeting of our own, know what I'm saying?"

"I know exactly what you're saying," I replied, glad we were thinking alike.

~~*

The refugees were at the dock for another forty-five minutes before they were dismissed and shown to their apartments. We followed Jaeger, staying behind him but keeping our eyes glued to the back of his head. We were so intent on our goal, Vincent even ignored refugees asking him for directions.

Jaeger was assigned to the last apartment block, as were the rest of the security team from the Philadelphia lab. I was surprised, since Jaeger obviously wasn't part of that group anymore. But Vincent was right; Jaeger was once a soldier, and would remain that way in Perkins's eyes. A lot of soldiers lived in this block, too, which could only mean that Perkins was planning to make him a part of his flock. We hung back for a while so we wouldn't be recognized. We waited for twenty minutes, until everyone was in their assigned rooms. Vincent went up to a soldier holding a clipboard just inside the door and asked, "Can I get a room assignment? I have a message I need to deliver."

The soldier handed Vincent a piece of paper from his clipboard without a word, and I followed Vincent up the stairs. We went to the fourth floor and stopped in front of a door labeled Q452. Vincent glanced at the piece of paper and back at the door.

"Is this it?" I asked, antsy.

"It says here: Peter Jaeger and Braden Tyler."

I realized I'd never known Jaeger's or Tyler's first names, but that was highly insignificant at the moment. "Good," I said. "I owe Tyler a proper greeting as well."

Taking out the hand gun on his belt, Vincent pointed it at the door and kicked it hard. It burst open and we both rushed in. We'd definitely taken the two men by surprise; Tyler was in the middle of changing his pants, and Jaeger was making a sandwich. Their heads snapped in our direction, their eyes wide with fear, and Jaeger went for a kitchen knife.

"Don't!" Vincent shouted, turning his gun on him.

I kept going for Tyler. "Hey, man," I said. "Remember me? You broke my arm." I decked him across the face and he went down hard, hitting his head on the wall.

"Do *you* remember us?" Vincent demanded, baring his teeth at Jaeger. "I sure hope so."

Jaeger had his hands in the air, true fear on his face. This pleased me; it was great to see him cowering in his boots, knowing his life was in our hands instead of the other way around.

"You tried to kill us, you piece of shit!" I shouted at him, once again forgetting my promise to myself. "After we gave you a second chance! We could have left you there on the side of the road! You tried to *kill* us!"

"I'm sorry," he whispered.

"Shut up!" Vincent snapped.

"Did you really think you could try to kill your own kind and then run back to us so we could take care of you?" I spit at him. "Did you really think it would be that easy?"

"I didn't want to hurt you—" Jaeger tried to explain.

"You *lied* to us!" I screamed.

"Everything I told you was true," Jaeger insisted, swallowing hard. "All of it."

"Bullshit!" Vincent said.

"I'm not lying!" Jaeger pleaded. "Read my mind! All of it was true. The lab changed me, and I pulled away from my team in D.C. I wanted to stay with you, fight with you." He paused, shaking his head. Tears started falling from his eyes. "He said he'd kill my family, Austin!"

"Hillerman?" As much as it angered me, he was making sense. This explained why I was so sure of Jaeger when we picked him up. He really *had* wanted to stay with us.

He nodded. "He found me before I found you. He said if I didn't do it, he'd kill my family. You understand my dilemma, don't you? If you were in my position, would you have picked me over your family?"

I wouldn't have. I would have done whatever Hillerman asked of me.

"He gave me a tracking beacon," Jaeger continued. "He said to keep it with me and he'd launch a missile strike at my position. I didn't want to do it, I swear! But I had to think about my daughters, just like you would have had to think of your son." He sighed. "I saw the missile coming from the back of the truck, and I suddenly had an idea. I threw the tracker as far as I could, and the missiles missed. I figured I could convince Hillerman that the tracker had a glitch, that it registered on the computers as being slightly off target. I did this so I wouldn't have to choose. I thought I could save everyone."

"You set your dog on Lee!" Vincent protested. "You expect us to believe that wasn't your fault?"

"I had to make it look convincing, Vincent! I didn't want her to kill your friend, just injure him enough to make it look like I really tried."

"So what happened then?" I asked, not sure if I should believe the whole story.

He shrugged. "The Colicians were suddenly there, just...*there*. They came out of nowhere. They got you all out of there just in time, because a team came in to pick up the remains. They flew me back to Philadelphia, where Hillerman was waiting. I thought I could convince him of my lie, but he knew. He always knows."

"What happened to your family?" I asked.

Jaeger glared at me. "What do you *think* happened?"

I felt a surge of pity, but it soon left me. Vincent made it perfectly clear that he didn't feel an ounce of pity, either.

"You expect us to feel sorry for you?" He lowered his gun.

"Of course not," Jaeger said. "I just want you to understand why I did what I did."

"You deserved it," Vincent blurted, his words slung together.

Jaeger blinked, taken aback. "I deserved it?"

"Yes." Vincent knocked Jaeger's half made sandwich onto the floor. "I guess you can call it karma. You kill families. You had it coming."

"I don't kill families!" Jaeger protested.

"You killed mine!" Vincent shouted, and I thought for a moment that he might shoot Jaeger. Instead, he said, "I see you again, you're dead," and stormed out.

I glanced over at Tyler, who hadn't moved from the floor. "You should check to make sure he didn't pee his pants," I said, and left as well.

~~*

Miriam didn't appreciate the news any more than Vincent or I did. "That bastard," she growled as she fed James. Our apartment wasn't any different than it was before we got married. It was still tiny, plain, simple, and the familiar nasty smell from when we'd first moved in had returned. It was time to start looking for dead rats again. "How did Vincent handle it?"

"No better than I did." I explained the confrontation to her, and at the end she nodded.

"I'm still not forgiving him," she informed me.

"Good," I said. "I'd be worried if you did."

"How many people did you say arrived?" she asked, clearly wanting to shake the topic of Jaeger.

"There had to be at least six hundred people," I told her. "They must have evacuated over half of the Philadelphia lab."

"How could they do that?" Miriam asked skeptically. "It was hard enough for four of us to escape! How could they evacuate half the complex?"

"I don't know," I answered. "Something isn't right. So many things aren't right, but this makes me really nervous. I feel like Hillerman *gave* them all to Perkins."

"Why would Hillerman do that?" Miriam asked, her expression scared.

"I don't know why. I don't understand Hillerman, or Perkins. But something is seriously wrong with this situation, and we need to find out what's going on. Perkins has something scary planned, and I think Hillerman's in on it."

Before Miriam could tell me how crazy that notion was, we turned to the sound of rustling at our door. A piece of paper was pushed under, and Miriam went to pick it up. She read it, her brow furrowing.

"What is it?" I asked, taking James from her.

"It's a flier," she said, and looked up at me with a sideways grin. "There's a sale at Ulysses's hardware store today."

~~*

Nine o'clock couldn't come fast enough. Apparently, that was the case for most people. The whole group of rebels had assembled beneath Ulysses's store, and they were all yelling at Lois, Quinn, and Olson for explanations. I couldn't distinguish one word from the other it was so loud and frantic down there. It took Lois five minutes just to shut everyone up.

"One at a time, *please*," she cried, out of breath and flustered. "Thank you," she said when the voices were just murmurs. "Now, I know you all have a ton of questions. We all do."

Voices erupted again, but Les bellowed. "SHUT UP!" It sounded more like a roar than a yell. Everyone went silent and shrank away from him.

"We need to have some order here!" Lois insisted. "Raise your hand if you have a question. We had this issue the last time something important occurred." She turned to her twin. "Quinn, will you tell everyone what you know?"

Quinn cleared his throat. "All Olson and I know so far is that Perkins is bringing in every living Caiten. He and his men are clearing out all the labs across the country. How he's doing it, we have no idea, but we have a guess as to *why* he's doing it. We all knew we wouldn't be able to stay in this town forever. There just isn't enough space here for all of us. We think that the ship is not just a battleship. We think Perkins is also planning to transport our entire population elsewhere."

Nervous chatter buzzed about the room, but no one dared raise their voices again after Les's outburst.

"We still don't know where Perkins is planning his attack," Quinn continued, shooting a slightly accusatory glance at me. "And we don't know where we'd go if our assumption is correct. Considering we're building an enormous ship, it must be somewhere overseas."

"We're overpopulated," Lois declared. "In case anyone hasn't noticed, we were running out of space before Perkins brought in the Philadelphia Caitens. Things are only going to get more crowded as he brings in more and more of us. Space, food, and utilities are going to be scarce. But while this is an inconvenience, it is also an opportunity. Make new friends, new allies. Find others like us, who are willing to fight. There will be thousands more of us soon. Not many of them will appreciate the conditions we're in. For every soldier who joins him, twenty more will join us. Overpopulation may be the chance we need to start afresh as a species."

Everyone nodded in agreement, including Miriam and I. She was completely right. Overpopulation could ultimately be our salvation.

Lois, Quinn, and Olson went on for another half hour, answering questions and revealing information about the new arrivals. People slowly ambled out after it was over. Miriam and I, as well as another dozen or so, remained behind like last time. I recognized everyone here, and realized that we were all making a habit of staying behind after meetings. Lois, Quinn, and Olson were here, big surprise, as well as Annabelle, Lee, and Vincent, none of whom I'd noticed at tonight's meeting until now. There were also Les, Kevin, Gary, Anne, Vincent's lady friend Kathy, Ingrid, and Jay and Amy, the couple who we helped during the storm. After the last of the other people trickled out of the basement, we waited a few more minutes for Ulysses, who closed the shop and came down to join us.

"I need to make a proposal to you all," Lois said, playing with her hair and looking at the floor. "As we all know, all of us have been contributing extra to this cause in one way or the other. Most of us stay late after every meeting to work logistics. We found ways to communicate with everyone without Perkins knowing about it. We're the spies. All this being said, we don't have an official chain of command, and that is something we desperately need. You all saw how the meeting started. There was no control, no order. We need to establish rank among the rebels, so we can have some sense of order." She sighed. "I realize that what I'm about to do is against our beliefs and against what we're fighting for. I want to do this democratically, but with the way things are escalating, we don't have a choice."

"What are you saying?" Kathy asked.

"We need a leader," Lois explained. "A leader for the rebels. Formally establishing a leader and a chain of command is going to help our situation."

"You think that leader should be you?" Les asked, raising his eyebrows.

Lois was quick to defend herself. "When people want answers, they come to me! If they want permission to do something, they come to me. I run the meetings."

"I wasn't going to disagree with you," Les said. "I was just trying to clear up what you were trying to say."

Lois blushed. "Oh. Sorry."

He shrugged. "I agree completely. Everyone looks up to you. You're a great leader. Even if we elected someone democratically, it would still be you." He looked around at us. "Does anyone disagree?"

We all shook our heads.

"Okay." Les looked back to Lois. "Then it's settled. You're the formal leader of the Caiten rebels."

"I need others in leadership positions along with me," Lois said. "So people have others to go to for varying situations. Les, you're my second in command. Austin, you're my third."

"What?" I said, surprised.

She ignored me. "Quinn, you're my adviser. Miriam, you're in charge of communication of all forms, physical and mental. See if you can find a hole in Perkins's telepathic web. We've tried before, but we may find something new. Ingrid, Ulysses, Gary, and Anne, since you'll be seeing a lot of new people over the next several weeks at your businesses, you're in charge of scoping out new members. Take a quick peak in everyone's mind to see what they think of this place. Then Kathy, Annabelle, and Amy will talk to those who aren't happy here and see if they're interested in joining us. Do it quietly though; don't just ask them if they want to join the resistance. Olson." She turned to him and put her hands on his shoulders. "I love you, but you really need to get a promotion."

We all laughed.

"I'll do my best," Olson replied.

Lois finished up her job list. "Vincent, keep doing what you're doing, but try to get as much as you possibly can. We've gone two months without any new information, and that ship is close to completion. Lee, I need you to try to get on that ship again. We need you in there with Austin. Jay and Kevin, stay where you are but try to get information from the soldiers patrolling the ship. They'll be distracted from all the noise, so try to get in their heads when they can't detect it. I think that's everyone." She took a deep breath and let it out loudly. "Okay. I need all this information up on the message boards, preferably right away. Please emphasize that this is all temporary. Let everyone know that we'll have a democratic election once we're rid of that monster."

~~*

News of Lois's new official position traveled fast. Miriam was quick to get everything onto the message boards, pleased at every opportunity to do something important.

About two weeks after rumors of a mole had spread, people started filtering back into the message boards. Perkins hadn't made a counterattack, and we hadn't heard anything else about the mole since Vincent's initial claim, so we started wondering if Vincent had simply misunderstood Perkins's thoughts. Vincent was ticked off that everyone was doubting him, but I thought that might be because he doubted himself. I shrugged off the conversation Jackson and I'd had about it. I didn't trust the man anyway.

Seeing him at work was weird. We hadn't made many attempts to talk to each other about our situations, so working with him and pretending we were just regular work partners was a bit uncomfortable.

The guy who had started to teach us to do our job, Blake Conover, never came back after the first day. No one told us what happened to him, and I wondered for a while if he had died from his illness. I didn't really want to know, because if he had it would drop my spirits lower than they already were. The guy in charge of the weapons design unit, Phil Eldritch, led the rest of our training and then it was pretty much just Jackson and me from then on out.

A few days after our emergency meeting about the new arrivals, Jackson and I were checking out the sixteen brand new big guns and twelve missiles set up in an outbuilding. These were the experimental weapons; Jackson and I were measuring them and verifying the specs, and if they checked out all right, they would be taken somewhere—somewhere none of us were allowed to know about—and tested. If the range and destructive force of the weapons were as Perkins wanted, then the manufacturing team would finish and deliver the rest of the eighty guns and sixty-five missile launchers.

Jackson and I may have been supervising the design of the weapons, but we didn't know what ammunition would be loaded into them. We had only received specs and dimensions.

"Have you heard anything more about where these things are going to be used?" Jackson asked me out of the blue when we were back on the ship.

"No," I replied. "We've come up with several possible scenarios, but we really don't know." I glanced over at him. "Why? Have you?"

Jackson stared at his notebook in which he was entering some calculations, but he wouldn't answer.

"Jackson!" I snapped. "What did you find out?"

"Please don't say my actual name out loud," Jackson said disapprovingly. "I'd like to make it out of this place alive."

"Would you just tell me what you found out, *Roy*?"

Jackson went to the door of the cabin and looked up and down the corridor. Once he was satisfied that no one was close enough to hear us, he closed and locked the door. "I wasn't finding enough information by just doing this job," he said. "So I broke into a few other places."

My jaw dropped. "And no one found out?"

He shrugged. "I'm still here, so I guess not. Anyway, I broke into three different places, and found something interesting at each of them." He stopped talking as a pair of laughing voices passed our cabin and slowly faded away. "I went to weapon construction first. Not an easy place to break into, mind you, considering it's offshore. But I got there, and I found out they're lying to us."

"*No way.*" I rolled my eyes. "What else is new?"

"I mean to *us*." He pointed at me and then himself. "We've been feeding them numbers for how to build these weapons based on what they told us, but once they received all of our initial calculations, they were modified."

"Which calculations?" I asked. "We gave them a ton of numbers."

"The calculations for distance."

This made a world of difference for us. Perkins was lying to us about the distance he wanted the missiles to reach, because he knew there were spies. "He wants the missiles to go farther," I said, certain that Perkins was aiming for somewhere farther inland.

But Jackson shook his head. "No. He doesn't need the missiles to go as far as we were told. He's planning to attack something near the shore."

This was interesting. "Closer? Hmm." I pondered over this, but could only come up with what had already been suggested; Perkins was aiming for a Navy fleet or a military base close to shore.

"I found something else. The missiles are remote controlled. Once they are armed and in the air, they will be under Perkins' control. He's planning to fly them directly into his target."

"Then what's the point of going through all these calculations?"

"To throw you off." Jackson raised his eyebrows. "He knows he has people like you trying to thwart him. This is all just a waste of our time. There's really no point to continue doing this, except that they'd figure us out. This is to make you believe what he wants you to believe."

"Goddamn it," I grumbled. "Everyone's gonna be pissed when they hear about this."

"Oh, that's not all. I went to the bridge next. The poor sucker plotting the course suddenly became violently ill, allowing me to step in and look at the course layout."

I stared at him. "You're a scary guy. I hope you know that."

"I didn't have a chance to look at the whole layout, because someone else was stepping in to take over for the guy who I—who got sick, but I saw enough to know that they're not going north. They're going south."

"South?" This was more confusing than interesting. "Why the hell would they be going south?"

"I was hoping you might know the answer to that."

"We all thought the likely target was somewhere north of here. We were thinking it was either Philadelphia, New York, D.C., or Norfolk, a naval base in Virginia."

"I know where Norfolk is, Austin."

"Well, you never know! So are they heading into the Gulf? I wonder what city along the Gulf Coast is a more likely target than D.C. or Philadelphia..."

"Did you ever take geography? I said they're going south, not west."

"You have to go south first to get into the Gulf!"

Jackson rubbed his brow, clearly frustrated with me. "No, I meant they're going *south*. They're not going around the Florida Peninsula."

My own confusion was now frustrating myself. "Okay, you've lost me. What the hell is south of here that's in the United States..." That's when it finally hit me, and I wanted to smack myself for not realizing it right away. "They're not attacking somewhere in the United States."

Jackson shook his head. "You know, considering how intelligent you are, you're not too bright."

"Shut up," I snapped. "Where are they going?"

He shrugged. "I told you I didn't see that much."

"Good God…is Perkins trying to start World War III? How stupid is he?"

"I don't know where he's going or who he's planning to attack, but you better find out soon," Jackson told me. "For the sake of both of us."

"Where was the last place you went?" I asked, eager to find out any more information.

"Oh." Jackson didn't seem too interested in that. He waved his hand dismissively. "I stopped in Eldritch's private office—another cabin on Deck 7—and the only thing I found that was of interest was a piece of paper with '110,860 square kilometers' written on it, which translates to 42,803 square miles if you don't get the kilometer thing."

"Someday you're gonna get smacked for that mouth, just saying," I told him. "Trust me, I know from experience."

"Okay, let's be serious for a moment," Jackson said, slapping his knees in a quick rhythm as he thought. "I don't suppose that number means anything to you? It doesn't mean anything to me."

"I got nothing," I said. "If we had access to the internet we could just Google it, but…"

"I'll have to look it up when I get out of here."

"How are you going to tell me what it means then?"

He glanced at me, shrugging as if he couldn't care less. "I'm not. You'll have to figure it out on your own, because once I'm out, I'm not coming back."

"Why not?" I demanded, the feeling of abandonment I got from his declaration hitting me harder than I thought. "You got in once before! You can do it a second time."

"Once I leave, and they realize who I was, it will be damn near impossible to get back in."

I sighed. "Awesome. So I guess we're both on our own with this one."

"Looks that way," Jackson agreed, picking up his notebook and getting back to work.

~~*

After work, I went to the hospital, claiming I had an unbearable pain in my right side. I was quickly admitted and Lois came to check me out, looking very concerned.

"I feel like I see you in here every other day," she said.

"I know," I replied, giving her a grin. "I'm actually okay this time."

Lois wasn't convinced. "Taryn said you thought you had appendicitis."

"I made that up. I got my appendix out when I was nine."

She folded her arms across her chest, really annoyed. "What the hell are you doing faking something like that?"

"I know, and I'm really sorry, but I needed to see you immediately and knew this was the best way to do it without drawing suspicion."

"What am I supposed to tell everyone, then?"

"Tell them it was just really bad gas from the crappy food we're given."

Lois shook her head. "What is so urgent that you needed to fake a life-threatening condition to see me?"

"I found out some information about where the *Defiant* is going."

She immediately lost her irritation toward me. She set her clipboard down and sat next to me on the observation table. "What did you find out? *How* did you find it out?"

"I have a friend who wishes to remain anonymous, and he's really smart and sneaky and broke into a couple places. He told me about it today and I had to tell you right away."

"Hold on." Lois went to the door and locked it. She came back and sat down again. "Talk quietly. I don't know who's around."

I told her everything Jackson had told me. She listened intently, especially interested in the fact that Perkins's target was not in the U.S.

"You're sure this source is reliable?"

"I'm sure. He just doesn't want to get involved with us."

"How did he get all of this information without getting caught?" Lois still wasn't buying it.

"He's..." I waved my index finger in a circle next to my head, "...a little cuckoo."

She nodded slowly. "Well, this certainly changes things. Did you put this information up on the message boards yet?"

"No. I wanted to tell you first."

She nodded again. "Okay. Put it up immediately, and I'll set up an emergency meeting for tonight."

"Yes, ma'am," I said, hopping off the table.

~~*

By the time I walked to my apartment the flier for the sale at Ulysses's store was already under the door. "Miriam," I called as I entered, picking up the flier and waving it around. "There's a sale at Ulysses's store again today." I didn't get an answer, but Miriam was there. She was sitting on the bed, hunched over, staring at the floor. "Miriam?" I said, going to her. "Are you okay, babe? What's wrong?" I looked at James in his cradle to make sure he was okay. He looked fine to me. "Did something happen to Vincent? Annabelle? Lee?"

She raised her eyes slowly, and I saw fear in them. "Something's happening outside," she whispered hoarsely. "It's not good."

I didn't question her. I turned and ran outside. When I burst through the door I tripped on the three steps leading to the ground and sprawled face first into the dirt. I glanced around, trying to see what it was that Miriam was seeing. It was down the street, in front of the shops. A group of people had gathered, and I could sense that something was really wrong. I got up and ran over. The crowd was really quiet, but as I got closer I could hear what sounded like a fight. I pushed through the onlookers and gasped when I got to the front. It wasn't a fight. It was a beating. Ulysses was on the ground, a bloody mess, and two soldiers were beating him mercilessly. I recognized one of the soldiers as the guy who almost broke my neck, and the second soldier was—

"Stop!" I shouted, running forward and plowing into Diereks, tackling him to the ground. "Really?!" I punched him in the face, and kept punching him. "You're here for a week and you're already hurting people? What is *wrong* with—"

The younger soldier punched me in the back of the head, but I was too angry for it to hurt me. I got up and punched him so hard that I felt his jaw break, and he backed away quickly, clutching his jaw and moaning. I turned back to Diereks, but he was already back on his feet. He tackled me before I could react. He started pummeling me, and I head-butted him, but that only caused us both to groan and clutch our heads before going back to beating each other

People had started yelling for help by now. I didn't know if they were soldiers, civilians, or both, and I didn't care.

Someone grabbed Diereks and ripped him off of me, throwing him backwards. When I looked up, I couldn't believe who I saw standing over me.

"Enough!" Jaeger shouted at Diereks, who was picking himself off the ground. "We're not here to fight with each other!"

I looked back and forth between Jaeger and Diereks, who were scowling at each other. Jaeger wasn't in uniform like Diereks, but Diereks still seemed afraid of him.

Jaeger looked down at me, his lips tight and body tense, ready for anything. He reached out a hand to help me up.

I glared at him, still hating him for what he did to my friends, but I took his hand. If he was going to defend me from one of his own, I could at least return a small gesture of respect.

"He's interfering with a direct order from Captain Perkins!" Diereks snapped, taking a defensive stance.

"Beating a civilian?" Jaeger turned to Ulysses, who was trying to push himself up. Gesturing for me to help as well, Jaeger started to help my friend to his feet. I took Ulysses's other side and helped raise him. Ulysses swayed a bit, and coughed a tooth out of his mouth, but he pushed our hands off of him and stood defiantly, glaring at Diereks.

"What's this about?" I demanded.

Diereks made a face at me. "Piss off, Rockwell! I'd be happy to beat your ass again."

"Answer the question!" Jaeger bellowed. "Why were you beating this man?"

Reaching into his belt, Diereks pulled out the flier for Ulysses's sale. "This is the second time this week that these fliers have been distributed. Captain Perkins was suspicious, so he sent Jared and I to search the place. We found the meeting place for the rebels, hidden below the building! He's the leader of the rebels!"

"That's ridiculous!" I said, stepping in front of Ulysses. "Finding a basement is not proof that he's the leader of the rebels!"

"It's proof enough for me," Diereks replied. "The captain didn't even know of its existence. What other purpose could it serve?"

"Even if he is the rebel leader," Jaeger said, trying to calm the situation, "that is no excuse for what you just did."

"We received orders to do so if we found evidence," Diereks snapped.

"If Perkins ordered you to shoot yourself in the head *right now*, would you do it?" Jaeger stared long and hard at him.

"That's *Captain* Perkins to you!"

"And as far as I'm concerned, you can still call me *Sergeant*!" Jaeger shouted. "You have exactly five seconds to move along before *you* also end up with a broken jaw!"

Diereks pulled something out of his belt that looked like a nightstick, something that a cop would carry. He glared hard at Jaeger. "You stepped down! You're in no position to be giving *me* orders!" He lunged forward.

Jaeger acted quickly, shoving Ulysses out of the way and reaching forward to catch Diereks's arm before it slammed the nightstick into his head. Before either of them made contact with the other, I had moved in between them. I caught Diereks's raised wrist in my hand, and I braced my other hand against his chest to stop his momentum. I soon realized that wasn't at all what I was doing.

The nightstick fell out of Diereks's hand and a horrible expression came across his face. It was terrified but also pained, as if he needed to take a breath but couldn't. It was the most horrible expression I'd ever seen, and it took me a moment to realize that I was causing it.

I could feel it in my hand, running up my arm and into my chest and head. It was energy. *Diereks's energy*. I was absorbing it through my own palm. I was adding his energy to my own. I'd never felt stronger. I kept pulling it from his body. It was as if I was hungry—*starving*—for more energy. Once I got a taste of someone else's, I couldn't stop draining it.

"Oh my God, Rockwell," Jaeger whispered in horror.

I looked back at Diereks's face, and scared myself even more. His skin had turned snow white, and the whites of his eyes turned red. I was killing him.

"Austin, stop it!" Jaeger grabbed my arm. "You're killing him!"

"Don't touch me!" I cried, letting go of Diereks and pulling away from Jaeger. I stared at my hands; they were buzzing with Diereks's energy, red and raw.

Diereks fell to the ground, convulsing and gasping for breath.

"Call for help!" Jaeger ordered, dropping down beside Diereks. He checked his pulse and tilted his head back so he could breathe better. While passersby ran for help, the remaining people stared at me, scared out of their minds. I didn't blame them. Many of them turned and ran away from the scene. Jaeger looked back up at me, angry but scared. "What did you do? *How* did you do it?"

I shook my head, terrified and confused. I was scared of myself. "I don't know what's wrong with me," I said, my whole body quivering. "Just…nobody touch me!" I turned and started running. I didn't know where; I just wanted to get away from all those people. I could have killed Diereks, just by touching him. I didn't want to hurt anyone by mistake.

I stopped when I reached the perimeter fence, doubling over and breathing hard. Once I caught my breath, I stared at my hands for a long time, trying to figure out how I could do what I just did. No Caiten had ever shown any ability apart from telepathy, so how was it that I—completely out of the blue—almost managed to kill a man with a single touch?

My hands weren't red anymore. They were back to their normal color, but my whole body was still vibrating. Panicking, afraid of my own power, I sat down in the dirt and rested my back against the fence. I covered my face with my hands. *What the hell did Hillerman do to me?* I wondered, hating him even more now. *And why am I the only one who can do it?*

"Rough day?"

My head snapped up. "What are you doing here?" I demanded.

"Nice to see you too," Jackson replied, walking over to me.

"Don't touch me!" I warned, jumping to my feet and edging away from him. "Don't…don't even come near me."

Jackson, barely fazed by my outburst, lifted his arm and took a whiff of his pit. "Did I forget to shower?"

"It's not you I'm worried about," I mumbled, shoving my hands into my own pits so I wouldn't accidentally touch him.

"You're not the only one, you know."

"What?"

"The only one who can do what you just did." He offered me a smile. "I got there just in time to see you drain that guy. He must have pissed you off pretty bad."

"He was trying to kill my friend," I said. "How do you know I'm not the only one who can do that? I've never seen that kind of power among us! *What did I even do?*"

"Calm down, buddy," Jackson said, leaning against the fence a few feet down from me. "I don't really know what you did, and I don't know how you can do it, but something I've noticed about the Caitens is that similar strains produce similar capabilities."

"What?"

"The Caiten Strain was mutated dozens of times. The scientists experimenting with it wanted to get it perfect, and they infected thousands of people with varying strains along the way. Hundreds of people were infected with one strain while hundreds more were infected with another. But there were some strains I heard about that were only given to a few individuals, and I'm guessing you received one of those rare strains. So you, and whoever else was infected with you, have this new capability."

"Oh no," I muttered. That meant Miriam and Jeff both had this power as well, and probably James, too.

Jackson cocked his head at me. "Someone else close to home, I'm assuming?"

"Yeah," I said.

Sighing, Jackson clapped his hands once. "Well, at least you and your wife don't have to worry about being outmatched."

"Perkins outmatches us all together," I replied hopelessly.

"I wouldn't be so sure of that. But if you want to believe that, that's fine. Feeling outmatched might do you some good. It'll keep you from trying to bust out of here."

"What makes you think we wouldn't try to bust out of here?" I demanded. "Even if we are outmatched?"

He shrugged. "You may not want to believe it, but sacrificing your freedom right now is probably for the best."

"You've seen what conditions we're living in here!"

"Are you sure it will be any different outside of this fence?"

I stared at him, confused. "What are you talking about?"

"Where were you before you settled here? In a lab? I'm suggesting that getting out of this place may not be your best option."

"Then what *is* our best option?" I snapped. "Since you *clearly* know everything."

Jackson smirked at me. "I think your best option is to wait for Perkins to carry out his plan with the ship before you overthrow him. I think you may find the end result to be worth the wait."

I laughed. "You want us to wait for him to attack another country and start a war that we have no hope of winning? That seems very worth the wait, *Roy*."

Jackson chuckled. "I love how you are all so stuck on the idea that attacking someone is a *bad* thing. I think if you wait and find out what he's really up to, you'll realize that he actually has your best interests at heart."

I suddenly understood what he was saying. "You figured it all out, didn't you? You know what he's doing!"

"That's correct."

I waited for him to explain, but he didn't continue. "Well?"

He shook his head. "You're smart, Austin. I'm not going to give you all the answers." He grabbed hold of the fence and started scaling it.

"Where the hell are you going?" I asked, realizing that he had a small duffel bag slung over his shoulder.

"My business here is done," he replied. "I'll be on my way now."

"You know that's barbed wire at the top?"

"Got it covered." He patted his belt.

I hated myself for saying this. "I need your help, man! This isn't just affecting humans!"

"My job is to help humans, not you." He paused at the top of the fence to pull something out of his belt: a wire cutter. He began cutting away a section of barbed wire so he could climb over.

"I thought we were going to help each other!" I couldn't believe this jerk!

Sighing, Jackson looked down at me. "Don't take it personally. You seem like a really good guy. I think you could be a really good leader for these people if things work out for you. But my job is to protect the human race, not the Caiten race. Good luck to you, my friend."

I laughed scornfully. "We're not friends, pal. You lied to me."

He finished cutting through the barbed wire, climbed over, and dropped to the ground on the other side. "That's what I do. But now I'm going to give you some truth. Find your mole. Trust me when I tell you that he's closer than you think. *Much* closer."

The mole? Why was he bringing up the mole? We hadn't heard anything about the mole or a counterattack by Perkins since it was first mentioned. Most of us were confident that there *wasn't* a mole. "Why does that matter now? We haven't had any issues with the supposed mole."

"Trust me. There is a mole, and he's much closer to you than you'd think."

"Why would I trust you now? You've been lying to me from the start! How do I know your name is even Jackson?"

"Because even though I had to lie my way through this place, I still think you have good people here. Why else would I have stopped Barnes from killing you? Your mole is very close to you, and if you don't stop him you'll get yourself, your family, and all the good people in this town killed. Don't trust your allies."

"Whatever," I snapped, glaring at him through the fence. "Go enjoy your free life." I turned and started walking back toward town.

"Austin," Jackson called. When I ignored him, he called louder. "Austin!"

"What!" I turned around, throwing my arms in the air angrily. "What?"

His face darkened, expressing a hate and rage that made me take a step back. "Don't trust the Colicians, either." His face softened again after a moment, and he said, "Good luck to you," before turning and walking away from Rebellion.

I watched him for a while, but eventually turned away without calling out to him. I wasn't going to listen to him. He was a liar, and had been from the start. He was trying to divert our attention and turn us on each other. *Don't trust the Colicians?* That was rich coming from a human. I wasn't going to listen to anything he said.

Before I headed back to town, I decided to contact Jeff. We hadn't been in touch for a few weeks, and I was certain he and the Colicians were very worried about how things were going here. I was also worried about him being alone on the Parallel Earth.

I let my mind stretch as far as it could reach and called out to Jeff. He answered much faster than usual.

Austin? Oh my God! Where have you been? I've been stressed out of my mind waiting for you to contact me! I thought you might be...

I'm fine, Jeff, I assured him. *I'm sorry I haven't been in touch for so long.*

Two weeks is really pushing it, dude, Jeff replied flatly. *How's everything in Rebeltown?*

No change really. I paused, unsure if I should trust Jackson about the information regarding the battleship. He hadn't proved to be very trustworthy. I gave in, knowing it would be on my hands if Jackson was telling the truth and I ignored him. *We have learned some new information about the battleship, though.*

I'm not sure I want to know.

You need to tell Walter this as soon as you can so he can look into it for us. We got someone on the inside and he found out that Perkins isn't attacking a city in the United States.

Oh, Lord. I could hear Jeff mentally groaning. *Where's he going?*

We don't know yet. That's why we need you and Walter to help us figure that out. If Perkins attacks internationally, the world will soon find out about our species, and then there's nothing left we can do to protect ourselves. We'll be annihilated.

This is intense. I'll talk to Walter about it right away.

Perkins and his soldiers are starting to crack down on us, I said. *A friend of mine was attacked about twenty minutes ago. They figured out where the rebels meet and know my friend is involved. I'm pretty sure they were going to have him killed. I probably saved his life.* I bit my lip, wondering if Ulysses was still okay, or if Perkins and his soldiers had already finished the job and were waiting for me to come back.

How did you manage that? Jeff asked skeptically.

For a moment, I considered not telling him about my new ability. I was scared of myself; I didn't know how others were going to react to this. But I had to tell him. He was going to find out sooner or later, after all.

We're not just telepaths, Jeff, I told him. *We have another ability, and possibly more.*

There was a pause on the other end. *What are you talking about, Austin? Another ability?*

I just used it. That's how I saved my friend. I had no idea I had it. I just…did it.

What did you do?

I'm not even totally sure. I put my hand on Diereks's chest—oh yeah, I forgot to mention that Jaeger, Diereks, Tyler, and Anders are all here now. Perkins rescued them from the lab and now Diereks is one of Perkins's soldiers. Still a douche. Anyway, I put my hand on his chest and it was like I was sucking the life out of him. He turned all white and the whites of his eyes were going red. I could literally feel myself pulling the life from his body. It was really scary, Jeff.

Jeff didn't reply for a while, and I thought maybe he'd pulled away from the conversation. Finally, he said, *Have you done anything else?*

No, I said. Thankfully that's it, but who knows what else we can do if we've gone this long without knowing about this second ability.

Okay. I'm going to talk to Walter and Dr. Perry about this. Call me again tomorrow and I'll let you know what their reactions were.

I will if I can. But that's not it, Jeff. If I have this ability, then everyone who was infected with the same strain should have it too.

Don't tell me that! Please don't tell me that! One ability is bad enough! He sighed. *I'm gonna go. Let me know if you find anything else.*

Will do.

Oh, and Austin, are you still lying to Perkins about me being sick?

I have to. But he's not going to keep believing me for long. I don't think he even believes that I'm on his side.

Okay. Well, hopefully you can bust yourselves out of there soon. Keep me posted.

Later.

~~*

I quickly returned to Rebellion. There were going to be at least a few angry people in town, most likely soldiers. I had no desire to run into any of them. Most of all, though, I just wanted to get to my family before anyone else did.

I dodged in and out of the thin alleys between buildings and snuck in through the back door of my apartment complex. I ran up to my floor and stopped dead in my tracks at the top of the stairs. The door to my apartment was busted off the hinges, lying in splinters. My stomach dropped and I couldn't breathe. My entire body was shaking as I walked forward and climbed over the remnants of my door into my apartment.

It seemed like the entire room was turned upside down. The bed was flipped over; the mattress hung out the broken window. Everything was pulled out of the cupboards and the refrigerator and the doors remained open. James's cradle was overturned.

I went into the bathroom, only to find a similar mess. "Miriam?" I said, even though I knew she was gone. I looked around at the mess, my body shaking even harder. My eyes landed on James's cradle. "James…"

I turned when I heard a gasp. Annabelle was standing in the doorway with Penny on her hip. Annabelle's hand was over her mouth, and she was staring wide-eyed at the destroyed apartment. She dropped her hand when she met my gaze. "Miriam…?"

I shrugged. Annabelle let out a sob, but I wasn't going to give up just yet. I closed my eyes and reached out my mind as far as it could possibly go. I could feel the mind of every human, Caiten, and Colician in existence. But I couldn't feel Miriam's. She was gone. She and my son were gone.

"Where are they?" I thought the fury I'd felt toward Diereks when he was beating Ulysses was the angriest I could possibly be, but I was wrong. The fury I felt right now was far beyond that. I felt like I could rip somebody's head off with my bare hands. I let out a scream of rage, and I knew that everyone in Rebellion could hear it. I stormed out of the room; Annabelle quickly moved out of the way when she realized I would walk right over her if I had to. As I left the apartment, Vincent came running up the stairs, frantic.

"Where's my sister?" he cried, running up to me. "James, Miriam... Where are they?"

I grabbed Vincent by the throat, too angry to care if I hurt him or not. "You tell me, you bastard." I felt the energy beginning to drain out of him. His face turned white and he made the same choking sound that Diereks had made. He couldn't speak, but he did what he could to mentally talk me out of killing him.

Austin...stop! I didn't take them anywhere; I ran as fast as I could to get them out of here before Perkins could get to them! Please stop! We have to find them together!

"Austin! You're killing him! Stop it!" Annabelle pleaded with me but didn't dare touch me.

I released Vincent, and he doubled over and gasped for breath. His color quickly returned, and he regarded me warily as he said, "They're coming for you, Austin. They came here for Miriam and James the first time. Now they're coming for you. They'll be here any second. Annabelle." He turned to her. "Run. Get out of here."

Normally, Annabelle would have stayed by our sides, but when she saw the gravity of the situation in Vincent's eyes, she turned and ran up the stairs with her daughter as fast as she could.

She got out of there just in time, because just as she disappeared up to the next floor, a lot of soldiers, led by Perkins, came running up the stairs and burst onto our floor.

Perkins's eyes landed on me, and Vincent quickly took a protective stance in between us. "Lobner," Perkins ordered, "arrest him."

"Where's my sister?" Vincent demanded. "Where's my nephew?"

"I gave you an order, Lobner!" Perkins snapped, but he didn't seem angry. He already knew that Vincent wasn't going to comply.

"I don't give a rat's ass about your orders!" Vincent snarled. "I want to know what you did with my sister and nephew!"

Perkins looked bored. "You've decided your own fate then. Arrest them both."

The group of soldiers advanced on us, but Vincent halted them as he whipped out his gun and aimed it at Perkins. The other soldiers quickly pointed their firearms at Vincent. "I'll shoot you," he threatened Perkins. "It would be an honor to shoot you."

Vincent and Perkins stared each other down, and I was certain Perkins was going to give the order to shoot. I knew both of us would be killed, and Miriam and James would have no chance. "Stop!" I commanded, pushing Vincent behind me. "I'm the one he wants, and he knows I'll go with him."

"You're being stupid, Austin!" Vincent said, refusing to lower his gun.

"Get out of here," I told him. "Go. I'll take care of myself."

"I'm not leaving without my family!"

"I'll take care of them, too. Get out of here, Vincent. Go find Walter and stay with him until this all blows over. I'll keep them from coming after you."

"You can't stop bullets, Austin," Perkins reminded me. "And from what I heard, you have to be touching someone to keep him from firing."

"I'm not so sure you're willing to take a chance with me, pal," I replied coolly, staring him down. "I mean it, Vincent. *Go.*"

With a frustrated groan, Vincent turned and high-tailed it after Annabelle. I trusted him to find his own way out of Rebellion.

I took a deep breath, still staring at Perkins. "All right, buddy. Where's my family?"

"Come with me and I won't hurt them," Perkins replied, glaring at me. Before I was hauled away, I saw the slightest flicker of fear in his eyes.

22

Uprising

I never thought I'd be experimented on in Rebellion, a town created to escape experimentation, but living here had provided me with plenty of surprises. For the last hour I'd been strapped to a chair in the hospital. Lois had drawn vial after vial of blood, shooting me a quick apologetic look every time. Perkins was ordering her to run test after test, and for the sake of keeping her infant twins—whom Perkins was threatening to take away from her—she didn't dare defy him.

"What are you finding?" Perkins demanded of Lois as she drew another vial of blood.

"I'm not sure," Lois replied nervously, capping the small IV in my arm.

"What do you mean you don't know? You're a doctor!" It was obvious he was getting extremely impatient, and Lois was getting more and more uneasy around him.

"I'm a physician, not a geneticist!" Lois protested, shrinking away from him. "I don't know what I'm looking for!"

Perkins cornered her behind me, getting in her face. "You'd better figure it out fast, or else our children are going to grow up without their mother!"

"Leave her alone," I snapped. "She didn't do anything to you."

Turning on me, Perkins asked, "You mean to tell me she isn't involved with the rebels, that she isn't the *leader* of the rebels? I know everything, Austin. I've known it for a long time."

"Then why didn't you just kill us?" I asked. There were too many twists and turns with this man; I couldn't tell what he knew and what he was pretending to not know.

"Because you're far too important to kill." Perkins hovered over Lois as she looked at my blood under a microscope.

"And what about everyone else? Certainly not everyone here is valuable to you."

"You'd be surprised," Perkins said. He addressed Lois. "Did you find it yet?"

"I told you I don't know what I'm looking for!"

Grabbing Lois by her ponytail, he yanked her away from the microscope and threw her to the floor. She collapsed in front of me, and when she looked up I could see the tears in her eyes. I'd never seen her come close to crying before.

As Perkins took Lois's place and began studying my blood thoroughly, Lois glanced at me. *Untie me, Lois.* I told her. Her eyes wide, she gave me the slightest shake of her head.

"Don't talk to her!" Perkins ordered without looking up from the microscope. "Dallas, remove my wife, please."

A short but broad young black man stepped into the room and grabbed Lois's arm. "Where would you like me to take her, sir?"

"Put her in a cell."

Lois looked at me pleadingly as she was dragged away, but there was nothing I could do for her. Nothing I could do without getting angry, anyway.

"Find a geneticist," Perkins commanded the dozen other soldiers outside the door. "I don't care if it's a human. Just bring me a geneticist, and do it fast."

Seven of the soldiers quickly left, and the others entered the room and stood against the opposite wall, eyeing me nervously.

"What do you need a geneticist for?" I asked.

"You really think I'm going to let *you* walk around with that kind of power? I don't think so. Someone needs to find a way to take it from you and transfer it to me. You're no leader, Austin. No one except a leader can have this power."

"I couldn't do any worse at it than you already have," I snapped.

He ignored me. "I've been waiting for this to happen, you know," he said, finally looking away from my blood sample. He put his hands in his pockets and stepped in front of me. "A phenomenon such as this was bound to happen after so many variations of the Caiten Virus were created. It was only a matter of time before a rogue variation appeared. How ironic it turned out to be your variation."

"Yes, and I'm so thrilled," I muttered. "What's so ironic about it?"

Perkins snickered. "You and your wife were the first on the list to be killed after this glitch appeared. Your new abilities saved your life. For now, at least."

"Fabulous," I said sarcastically. "This is wonderful and all, but I'd really appreciate it if you'd tell me where my wife and son are."

"You can see them soon," he replied, looking away from me quickly. There was something suspicious about his behavior whenever I brought up my family. "First, I need to find out exactly what you can do."

"I'm sure you heard from Diereks exactly what I did," I grumbled.

"No." Perkins shook his head. "There's more to it than just that. There's more you can do."

"How could you possibly know that?"

"I know." Perkins's eyes were gleaming with anticipation. I thought he was going to start drooling over me.

"Yeah," I muttered. "I think you're just nuts."

"Do something," Perkins commanded.

"And for my next trick, I will do nothing because I can't move my arms." I shrugged at him. "I don't know what you expect me to do when I'm tied down. I used my hands last time."

"You don't need your hands," Perkins insisted. "The only things we need are our minds."

"Good God, you're insane…"

Pulling out his pistol, he pointed it at my head. "I know you can stop the bullet. I certainly hope you do, because your life depends on it."

"Dude, stop!" I cried. "I can't do it! I don't know how! The last time I only did what I did because I was angry!"

Perkins lowered the pistol. "You're right," he said. "This isn't the correct motivation." He turned and gestured toward the door. A soldier went out into the hall and came back a moment later, Annabelle in tow.

"Oh, shit," I said. Annabelle's hands were cuffed behind her back and she was gagged with a piece of cloth tied around her head. I had never seen her look more scared, even when Barnes had tried to kill me. Tears, snot, and blood were running down her face. She had a large cut above her right eyebrow and her nose appeared to be broken.

"Do you want to save your friend, Austin?" Perkins asked, raising the pistol and pointing it at Annabelle. "I know she's your friend, and I know you won't let me kill her. So stop me, Austin."

"Don't do this!" I begged, but I could feel my anger returning, and with it, a new energy. This one was different than when I'd almost killed Diereks and Vincent. This was more powerful.

"You can save her, Austin," Perkins told me, and pulled the trigger.

I screamed loud and long, waiting for Annabelle to drop to the floor. But she didn't, and it took me a moment to see what everyone else was staring at in astonishment. The bullet from Perkins's pistol was floating in midair, halfway between the barrel and Annabelle's head. It dropped to the floor a moment later. Annabelle sank to her knees, sobbing.

I had no idea how I did it; I didn't even feel anything, aside from terror, when the gun went off.

"See?" Perkins said, turning back to me once he'd gotten over his surprise. "Was that so hard?"

"I hate you," I replied.

"Get her out of here," Perkins told his soldiers, who had to carry her out because she was too shocked to stand.

"All right," I snapped. "Enough's enough. Where's my family?"

"Keep on cooperating and we won't hurt them." Perkins went back to the counter with the microscope, picking up one of the vials of my blood and holding it up to the light to study it.

"I'm not gonna play this game with you," I snapped. "No way. Prove my family is all right or I'll kill everyone in this room."

Perkins froze. The other soldiers started inching toward the door, not sure whether or not to believe me. Perkins turned on me. "You're bluffing. I know when you're bluffing. I'm a telepath too, remember? I'm the strongest one here."

"You don't believe that anymore," I said. "You're convinced that *I'm* the strongest one here. Actually, I think you believe that *Miriam* is the strongest one. Because she is, isn't she, Perkins?"

His jaw clenched angrily. So Perkins had an ego after all. "Miriam is not the strongest. I don't know why you think that."

"Oh, you do, pal. She's not here, is she? She left before you could get to her. That's why you brought Annabelle in here instead of Miriam. And that's why my apartment was torn to pieces, because you were looking for her. She knew you were coming so she took James and left. And she managed to get out without anyone knowing, not even you. You're pathetic compared to Miriam. You're lucky she decided to take our son and get out, because if she'd stayed she would have torn your mind to pieces!"

"That's enough!" Perkins advanced on me, holding the vial of blood over me like a weapon.

I laughed in his face. "Get out!" I snapped. "Get out before I kill you and your band of Nazis!"

"You can't hurt us," Perkins replied coolly.

"You'd better scram before I prove you wrong."

"Shut up! Just shut up! We aren't going anywhere! This is *my* town!"

"Get out!" I screamed. "Get out of Rebellion! This is *my* town now!"

Perkins brought the vial of blood down on my head. The moment before it made contact, it flew backwards out of his hands and exploded against the wall above the soldiers' heads. Blood flew everywhere, splattering against the wall, dripping down onto the soldiers. They cried out in fear and ran out of the room, stumbling and pushing each other out of the way to get away from me.

"Where are you going?" Perkins shouted, turning his back on me. That was a mistake.

He was the next thing to fly into the wall, and before I realized what was happening everything in the room was upended and smashed. The whole room shook around me, and a deafening crash sounded as the wall behind me blew out. As suddenly as it had all started, it stopped. Perkins stared at me in fury, still not afraid, as the straps holding me down broke free and I stood up, glaring right back.

I finally snapped out of my rage-induced violence, and took a look at what I'd done. Everything was broken or bent. There was glass everywhere. Sparks were falling from the ceiling where the lights used to be. There was an enormous hole in the side of the building, with a huge pile of debris scattered around it. I did this. I could cause this kind of destruction. There was no way I could allow a monster like Perkins to have this ability.

I turned and jumped out of the hole. I was three stories up, but, with my newfound power, I landed softly on the ground below. I started running toward the jail. This power I held could only be used in two ways: liberation or destruction. I was going to use it to save the people of Rebellion.

I sprinted the whole way to the jail, not even stopping when soldiers ran out and aimed their weapons at me.

"Don't shoot!" I heard a soldier yell, and the rest of them cleared a path for me as I ran past. "He's extremely dangerous! Don't shoot him!"

No one tried to stop me after that. Word was spreading fast that I was telekinetic, and no one dared confront me. I kicked down every cell door I came across, hoping to rescue Annabelle, Ulysses, and Lois. I had to get those who were already captured out of Rebellion, and then get the rest of the civilians as well.

None of the cells were occupied, except for the very last one. Lois was sitting in the far corner, weeping. "Lois!" I cried, running to her. "Where is everyone? Where's Annabelle and Ulysses?"

Lois jumped up and hugged me, sobbing into my shoulder. "They're executing them!"

"What?" I pulled away from her. "What are you talking about?"

"Perkins knows everything about the rebels, Austin! He knows about *everything*! He knows that I'm in charge and knows who was by my side planning the rebellion! He's executing everyone who held a leadership position!"

As my stomach sank to the floor, I became even more grateful that Miriam and Vincent had fled. But even though they were out of the line of fire, I had a long list of friends that were about to die: Annabelle, Lee, Les, Quinn, Kevin, Ulysses, Anne, Gary, Ingrid, Olson, Kathy, Amy, and Jay.

"What about you?" I asked, my mouth dry. I was so stunned that I didn't know what else to say. "Why aren't you out there with them?"

"Perkins still needs me." She shuddered.

"What for?"

"What do you think?"

My nose wrinkled in disgust. "Never again, Lois. Come on. We're getting out of here."

"My brother, Austin!" she cried, about to collapse in anguish.

"Has the execution started yet?"

"Not until Perkins gets there..."

"Then we still have time. Get out of here, Lois. Climb the fence. Run."

"Not without my brother and my babies!"

I pulled her out the cell door and put my hands on her shoulders. "Listen to me, Lois. You're not in the right state of mind to rescue anyone. Get out of Rebellion. I'll save your brother and your babies, and everyone else. I promise you."

"Austin—"

"*I promise you.*" I stared at her, waiting, until she nodded in agreement. "Let's go." I tried to pull her forward, but she groaned and clutched her stomach. "What's wrong?" I asked, immediately concerned. "Were you beaten?"

"I'm pregnant," she said. When she saw the horrified look in my eyes, she shook her head. "It's not his."

I was astonished at Lois's bravery and defiance, and knew that it was absolutely essential that she got out at once. If Perkins found out about Lois's infidelity... "We're going to get out of here, and you can raise your babies in peace." I took her hand and we left the jail.

While I ran back toward Rebellion, Lois ran to the fence fifty meters away and climbed over to the safety of the other side. Once she was across, she stopped and watched me as I ran; I called back to her, "Keep running!"

Reluctantly, Lois turned and kept running.

I knew I didn't have enough time to detour and get Lois's twins first, so I ran straight toward the main street, where I knew the executions would take place. There was a mass of people in the street; I could see the crowd before I even got close. As I reached the terrified citizens of Rebellion being forced to watch the execution of the people who had been trying to liberate them, people started crying out in fear and moving away from me.

I felt like Moses, parting the Red Sea. A clear path to the execution circle was made, and I was quickly inside and facing Perkins once again.

My friends were all lined up, gagged and on their knees with their hands cuffed behind their backs. I did a quick count and realized that Lee and Kathy were missing. I prayed they were both safe. I prayed Vincent had gotten Kathy out, but I wasn't so confident about Lee's whereabouts. My friends' backs were to me, and when I burst into the circle the soldiers who were aiming their weapons at them all jumped away and retreated back into the crowd, more terrified of me than of Perkins. He stood across the circle from me, his presence ushering fear into every person surrounding us. But when Annabelle and Les and the others turned to see who had arrived and saw that it was me, a spark of hope crossed their faces. It was now my job to make that spark a flame.

"Austin," Perkins said. That was all he had to say to me.

"I thought I told you to get out." I looked around at the onlookers, who were too afraid to stand up for themselves, but who might just start if they had the right person to lead them. "Nathaniel Perkins has been running this town on fear and lies! He doesn't care about any of you!" I gestured to my friends in front of me. "We do. That's why we were leading the rebels, to try and overthrow Perkins's oppressive reign. Now, Perkins is going to execute us for fighting for our—*your*— liberation, and go right back to his corrupt ways! There's a way we can prevent that from happening, but you have to help me. You have to help yourselves."

Perkins started laughing. "You think they're going to follow you, Rockwell? You're a boy! You're uncontrollable. You're not a leader."

I ignored him and kept talking. "I know you're afraid of what Perkins can do to you, but he can't fight us all! If we stand our ground together, he can't hurt us!"

"They're not just afraid of me, Austin," Perkins said, folding his arms. "They're afraid of *you*."

I gazed out at the faces of my fellow Caitens and knew his words were true. I could see the fear on each and every one of their faces. They knew what I could do and they feared it just as much as they feared Perkins. I was frustrated; I was also sad. My sadness for these people formed tears, and those tears dropped down my face. "I care about you," I whispered. "I care about what happens to you. That's why I was helping to lead the rebels. I want to *save* you!"

"He almost killed someone!" Perkins had stopped addressing me and was now addressing the crowd. "Less than three hours ago! He thinks he's better than me, but he won't lead you to a place any better than here."

"I am not your enemy!" I cried to the crowd.

"He has a different power than any Caiten has ever had before!" Perkins challenged. "It's more powerful than any telepathic ability any of you possess! None of you could match him!"

I realized he was avoiding telling everyone that he couldn't match me either. "It's true," I said. "I have a power more powerful than any of you possess, but it's also more powerful than Perkins'. Yes, I hurt someone, but it was to protect an innocent person from being murdered. I have this power, and I want to use it to help you. To protect you." I stabbed a finger toward Perkins. "He wants to take this power from me and find a way to use it for his own purposes. If that happens, he will only use this power to hurt more people. I only want to use this power to protect innocent people like you from people like him. If he steals this power, there's no telling what destruction will lie in his wake." I took a deep breath. I didn't know what else I could say to motivate these people. "It's up to you."

"I suppose it is," Perkins agreed, smirking at me confidently.

I was scared. If no one stood with me against Perkins, Perkins might destroy me, and if he did he would then destroy the rebels. Then there would be no hope for the Caitens. All I needed was one person to stand with me, one person to ignite the flame, but the bravest people I knew were all tied up in front of me.

I heard gasps from all around the circle, and I turned quickly, scared that someone was about to attack me from behind. My mouth fell open when I saw who had left the onlookers to join me.

Peter Jaeger clasped my shoulder and looked me in the eye. I saw all his regrets for the pain he had caused others. I also saw his readiness and willingness to change. I stared back at my past enemy and present ally, and realized that it didn't matter who he was or what he'd done. He was prepared to fight, to die, for the freedom of our race. That was all that mattered anymore.

Looking defiantly at Perkins, Jaeger growled, "After the violence I've endured the past few years, and the violence I've participated in, there comes a point when you decide that enough is enough. I'm at that point. Let this be the end of it."

A murmur started to buzz through the crowd. Perkins looked around, realizing with increasing anxiety what was about to happen. Jaeger wasn't the only one who'd had enough.

I stared with growing awe as the circle of civilians pulled away from Perkins and all backed up behind me. Even several soldiers inched over in support. There were still plenty of soldiers standing behind Perkins, but they were nothing compared to the mass standing beside me.

"The people have made their choice, Perkins," I said. "Now it's time to make yours. You and your soldiers can let us leave, and we'll leave in peace. Otherwise, you can fight and suffer the consequences."

Perkins just stared at me for a moment, but then he started laughing. "Oh, Austin. You're the one who's going to suffer the consequences."

It was the most excruciating pain I'd ever experienced. I felt like my head was imploding and exploding at the same time. I clutched the sides of my head, in too much pain to scream. I sank to my knees, waiting for someone to come to my aid or fight Perkins. That was when I realized that everyone on my side was being affected. People were screaming and crying out in pain. Babies shrieked. Children cried. No one on my side was left untouched. It was Perkins. No other Caiten could affect this many people at once. I knew by the pain in my head that I would not survive if this continued. Neither would anyone else. I had to do something.

I thought about what Jackson had told me before leaving Rebellion. He said Miriam and I never had to worry about being outmatched. I'd replied by saying no one could outmatch Perkins. I was right in a way, but I was also wrong. No one could outmatch Perkins telepathically—except maybe Miriam—but I definitely outmatched him telekinetically.

Fighting my pain, I did what I had to do to save my people. I slowly rose to my feet, and lowered my hands. I could barely see Perkins standing across from me through the red spots dotting my vision, but I only needed to know where he was. I focused every last bit of energy I had on him, and then punched the air in his direction, letting out a scream of agony as I did. The force I sent to Perkins knocked him clean off his feet and backwards several dozen yards. Dust was also picked up and was now spinning like a twister. Most of the soldiers backing up Perkins were also knocked to the ground.

The pain immediately subsided and my vision cleared. I felt like I was going to puke and pass out, but I forced myself to stay on my feet. Something was coming out of my eyes; I assumed it was tears, but when I wiped them away I saw blood on my hand. I couldn't let that stop me. I had to fight Perkins.

I stood, catching my breath, while Perkins caught his and climbed to his feet. The people behind me, and my friends in front of me, were all whimpering as they recovered from the attack. I glared at Perkins as he regained his composure and snarled back at me. "Leave them alone, Perkins!" I warned, pulling my fist back and getting ready to let loose another punch. "Last chance!"

"You really think you can lead them?" Perkins shouted at me. "You can't take care of your own family!"

"Stay back!" I yelled as he strode closer. I threw a punch at the ground right in front of him, leaving a crater in the street and releasing another cloud of dust. This didn't faze him at all.

"You can't lead these people!" Perkins finally stopped, only a few feet from my friends. He waved his hand at them. "And neither can they!"

My friends started screaming through their gags, falling over and convulsing.

"Stop!" I cried. They were the only ones he was targeting; if I didn't stop him now, they would die or be too brain damaged to function. I pulled my fist back and prepared to strike him with a blow so hard he wouldn't ever hurt anyone again. But before I could respond, the ground began shaking. I looked around, startled. Were we having an earthquake?

Perkins released my friends and they stopped convulsing, but now I could feel him beginning to target me. "Stop it, Rockwell!" he shouted.

"This isn't me!" I replied, looking around for the source of the quaking.

The people behind me started yelling again, but this time it was out of fear. They all started running toward the shops and apartments. Some ran inside the buildings, and some shrank down in the doorways and the alleys to watch. I looked at the person down the street who was causing the quaking, and almost screamed with joy. "Miriam!"

Miriam stood defiantly, her hair tied up in a bun, her eyes ablaze. Dust was spinning around her. She didn't even seem to notice me. "You were warned, Perkins!" she shouted, and then picked up her foot and slammed it back into the ground. When her foot made contact with the ground, the shaking became much more intense and an enormous crater formed around her. The ground began to split in front of her, and the crack traveled forward, past me, past our friends, and then around Perkins. Perkins stared at her, real fear finally taking over. He had known all along that Miriam was the strongest of us all, and now that she'd come back to assist in the uprising, Perkins didn't stand a chance and he knew it.

"Make a decision!" Miriam told him. "You can let us leave, and if you don't agree to that I'll drop the ground out from under you! Make your choice, Perkins, and make it now."

Perkins nodded quickly. "Okay," he said. "Okay."

"Go," Miriam ordered. "Take your soldiers and go to the beach. Stay there. In two hours, you can come back. You can have the town. Now go."

Nodding, Perkins gestured for his men to follow him, and they all took off toward the beach. Before he disappeared behind one of the shops, he shot me one last, hateful glance.

The quaking slowed to a halt, and the dust settled. Miriam exhaled heavily, and suddenly looked exhausted.

"Baby," I whispered, running to her. "You're amazing."

"I'm sorry I left," she said, out of breath. "I had to get James out of here. I had to get him somewhere safe before I came back."

"Where is he?"

"With Vincent and Kathy. They're going back to Wisconsin, to find somewhere near Lake Superior where we can all meet once we're out of here."

"Is Lee with them?" I asked.

"No." She looked confused. "Why?"

"Something's not right. He's not with the rest of them." I took her hand and pulled her toward our friends, who were still lying in the middle of the street. We untied them and helped them to their feet. They were still pretty unsteady and disoriented after the last attack. "Annabelle," I said as I pulled her up and steadied her. "Where's Lee? He's not with the rest of you. Where is he?"

"I don't know," she murmured, trying to focus her eyes. "I haven't seen him in a while..."

"What about Kathy and Vincent?" Anne asked, clinging to Gary.

"They're safe," Miriam promised. "We're going to rendezvous with them once we get everybody out of here."

"Austin," Annabelle whispered, gripping my arm tightly. "We have to find Lee and Penny. I think something's wrong."

"We'll find them," I promised. I glanced over at the rest of my friends as an angry commotion started. Several of them started shoving Jay around. "Hey!" I protested, pulling Jay away from them. "What's the deal, guys? We need to stick together here!"

"Jay's the mole!" Les shouted angrily. "He's the one who told Perkins everything!"

"I didn't, I swear!" Jay whimpered, but I could tell he was lying.

"Perkins told us!" Kevin snapped, giving Jay another shove. "You were there! Everybody was there! Everyone knows you're the traitor!"

Jay looked at me pleadingly as I backed away from him, astonished. Even though we hadn't known each other very well, I'd trusted him. We all had. "I didn't tell him everything. I swear, Austin. I told him a few things when he threatened my family, but I didn't give him any names! I swear. I didn't want anything like this to happen."

"You're a liar!" Olson shot back.

Jay looked at his wife, who wasn't saying anything. "Amy," he begged. "I didn't tell him."

Amy shook her head in disgust and looked away from him.

"We don't have time for this," I declared. "Jay, if you want to leave this place, you can come with us, but once we get out of here you're in a lot of trouble, understand?"

Jay nodded. "Just please get my family out of here!"

I shoved him aside and gestured for everyone else to come closer so I could give instructions. "We need to get everyone out of here," I told them hurriedly. "I have no doubt that Perkins is planning a counterattack. We need to be long gone before that happens. Make sure everyone gets their families and whatever they can carry, and then gets to the fence. We'll go from there."

"I'll take care of that fence," Ulysses said eagerly. He was still bruised and bloodied, but that didn't take any of the enthusiasm out of him. He turned and started toward his shop.

"I need some of you to grab food and other supplies. Whatever we can haul with us. Quinn, take Olson, Les, and Ingrid and get vehicles. Gary and Anne, get as much food and supplies from your store as you can. We'll load up and get out of here. I need someone to find Lois's twins, Harvey and Jessica, and get them to the fence. Get to them before Perkins does."

"I'm on it," Jaeger called from behind us. "I know where he's keeping them. I'll keep them safe."

"Thank you," I said. I addressed my friends again. "We're the leaders here. We have to help everyone get out safely. Now let's go!"

They all split up, each going their separate ways. Amy, Jay, and Kevin hurried to the buildings where people were hiding, informing them of what was happening.

"Miriam," I said. "Help get everyone out of here. I'll meet you at the fence as soon as I can."

"Where are you going?" she demanded, alarmed.

"I have to help Annabelle find Penny and Lee. I'll meet you at the fence!" I took Annabelle's hand and pulled her toward our apartment building.

"Why are we going here?" she asked as we dodged past people running into the streets, calling out for their families.

"It's as good a place to start looking as any," I replied. "They may just be holed up in your apartment."

It took a good five minutes just to get up the stairs to Annabelle's apartment; the hallways and stairwells were clogged with people scrambling to get out. We finally reached it, Annabelle fishing around in her pockets for her key. "I don't have it!" she cried. "They must have taken it when they arrested me!"

"Hold on." I pulled my fist back and punched at the door. It smashed in half and crumpled to the ground. Annabelle hurried past me. As I followed her in, I heard her scream of horror.

I only got a glimpse of Penny, but it was enough to sear that image into my brain forever. The baby was lying on the center of the bed, her arms splayed out. Blood covered her dress and her little legs. A bullet had left a gaping hole where her left eye once was. Blood was still gushing out of the wound. This had just happened.

Annabelle, wailing in a way that only a mother could, sank to her knees by the bed, reaching out a hand and stroking her baby's arm.

Words couldn't describe how I felt, and it wasn't even my child who was dead. I felt sick, but also numb. "Oh my God," I whispered, covering my mouth as I gagged. "Penny..."

I jumped as a figure slowly moved out of the bathroom. I grabbed Annabelle and pulled her to her feet. As the figure stepped into the light, I breathed a sigh of relief. "Oh, God, Lee! I..." I looked down at Penny again but couldn't keep my eyes on the horrific sight. "I'm sorry."

He didn't say anything. He simply stood there, staring at his dead daughter.

I was suddenly furious with Jay. "This is Jay's fault," I said angrily.

"Jay?" Lee muttered.

"Jay was the mole," Annabelle managed to choke out. "He gave us up."

"He wasn't the mole," Lee said softly, raising his arm.

I didn't see the gun in his hand until he'd already fired it, and by then it was too late to save Annabelle. She fell back into the refrigerator and sank to the floor. I screamed, falling to my knees beside her. The bullet hit her right in the sternum; I wasn't a doctor, but I knew she wasn't going to make it. She let out a few choked breaths and then stopped moving, her lifeless eyes staring across the room.

My hands shaking, I looked back to Lee, who was now pointing the gun at me. It suddenly all became clear; Lee was the mole. He had been all along. *The mole is closer than you think...* I never thought the mole could be *that* close. "It was you," I whispered. "It was you this whole time!"

"It's not my fault, Austin," Lee said, his arm beginning to shake. "I didn't want to do this."

I gazed into his eyes, but didn't see Lee. An emptiness, a void, was looking back at me. Lee wasn't there. Perkins had taken him over and made him do the unthinkable.

"Then stop. If any shred of Lee is still left in there, he'd stop this."

The shaking in his arm became worse and worse, until his arm dropped down to his side and he gasped for breath. "Don't ever let your family down, Austin," he whispered, and then put the gun to his own head.

"No!" I cried, but it was over. Lee's body fell to the floor.

I stood up slowly, still shaking. A rush of anguish washed over me and I wailed. This wasn't how things were supposed to happen. When I was in D.C. and I met Lee for the first time, he'd given me hope. That was where I'd learned about this place, and where I'd felt that we would all finally be okay. We had each other, a whole species to work together and to call family. Now my friends were dying. We were killing each other.

"This can't go on," I whispered. I forced myself to leave the room, unable to look at any of them. I had to get everybody out of here, and then find a safe place for my family. The violence had to end today.

The hallways were clear once I left the apartment. I could hear a few voices and pounding footsteps, but for the most part it seemed like everyone was out and heading toward the fence. I ran out of that building as fast as I could without looking back. I would never enter that building again, not after what just happened. I followed the stream of people moving toward the fence. As I got closer and the fence came into view, I saw that Ulysses had brought a forklift from his shop and was now pulling the fence up and out of the ground, creating a large space for people to climb through. I saw Miriam at the fence, ushering people out. She looked out at the crowd and her eyes landed on me. For a brief moment, I saw her lips move to form my name. That was the last thing I saw before the *Defiant* began firing at us from her port.

I was thrown through the air when the first missile struck the sand near me. I landed hard, the wind knocked out of me. My ears were ringing from the explosion. Another missile landed closer to me than the first one had, and the force of it rendered me unconscious.

The only thing I remembered was the screaming. Screams of fear, screams of pain, screams of anguish. People were dying all around me. Perkins and his soldiers were firing at us from the ship, and it was my fault that I didn't believe he would do such a thing.

At one point, I thought I heard Miriam screaming my name. I couldn't open my eyes or speak, so I sent her a message with my mind, telling her to get out, to find Vincent and take care of our baby boy.

When I was finally able to open my eyes, it took them a moment to adjust in the sunlight. I stared at the sun, peeking at me from behind a cloud, and I wanted to reach for it. I looked away, and saw the sea of bodies. Some were moving, but most weren't. Instead of praying to God, like most people would, I prayed to Walter.

"Help us, Walter," I breathed. "Help us be free from this."

I heard footsteps behind me, and then a gunshot. More footsteps, all around me, a pleading voice from an injured woman, and another gunshot. They were killing the survivors.

I tried to get up and fight, but I couldn't move. I was sure I was dying. I could feel burns all over my body, and my head was pounding.

A pair of boots stepped in front of me. I managed to raise my eyes. It was Perkins. He was staring down at me, gun in hand. I waited for him to raise it and pull the trigger, to end me, the rebel who finally fought back. He never did. He simply stared at me for a long time.

"What are you doing?" I whispered as he gestured for some of his men to come move me.

"Returning you to an old friend," he said.

23

Constant Mutation

Bright lights hung overhead. Soft voices murmured around me. I was moving, the lights growing brighter and dimmer, brighter and dimmer. I felt only calm. My eyelids were too heavy to open.

The movement continued for several minutes; I could even swear I was on an elevator at some point. When I came to a halt, I heard a louder, clearer voice above me, and it was all too familiar.

"Keep the sedative at this level. We don't need any surprises from him."

I forced my eyelids to lift. It took a minute to focus on the figures looming over me. There were three men in my line of sight: two nurses, one of whom was adjusting the IV going into my arm. The other was talking to the third figure, Dr. Hillerman.

"Doctor," the second nurse said, nodding to me. Dr. Hillerman looked down at me, and when he saw I was awake he smiled.

"Hello, Austin," he greeted warmly. "It's been awhile."

"My family," I muttered, barely able to speak. "Miriam. James."

Hillerman turned to the nurses. "Why don't you let me talk to him for a minute?" They both left, and Hillerman turned back to me.

I didn't know why I felt so calm. I should have been panicking, scared out of my wits, but all I felt was this eerie calm. "Why am I back here?" I asked, trying to raise myself up. I couldn't even lift my head. I gave up with an exhausted groan.

"Don't try to move," Hillerman instructed. "You were severely injured in Florida, but you'll be all right. You've been given a sedative, which is why you're so groggy."

That also explained why I felt so damn calm. "My family," I repeated. "Where are Miriam and James?"

"Who's James?"

"My baby."

I realized when I saw Hillerman's surprised and curious expression that I shouldn't have told him that. James was safer if Hillerman didn't know he existed. "I don't know," he replied. "Our friend Perkins didn't say. He only said there were a hundred and thirty dead bodies in his town and three thousand or more escapees."

"So everybody who made it out is okay?"

"I wouldn't get my hopes up. Labs, including mine, have been picking up escaped A Negatives for the past three days."

"It's been that long?" I whispered. "What are you doing with the ones you capture?"

"That's none of your concern, Austin."

"These are my people. Of course it's my concern."

Hillerman didn't reply. He gazed at me for a moment and then turned away, picking up a syringe off a table.

"And you don't have Miriam?" I asked hopefully.

Hillerman glanced at me and shook his head.

That meant she was either dead, caught by another laboratory, or on her way to meet Vincent in Wisconsin.

"I thought you wanted me dead?" I said skeptically. "You spent all that time trying to kill me. Why am I still alive?"

"You're alive because your variation is the one we were looking for after all," Hillerman explained. "Your DNA is mutating, constantly. That's what we have been trying to achieve. It just took a long time for it to start functioning the way we were hoping." He began injecting the contents of the syringe into my IV.

"So what are you going to do with me now?"

Hillerman smiled, the last thing I saw before I lost consciousness. "What we were planning to do all along."

~~*

My DNA was in a series of constant mutations. This was why I was discovering new abilities, and why I would continue to develop and lose abilities. As far as Hillerman could tell, my telepathy was here to stay. But the telekinesis and ability to draw out another's energy wouldn't be around for too much longer, and soon I would discover a new ability within myself. Well, Hillerman would discover it. I was simply sedated twenty-four seven, unable to use my abilities due to the drugs in my system. That was how Hillerman was planning to keep me. When I asked him how long, he merely said, "Indefinitely." I knew in his eyes that meant for the rest of my life.

I couldn't fight him. I could hardly move when I was conscious, which was only for a short time each day. Day after day I was awakened and asked the same questions over and over again:

"How did you first discover these secondary abilities?"

"How did you feel after using them?"

"Have Miriam Lobner and Jeff Robinson shown signs of similar capabilities?"

"Does your infant possess any abilities?"

And so on.

I mostly just shrugged or offered short, mumbled answers, but whenever Miriam or James were brought up I would get angry and defensive, sometimes screaming at Hillerman and the other doctors until they sedated me again. I didn't want them brought into this at all. If they were found, I knew they would suffer the same fate as me.

As the days turned into weeks, my hope grew. Hillerman continued to ask me about Miriam and James, and each day he became more and more frustrated. This meant that Miriam and James hadn't been captured. I was certain Hillerman was in communication with the other labs searching for them. They would have been turned over to Philadelphia immediately if they were among the captured.

"How long is your refusal to cooperate going to last, Austin?" Hillerman asked one day, after several weeks had passed.

"You have nothing to threaten me with," I replied. "I have no reason to cooperate."

"I could make it worse for you, you know." Hillerman frowned down at me.

"Go for it," I said. "I honestly don't care."

Hillerman sighed, shaking his head.

"Have you made more?" I asked. "More of me?"

He didn't respond. He stared at the wall, lost in thought.

"Perkins was going to steal it, you know."

He glanced at me. "Steal what?"

"My abilities. He wanted to be like me." I paused. "You're not helping him, are you?"

He looked down at the floor.

I laughed bitterly. "So he gives you me and in return you make him into an even deadlier tyrant? You have no idea what you're doing."

"Don't pretend you understand me, Austin."

"I don't need to. I know you're one of us, Hillerman. You're a Caiten."

Again, he didn't respond.

"Your wife died, didn't she? She was killed after she was turned."

"Stop," Hillerman warned.

"This was never about curing the Colicians, was it? This was about getting back at the humans for killing your wife."

"You don't understand any of this." Hillerman's anger was rising.

"You were trying to create a variation that would cause this constant mutation like mine, so you would have enough power to get your revenge. This was always about you. That's all it ever was about."

Hillerman turned his back on me. I thought he might say something, but he just stood there for a minute before leaving. He didn't even bother sedating me.

~~*

I was there for a long time. That gave me, thankfully, plenty of time to think.

I mostly thought about Miriam and James, wondering what they were doing in my absence. But I oftentimes found my thoughts drifting to Lee, Annabelle, and Penny, and how I had failed them all. How could I have missed it? My mind had been astray for so long over the course of my stay in Rebellion that I hadn't even recognized the warnings I'd received. I'd been told that Lee was a traitor, even if his treachery was forced upon him. Unfortunately, I hadn't recognized the warnings until now, and now was much too late to save my friends.

Gorilla Man had been the warning. He was more of a clue, but a warning all the same. The first few times I'd seen him, it was to elicit my first encounter with Lee and keep me from getting killed at the D.C. safe house. But, even after I'd joined forces with Lee, I'd seen Gorilla Man two more times. Those were the warnings, warnings that Lee was the mole. I hadn't made the connection between the existence of a mole and the Gorilla Man sightings, which pointed to Lee as the culprit. Now, I wanted to smack myself for not seeing it sooner. It had all been laid out right in front of me, and yet I hadn't been able to prevent the carnage in Rebellion.

I was a failure. I'd failed my friends, and now I was failing my family by not being with them, wherever they were.

~~*

One day, after I'd lost count of how many days and weeks had passed, after the repetition of procedures and questions became a blur, something weird happened. I woke up, but not in the usual way. I woke up feeling stiff and sore, but I didn't feel groggy. I blinked several times, letting my eyes adjust to the bright lights above me. I lifted my arms, wiggled my fingers. Confused, I looked at the bag of fluid that drained into my IV. It was empty. Pulling the IV out of my arm, I sat up, rubbing my aching head.

I didn't understand what was going on. Did Hillerman seriously forget to refill my bag, to keep on sedating me so I wouldn't wake up on my own? I felt neglected, but in a good way. I didn't even have restraints holding me down.

"You must have been relying too heavily on those sedatives, Jack," I muttered, standing up and going to the door. There was a handle, but it wouldn't turn. "But you still remembered to lock the door." I huffed, putting my hands on my hips and thinking. This door was key locked, not electronic, so I couldn't get the computer system to let me out. At least they were learning. "Come on, telekinesis," I said, raising the palm of my hand toward the door handle. "Please still be here." I sent a short burst of energy through my hand and I heard a loud click in the handle of the door. I grabbed the handle again, and this time it turned. I laughed happily and opened the door, bracing myself for whatever was outside.

That turned out to be nothing. I was in another medical room, with a table and counters covered in various vials of drugs and other things. But there were no people. I listened carefully, stretching my mind out far. Hillerman and his doctors were nowhere to be found. The hallways and medical rooms were completely empty.

The building, however, was not empty. I could feel the minds of three hundred and forty-seven other Caitens, all waking up or already awake. *Hello?* I called, hoping for a familiar voice to respond.

Voices started popping in my head immediately after I sent the call.
What's going on?
Where are the doctors?
How can we use our abilities?
Are they letting us go?
And then: *Austin!*

Les! I shouted back. *Are you okay?*

Yeah, man. Are you busting us out?

I'm on my way. I left the medical room and hurried down a long corridor, following the mental and physical voices as well as the banging I could hear a floor above me. I hurried up a flight of stairs and found where many of them were being held. The hallway was long, and every few feet there was an identical door with an identical keypad, as far as the eye could see. Unlike my room, theirs were controlled electronically, so I could free everyone at once. I went to the closest door and put my hand on the keypad, thinking to it what I wanted to happen. *You're connected to all the doors, so open all the doors…*

Hundreds of loud clicks, like the one in my door, sounded, and the doors all swung open.

What happened next was beautiful chaos. Every captured Caiten in the facility burst out of their rooms and started yelling with joy. Hugs, kisses, and tears were shared, as everyone realized we'd been abandoned and were now free. As I pushed past people, searching for Les, I was grabbed, hugged, kissed, and thanked for my bravery and initiative. I felt bad for ignoring them, but it was very important that I find Les.

"Austin!"

I turned at the sound of his voice. I'd almost walked right past him. Laughing and smiling ear to ear, he squeezed me in a bear hug and lifted me off the ground. When he put me down, I asked, "Is my family okay, Les?"

He nodded. "They're great, Austin."

"What about the rest of us? Ulysses and Anne and Gary and the rest. Do you know what happened to them?"

Les's expression fell, and I knew by the grief in his eyes that the news wasn't good. "I was only picked up a month ago," he said. "I don't know what's happened since then, but I can tell you what I know."

"Okay," I said, fearing the worst.

"Ulysses, Jay, Ingrid, Olson and Quinn are all dead. Jay, Ingrid, and Olson were shot down in Rebellion while gathering supplies. Ulysses refused to leave the forklift until everybody was out. He was killed when the bombs dropped. Quinn broke his leg while we were fleeing to Wisconsin. He had a blood clot and died before we could get him help."

"Jesus," I whispered. "And everybody else?"

"Lois, Miriam, Vincent, and Kathy are all in Wisconsin, hiding up along Lake Superior with five hundred of us. Amy is in New Mexico with another group. We split into four different groups, hiding all around the country. It's snowing up in Superior now, so there aren't a whole lot of people in the area to bother us."

"What about Anne and Gary and Kevin?" I asked hopefully.

"Anne and Gary barely made it out alive," Les said. "They were trapped in Rebellion for a day after the attack, and managed to sneak out along the beach. They're hiding out in South Carolina. We haven't had any word from Kevin, so he's either dead or still in Rebellion." He took a breath. "Do you know what happened to Lee, Annabelle, and Penny? We haven't seen them since the uprising, and haven't heard anything about them."

My stomach dropped and I shook my head. "They're dead."

Les wrung his hands together. "All of them?"

"All three of them. Jay wasn't the mole, Les. It was Lee all along."

"Lee?" Les was skeptical. "That's impossible. How could Lee be the mole?"

"Perkins took control of him when he made Lee go insane," I explained. "He was always controlling Lee. He made us come to Rebellion in the first place. He told Perkins everything about the rebels. Then, when the uprising began, he killed Penny, Annabelle, and then himself."

Les covered his mouth. His eyes were horrified.

I didn't want to think about them anymore. "Did Jaeger get Lois's twins to her safely?"

Les nodded, trying to mask his horror. "They're fine. Jaeger's taken charge of the group hiding out in New Hampshire."

"Where's the last group?"

"Montana."

I nodded. "How long has it been?" I asked. "How long since we left Rebellion?"

Les thought. "I was captured a month ago, and we were hiding out for three months before that."

"So four months. Wow." That meant it was the start of December. I had missed my twenty-second birthday while trapped here.

2021 was almost over.

I looked at the people around us, who were starting to calm down and look to me for instructions. "We need to get these people out of here," I said.

"Why did they leave us behind?" Les asked, confused. He followed me as I started back the way I'd come.

"I don't know, but I don't like this." I turned and stood in front of everyone. "We need to get out of here before they decide to come back." *Listen up, everyone,* I called, and everyone went quiet. *I don't know what's happening, but we can't stick around to find out. Stay together, and follow the people in front of you. I'll lead us out of here.* I turned, and Les and I began leading the way up the stairwell to ground level. "We're several floors below ground," I told Les.

"What do we do once we get there?" he asked me uncertainly. He didn't say, but I knew he was talking about Rebellion. We were going back. We had to, to rescue anyone still trapped in that awful place. No doubt Perkins had rounded up escapees and forced them back into the town.

"I haven't thought that through yet," I admitted. "But we'll figure this out together."

With Les and I in the lead, all three hundred and forty-eight of us climbed eight flights to reach the surface. We flooded down the hallway, the walls echoing with our chatter. I asked others to inform me once everyone was out of the stairwell and on ground level.

"Everyone's up, Austin!" people were calling from behind me.

I wasn't focusing on them. I was too busy focusing on the three dozen other minds that had just entered the building. *Everybody, freeze and be silent!* I shouted, and at first people started to protest in fear but quickly quieted down and huddled amongst each other.

"What do you hear?" Les started to ask, but I hushed him with a wave of my hand.

There were thirty-four new arrivals in total. They had come in the front doors, and we had just come up the back stairwell. We had a lot of ground between us.

How many? Les asked in growing fear.

Thirty-four, I said. I looked closer, just lightly grazing their minds. *They're all Caiten. All except one.*

One Colician?

No. One human.

Les started to panic. *One human? Shit. It's gotta be Perkins! He came back for us with reinforcements…*

Get everyone out the back, I ordered. *I was here for a few months. There's a door not far from here. Go back past the stairwell and take a left. Go all the way to the end and take a right. You'll see the door.*

What about you? Les grabbed hold of my arm when I started moving forward. *You're not going alone.*

I can't risk anyone else getting hurt or killed, I said. *Besides, you've seen what I can do. I'll be fine. Get these people out of here, Les.*

Where are we supposed to go?

I thought. *There should be some buses in the parking lot back there. They were there in case we had to evacuate or relocate. Take them. Go back to Wisconsin. Make sure they get there safely.* I took a deep breath. *I'll meet you there.*

Les wanted to keep arguing, and I felt shame when I saw his distraught expression. None of us wanted to be separated again, but that was why I had to do what I was about to do. *I'll meet you there,* I promised.

Nodding, Les turned back to the others and started giving telepathic commands, ordering them to move quickly but silently back the way they'd come.

I watched as they left, praying the buses were still out back and that they would make it safely to Superior. Taking a deep breath, I started jogging toward the front of the building.

We met at the center, and I could hear them calling verbal commands to one another. I waited behind a wall as they drew closer, planning to strike as soon as the first one came around the corner. I waited patiently, my heart pounding in my chest. The first person, the human, appeared from around the corner...

I punched in the direction of his chest, but he caught me by the wrist and pushed it away from him just as the energy released, sending it into the wall. Chunks of plaster exploded everywhere. The human kicked me in the chest and sent me sprawling backwards. I punched at him again, but he dodged it. I was about to throw another, but he suddenly shouted my name.

"Austin! Calm down!"

Now that we had both stopped moving, I could actually see his face. "Jackson?" I asked.

He nodded. "Nice to see you too, my friend. Now will you stop trying to blast my face off?"

"Sorry," I said. "I thought you were...it doesn't matter."

He helped me to my feet, as the group of Caitens came around the corner, guns drawn. Several of them said my name too, surprised and relieved to see me. Among the group I recognized a very pregnant Lois, Jaeger, and…

"Vincent!" We both plowed into each other, hugging and slapping each other on the back.

"We thought you were dead, man," Vincent told me, beaming. "We seriously thought you were dead."

"Everyone except Miriam," Lois said. "She kept telling us that you were alive, even after you were caught up in the missile strike in Rebellion."

"How is she?" I asked. "How's my boy?"

"Getting big," Vincent said. "You won't believe how different he looks. And Miriam's fine, too." He paused. "She's been sad, but she'll be okay."

I felt a pang in my chest, a longing for my family, and the guilt of being absent for so long overwhelmed me.

Vincent forced a small smile. "It's okay, dude. It wasn't your fault. You'll be with her again soon."

"How did you know I was here?" I asked.

"We didn't," Jaeger said. "But we knew there were a lot of Caitens here. We've been watching this place for two months."

"Oh!" I turned and started running toward the back of the building again. "They're out back! We thought you guys were trouble, so I told them to get on the buses and get out of here."

"Oh, Lord," I heard Jaeger mutter, and then dozens of pounding footsteps followed me. We made it out back while people were still filing into the buses, and when they saw everyone run out with their guns, screams and yells erupted. People pushed and shoved, trying to get on the bus before we reached them.

It's all right! I shouted to them, waving my hands over my head. *They're with us! They're here to rescue us!*

There was a pause as everyone took in this new information, and then they all began cheering.

I laughed as everyone came running toward us, but Jackson pulled me aside. "They can't leave on those buses, Austin," he insisted. "A fleet of buses going in the same direction will draw too much attention. They'll be bombed before we get out of the county, without a doubt."

"Well, then what do we do?" I asked. "They can't stay here!"

"We each drove a different vehicle down here," Jackson explained. "We left at different times and took different routes so we wouldn't attract attention. That's thirty-four vehicles up front, and while we'll need approximately six of them, that still leaves about two hundred and twenty seats in total. We can load one of these buses, and load the rest on another—"

"Wait a minute," I said, stopping him. "Why do *we* need vehicles? What's going on?"

Jackson stared at me, his mouth half open. He was debating whether or not to tell me the truth right now.

"Jackson," I said firmly, taking a step closer to him. "What is going on? What are you even doing here?"

He sighed. "I'm here, Austin, because I need your help."

"This can't be good," I muttered.

"The reason we're all here, why you managed to get out of your cells, is because the doctors abandoned this place."

"And why did they abandon it?"

"Because they found what they needed."

My stomach dropped. "They figured out how to give themselves my DNA mutation."

Jackson nodded gravely.

"So where are they going? What are they going to do with it?"

All Jackson did was raise his eyebrows, and I knew. "We need to get to Miami! Now!" I knew we would have to go back to Rebellion, but I didn't realize it would be so soon, and under such terrible circumstances.

"That's where we're going," Jackson said, taking my arm and leading me away from the parking lot, toward the highway. "Ten Caitens who came with me will stay behind and help get everyone loaded. They'll make sure everyone gets to one of your havens. The rest of us are leaving for Miami, *immediately*."

I looked back at the growing crowd of people. "Lois! Vincent! We have to leave *now!*"

Before our group started running over to join Jackson and me, I caught Les and Lois in an embrace. When they pulled away, Les lightly touched Lois's now bulging stomach. That was when I made the connection. I almost smacked myself in the head for not realizing it sooner.

The moment was quickly over, and Lois and Les were once again in business mode. Those who were going to Miami quickly huddled around us, and that included Les.

"I'm going too," Les insisted. "Don't try to tell me no."

"I wasn't going to," I replied, glancing at Lois and then right back to Les. His face started going red, and I heard Lois tell him softly, *He knows.*

~~*

We were on the road, headed toward Miami, in less than five minutes. I was riding in a stolen squad car driven by Jackson, accompanied by Lois and Les.

"Are you sure you should be doing this when you're...this pregnant?" I asked.

"This is something I have to do," Lois said firmly.

"There are plenty of us," I said. "You don't need to put yourself at risk..."

"There are still people trapped in Rebellion!" Lois sighed. "Not everyone made it out. Some were killed, but some weren't. It was my job to protect them, and they're still trapped with that monster. I have to redeem myself."

I nodded, trying to understand even though I strongly disagreed with her. I saw her and Les holding hands, trying to hide it, and I grinned. "I don't have a problem with you two. I think the only person who would is Perkins, and he's not here, is he?"

"It's just not something we're used to," Lois replied uncomfortably. "Being...open about our relationship."

"How long have you two been together?" I asked.

Les glanced at Lois, but didn't answer.

"Well, congrats on the baby. Do you know what it is?"

"A girl," they said simultaneously.

"You picked out a name yet?"

At the exact same time, Les said "Karina" while Lois said "Aurelia." They both scowled at each other. They'd clearly been at war over this matter for a long time. It made me think back to our meetings in Rebellion, when they argued over the smallest things like an old married couple.

"You two were made for each other," I told them, laughing and turning to talk to Jackson. "How long until we get there?"

"Well," he said, "considering the high speeds we'll be able to go because of my 'police' escort, we should be able to reach it a few hours sooner than we normally would."

"That doesn't answer my question."

"About sixteen hours, Austin."

"Sixteen hours? Will we make it in time?"

"I don't know," Jackson admitted.

I was anxious and frustrated. "Couldn't we have flown or something?"

"There's no way we could have gotten a flight in time. Security takes too long."

"You're working for the government! Couldn't you have made a call and they'd have someone to pick us up in fifteen freaking minutes?"

"The government doesn't know I'm doing this, Austin," Jackson explained. "Your pal Perkins has somehow blocked our satellite view of your town. We can't see anything. I gathered intel for them while I was there, so it didn't matter if we couldn't get a view of the ship. There is a three-mile block surrounding that town. We can't see any of it. I told them they needed to destroy the ship before it launched, but they didn't want to risk sending someone in blind. They aren't going to do anything. I decided that you were the only other people I could trust to help me end this. We're on our own."

I sighed. "Okay. But what are we going to do if we get there and the ship's left port?"

He shrugged. "I honestly don't know. Let's just hope we get there in time."

"Do you know when Hillerman and the other doctors left?"

"About three or four hours ago. They have a head start, but maybe we can catch up to them."

"Maybe you could drive a little faster?" I suggested, even though he was going eighty-five.

"I don't want to push it."

We drove in silence for hours. There was too much tension in the air, too much pressure on our shoulders, for us to converse. Les and Lois eventually fell asleep in the backseat. I was too anxious to sleep; I had no idea how they managed to do it.

Jackson started yawning right after we crossed the Georgia border.

"You gonna make it?" I asked, concerned that he might zonk out at the wheel.

"I'm fine," he assured. "Don't worry about me."

"Let me know if you need a break," I said.

"Will do."

While we cruised through Georgia, I tried to relax and get some rest.

There was no way I could fall asleep, but I closed my eyes anyway. As soon as I did, I saw Miriam and James. I opened my eyes again. I couldn't bear to see them right now, even if they were only mental pictures. I bore too much guilt on my shoulders, guilt for being absent from their lives for four long months. My wife had been raising our child on her own, and my child had been without his daddy. Would my son even recognize me? Would *I* even recognize *him*?

I wanted to see my wife and son so badly. I could hardly bear to think of them; the pain in my chest was too much. Taking a deep breath, I told myself that I would see them soon. Just one more job, one more mission, and I could be with them again.

I'm okay. I sent the message to Miriam, projecting my thoughts back toward Wisconsin. *I'm okay, and I'll be with you again soon.*

I looked ahead, down the endless highway. I told myself it would all be over soon, even though I had doubts about the outcome of our mission.

~~*

We crossed the border into Florida just after 5:00 p.m. I thought we were going to have issues when crossing like the last time, but we sailed on through without even having to slow down. I turned and looked back at the border, where the gates that were usually closed stood wide open, without even a single officer patrolling the area.

"What's going on?" I asked, bewildered. "Did one of the states surrender?"

"Georgia called a cease-fire two months ago," Jackson explained. "Florida signed a tentative peace treaty with them. There's still tension, but at least the borders are open and there aren't missiles flying left and right."

We sat in silence again. Les and Lois were still dozing in the back seat. We had several hours left to go before we'd reach Miami.

"So where is Perkins going?" I asked, hoping Jackson would finally tell me the truth. "I know you wanted me to figure it out on my own, but he's about to leave port. We're out of time."

For a while, Jackson remained silent and I was sure he was ignoring me. I sighed in frustration and crossed my arms over my chest. I gazed out my window, trying to think of where Perkins was going, and a logical explanation for why he was going there.

"The course of the *Defiant*, once it leaves port, is directly south of Florida," Jackson said.

"That doesn't answer my question." I rubbed my eyes, frustrated with his cryptic answers. "What's directly south of Florida?"

Jackson looked at me, eyebrows raised. "I don't know, Austin. What *is* directly south of Florida?"

"Antarctica?" When he gave me a dirty look, I protested, "I didn't do well in geography, okay? Can you just tell me…?"

While he stared at me in annoyance, my memory of the map in the room under Ulysses's store, where the rebels met, and the map on the message boards, came back to me. I suddenly remembered the large island nation situated just south of Florida.

"They're going to Cuba," I said. "Why are they attacking Cuba?"

"Thank you for figuring it out," Jackson said, rolling his eyes.

"But why are they attacking Cuba? What's the point? They haven't done anything to him and he doesn't have anything to gain from going there."

"Are you sure about that? I think they have something very valuable to him. To you, too."

I put my elbows on my knees and put my face in my hands. I didn't see any logical reason to attack Cuba, unless they were doing something I didn't know about.

"Think about what you saw in Rebellion," Jackson told me as I thought. "Especially the events that occurred toward the end of your stay."

My immediate thoughts were of the uprising, of Miriam and I revealing our true power and liberating the people of Rebellion, only to have over a hundred of us killed and several hundred more recaptured and imprisoned in labs. I couldn't see a relationship between those events and Cuba, so I thought back to things Perkins had done. I thought of the wonderful wedding he allowed our friends to throw for Miriam and I, and how skeptical we were that he did something that kind for every married couple in Rebellion.

The wedding didn't add anything to my understanding of Perkins's motives. However, the next significant event I recalled, following the wedding, was the rescue of fellow Caitens from labs around the country. Perkins had been bringing in Caitens by the hundreds, probably thousands. I thought back to the rebel meeting the day I confronted

Jaeger. Lois had declared we had a population problem. We were overpopulated.

Overpopulation…

"Oh no," I whispered. Perkins's plan was more horrible than I'd ever imagined. We'd thought he was going to attack a U.S. city as an act of revenge, or to simply wipe out the United States government. That was why I was so confused when Jackson insisted Perkins was planning to attack another country; I couldn't understand how attacking another country would benefit him. But his overall goal wasn't to bring down a government. "He's going to invade Cuba, and wipe out Cuba's population to make room for the Caitens. He's planning to make Cuba the new Caiten homeland. Jesus…" It would be successful, too. The civil war in Cuba had thrown the country into a state of anarchy. There was no government, no one to protect the island. Much of the population had already been decimated.

"That's what those numbers were, the ones I found in Eldritch's office. It's the square mileage of the country."

"He's going to kill everyone there." I shook my head. The weapons of the battleship were for the first initial strike, to render the country helpless. Then Perkins and his men would invade the country to wipe out the remaining population.

"That's why we need to stop this from happening," Jackson said. "If the Caitens attack Cuba and the U.S. denies responsibility, which it will, it will only be a matter of time before the world realizes what you are, and who created you. The entire world will declare war on the United States."

I turned to him, astonished. "Is that all you care about?" I demanded. "What about the millions of innocent people on that island? Does it matter at all to you that they'll all be dead? And hold on just one second! A few months ago, you were telling me I should go along with Perkins! Now you're helping us stop him? Will you make up your damn mind!"

Jackson didn't look at me. He kept his eyes on the road, his expression calm. "We're not the same species. We have different interests. My interest is in the safety and security of the United States, and so long as you're helping me with that it doesn't matter to me where your interests lie."

"You're sick," I said, disgusted.

"If you were in my position, you'd understand."

"No. If I was in your position, I wouldn't have waited this long."

I saw Jackson's mouth twitch the slightest bit, and for a second I was afraid. Although he was helping us stop Perkins and save whoever was still trapped in Rebellion, I knew, deep down, that Jackson Odau was not a good person. There was evil inside him. I didn't need to read his mind to know that.

I turned away, deciding to end the conversation. I knew what I knew, and saying it out loud would only get me into trouble. Surprise, surprise. I was finally learning when to keep my mouth shut.

24

Defiant

As we drew closer to Miami, the miles seemed to drag on and on. Time felt like it was slowing down, taunting us, reminding us that it was limited. Les and Lois finally woke up two hours out, but to my surprise they didn't talk at all, except to ask where we were and how long we had until we reached Miami. Eventually, my frustration with their silence got the better of me.

"Does anyone have a plan?" I demanded. "What are we going to do once we get there?"

Les and Lois looked at each other, their expressions uncertain. "We don't have a plan," Les replied.

I groaned. "Awesome."

"We honestly just don't know what to do," Lois admitted. "Our original plan was to find a way to sabotage the ship before it was ready to leave port. But after we escaped, we lost our chance to do so. Now that Perkins and Hillerman found a way to steal your ability, our task is far more challenging."

"No shit," I muttered.

"I think we just have to play this by ear," Lois said. "This is really too complicated and there are too many unknowns to do much else."

"So basically your plan is me?" I glowered at them in the rear-view mirror. "I'm the only one on this mission with the capability of fighting Perkins."

"That's true," Les said. "We need you in order to get us onto that ship, and we do need you to take down Perkins. But you can't do this on your own, either. We'll be watching your back."

"Can't I just open up a pit large enough to swallow the ship?" I asked. "Problem solved in thirty seconds."

"Some of our people will be on that ship," Lois told me. "I'll be damned if he doesn't know we're coming. He'll use civilians in an attempt to deter an attack. You can't take the whole ship down; we have to take out Perkins and Hillerman individually."

"And what about the guys defending them? Are we supposed to let them go free?"

"We give them a second chance. Some people only follow others out of fear. If they side with us, then we'll let them. If they don't, then we'll deal with that when the time comes."

"It's a good thing you're in charge," I mumbled. "If I were in charge I'd let them all rot in a lab."

"If you were in charge, none of us would have made it this far," she replied. "No offense."

"This argument is lovely to listen to and all," Jackson told us, "but I think you should listen to this." He turned the volume of the radio up.

We started listening mid-broadcast, and my stomach dropped before the first sentence was finished.

"…*word that an undocumented ship has just sailed past Miami. It is a New Age cruise liner labeled as the* Defiant, *but we are receiving information that suggests the ship may not actually be property of New Age Cruise Line, a popular cruise line for vacationers. The* Defiant's *departure was unscheduled, and when Coast Guard personnel attempted to make contact with the ship, they did not get a response. New Age Lines is currently denying responsibility for the undocumented liner, which leads us all to wonder who is behind the wheel of this massive ship, and where they are going. This is Curtis Taylor with GH114.3 Miami news, and I'll be back soon with more updates about…*"

"Fabulous!" I dropped my head in my hands. "We're too late."

"We'll figure this out," Jackson assured me.

"They left port already!" I cried. "We still have over two hours until we reach Rebellion, and by the time we get there we won't be able to catch up!"

"He's right," Les sighed. "I don't see how we could ever catch up…"

"We're not giving up," Lois said firmly. "Jackson's right. We'll figure this out. We always do."

I shook my head, convinced that it was all over. Cuba was going to be decimated.

"There are millions of lives in our hands," Lois continued. "People are depending on us, Caitens and humans alike. So we're going to face this problem and work our way through it."

"I think it's about time I tried some speeds that are not usually recommended," Jackson said, grinning. "Now I finally have an excuse to use the siren." He flipped a switch and the siren began to blare, and Jackson soon had us traveling at speeds close to one hundred and ten. I was glad the terrain was flat and the roads fairly straight; there was no way we could have kept up this speed if we were in Pennsylvania or Wisconsin. One of us kept looking back, making sure the others could keep up with us. They were, but a few of the vehicles didn't look like they were handling it very well.

I thought about contacting Walter, knowing that he had the means to get us onto that ship, but I knew that would be a huge risk for him and his people. If they got involved, Earth could declare war on them, so Walter and the Colicians were out of the question.

I didn't know who else could help us. Of the billions of people on Earth and on the Parallel Earth, I couldn't think of anyone else capable of helping us end this conflict. We were alone.

"We need more people," I muttered.

"What?" Jackson asked.

"I said we need more people. The group we have isn't going to be enough to get on that ship *and* take out Perkins."

"Well it's a little late to call for backup," Jackson replied. "Unless one of you can teleport."

I shook my head. "I don't know how we're going to be able to pull this off…"

Jackson glanced at me, his brow furrowed "Did you ever see *300*?"

"Three hundred what?"

"No. *300*. It's a movie. It was made in the early 2000's, when we were kids."

"I don't think I've even heard of it," I said, searching my memory for the name.

"Well, I hope you don't mind spoilers," he said. "The movie is about the Battle of Thermopylae. I'm going to take a guess and say you don't know what that is either."

"You know me well."

"The Battle of Thermopylae was a three day battle between the Greeks and the Persians. Small armies from the Greek city states blocked the approaches to Thermopylae, trying to keep the Persians from passing and invading Greece. The most well known army of the bunch was that of King Leonidas of Sparta, who led an army of 300 men, hence the title. They held off the Persian army, which was rumored to be over a million strong, for more than two days while they waited for reinforcements to arrive. Three hundred men managed to hold off a million. Strength is not necessarily in numbers, but in the men and women who make up those numbers." He glanced at me again, offering me a reassuring smile. "We can still do this, Austin."

"That was an inspiring story," I said, "but I hate to remind you that we don't have any reinforcements."

"Miracles *do* happen," he told me.

I thought about what he'd just told me, seeing a hole in the story. "What happened to the 300?" I asked. "After the two days? What happened to them?"

Jackson's expression didn't change. "They were overrun. They all died."

"And the Persians won?"

"Yes."

"That's reassuring."

"That doesn't have to be our ending. This is our own battle. I was just trying to say that we haven't lost yet."

"*Yet...*" I stared out my window, at the swamps and palm trees rolling by. "By the look of things, we've already lost."

"I have faith in us," Jackson replied.

"I'm glad somebody does."

We reached Miami ninety minutes later. The traffic was ridiculous. Even with the siren blaring, we were still weaving our way through the city at a crawl. Jackson honked angrily to try to get people to move, but it was no use. The highway was gridlocked.

"I told you not to take the highway!" Lois said, frustrated.

"I don't need a lecture right now," Jackson snapped. "What I need is a way out of here."

"Try to get onto the shoulder," I instructed. "We can start moving again if we get over there."

"I can try," Jackson muttered. "I don't know how fast we can go though. It's pretty narrow over there."

"I've lost sight of Vincent," Les reported. He'd been staring out the back window for the past half hour, trying to keep track of everyone behind us. He'd lost sight of everyone except for Vincent, but now we'd lost him too.

"If we get to the shoulder, maybe they'll follow our lead," I said hopefully.

"I said I lost sight of him, Austin. That means he can't see me either."

"Well, maybe he'll have the same idea!"

"Can't you send him a message?" Jackson asked.

Exasperated, I said, "I can try, but there are a lot of people close together. It's a lot harder to find one specific person when—"

Lois interrupted. "Jackson, please do your best to get to the shoulder. Austin, do your best to contact Vincent, and I'll try to contact Jaeger. Les, dear, just keep an eye out for one of our vehicles."

We went silent and focused on our assignment. I searched the sea of minds for Vincent, hoping I could find him. To my surprise, our minds bumped into each other. Vincent had been searching for me too.

Vincent! I said, relieved.

Great minds think alike, huh? he replied.

I suppose they do. Can you see us?

No. Where are you guys?

Up ahead. We're trying to get to the shoulder and drive past whatever's going on up there. You should do the same.

Already working on it. We're still two lanes away.

"I can't find Jaeger," Lois said. She looked at me. "Did you find Vincent?"

I nodded. *Vincent, can you find Jaeger and tell him to follow our lead?* As I said this, Jackson slipped into the far left lane, and a big black Hummer came flying down the shoulder toward us. As it passed us, a woman named Tracy stuck her head out the window and saluted us. "Was that Jaeger?" I asked.

"Yep," Les said, rolling his eyes.

Never mind, Vincent. He's already on top of it. See you soon.

Tell Odau not to crash that thing.

"All right, let's go," I said, and Jackson slipped onto the shoulder. It turned out to be wider than Jackson thought; it had to be for that Hummer to go flying by at such a speed. We had no problem sailing past the halted traffic.

"Did you guys notice that there's no one going the other way?" Les said as we trailed after Jaeger.

"Did you guys notice the red and blue flashing lights up ahead?" Jackson muttered.

"Vincent's behind us and catching up fast," Lois told us, and then turned back around. "What did you say?"

"No one's going in the other direction and the cops have the highway blocked off," I pointed out, my stomach clenching at the sight of the massive roadblock half a mile down the road. "That's why the highway's turned into a parking lot."

"What do you want me to do?" Jackson asked, gripping the steering wheel tightly. "I need to know *now* what you want me to do."

"You don't have some kind of security clearance to get us through?" I demanded, even though I already knew the answer.

"We can't stop," Lois said. "We're so close. We can't give up now."

"I need to know what you want me to do!" Jackson said.

Before Lois could make her decision, Jaeger made it for her. When the police saw his vehicle approaching on the shoulder, they immediately put up another plastic barrier, blocking our way. Jaeger didn't even slow down. He barreled right through that roadblock, sending the half dozen police officers sprawling in the dirt to avoid getting hit.

"I guess that's what we're doing," I told Jackson, but he was already stomping on the gas.

"Perhaps I can make this look convincing," he replied, turning the siren back on and flying past the roadblock before the cops could put it back up. Vincent was quick to follow our lead.

"Heads down!" Les shouted, right before the cops rained bullets on us. Thankfully the vehicle was bullet proof.

"What the hell?" I said. "We're in a cop car! We're one of them! Why are they shooting at us?"

"Your friends got this car back in Wisconsin," Jackson said, being careful to avoid the remaining police cars blocking our path. "It says Bayfield Police Department on the side. We're clearly not one of them."

"Would they really shoot at us just because we're from Wisconsin?" Lois asked skeptically.

"I think they're shooting at just about anything out of place right now," Jackson replied. "They'll ask questions later."

I glanced out the rear window. Vincent was following awfully close to us, but at least he'd made it through okay. It looked like everyone else in the car was okay too. We had a decent head start ahead of the Miami cops, but I could see a swarm of red and blue flashing lights steadily gaining on us. "Do you know how far we have until we reach Rebellion?" I asked uncertainly.

"At this speed, and assuming we don't run into any more road blocks, about five or six minutes." Jackson stole a quick glance at him. "Why?"

"I was just wondering if we can make it before they catch up."

Jackson glanced in the rear-view mirror and cleared his throat.

"Would you mind helping out a friend?" When all I did was look at him quizzically, he said, stress in his voice, "Do something, please!"

"Oh." I turned around again and made eye contact with Vincent. He pointed with his thumb at the approaching cluster of cops.

What do we do? he asked nervously.

Move over, I instructed, and he swung to the right and pulled up alongside us. I focused on the road, the pavement whizzing by behind us. I tried to slow everything down, so I could focus on one particular spot.

"Let's not hurt anyone, yeah?" Jackson said. "They may not be your people, but they're mine."

I didn't reply, but I obeyed his wishes. I focused on the road passing just behind our car, made a fist, and punched upward. Nothing happened. I tried again.

"What are you doing?" Les asked.

"It's not working!" I protested, continuing to try to rip up the pavement.

Lois looked out the back. "They're getting closer, Austin!"

"My telekinesis is gone!" I groaned and slammed my fist down on the dashboard. The car suddenly went dead, the lights and engine going out. We drifted for a few seconds, all of us silent in our confusion, and then the lights and engine sputtered back to life.

"What did you just do?" Jackson demanded.

I suddenly remembered what Dr. Hillerman told me when I was back in the lab. "Constant mutation." I laughed.

"What did you say?" Lois bit her lip, confused and frustrated. "Will you explain what's going on?"

"The strain of the Caiten Virus I was given is constantly mutating," I told her, looking at my hands. I could feel the electricity, the energy, pulsing in my palms. "My abilities keep changing."

The others seemed to understand. "As long as you can keep them from catching up to us," Jackson said, "I really don't care what ability you have right now."

I pointed two fingers at the cars behind us, focused on the engines, and released the energy stored in my hands. I completely blew out our back window, spraying glass all over Les and Lois, but my invisible bolt of electricity hit the two cop cars leading the pack. Their lights went out, and they drifted into each other before bouncing into the cars behind them. One vehicle flipped, and the rest of the cars piled into each other.

"Thanks for the warning!" Lois muttered, shaking glass out of her hair.

"What did I say?" Jackson snapped, that terrifying expression of his back.

"I didn't try to do that!" I insisted. "All I did was shock the car."

"Some of them are still coming!" Les said.

I looked back, and four cars were pulling around the mess and pursuing us.

"Austin!" Lois said urgently.

We had just gone through an intersection with stoplights, and I pointed my fingers at the base of one. Again, the pulse of electricity left my hand and hit the metal base. There was a mini explosion as the circuits blew, and then it simply tipped forward, falling into the street and completely blocking the cops' path. They would have to go up over the curb and through a ditch before they could get past it. "That'll keep them busy for a while," I said.

"It'll give us enough time," Jackson agreed.

A few minutes later, we made it to the gates of Rebellion. Someone in Jaeger's car had left them open for us, so we simply sailed on through with Vincent following.

"Do you think…" I started to ask, but I already knew the answer.

"What?" Lois asked.

"Do you think anybody else from our group will make it here in time to help?"

"I doubt it," Jackson answered. "We're going to have to figure this out on our own."

We sped down the dusty roads until we made it to the port. Jaeger and his crew were already parked and on the dock, shielding their eyes and looking out at the open sea. With him he had the woman who'd saluted us back on the freeway, Tracy, another woman who looked like she could be her sister, and a young African American man. I could tell by their body language that they felt pretty hopeless.

Once parked, we got out and joined the others on the dock. "What's going on?" I asked Jaeger.

He turned toward me, dropping the hand over his eyes. "Listen, Austin, I know we don't have a particularly good relationship, but I hope we can set that aside, at least for now." He held out his hand.

"I asked what was going on," I replied flatly, letting him know that I was doing exactly what he asked.

A small smile formed, but then quickly disappeared. "We can't see the *Defiant* at all. It's long gone, and the other boats they had are gone too, so we can't use them to catch up to it. We're stuck here."

Tracy's younger sister's name was Izzy, and the young black man's name was Otto. Vincent and his group came to join us on the dock; with him were Kathy and Amy, and two Hispanic men whom I didn't recognize. I learned their names were Jaime and Gabe. There were thirteen of us, a pathetic number compared to what Perkins had on that ship. And it didn't even matter, because we didn't have a way to get to the ship. Nobody had any logical ideas how to get there.

"You're sure you can't fly, Austin?" Vincent asked. I shot him a dirty look and he shrugged. "Can't blame me for trying."

I glanced at Kathy, who refused to leave his side, and smirked at him. "I didn't think you'd actually let her come."

"She was insistent," Vincent replied, and Kathy shot me a sarcastically sweet smile. "So," he said, coming to my side and slapping a hand on my shoulder. "We don't have a plan, do we?"

"Our plan was to get on that ship," I replied.

"But we have no way to do that."

"Right." I sighed. "How did Walter Reifert manage to lead his people when they were in turmoil like this? He was still just a kid. How did he save all those people?"

"I don't know," Vincent murmured. "I don't know." He looked up at the sky, at the gentle pinks and oranges signaling the end of another lost day. He shrugged. "Maybe he was just smarter than us."

"Maybe." I gazed sadly at him. "Perkins is going to destroy our chances at a normal life. When he invades Cuba, and kills all those people, the world is going to come for us, just like they did for the Colicians."

"I know," Vincent said.

Helplessly, I asked, "What do we do then?"

Vincent dropped his eyes from the sky, and turned them on me. They were fierce, defiant. He turned his head and gazed across the dock at Kathy, who was arguing with the others about what to do next. "We keep fighting," he said. "We never give up. Not when we have so much to lose."

In the distance, I could hear the whirring of a helicopter, probably a news chopper trying to get an up-close look at the *Defiant*. "But how do a few thousand of us fight against the entire world?"

Vincent shook his head. "It doesn't matter. The moment we give up is the moment we lose everything."

I nodded. "I guess I'm just not as optimistic as you about this whole situation." The whirring of the helicopter grew louder. It sounded like there might be a couple of them heading out together.

Chuckling, Vincent said, "I wouldn't go so far as to say I'm optimistic. I just..." He looked at Kathy again. "I have too much worth protecting." He looked back at me. "And so do you."

"I know, I just don't know how I'm supposed to—" I shielded my eyes and looked around as the helicopter rotors became almost deafening. "Where is that coming from?"

Everyone else was now on high alert. The chopper sounded very close, but so far no one could see it. And then...

"There it is!" Jaime shouted, pointing toward Rebellion. It took my eyes a moment to spot it, but that was because it was flying very low. Too low. It was lower than the apartments, flying in between buildings like whoever was at the controls was looking for something.

"Get under the dock!" Lois ordered, and several of us began jumping into the shallow water and ducking under the wooden beams.

"No, wait," I said, staring at the chopper. It was still too far away to see anybody inside, but I could hear something. An echoing inside my head. Someone was calling out for us. I started running toward the town, where the chopper was hovering. "Jeff!" I shouted, waving my arms. *Jeff, we're over here!*

The chopper lifted up out of the town and started toward the beach. I continued to wave my arms, too excited to stand still even though Jeff knew where we were. I let out a bellowing laugh, surprising myself with its volume.

"My man, Jeff?" Vincent asked, running up to meet me.

"That's him!" I confirmed, and then we were both jumping up and down, waving our arms and cackling. The rest of our group climbed off the dock or out of the water and came to join us, curious. When they found out who was in the chopper, there was nothing but smiles and laughter.

As the chopper touched down several yards from us, I saw Danny Bennett at the controls, sitting next to Jeff, who was smiling more broadly than I thought possible. Once the rotors had slowed down enough, Jeff jumped out and hurried over to us. I jumped on him so hard that we fell to the sand laughing. Vincent landed on top of us. After a brief reunion, we untangled ourselves and stood, tears of happiness clouding our eyes.

"You're okay!" Jeff cried, half sobbing and half laughing.

"We're fine! What about you?"

"Fine," he said. "I've been worried about you guys." He looked around at everyone. "New friends?" His eyes landed on Jaeger and he took a step back.

"Long story short, he's with us," I said. "I'll explain everything when we have time. Everyone here is with us. We need to get to that ship! Care to give us a lift?"

"That's what we're here for." Jeff turned and looked at the chopper, the rotors still spinning and Danny gazing out at us expectantly. "I'm not sure if we can fit everyone on board, but we'll do our best. Let's go!" He waved us forward and, ducking down, we hurried onto the helicopter, squeezing together to fit everyone.

Jeff yelled something at me as I got situated. "What?" I yelled back, and Jeff pointed to a headset behind me. Understanding, I slipped it on, and the noise around me was partially blocked out. Across from me, Jackson was doing the same. Lois and Les took the remaining two headsets in the back of the chopper, while Danny and Jeff slipped theirs on up front.

"Danny!" I said. "I've never been happier to see a human in my life!"

Laughing, Danny said, "Good to see you, too!"

As he lifted the chopper back off the ground, I asked, "Aren't you a little young to be flying one of these?"

"Legally?" Danny grinned at me in a rear-view mirror above him. "Absolutely."

"So what's your game plan, Austin?" Jeff asked me as we sailed over the dock and out to sea.

"Hello," Lois called, trying to adjust the volume dial on her headset. "Lois Royalty, nice to meet you."

Jeff and Danny introduced themselves.

"Lois is in charge," I told them.

"*Temporarily* in charge," she corrected. "So far, the only plan we have is to get on that ship and stop it from reaching its destination. We're not really sure what to expect other than a lot of resistance."

"Well, I can get you on the ship," Danny replied. "I'm not sure how easy it'll be. We're overloaded, so we can't fly as high or as fast. They'll see us coming and will have plenty of opportunities to take us out."

"Austin and I will take care of any opposition headed our way," Jeff assured him. "You just focus on landing this thing."

"Did you discover some new talents, Jeff?" I asked, grinning.

"Excuse me," Jackson interjected, "but I think the wisest thing would be to take out the ship as soon as possible. Disable the engines, I mean. Austin can do that before we even land. That's one half of our problem solved right there."

"Who's that?" Jeff asked, cranking his head over his shoulder to see who spoke.

"Jackson Odau," he replied. "I'm not one of you."

"He's been helping us for a while," I explained to Jeff and Danny. "He works for the U.S. government."

"What part?"

"Doesn't matter," Jackson said quickly, turning his cold gaze on me. "But do you understand what I'm saying, Austin? Shock the ship, and they can't continue. Then all we have to worry about is the people on board."

"Most of them are there as hostages," Lois added. "Or they're only obeying out of fear. Our main targets are Hillerman and Perkins. Once they're dealt with, we'll see who else is still eager for Cuban domination and deal with them."

"How are we planning to deal with Hillerman and Perkins?" Les asked.

There was a moment's pause. "We'll figure that out when we get there," Lois said through her teeth. "Oh, and by the way, Perkins is mine."

Out of the corner of my eye, I saw Les take her hand. "I'm right there with you," he murmured.

"I don't mean to be...uh...racist or anything," I said to Jackson, not really sure what other word to use in this case. "But what exactly do you plan on doing once we get on board? It's not exactly a fair fight..."

Jackson raised an eyebrow at me, and I knew what he was thinking. It *was* a fair fight. I didn't know if anyone else knew about Jackson's impenetrable mind, but those opposing us would be finding out soon enough.

"Military training does pay off," Jackson replied smoothly, his lips turning up in a slight smirk.

For forty-five minutes, we sat anxiously, one of us occasionally asking a question and someone providing a quick answer before returning to our nervous silence, the thundering rotors our only company. We refrained from asking the inevitable: where would we go afterwards, if we did manage to stop the ship and rescue our people? What home did we have on earth anymore?

Vincent, who had found a pair of binoculars under Kathy's seat and had been staring out to sea through them the entire ride, suddenly elbowed me and pointed. There it was, just a smudge on the horizon steadily growing bigger: the *Defiant*. The ship with weapons I helped design.

"Do you see it, Danny?" I said into my headset.

"We got a missile!" was Danny's response, and he did his best to maneuver his way out of the missile's path.

"They're not heat-seeking!" I said. "Just get out of the way and we'll be fine."

"These aren't advanced enough to hit moving targets," Jackson agreed. "And their supply is limited, so they won't be firing too many. This is just a warning shot." He glanced at me. "This is about to get real interesting."

"If they're not that advanced, then why the hell hasn't the military destroyed it yet?" Danny demanded.

"Perkins and Hillerman aren't ordinary Caitens," I explained. "Not anymore. They're like me, Jeff, and Miriam. They can deflect just about anything with only their minds."

"Another missile!" Danny shouted, and we all held on as we turned sharply again. "I sure do hope you and Jeff have a few tricks up your sleeves, Austin, because this is *not* fun!"

We flew for several more minutes without having to worry about dodging any more missiles, but then, as the ship grew closer and closer, we saw something peculiar radiating from it.

"What is that?" Danny asked, turning the chopper sideways and then pulling up. "I can't avoid this! Brace for impact!"

"Jackson!" I yelled. "We didn't design anything like that! What is that?"

Jackson was already leaning his head out of the chopper to get a look, his sandy hair blowing every which way. What we saw coming toward us was a bright blue light, starting as a small dome and expanding quickly outwards, growing in size at a very fast rate. It glistened like an electrical pulse. There was no way to avoid contact as it expanded.

"What is that?" I repeated.

"EMP!" Jackson shouted, his head snapping toward me. I knew in that moment that this was not a weapon; this was Perkins. I saw Jackson's expression of horror a moment before the blue shock wave struck us, throwing us backwards and completely frying the engine. I heard a few sputtering screeches as the rotors died before silence. And then we were falling.

I heard screaming. I was scared, and my eyes were wide, but as I gripped the bar on the wall beside me, a sudden clarity came over me.

I finally understood what I was. I had known for a while now that my genes were constantly mutating, but that also meant something else: *I* was constantly mutating. *I* was evolving. My mind was growing in strength and ability. I couldn't have come to this realization at a more convenient moment: I could also manipulate these mutations. I could choose which direction, so to speak, my genes went. And I knew just where I wanted them to go.

I squeezed my eyes shut, the feeling of free-falling making my stomach clench. A moment later, my ears popped several times, and instead of striking water, the helicopter crashed down onto the top deck of the *Defiant*. As the helicopter skidded across the deck, I was thrown from it, slamming my head into the deck's overhang before crashing to the floor in a daze.

I'd landed in the skid trail left by the helicopter, leaving me laying in a heap of broken wood flooring. When I groaned and sat up, I felt a sharp pain in my side and saw a large piece of wood poking out of me. Thankfully, it wasn't too deep and I was able to pull it out easily, and without too much bleeding.

My head was spinning from the impact, but it didn't feel worse than anything I'd experienced this past year. I would be all right. I carefully climbed to my feet. Jackson had also been ejected from the chopper, and he was sitting where he'd fallen, clutching his right arm. I ran to him, grabbing his other arm and pulling him to his feet. "You okay, man?"

"Wrist," he grunted, and I saw that his right wrist was rapidly swelling, most likely broken in the crash. "Good thing I'm a leftie," he said, and pulled a gun out of a holster hidden in his jacket. He pointed it at something over my shoulder and pulled the trigger one, two, three times. Instead of a loud bang, it only emitted a high pitched pop. I turned, and saw three Caitens in soldier attire falling to the floor on the other side of the wreckage. "Tranquilizer," he told me. "You don't kill my people, I'll return the favor and won't kill yours."

"I appreciate it," I said, moving toward the wreckage. "You going to be okay?"

"Don't worry about me!" he called back. "Get them out of there! I'll cover you."

The chopper was on its belly but tilted to the right at a forty-five degree angle. The tail of the chopper had snapped and now rested under the right side, blocking that exit. Vincent was pulling Kathy out of the left side. He jumped down after her. They had cuts and bruises, but overall they looked fine.

"You guys okay?" I asked hurriedly.

They were both staring at me, awestruck. "What in the high hell did you *do*?" Vincent demanded. "We could have used your teleporting about six states ago!"

"I didn't know I could do it," I explained. "I just figured out how. I'll explain later." I reached up and took Izzy's hand as she climbed out. She held her sweatshirt sleeve to a gash in her forehead. "You okay?"

Once down, she pushed me aside and sat down on the deck. "Take care of her!" I told Vincent, and pulled myself up to the opening. Otto was pulling himself up. "Here," I said, extending my hand. He took it, wetting my hand with his blood, and I helped him climb out. Lois and Les, bloodied and bruised, were pulling themselves over mangled seats to get to me.

"Austin!" Lois moaned, clutching her bulging belly. "The baby..."

I jumped inside the totaled helicopter, my heart pounding in fear for Lois's unborn child. Les was clinging to her, afraid but desperately trying to hide it. When I reached them, I put a hand on Lois's belly. It was as hard as a rock. "I think you're having a contraction," I said. "It's probably just because of the trauma of the crash." I quickly added, "But I'm no doctor."

"It hurts so bad!" Lois moaned as Les and I each took an arm and pulled her up over the side. "Is the baby okay?"

"She's fine," Les promised, but he glanced at me and I could see he wasn't convinced.

Otto, although visibly injured, helped us lower Lois down to the deck. "I gotta help the others," I told Les, and turned back to hoist up Jaime and Tracy. "Are you guys okay?"

"Where's Izzy?" Tracy demanded, her words slurred.

"She's out there, she's fine," I assured her, and she hurried out. "What about you, Jaime? Are you—"

"It's Gabe," he choked out, tears in his eyes.

I looked down, and saw Jaeger assisting Amy in CPR on Gabe, who had taken a large piece of shrapnel through the chest. "Go on, get out of here," I told Jaime, and jumped into the chopper. I knew immediately that Gabe was dead. The shrapnel was at least six inches wide and three feet long, and it had punctured him on the left side of his chest just below the breast. His eyes were closed, and a continuous trickle of blood was falling from his mouth. "Guys," I said, and put a hand out to stop Amy's rigorous chest compressions. "He's dead. I'm sorry."

Amy had tears running down her face, and Jaeger was shaking his head, like he couldn't believe it. Neither of them appeared to be significantly hurt. "Why don't you get out of here and help the others? I'll help Jeff and Danny."

Nodding solemnly, Amy climbed out of the chopper. Jaeger, still shaking his head, followed her without looking at me.

As much as I wanted to, I couldn't let guilt get the better of me. Not now. Lois was injured, and I knew Les wouldn't leave her side. That left me in charge. And I had people to protect.

I pulled myself to the cockpit, where Jeff was holding a torn piece of his shirt to Danny's head. "How bad is it?" I asked as gunshots rang out. I could hear my friends shouting as they took cover.

"His head's bleeding pretty bad," Jeff replied, glancing at me. "Do you have a shoelace or something I can tie this with?"

"No, but here." With effort, I tore a long strip off my shirt and helped tie it around Danny's head, securing the blood-soaked piece of Jeff's shirt in place over the gash.

Outside, I heard a few more gunshots, followed by Vincent's voice: "Don't shoot! Don't shoot! Hold your fire!"

"I'm okay, I'm okay," Danny kept whispering, his eyes rolling back. "I'm okay…"

"We need to get him out," I said, slinging one of the kid's arms over my shoulder.

Jeff took Danny's other arm and helped me carry him up and over the side. "It would've been nice if you'd learned your new skill a little earlier." He stopped when we got a view of what was going on outside. There were about a hundred people on deck now, but none of them were firing or fighting. In fact, many people were embracing, laughing, and crying tears of joy.

"What the hell?" I said, and then saw a familiar face I'd been missing. "Kevin!"

Kevin and I had become pals while in Rebellion. He was like my little brother, part of my new family. We hadn't seen much of each other the last few weeks in Rebellion, and after the uprising I'd lost hope of ever seeing anyone I loved again. But now, it felt like no time had passed.

"I can't tell you how happy I am to see you!" Kevin replied, grinning from ear to ear as he and a few others came to help us lower Danny down. "We were just waiting for an opportunity to take this ship down."

"Well, now that we're here, that shouldn't be as hard as you thought." I gestured to Jeff. "Kevin, Jeff. Jeff, Kevin."

"I've heard good things," Kevin said as he shook Jeff's hand.

"I'd hope so, considering there's nothing bad to say about me." Jeff sneered at me.

"How many on board will side with us?" I asked Kevin, trying to do a quick head count. More and more people were joining the reunion on deck, and there were probably close to three hundred of us now.

Snorting, Kevin said, "Probably about ninety to ninety-five percent of the ship. Few of us are fond of Captain Perky." He grinned, hoping he did well with the nickname.

I winced. "Try again later, dude." I glanced at the group I had come with. Lois was half sitting, half laying, breathing heavily as she clutched her stomach. Les was holding her, trying to comfort her. Amy was tending to her and Otto, who was bleeding heavily from his arm. Tracy and Izzy didn't look in the best shape either. "A lot of us were hurt in the crash," I told Kevin. "I need help taking out this ship."

"Can I be of assistance?" Jackson stepped forward, keeping his injured wrist cradled to his chest.

"You're hurt. I don't think that's the best idea."

"You could use my mind right now, Austin."

Cockiness aside, he was right. He was the smartest person I had with me, and broken wrist or not, he was very valuable. "Okay," I agreed. "You can come. I need a large group in order to take out Perkins."

"No," Jackson interrupted quickly. "You need to take out the engines first."

"Jackson, I don't—"

"We need to go one step at a time. Take out the ship. Once it's rendered useless, then we can take out Perkins and Hillerman."

"I guess that makes sense," I replied reluctantly. "But I don't know if I can immobilize something this big. A car and a stop light are a lot different than a ship."

"You don't have to worry about shocking the whole ship," Jackson said. "Just the engines."

"That's great, except for the fact that I have no idea where that is."

"Good thing you have me with you!" Kevin declared proudly.

I sighed. "You're a wonderful human being Kevin. I'm sorry, you're a wonderful Caiten being, or whatever. Can you tell some of your pals here to come with us as an escort, some to stay behind to tend to the injured, and some to take out the weapons?"

"Sure thing." Kevin turned to the ever-increasing crowd and telepathically issued orders.

Jaeger, Vincent, and Kathy had come to my side, eager to help. "Jaeger, come with me to the engine room," I said. "Vincent and Kathy, go with Jeff and help take out the weapons. Just don't blow yourself up."

"No." Jeff turned to me. "We should stay together."

"This will get done a lot faster if we split up," I insisted. "Plus, they need you with them for defense. We've got the crazy powers, remember?"

Jeff shrugged. "Okay. Fine."

"Meet me back here in ten minutes," I instructed. "We'll go take out Hillerman and Perkins together."

"Don't think you're leaving me behind when you confront them." Lois, with the help of Les, had come to join the fight.

"Lois," I said, as sternly as I could, "if you're having contractions—"

"Braxton-Hicks," she replied, and I pretended to know what that meant. "I'll be fine. We'll wait here with the others until you get back."

"I just don't think—"

"You're not going onto the bridge without me," Lois said firmly, and I saw in her eyes that this was something she had to do. I nodded, agreeing. "Now go take out those engines," she ordered.

As our groups parted ways, I leaned in and asked in Jackson's ear, "If we disable this ship, how are we supposed to get off of it once this is over?"

I saw Jackson tense beside me, and he was silent for so long that I thought he wasn't going to answer. But as we left the open air of the deck and entered the ship, I heard him mutter, "Let's hope there are enough lifeboats."

Kevin, Jackson, Jaeger, and I were accompanied by two dozen Caitens from the ship who were eager to help. They all had a gun of some sort; some of them were soldiers who had stolen more weapons from the armory to distribute to the others. I was offered one, but I simply gave them a look that stated, "I don't need it."

Kevin led us to the main stairwell and we started our descent. Two levels down, several people came running up to us, begging us to stay and protect them. We explained where we were going, but that did nothing to comfort them. They were civilians being held hostage, and were terrified of what might happen to them with a mutiny onboard. We left them there with two of our own to protect them.

At the third level down, we didn't hear anything until we were all within full view of the soldiers waiting for us. They then opened fire. Two of us were hit before I sent a wave of electricity their way, knocking them all out cold. I couldn't say for sure they were only knocked out—and not dead—but that was what I was hoping for. Our two who were hit didn't seem seriously injured; they insisted they would be all right and we should continue on without them.

On the fourth level down, we bumped into some of the guys taking out the weapons. They explained that the people guarding the weapons destroyed them once they heard what was going on, so their job was done. They decided to continue on with us, since we'd lost a couple of our own already.

By the time we reached the fifth level down, nerves were high, but that didn't prepare us for what we encountered there. I don't remember the first grenade being thrown; all I remember is feeling like a five-ton brick hit me in the chest, sending me flying over the railing and down another half level. I laid there, stunned, ears ringing, while more and more explosives went off. More and more bodies went flying, and I was certain this was it until I saw Jaeger vault over the railing, followed by Kevin and Jackson a moment before the railing was blown to bits. Jaeger grabbed me and threw me over his shoulder with barely any effort. He carried me, following Kevin down several more flights of stairs until the decorative carpeting and paintings disappeared and everything looked unfinished, like a house half completed. It was dark and dank and smelled like mold.

"It's right through here," Kevin said, and I saw, upside down, that he was pointing at a small steel door just around the corner from the stairwell. He took out a keycard and tried to open it, but the lock just beeped back at him and flashed red. "They changed the access code!" he cried, slumping against the wall in defeat.

Jaeger set me down, propping my upper body up against the same wall. He shook me gently. "Hey," he said. "We need your help now. Can you snap out of it?"

I blinked a few times and tried to get up, but I could barely move. My head was ringing and spinning and I couldn't focus on any of their faces. "Help me up," I said, but it didn't come out sounding that way.

Jackson shook his head. "He got hit pretty hard. He's going to be out of it for a while."

Kevin threw up his arms. "Well, what are we supposed to do?"

"Hey!" Jeff said, running down the last flight of stairs and rounding the corner to join us. He tapped his head. "I heard you guys were in trouble. I came to help."

"Thank God!" Kevin breathed.

"Austin's hurt," Jaeger said, pointing at me on the floor. "We need this door open."

Jeff glanced at me with an apologetic look. He wanted to stay with me to make sure I would be okay, but he had to take charge and finish this. "I'll see what I can do. You might want to stand back."

They did what he asked, and Jeff stared hard at the door. He raised both his hands, clapped them together, and then pulled them apart quickly. I couldn't see from where I was, but it sounded like the door split right down the middle. The screech of metal ripping apart was not pleasant.

The others all laughed in relief. "Will you stay with Austin?" Jeff asked, and Jackson replied that he would. The other three then entered the engine room, and my fear level began to rise. Something was very wrong.

I began breathing rapidly, panic overwhelming me. Jackson knelt down in front of me, studying my face. "You'll be okay, Austin. Just breathe. It'll pass soon."

"Get them out!" I tried to yell, but it came out as more of a whisper. "Get them out of there!"

Jackson seemed to understand what I was saying and looked toward the engine room. He started to raise his gun, standing up. That was when we both heard Jaeger, Jeff, and Kevin start yelling. It was only for a brief moment, their frightened voices abruptly cut off, followed by three audible thumps.

"Hold on," Jackson said, but I was already struggling to my feet.

"Don't!" I told him, pushing him away from the door. "Stay back!" I stumbled inside, the extreme heat and smell of gasoline overpowering me. I blinked rapidly to keep my vision clear. As I moved forward into the dark engine room, my eyes adjusted and I saw Kevin laying on the floor in front of me, unconscious. I reached out telepathically and felt that he was still alive, but he was badly hurt. I hurried past him and soon came upon the unconscious forms of Jeff and Jaeger, both in the same condition as Kevin. It was strange. I didn't see anyone around. What had happened here?

"Nice to see you again, Austin."

"Are you ever going to cut us a break?" I demanded.

Hillerman smiled at me, but it wasn't a kind smile anymore. It was mocking.

"What did you do to them?" I asked.

The old doctor was standing several yards in front of me, right in front of one of the engines. There was a clear but shimmering shield surrounding him and the engines. He was generating the force field, preventing anyone from taking out the ship.

It was weird seeing him in casual clothes. He was wearing jeans and a graphic t-shirt, something that looked strange and almost comical after only seeing him in a lab coat. "Let me ask you a question first," he replied. "Why are you trying to stop this ship?"

"Why do you think?" I snapped.

"Isn't this outcome better for all of us?" he asked, raising his hands questioningly. "We'll all have a safe place to call home, something we would never have back in the States."

"We wouldn't have had this problem to begin with if you hadn't turned us all into freaks," I reminded him.

He took a step toward me. "Isn't this what you want? A safe place for your family and friends? That's what we'll have, Austin."

"At the expense of millions of innocent lives?" I shook my head. "I don't think so." I pointed two fingers at him and shot a jolt of electricity his way. Hillerman didn't even flinch as the force field absorbed my energy. He just continued smiling that snide smile. I tried again, but still nothing. My head was starting to feel better; it had stopped spinning and my vision was clearer. I gathered up all the energy I could muster inside me and let it all out at him. As I did this, Hillerman, who looked pretty annoyed by now, strode up to me and knocked my hand away. The electricity I was directing at him was redirected, striking a pipe overhead. I looked up, surprised, and saw my electricity, now blue, moving up through the pipe until it struck a wall and dissipated.

I suddenly had an idea. But before I could carry it out, Hillerman grabbed me by the throat and lifted me clean off the ground. I stared, eyes wide, unable to breathe. How could he lift me up like this? My DNA must have given him some extra strength with all that extra power.

"I really don't want to kill you," he said quietly, glaring up at me. "But you're not giving me much of a choice." He threw me backwards. I struck the wall and went down hard, but I was right back up again. Before I could throw another shot, Hillerman raised a hand toward me and squeezed it into a fist.

I cried out in agony, but my air supply was quickly cut off. I dropped to the ground like a rock, convulsing violently. The pain was unreal. It felt like my insides were being squeezed, my organs about ready to pop. Hillerman sneered down at me as the pain made me see blue, something I didn't know was possible. Through the pain, I managed to look down at Hillerman's feet. He was standing about two feet in front of a large metal grate. If I could somehow get him to step backwards far enough... But then there was always the possibility that Hillerman actually *did* have the force field under his feet...

My gut told me that Hillerman didn't have the force field covering the bottom of his feet, so this was the best chance I had at removing him from the equation.

"I didn't want it to end this way," Hillerman told me, clenching his fist harder and making my insides hurt even more.

The sudden sound of gunfire was loud, amplified in the large, metal-walled room. Bullets ricocheted off of the pipes and grates, adding to the noise. Startled, Hillerman's eyes widened and he stepped back, moving away from the source of the noise. In his surprise, he released me, and I could breathe again. I rolled over and saw Jackson raining lead down on Hillerman. But none of the bullets were actually hitting the doctor and his force field. They all missed, hitting just to the sides of him and over his head. I knew Jackson was a better shot than this. He wasn't trying to hit Hillerman; he was trying to scare him into stepping backwards. He knew what I had been thinking.

Now that Hillerman had recovered from his surprise, his expression sharpened and he reached out toward Jackson, doing the same to him as he had to me. Jackson's entire body clenched and he dropped his gun, the shock pushing the air from his lungs. Before he lost the ability to speak, his eyes landed on me. "Finish it!" he said through clenched teeth.

Hillerman was standing on the grate, but was stepping forward and in a moment it would be too late. As he raised his other hand to grab me again, I raised mine and fired one last shot, aiming at the grate under his feet, hoping that my gut feeling was right.

With a sharp jerk, Hillerman's limbs swung out of control and he fell to the deck. The shimmering of the force field was gone from him and the engines. Jackson gasped for breath on the floor where he fell. I stood back up, supporting myself on the wall. I stared at Hillerman's eyes, glazed over and looking straight up at the ceiling. His mouth hung ajar, as if he'd realized in his last moment of conscious thought, "Oh yeah, I probably should have thought of that."

My stomach lurched at the sight of his body. As much as I hated the guy, deep down I never wanted him dead. I never wanted to kill anybody, despite my previous attempts to convince myself otherwise.

Jackson came to my side, still catching his breath. "Nice work. Great minds think alike, eh?" When he saw my expression, he asked, "Are you all right?"

"When I was on the Parallel Earth, Walter Reifert told me that, even after his entire family was killed, even when his people were under siege, he never killed anyone. Not anyone." I looked at Jackson. "What does that make me?"

I saw the slightest amount of contempt on his face at the mention of Walter's name, but then his expression softened. He put a hand on my shoulder. "Sometimes things don't always play out the way you'd expect. Sometimes you have to do things you never thought you'd do, that you never wanted to do, for the sake of others."

I couldn't bear to look at Hillerman's corpse any longer. I looked down, battling the guilt and regret building in my chest.

With a friendly pat, Jackson said, "Let's finish this."

I heard Kevin and the others beginning to stir. "Get them out of here," I instructed. "I don't know if this will blow up once I shock it." I waited as Jackson helped my friends get on their feet and leave the engine room. Once I heard their last footsteps disappear around the corner, I stepped back as far as I could while still seeing the engines. I pointed two fingers at them, fired, and quickly ran out of the room. I was wise to do so. The engines exploded moments after being shocked, and I escaped into the stairwell just as fire and molten metal shot out of the door, blowing a hole in the hull. We were far enough down in the ship that we were below sea level, and water began rushing in. "Go, go!" I shouted, leading my group up a flight and then down a hallway to another stairwell that hadn't been reduced to rubble. We thankfully made it away from there before the incoming wall of water could swallow us.

"New plan," I yelled as we ran as fast as we could up to the top deck. "Start evacuating the ship. Get everyone on the lifeboats before this whole thing goes down!"

Jaeger, Jackson, and Kevin each took a separate deck, spreading the word and leading our people to safety. Kevin knew how to issue a ship-wide announcement, and moments later I heard him over the speakers: "Attention, passengers and crew of the *Defiant*. There is a hull breech. Repeat, there is a hull breach. Evacuate to the lifeboats immediately…"

"I'm going with you," Jeff said, knowing I was still planning to face Perkins.

"I need you to help with the evacuation," I replied, not slowing down.

"You can't do this alone!"

"Rescuing our people is more important than eliminating this guy!" I turned to Jeff. "I know I can't do this alone, but I can at least distract him long enough for you and the others to get off this ship."

Jeff rolled his eyes. "So noble. Why are you the one who has to sacrifice himself? Others can help with the evacuation. I'm not letting you die!" I tried to push him away from me, toward the level we'd just passed, but he grabbed my arm and made me look him in the eye. "We were in this together from the start. We're going to end it together, too."

I knew there was no convincing him otherwise, so I consented. When we reached the top deck, an older woman was waiting there, and she turned and shouted, "Lois! They're back!"

Dozens of people surged toward us, shouting questions at us. Lois finally pushed her way through and shouted for everyone to be quiet. "What happened, Austin? Where's everyone else?"

"Jaeger, Kevin, and Jackson are helping with the evacuation," I explained. "Did anyone else from our group come back up?"

She shook her head solemnly.

Another pang of guilt pulsed in my chest, but I pushed it aside. "Everyone needs to get off this ship!" I instructed. "The message over the com was true. There's a hole in the ship and water's rushing in.

Everyone who's not coming with me needs to get on a lifeboat immediately. Now go!"

Everyone began scrambling about, rushing to the lifeboats. Lois grabbed my arm as we shoved through the crowd. "What happened?" she repeated. "Why is there a hole in the ship?"

"The engines exploded when I shocked them, and it blew a hole in the side." I looked around. "Where's Les?"

"He went looking for you," she said, and I heard the fear in her voice. "We heard explosions and gunshots down below, and he went to make sure you guys made it…" She looked moments from tears. "Tell me he's okay, Austin! Tell me he's okay!"

"I didn't see him when we were down there," I said, "so I really don't know. Where are Vincent and Kathy?"

"They haven't come back yet."

We could no longer hear the loud whirring of the engines; now something more ominous could be heard through the fading light of dusk. A low, metallic creaking punctuated the air, and ever so slightly, the front of the ship was beginning to dip downward. I turned to Jeff, who was still by my side. "Go with Lois," I ordered. "Find Perkins. But don't engage him until I get back."

"Wait, where are you going *now*?" Jeff demanded.

There was something I had to do before I took on Perkins. It was much more important to me than finishing him off. "To find Vincent and Kathy," I said, and looked back at Lois. "And Les."

This was the last time. There was one more thing I had to do. I left my sleeping wife behind again, careful not to disturb her. Many nights had passed since my first visit to the young man, and now I was certain this would be my last. I prayed he would listen and pay attention to the signals I would give him.

I slipped out the bedroom door and padded softly down the hall, to the closet outside the powder room. As quickly and as quietly as I could, I pulled on the itchy suit and pulled the mask over my head. This would be the last time. After it was over, I would dispose of the suit, burn it, for I never wanted to see or touch it ever again. So much pain and confusion had been sewn into this suit, long ago when I was young and laid eyes on it for the first time.

I knew what I had to do: stop him from finding the captain as soon as he would. A confrontation with Perkins was inevitable, but if I managed to redirect his route and have him reach the lifeboats first, a point at which he would sense the Colician presence, he might be able to stop the calamity that the Colicians were about to bring down upon him and his people.

I knew he would recognize me this time. There was no way he wouldn't. Lee was gone. There was only one person left alive who knew what this suit represented. Maybe if he recognized me, he would listen, knowing that I above all people would know what he needed to do.

25

Endgame

Getting down one level was a chore. The stairwell was so packed full of people trying to get to the lifeboats that it took about five minutes for me to squeeze past. When I finally made it, I breathed a sigh of relief, and then realized how stupid I was being. How in the hell was I going to find Vincent, Kathy, and Les in this chaos? There were too many people clustered together for me to call out and find them. Plus, there were at least twelve other decks. What was I doing?

It didn't matter. I wasn't going to lose anyone else today. We were all going to walk off this ship together.

I ran down the corridor, dodging people as I went. I called out for them verbally and mentally, hoping they would hear me and answer. This continued on four other decks, when I finally stopped running into people and the hallways were quiet. The ship was tilted at a much steeper angle now. There wasn't much time left.

I kept searching, wondering if maybe they'd evacuated with everyone else. That didn't seem like them; they would stick with me until the very end.

At one point, I rounded a corner from the stairwell into the corridor, and then skidded to a halt. Facing me, dozens of yards down the expansive hallway, was an old pal I'd long forgotten.

Gorilla Man stared back at me, unmoving. He didn't speak, gesture, or acknowledge me. For a long time, I stared back at him, stunned. I'd never considered that I'd see him again, especially after Lee's death, yet here he was. And that was when I realized something, something I should have realized a long time ago.

"You're not Lee," I whispered. I closed the distance between us, walking as briskly as I could until we were nearly nose to nose. "You never *were* Lee."

Gorilla Man didn't respond, didn't move. I analyzed him, noticing for the first time that he was my height, my *exact* height. I grinned and shook my head, amazed at what I was seeing. At *who* I was seeing.

"Hello, *me*," I greeted, wanting to reach out and touch my future self dressed in that ridiculous costume, but knowing there was nothing there to touch.

At some point in the future, when I was who knew how old, I was dressing up in Lee's old gorilla suit and projecting images of myself to my past, younger self. I'd warned myself of the attack on the D.C. safe house, and then attempted to warn myself of Lee's unintended treachery. Now, here I was again, warning myself of…something.

"Where's Vincent?" I asked, hoping my future self had the answer. "Where are my friends?"

My future self turned and pointed his fuzzy hand down the corridor behind him. "Go," he said, still in the same, familiar deep voice he had always talked in. I didn't understand why I would one day project an image of myself into my past, while disguising my voice.

"They're down there?" I asked, unsure of the message I was receiving.

"Go," he said again.

Then, a scream erupted in my head and through the ship: "AUSTIN! AUSTIN!"

It was Vincent. He was screaming in agony. But he wasn't down the corridor Gorilla Man was pointing to. He was two decks down, dangerously close to the flooding. He was projecting his location to me, begging me to help him. I turned to go to him, forgetting what my future self was trying to tell me.

"Don't," he said sharply.

I glanced back at him. "I don't know why you're telling me to leave Vincent behind, but I'm not going to listen to you."

"Please," he said, and this time I heard my own voice, aged but recognizable. I was begging myself to abandon Vincent.

"No." I couldn't do it, no matter what the consequence would be.

I took off running, back toward the stairwell, turning my back on my future self. I rushed to save my friend, taking the stairs four at a time and twisting my ankle in the process. When I reached the deck he was on, I landed in a shallow pool of water about four inches deep. The water was rising quickly as the ship sank further.

Vincent was still screaming, and when I found him, I gasped. He was halfway down the hallway, on his knees. His arms and fingers were twisted in such a way that I knew instantly they were all broken. His head was cranked back and his mouth hung open wide in a never-ending howl of pain. His back was arched, and I knew if he went back much farther that would break too. I was about ten paces from him when whatever force holding him was released, and he fell forward hard, face first into the water. I slid down beside him and gently turned him, lifting his head up onto my lap so he could breathe. I'd never seen any expression as pained as his was in that moment.

"Good. You made it."

I looked up. Perkins was standing behind me, his expression neutral, but fire lighting up his eyes. He enjoyed what he'd just done to Vincent.

"Why would you do something like this?" I shouted, cradling Vincent to me. He was shaking, his broken limbs twitching.

"You weren't moving fast enough. I had to speed you up. Speaking of which…" He looked past me, and from around the corner I could hear that same agonized scream, but this time it was coming from Les. "Call her!" Perkins ordered.

"I won't!" came Les's reply, and a moment later his screams intensified and he began shouting, "LOIS! LOIS!"

I looked down at Vincent, who was fighting to stay conscious. "Where's Kathy?" I whispered.

"I don't know," he croaked. "We got separated before he found me."

That gave me hope for her. I apologized to Vincent before grabbing him under the arms and dragging him through the water, away from Perkins and toward the sounds of Les's screaming.

"I don't think so," was Perkins response, and then Vincent was writhing and screaming in my arms.

"Stop it!" I begged, sitting back down. "Your problem is with me and Lois! Leave Vincent and Les out of it!"

"What leverage would I have without these two?" Perkins asked, smirking. "It would have been Miriam for you, but she decided to stay behind. Wise decision."

Blind rage coursed through me. The thought of him doing this to Miriam was too much, too infuriating. I raised my hand to fire a bolt of electricity at him, but my arm cranked back and a moment later I felt my forearm snap. I screamed, and Perkins said over my pained cries, "If you shock me, or anything right now, you'll electrocute everyone in the water. Use your brain, Austin."

My right arm hung beside Vincent now, cracked at an angle much like Vincent's arms. I clenched my teeth together, trying to keep calm even through the pain. I clutched Vincent with my left arm, the only way

I was keeping his head above the rising water. Behind us, Les was still screaming for Lois, and I wondered how long it would take before she walked into the trap as well. I considered calling out to her, telling her not to follow the screams, but I knew Perkins would only break my other arm, and then Vincent would drown. Besides, I knew Lois wouldn't listen to me. Les meant too much to her.

"I don't wanna die!" Vincent whispered to me, and I felt his fear.

"We're gonna get out of this," I lied. "We'll be okay."

Perkins was stronger than me, Jeff, and Miriam put together. I felt it when he broke my arm. It was almost effortless for him. He was a monster, worse than he had ever been before. And my DNA made him this way.

"What do you want?" I asked Perkins as he sloshed past me, planning to hide around the corner until Lois found Les. "The ship's dead! Why are you still fighting us?"

"After I kill your loved ones, slowly, and in front of you, I'll do the same to you. Then, when your bodies look like a couple of mangled chew toys, I will push all of this water back out into the ocean and seal that hole. Once I get this boat moving again, I will finish what I started."

"You're insane!" I told him, but I knew he wasn't lying. If he could shatter our bones with barely lifting a finger, I was certain he would have no problem fixing this ship on his own. Even after all the damage we'd done, Cuba would still be leveled.

There was something I had to ask, something I had wanted to know four months ago but hadn't had the chance to find out until now. "How long have you known we were a part of the rebels?" I demanded. "How long were you playing us?"

"From the very beginning," he replied, not seeming very interested in the subject. "You were all so convinced I was clueless, but you were the clueless ones."

"Les? Les! Oh my God, Les!" Lois's cries came from around the corner, where Les was still howling in agony. A moment later, Lois was screaming in agony too, and the two of them were slowly dragged around the corner by Perkins's mental hold.

Les was worse off than Vincent, and I knew it was because Les's crimes against Perkins were greater. While Vincent had merely betrayed him, Les had humiliated him. He had gone behind his back and slept with his wife. He and Lois were about to bear the brunt of Perkins's fury.

Les's legs were also broken, one snapped backwards at the knee and the other with a broken femur and tibia. His arms looked like spaghetti noodles; they weren't recognizable anymore. Lois's back was arched, just like Vincent's had been, her pregnant belly bulging forward.

"Nathaniel…!" Lois whimpered, her eyes wide with terror. At the mention of the name, Lois's upper body snapped even farther backwards, and I heard her back break. She screamed, and I knew I had to do something.

"Leave them alone!" I shouted, forgetting my own fear. Perkins was too focused on them, too angry at them, to pay any attention to me.

"Do you have anything to say?" Perkins asked quietly, standing over Les and Lois. Both of them quivered and twitched in pain and fear, but said nothing. "Say something, damn it!" Both of them screamed in pain again.

I couldn't shock him. He was right when he said I'd electrocute everyone. I supposed it was a good thing I'd figured out how to teleport. I focused on the deck a few levels below us, where a few lifeboats were still left. I squeezed my eyes shut, just as Perkins realized what I was doing and whipped around. He was too late, and Vincent and I were now on an open deck beside an almost full lifeboat.

"Vincent?!" I heard Kathy's voice and locked up. She stumbled off of the boat, crying over the sight of Vincent's broken body. "What happened, Austin? Oh my God, your arm, too!"

"Get him off the ship," I wheezed. "Get him away from here!" The smell of sea salt and the feeling of the cool wind running through my hair made me hesitate, made me want to stay where it was safe. But I had to go back. I teleported back down, behind Les and Lois. Perkins whipped around again, yelling, "Austin!" I was too far away to grab both of them, so I grabbed Les's arm and teleported us back to the lifeboat, and then went back for Lois.

Perkins was ready for me this time. Before I could grab Lois, he grabbed me in his mental grip and made me feel as if my body was going to implode. I was seeing that blue light again, just like I'd seen when Hillerman had tried to hurt me. Perkins was stringing together a series of violent curses, furious that I'd gotten the better of him. I could feel my ribs cracking. My sternum, my pelvis. Even my skull.

"What did I say?!" Perkins was shouting, spittle flying from his mouth. "What did I say?!"

I was moments away from my brain squirting out my ears. My organs were squished together, about to become liquid.

"Hey!"

The shout came from behind Perkins. He turned, startled, and then was struck by a stream of water about two feet in diameter. He was thrown backwards, over Lois and I, and went splashing down the hallway, blown away by the force of the water. I looked up as my hair was sprinkled with salt water. It was Jeff, standing down the hall in a fighting stance, a challenging expression on his face. He looked at Lois and I, reached toward us, and then pulled his arms backwards like he was pulling on a rope. Lois and I slid through the rising water toward him, coming to a halt at his feet.

Exhausted, my head sank below the water. My eyes opened, the salt water burning them. Jeff was sending more water at Perkins, refusing to give the old captain a break. I heard him shout to me through the water, "Sit up, Austin! Breathe! I need your help!"

I couldn't. Consciousness was slipping. I had nothing left. I'd already given it all in the fight. My eyes started to close, but they opened again when I felt the ship rising up. The fight between Perkins and Jeff paused as they too looked about in alarm. As the ship rose, it began to lean sideways. Gravity took the water off of me, and I blinked the stinging salt out of my vision.

I didn't know this at the time, but I later heard a first-hand account of how the wave rose to nearly a thousand feet. It hung in the air, showing the true power of a single Colician.

A moment later it came crashing down on the *Defiant*.

✻~✳~✻

I remembered floating in the open ocean, a long way below the surface. My eyes opened and I saw the *Defiant*, completely submerged and slowly sinking. I had no idea how I ended up outside the ship, way over here. My guess was that I teleported out, and that was confirmed a few days later when I was reunited with Jeff. It was night now, the only light coming from the sinking ship.

I thought about letting go, taking a deep breath and letting it all end. I had nothing left to give. Every last drop of energy had been sucked out of me. It would be so easy to just let go…

An image appeared in my mind, of Kathy and Vincent, several years down the road, playing with their three kids, two girls and a boy. They were laughing and smiling, the kids happy and healthy. Behind them, I saw Miriam, sitting alone. James was about ten, briefly playing with his younger cousins before turning and heading away from the group, lonely, his family having been broken long ago.

I found the strength. I kicked upwards.

~~*

A lot of things happened in the three weeks following the destruction of the *Defiant*, the first being the memorials. Three hundred and twenty-seven Caitens were either dead or missing, all due to that single, massive wave the Colicians had brought down upon us.

"Nathaniel Perkins was going to kill you," Walter told me when I confronted him. "And everyone else within his reach. He would have fixed the ship and continued on his way to Cuba. Millions of people would have died. Your race would have been discovered by the world in a horrible way and a whole new war would have begun. We did what we had to do to protect all three species." I must have punched Walter at least three times after that conversation, before I was restrained and escorted to a jail cell on the Parallel Earth.

Many of the dead or missing were children or the elderly, who couldn't swim or who didn't have enough energy to keep afloat. The ship was almost completely evacuated when the Colicians unleashed the wave, the lifeboats a good distance away, but the wave was so massive that it flipped many of them, sending more people to their deaths. Many of those still on board at the time were dead. Jeff and I were two of the few exceptions.

Yes, Perkins was dead, but so was Lois. So was Les, and Izzy, and Tracy, and Otto. And hundreds more.

Lois was brain dead by the time the Colician doctors could escort us through the rift. The cause of death was drowning, as were most of the deaths. Dr. Perry managed to get her on life support fast enough to save her daughter. "Once the brain is dead, there's no way to bring her back," he explained when I asked why he couldn't give Lois some of his regenerative blood. "I'm sorry, but she's gone."

Les died of his wounds. His body was so heavily damaged that Dr. Perry didn't think he could have saved him even if he'd lasted long enough to receive treatment.

Izzy, Tracy, and Otto were among the drowned.

I told Dr. Perry that Lois and Les's daughter was to be named Aurelia Karina Blackwood-Royalty. Despite how close Les and I had been, I'd never even known his last name. Someone else had to let me know what it was so I could fill in the birth certificate. Baby Aurelia would be adopted out to a Caiten family, as would Lois's twins and all the other orphans.

I woke up three days after the *Defiant*'s destruction, with Jeff sitting beside my bed. My arm was set and wrapped in a cast, the pain a dull throb. We were in Reifert City General Hospital, a whole wing used for the incoming Caiten refugees. I was groggy and weak at first, but then I was overcome with anger when Jeff explained what had happened. That led to my confrontation with Walter, which led to my occupancy of a jail cell for four days. And that was where I met Ulysses's son.

Two days after I'd been escorted to this cell, I was pacing back and forth, angry and grief-stricken. I wanted to hurt Walter badly for what he'd done to my people, and knew I would if I ever saw him again. There was still a chance we could have stopped Perkins on our own, and then there would have been no reason for all the death.

My cell was in a separate room from the others; it was considered maximum security, for the inmates with powerful abilities. A transparent force field separated me from the other half of the room, and my fists bounced off of it like it was Jell-O. I found I couldn't use any of my abilities in there; it was built to suppress such things. The cell wasn't uncomfortable though; the toilet and sink were clean, the bed small but soft. The second day of my imprisonment, the door to the room opened and in stepped a guard. He scowled at me before saying, "There's someone here to see you."

He was a young man, a few years older than me. His hair was dark brown, his eyes hazel and wide like a frightened child's. He wrung his hands together nervously, and I was suddenly reminded of Lee's nervous wrist rubbing, back when he'd still been alive and happy. I looked away, overcome by another wave of grief.

"Hi," the young man said, stepping up to the force field and peering in at me.

"What do you want?" I snapped, refusing to look at him. I struggled to hide the tears threatening to leak down my face.

"I heard you punched President Reifert," he said sheepishly, as if this was the most amazing thing ever. "That's why you're in here?"

"Yeah, yeah." I rolled my eyes and sat on my bed. "I'd probably punch you too if this dumb force field wasn't in the way." When the man stepped back, startled by my hostility, I sighed. "Look, just tell me what you want and then leave. *Please.*"

Sheepishly, he said, "My name is Oliver Branson. My father was Ulysses Branson. I was wondering if you knew him?"

Shocked, I looked up. I hadn't seen it before, but now I could see the distinguishable facial features: the round face, high cheekbones, and bottom jaw that poked out ever so slightly. I remembered, all that time ago when I was back in Rebellion, when Annabelle told me Ulysses's sad story. He had a wife and two children. His wife and son were changed during the Colician outbreak. His wife was killed, but Ulysses never knew what happened to his son.

Seeing my confused look, Oliver continued. "I know he had A negative blood... they made us all get tested after the Colician outbreak... and you were the only Caiten I could get in to see. The rest are all being quarantined at the hospital. you know. I was just wondering if maybe, on the off chance, you'd met my father." When I still just stared at him, he said, "I know it's a long shot...there were a lot of you..."

"He was one of the groomsmen in my wedding," I blurted, finally finding my voice. "He was a good friend of mine."

Oliver's face lit up in a relieved smile. "Oh, thank God!" he said. "You know him?"

"You're really his son?" I asked, amazed at this coincidence.

He nodded. "Do you know where he is? I hear once your population is moved to the refugee camp, they'll allow visitors..." He saw my expression and stopped. "What is it?" he stammered, although I could tell he was starting to realize the truth before I even said it.

"He died a few months ago. He was helping to free our people from that town in Florida. He died a hero."

Oliver's face crumbled, but he didn't cry. He looked at the ground. "Did his death have meaning?" he whispered.

"Yes," I promised. "It did indeed."

"What about my sister?" he asked. "Her name was Lilia. She was an A Negative too."

I didn't want to give him any more bad news, but I couldn't lie to him. Not about this. I shook my head.

Staring at the ground, Oliver took a deep breath and nodded. "Well, I'm just glad I found someone who knew them." He turned slowly to leave.

An emotion I couldn't describe overtook me in that moment. It was a combination of grief, relief, and acceptance. I wasn't the only one grieving over the events which had taken place. There were others in pain, too, and in some strange, sick way that comforted me.

I didn't tell him that I'd never met his sister. I didn't tell him the story of how she died, either. He didn't need to hear that. But there was one more thing he needed to know. "He didn't know what happened to you." When he turned to look at me quizzically, I continued, "Your dad. He didn't know what happened to you after you were taken." I forced a smile. "It would have made him very happy to see you here today."

Oliver forced a smile in return and mouthed a thank you. That was the first and only time I ever saw Oliver Branson, and in a way I was grateful for that.

Two days later, the Caiten population was moved to a large school on the edge of the city that was to be used as a temporary refugee camp. Cots were set up neatly throughout the building, all made up with clean sheets and blankets. There was room for every single Caiten refugee; there were even cradles for the infants. I was released from jail and sent to join the rest of my people, scolded for my actions and instructed to improve my behavior. I wasn't charged with anything. Walter had let me go, choosing not to press charges.

Jeff, Vincent, Kathy, and Kevin were all waiting for me. When I arrived, we exchanged somber, silent hugs and then walked to the classroom we were assigned. The Colicians were kind and allowed friends to stay together, clearly a way to make up for what they'd done to us a week earlier. We all sat down in the cluttered room, the rest of the room's inhabitants clearing out so we could talk. For a while we all sat in silence without meeting each other's gazes.

"Jaeger should be here soon," Kathy said finally, breaking the silence. "He'll be staying with us."

"Do you guys know what happened to Jackson and Danny?" I asked.

"Danny was treated and then returned to his family," Jeff said. "None of the humans know about his involvement."

"What about Jackson?"

The others glanced at each other. "None of us saw him after the ship went down," Kevin said softly. "We think he might be dead."

Somehow I doubted that, but I didn't say it. I just nodded. I still felt numb from my grief. Kevin told me that Jaime and Amy had made it, that they were on the top floor, Amy with her two kids. I was relieved to hear it. "Has anyone told you guys what's going on? How long are they making us stay here?"

"Dr. Perry met with us a few days ago, since we're all that's left of our makeshift government," Vincent explained. His arms were wrapped up in casts and Kathy was helping him with pretty much everything. "He said the Colicians are clearing out of the Eastern Continent and coming back here."

"How many continents are there here?"

"Just two. The western one is the largest, covering about a third of the planet, or so I was told. The eastern one is much smaller, but still plenty big. Since the Caiten population is smaller, we're taking the smaller continent."

"Why are they giving us an entire continent?" I knew why Walter was doing this, and although the generosity was appreciated, it didn't make up for what he'd done to us. Nothing he did ever could.

Vincent shrugged. "We need to build a home for ourselves, just like they did three years ago. We may all hate them right now, Austin, but they understand what we need, and what we need is our own space so we can rebuild our lives."

I didn't want to admit he was right, so I looked down at my hands. Thankfully, Jaeger entered, carrying a squirming bundle of blankets and distracting us.

"What is that?" I asked.

"Aurelia," Jaeger said, pulling a bottle out of a bag slung over his shoulder and sticking it into the bundle.

"Why do you have Aurelia?"

Jaeger looked confused. "Did no one tell you?"

The others looked at me, surprised. "Sorry," Jeff said. "We thought you knew…"

"Knew what?"

"I adopted her," Jaeger said. "I'd have taken the twins too, but I can't take care of three infants by myself. Whoever ends up adopting them will have to keep in close contact with me, so Aurelia will know her siblings."

I thought that was sweet of Jaeger, taking in a baby whose parents he barely even knew. It was hard to believe how he'd changed over this past year, from a ruthless murderer to a loving and doting father.

He shrugged. "It was the least I could do to thank Les and Lois for giving me a second chance."

I felt the tears coming again, so I quickly changed the subject. "So how long until we all move?"

"As long as it takes for them to clear out their people and get them situated in homes here. Since there were a lot of people living on the Eastern Continent, there are a lot of houses and buildings already there. Once everyone gets situated, we should be able to get everyone to work and have things up and running shortly. The climate there is like the climate in the southern U.S., so we shouldn't have to worry about being cold, at least this time of year…"

"How are we going to function?" I said. "I don't see how you expect everyone to just get up and go to work when we have no real government."

"That's where we come in," Jeff said. "We'll be the temporary authority figures, until we're all settled and organized, and can hold a real election. People will listen to us, Austin, especially after what happened on the *Defiant*."

I laughed bitterly. "What happened on the *Defiant* is exactly why they *shouldn't* listen to us."

Kathy's face scrunched up in confusion, and she looked offended. "We laid our lives on the line to save everyone. We came back for them when Perkins was holding them hostage. The wave wasn't ours, Austin. All those deaths were not our fault. As far as those people out there are concerned, we're their saviors."

I didn't argue. I rubbed my head, which was beginning to ache from lack of food and sleep.

They all knew I was angry and resentful. Kevin patted me on the back. "I know something that'll cheer you up. Tomorrow, the Caitens hiding in North America are going to come join us. That means you'll be back with James and Miriam!"

That did cheer me up. I finally smiled, after a week of constant scowling. "How are they managing that?"

Vincent snorted. "The Colicians made a deal with the United States after the ship went down. They demanded that they allow the Colicians into the country in order to round up all the Caitens, and any of the Caiten Strain still remaining in labs, in exchange for silence."

"Silence?" I inquired.

They were all grinning, as if this was a joke I'd been left out of. Jaeger cleared his throat and explained. "Walter told President Kingsley that if he didn't cooperate, he'd tell the rest of the world about the U.S.'s attempt to recreate the Colician Virus. Even though he's an idiot, Kingsley knew better than to refuse."

Relief took grief's place inside me, and I sent a silent prayer to God that everyone would get here safely.

They did.

There were about twelve thousand of us in total, and the school wasn't big enough. People were reassigned to different locations so families could be reunited. The others in our classroom were reassigned to an alternate location so Miriam, James, Anne, and Gary could join us.

The reunions were full of tears. Anne and Gary arrived first, and we almost knocked the old couple over as we greeted them with tight embraces, tears streaming down our faces. When we'd settled down a little, we showed them to their beds and they sat down, both breathing sighs of relief. They told us that they'd hidden in South Carolina for the past few months, never staying in one place for very long. Whenever suspicions arose, they'd be on the move again. Gary said he'd actually collapsed when they got the news about the *Defiant*, and that they would be moving to the Parallel Earth, where they'd finally be safe. We all hugged again, glad to have part of our Rebellion family back. I was hugging Anne tightly when I saw Miriam appear in the doorway.

I pulled away from Anne and stared at my wife. She looked older, tougher. Her face was etched with lines that weren't there the last time I saw her, and I blamed myself for that. She was wheeling a small suitcase behind her and carrying a heavy backpack. James was strapped to her, hanging loosely from her hip. My son was almost seven months old now, and he'd put on some weight. His cheeks were pudgy and red, his arms and legs covered in baby fat. He looked to be the size of at least a twelve-month-old human baby. His hair wasn't as dark as it had been at his birth; it had lightened, and I wondered if it would ever be my color. He looked so much like me, it was stunning. His eyes landed on me, and he stared at me for a moment. My heart pounded. I feared he wouldn't recognize me, wouldn't know I was his daddy. But a moment later his face lit up, and he reached for me and shouted, "Da!"

Tears were pouring out of Miriam's eyes as she dropped the suitcase and ran to me. We sobbed as we held each other. James patted my shoulder, pulled my hair, oblivious to the exchange of emotions occurring.

"Don't you ever leave me again!" Miriam whispered fiercely, her voice wavering. "Don't you dare leave me again!"

"Never," I breathed. "Never."

~~*

That same day, while Miriam slept in my arms and James slept in the cradle beside our bed, a Colician volunteer entered our room and lightly tapped me on the shoulder. "Pardon me," the woman said, clasping her hands in front of her. "But there's someone here who'd like to see you."

For a moment I thought I was in trouble again, but I hadn't done anything wrong since my encounter with Walter. I then thought it might be Oliver Branson, but I couldn't see him ever coming to talk to me again, not after our last conversation. Glancing down at Miriam, I considered staying and telling the woman to tell my visitor that now wasn't a good time. I'd been apart from her and our son for so long that I never wanted to lose sight of them again. But they were both asleep. I would be back before they realized I was gone. Gently, I pulled my arms out from under Miriam. She stirred, pulling the blanket tighter around herself, but didn't wake. I looked at the Colician and put a finger to my lips. She nodded and gestured for me to follow her.

It was about nine o'clock in the evening, so a lot of people were heading to bed or down to the cafeteria to get a late night snack. We passed lots of yawning folks, who smiled and nodded to me as I passed. Kathy was right; despite what happened to the *Defiant*, my friends and I were still viewed as saviors.

The woman led me to the room that once functioned as the main office of the school. It was currently used for registration and "customer service," as we called it, so no Caitens were sleeping there. I entered the main office and the woman stepped aside, extending an arm toward my visitor. My eyes landed on him and my mouth fell open. The breath caught in my throat. "Oh my God!" I cried, covering my mouth.

My dad, Nathan Rockwell, stood in front of me, smiling. He didn't look any different than he had the last time I saw him. His hair was still overgrown and wiry. His glasses still had thin frames that looked like they would snap at the slightest amount of applied pressure. His eyes were brighter, like those of all Colicians, but they were also sadder. He stood with his hands in his pockets, lost for words, as was I.

I was so shocked and overcome with emotion that I sank to my knees. The woman started forward to help me, but my dad waved her away and asked her to give us some time alone. He came to me, kneeling in front me and taking my shoulders in his hands.

I was crying. I couldn't help it. I'd waited for this moment for almost four years, and now that it was here, I didn't know what to do with myself.

"Are you okay?" he murmured softly.

"Am I okay?" I repeated, unable to look at his face. "What about you? What... how...?"

He shushed me and pulled me to him. We sat there for a while, while I struggled to get a grip. I soon realized that I wasn't the only one crying, though. I could feel my dad's chest lurching as he fought back sobs. He took a few slow breaths and pulled away to study me. "You haven't been staying out of trouble, I see."

I laughed. "No, I haven't."

Dad took another deep breath. "This has been all over the news for the past year. I knew you were an A Negative, but I couldn't get any information about whether you were all right. Then, a few days ago, President Reifert released a statement about the recent incident, and he mentioned your name in the report." He shook his head and laughed. "I couldn't believe it, so I had to watch it again. I finally managed to get in to talk to you."

"You have no idea how much I've missed you," I croaked, and the tears started flowing all over again. "It was so hard trying to move on after you left." I suddenly remembered my little sister, and felt a flash of guilt for being so caught up in the moment. "Chrissy! Where's Chrissy?"

Dad's face fell, and I knew. "I never found her after we got out of the labs. Those who were never found..."

"Are most likely dead," I finished. I didn't have room in my heart for any more grief. All I felt was this numbness, this detachment, like I was watching a movie of somebody else's traumatizing life.

Dad pulled me up and we went to a pair of chairs to sit and talk. "So tell me," he said. "Tell me everything that's happened. I want to know everything."

I thought about everything I had to tell him, and how long it would take to tell my story. I started after the Colician outbreak, when I dropped out of school and got into trouble with the law. I told him about the lab and the experiments that went on there. I told him about Miriam, how she'd started out as my only friend, my best friend, and then became my wife. I told him about James, his first grandchild. I told him about all the friends I'd lost, starting with Kost and ending with Lois. I told him about Rebellion, about the *Defiant*, about all the events and trying times that the past few years had dealt me.

Epilogue

The boys jumped on top of us, waking Miriam and I from our afternoon snooze.

"*Oof!*" I cried as the air was knocked out of me. James had landed square on my chest. He grinned at me, knowing I was mad but also knowing he'd get away with it. He had always been Daddy's little boy.

James was ten years old now, but a lot of people mistook him as a fourteen- or fifteen-year-old. He was muscular, broad-chested, and had a vocabulary that would stun most scholars. His hair was even lighter now, almost my color but not quite, and except for the hair and slightly darker skin tone, he was a mirror image of me at ten years old.

Miriam was tickling our second son, Bobby, or Bo as James called him. Bobby was shrieking as he fought to escape his mother's grasp. He was a mama's boy. Miriam adored him. He was soft-spoken but fierce when need be, just like Miriam, and was gentle and kind; the complete opposite of James, yet the two were inseparable friends. Bobby was eight, but much smaller than James and much meeker. He had Miriam's dark hair, skin, and eyes, and was thin and quick.

Kathy and Vincent laughed at us from across the lawn. They sat together on their blanket, sipping fruity drinks and telling stories as their kids played in the yard, soon joined again by their cousins. Kathy and Vincent had three children: twin girls and a boy. The girls were named Annabelle and Lois, and the boy was called LesLee. The girls were seven and Les was six. We all got together every weekend, and sometimes during the week as well. We had fun together, our family. My father even came to visit, usually every other weekend if tensions weren't high between our races. He had, as I'd once feared, started a family of his own on the Parallel Earth, but it was not as I expected. He'd adopted two brothers after he crossed over, named Alan and Eric Brown. The boys had been in separate labs during the Colician outbreak, but were reunited after relocating to the Parallel Earth and were then adopted by my dad. Dad brought them almost every time he came, and I considered them my little brothers. Dad and the boys were welcomed with open arms by our family, but not everyone felt the same way. The relationship between our races still suffered because of what happened on the *Defiant* ten years ago. I still felt a raw bitterness toward Walter Reifert, but maybe one day things would change.

Miriam slipped an arm around me and kissed my shoulder. I smiled. I watched my sons and my nieces and nephew play together in our backyard, and remembered back ten years, when I didn't think my family would have a chance to be happy. Back then, I never thought of Bobby as a possibility. Our race had had a rough start, on Earth *and* on the Parallel Earth. We struggled to keep our society running. Jeff was sworn in as president a year after we settled on the Eastern Continent. He was still president, having been reelected twice. We were still close, and he told me he wasn't planning on running again after this term. He told me I should run. I laughed and said, "Not a chance." Maybe in a few years, when my boys were a little older, I'd think about it.

Jaeger and I had lost touch a few years back. He, Aurelia, and Lois's twins, Harvey and Jessica, had gone out east to explore uncharted territory once the kids were old enough, and he eventually stopped sending letters. In the end, the ex-sergeant had decided to adopt Lois's twins as well as their half-sister, and with some help from friends he successfully raised them.

Kevin lived with us for two years until he started his own family. He lived down the block with his wife and son.

Jeff lived in the capital city—named Defiant in memoriam of those we'd lost—governing our race. A few years ago, he married a lovely woman named Anna. He had two young daughters, and seemed to be loving life with his new family. He even kept in close contact with Amelia, his previous wife, and their families seemed to get along well. I was happy for him, because this meant he still got to see Olivia, his and Amelia's daughter. Jeff and I kept in close contact.

Anne passed away in her sleep a year ago, and then Gary followed a few months later. I missed them greatly, just like I missed everyone we'd lost, but I was thankful they died happy, safe.

Danny Bennett kept in close contact with Walter and Jeff, keeping them informed of what was happening on his side of the rift.

I hadn't heard anything more about Jackson Odau. I hoped he was happy despite our differences. I realized he was right when he told me to never give up, to always strive for what I wanted.

In the decade following our settlement on the Parallel Earth, I learned many things, but there was one that stuck out in my mind. The constantly mutating strain Miriam, Jeff, and I were given was genetic. James now had the same capabilities as us, and both of Jeff's young daughters did as well. Bobby seemed to be the only one in our lines who hadn't been affected by this strain, and I hoped he would never have to bear the burden of carrying such power. Our race had named us "Royal Caitens," since only Caitens in our bloodlines could develop these abilities.

~~*

I sighed happily, resting my chin on the top of Miriam's head. Our lives had led us in crazy directions, but they had ultimately led us to each other. Now that the storm had passed, life on the Eastern Continent of the Parallel Earth was calm, peaceful. I had my wife and sons. I had Vincent and Kathy and their kids. I had my father and my adopted brothers. I had Jeff and Kevin and their families and the other friends I had come to know and love throughout the years.

As a slow and steady breeze ruffled my hair, I watched my kids as they created a variation of tag with their younger cousins. I found myself thinking back to ten years ago again, back to when the *Defiant* was sinking and I was certain I'd drown. I thought about giving up, how it would be so much easier than swimming to the surface and taking that fresh breath of air.

Life was never easy. When you gave up, you lost everything, the good and the bad. You could never take it back.

I was glad I'd found the strength to take that breath.

ABOUT THE AUTHOR

Author photo by Amber Blanchard Photography

Ms. King resides in Southern Wisconsin. She enjoys creative writing, reading, martial arts, and playing saxophone. To contact the author visit CSJ King Publishing at www.repeatproductions.samsbiz.com, email her at csjkingpublishing@gmail.com, or follow her on Facebook.

Also enjoy these novels from Cassandra Lynn King:
Parallels (Parallels Vol. 1)
O Negative (Parallels Vol. 2)

Coming soon:
2048 A.D. (Parallels Vol. 4)